Austin Dobson

The Poems and Plays of Oliver Goldsmith

Austin Dobson

The Poems and Plays of Oliver Goldsmith

ISBN/EAN: 9783742897657

Manufactured in Europe, USA, Canada, Australia, Japa

Cover: Foto ©Andreas Hilbeck / pixelio.de

Manufactured and distributed by brebook publishing software
(www.brebook.com)

Austin Dobson

The Poems and Plays of Oliver Goldsmith

Canonbury Tower

THE
POEMS AND PLAYS
OF
OLIVER GOLDSMITH

EDITED BY
AUSTIN DOBSON
WITH FRONTISPIECE BY HERBERT RAILTON

LONDON
J. M. DENT AND CO.
69 GREAT EASTERN STREET
1891

CONTENTS.

INTRODUCTION.

I.

THIRTY years of taking-in; fifteen years of giving out;—that, in brief, is Oliver Goldsmith's story. When, in 1758, his failure to pass at Surgeons' Hall finally threw him on letters for a living, the thirty years were finished, and the fifteen years had been begun. What was to come he knew not; but, from his bare-walled lodging in Green-Arbour Court, he could at least look back upon a sufficiently diversified past. He had been an idle, orchard-robbing schoolboy; a tuneful but intractable sizar of Trinity; a lounging, loitering, fair-haunting, flute-playing Irish "buckeen." He had tried both Law and Divinity, and crossed the threshold of neither. He had started for London and stopped at Dublin; he had set out for America and arrived at Cork. He had been many things:—a medical student, a strolling musician, a corrector of the press, an apothecary, an usher at a Peckham "academy." Judged by ordinary standards, he had wantonly wasted his time. And yet, as things fell out, it is doubtful whether his parti-coloured experiences were not of more service to him than any he could have obtained if his progress had been less erratic. Had he fulfilled the modest expectations of his family, he would probably have remained a simple curate in Westmeath, eking out his "forty pounds a year" by farming a field or two, migrating contentedly at the fitting season from the "blue bed to the brown," and (it may be) subsisting vaguely as a local poet upon the tradition of some youthful couplets to a pretty cousin, who had married a richer man. As it was, if he could not be said "to have seen life steadily, and seen it whole," he had, at all events, inspected it pretty narrowly in parts; and, at a time when he was most impressible, had preserved the impress of many things which, in his turn, he was to re-impress upon his writings. "No man"—says one of his biographers—"ever put so much of himself into his books as Goldsmith." To his last hour he was drawing upon the thoughts and reviving the memories of that "unhallowed time" when, to all appearance, he was hopelessly squandering his opportunities. To do as Goldsmith did, would scarcely enable a man to write a *Vicar of Wakefield* or a *Deserted Village*,—certainly his practice cannot be preached with safety "to those that eddy round and round." But viewing his entire career, it is difficult not to see how one part seems to have been an indispensable preparation for the other, and to marvel once more (with the philosopher Square) at "the eternal Fitness of Things."

II.

The events of Goldsmith's life have been too often narrated to need repetition here, and we shall not resort to the well-worn device of repeating them in order to say so. But, in a fresh reprint of his Poems and Plays, some brief preamble to those branches of his work may be excusable, and even useful. And, with regard to both, what strikes one first is the extreme tardiness of that late blossoming to which Johnson referred. When a man succeeds as Goldsmith succeeded, friends and critics speedily discover that he had shown signs of excellence even from his boyish years. But, setting aside those half-mythical ballads for the Dublin street-singers, and some doubtful verses for Jane Contarine, there is no definite evidence that, from a doggerel couplet in his childhood to an epigram not much better than doggerel composed when he was five and twenty, he had written a line of verse of the slightest importance; and even five years later, although he refers to himself in a private letter as a "poet," it must have been solely upon the strength of the unpublished fragment of *The Traveller*, which in the interval, he had sent to his brother Henry from abroad. It is even more remarkable that—although so skilful a correspondent must have been fully sensible of his gifts—until, under the pressure of circumstances, he drifted into literature, the craft of letters seems never to have been his ambition. He thinks of being a lawyer, a physician, a clergyman,—anything but an author ; and when at last he engages

in that profession, it is to free himself from a scho-
lastic servitude which he appears to have always
regarded with peculiar bitterness, yet to which,
after a first unsatisfactory trial of what was to be
his true vocation, he unhesitatingly returned. If
he went back once more to his pen, it was only to
enable him to escape from it more effectually, and
he was prepared to go as far as Coromandel. But
Literature—" *toute entière à sa proie attachée* "—refused to relinquish him ; and, although he con-
tinued to make spasmodic efforts to extricate
himself, detained him to the day of his death.

If there is no evidence that he had written much
when he entered upon what has been called his
second period, he had not the less formed his
opinions on many literary questions. Much of the
matter of the *Polite Learning* is plainly manufactured *ad hoc ;* but in its references to authorship and
criticism, there is a personal note which is absent
elsewhere ; and when he speaks of the tyranny
of publishers, the sordid standards of criticism, and
the forlorn and precarious existence of the hapless
writer for bread, he is evidently reproducing a
condition of things with which he had become
familiar during his brief bondage on the *Monthly
Review.* As to his personal views on poetry in
particular, it is easy to collect them from this, and
later utterances. Against blank verse he protests
from the first, as suited only to the sublimest
themes—which is a polite way of shelving it
altogether ; while in favour of rhyme he alleges
that the very restriction stimulates the fancy, as
a fountain plays higher when the aperture is

diminished. Blank verse, too (he asserted), imported into poetry a "disgusting solemnity of manner" which was fatal to "agreeable trifling," —an objection intimately connected with the feeling which afterwards made him the champion on the stage of character and humour. Among the poets who were his contemporaries and immediate predecessors, his likes and dislikes were strong. He fretted at the fashion which Gray's *Elegy* set in poetry; he considered it a fine poem, but "overloaded with epithet," and he deplored the remoteness and want of emotion which distinguished the Pindaric Odes. Yet from many indications in his own writings, he seems to have genuinely appreciated the work of Collins. Churchill, and Churchill's satire, he detested. With Young he had some personal acquaintance, and had attentively read his *Night Thoughts.* Of the poets of the last age, he admired Dryden, Pope and Gay, but more than any of these, if imitation is to be regarded as the proof of sympathy, Prior, Addison and Swift. By his inclinations and his training, indeed, he belonged to this school. But he was in advance of it in thinking that poetry, however didactic after the fashion of his own day, should be simple in its utterance and directed at the many rather than the few. This is what he meant when, from the critical elevation of Griffiths' back parlour, he recommended Gray to take the advice of Isocrates, and "study the people." If, with these ideas, he had been able to divest himself of the "warbling groves" and "finny deeps" of the Popesque vocabulary (of much of the more "mechanic art" of that supreme artificer he *did* successfully divest himself), it would have needed but little to make him a prominent pioneer of the new school which was coming with Cowper. As it is, his poetical attitude is a little that intermediate one of Longfellow's maiden—

> "Standing, with reluctant feet,
> Where the brook and river meet."

Most of his minor and earlier pieces are imitative In *A New Simile*, and *The Logicians Refuted*, Swift is his acknowledged model; in *The Double Transformation* it is Prior, modified by certain theories personal to himself. He was evidently well acquainted with collections like the *Ménagiana*, and with the French minor poets of the eighteenth century, many of which latter were among his books at his death. These he had carefully studied, probably during his continental wanderings, and from them he derives, like Prior, much of his grace and metrical buoyancy. The *Elegy on the Death of a Mad Dog*, and *Madam Blaize*, are both more or less constructed on the old French popular song of the hero of Pavia, Jacques de Chabannes, Seigneur de la Palice (sometimes Galisse), with, in the case of the former, a tag from an epigram by Voltaire, the original of which is in the Greek Anthology, though Voltaire simply "conveyed" his version from an anonymous French predecessor. Similarly the lively stanzas *To Iris, in Bow Street*, the lines to Myra, the quatrain called *A South American Ode*, and that *On a Beautiful Youth struck blind with Lightning*, are all confessed or unconfessed translations. It is possible that if Goldsmith had lived to collect his own works, he would have announced the source of his inspiration in these instances as well as in one or two other cases—the epitaph on Ned Purdon, for example,—where it has been reserved to his editors to discover his obligations. On the other hand, he might have contended, with perfect justice, that whatever the source of his ideas, he had made them his own when he got them ; and certainly in lilt and lightness, the lines *To Iris* are infinitely superior to those of La Monnoye, on which they are based. But even a fervent admirer may admit that, dwelling as he did in this very vitreous palace of Gallic adaptation, one does not expect to find him throwing stones at Prior for borrowing from the French, or commenting solemnly in the life of Parnell upon the heinousness of plagiarism. " It was the fashion," he says, " with the wits of the last age, to conceal the places from whence they took their hints or their subjects. A trifling acknowledgment would have made that lawful prize, which may now be considered as plunder." He might judiciously have added to this latter sentence the quotation which he struck out of the second issue of the *Polite Learning*,—" *Haud inexpertus loquor.*"

Of his longer pieces, *The Traveller* was apparently suggested to him by Addison's *Letter from Italy to Lord Halifax*, a poem to which, in his preliminary notes to the *Beauties of English Poesy*, he gives significant praise. " There is in it," he says, "a strain of political thinking that

was, at that time, new in our poetry." He
obviously intended that *The Traveller* should be
admired for the same reason; and both in that
poem and its successor, *The Deserted Village*, he
lays stress upon the political import of his work.
The one, we are told, is to illustrate the position
that the happiness of the subject is independent of
the goodness of the Sovereign; the other, to
deplore the increase of luxury and the miseries of
depopulation. But, as a crowd of commentators
have pointed out, it is hazardous for a poet to
meddle with "political thinking," however much,
under George the Second, it may have been needful to proclaim a serious purpose. If Goldsmith
had depended solely upon the professedly didactic
part of his attempt, his work would be as dead as
Freedom, or *Sympathy*, or any other of Dodsley's
forgotten *quartos*. Fortunately he did more than
this. Sensibly or insensibly, he suffused his work
with that philanthropy which is "not learned by
the royal road of tracts, and platform speeches, and
monthly magazines," but by personal commerce
with poverty and sorrow; and he made his appeal
to that clinging love of country, of old association,
of "home-bred happiness," of innocent pleasure,
which, with Englishmen, is never made in vain.
Employing the couplet of Pope and Johnson, he
has added to his measure a suavity that belonged to
neither; but the beauty of his humanity and the
tender melancholy of his wistful retrospect hold
us more strongly and securely than the studious
finish of his style.

" *Vingt fois sur le métier remettez votre ouvrage* "

—said the arch-critic whose name, according to Keats, the school of Pope displayed upon their "decrepit standard." Even in *The Traveller* and *The Deserted Village*, there are indications of over-labour; but in a poem which comes between them—the once famous *Edwin and Angelina*— Goldsmith certainly carried out Boileau's maxim to the full. The first privately-printed version differs considerably from that in the first edition of the *Vicar;* this again is altered in the fourth; and there are other variations in the piece as printed in the *Poems for Young Ladies.* "As to my 'Hermit'," said the poet complacently, "that poem, Cradock, cannot be amended," and undoubtedly it has been skilfully wrought. But it is impossible to look upon it now with the unpurged eyes of those upon whom the *Reliques of Ancient Poetry* had but recently dawned, still less to endorse the verdict of Sir John Hawkins that "it is one of the finest poems of the lyric kind that our language has to boast of." Its over-soft prettiness is too much that of the chromo-lithograph or the Parian bust (the porcelain, not the marble), and its "beautiful simplicity" is in parts perilously close upon that inanity which Johnson, whose sturdy good sense not even friendship could silence, declared to be the characteristic of much of Percy's collection. It is instructive as a study of poetical progress to contrast it with a ballad of our own day in the same measure—the *Talking Oak* of Tennyson.

The remaining poems of Goldsmith, excluding the *Captivity*, and the admittedly occasional

Threnodia Augustalis, are not open to the charge of fictitious simplicity, or of that hyper-elaboration, which, in the words of the poet just mentioned, makes for the "ripe and rotten." The gallery of kit-cats in *Retaliation*, and the delightful *bonhomie* of *The Haunch of Venison* need no commendation. In kindly humour and not unkindly satire Goldsmith was at his best, and the imperishable portraits of Burke and Garrick and Reynolds, and the inimitable dinner at which Lord Clare's pasty was *not*, are as well known as any of the stock passages of *The Deserted Village* or *The Traveller*, though they have never been babbled "*in extremis vicis*" by successive generations of schoolboys. It is usually said, probably with truth, that in these poems and the delightful *Letter to Mrs. Bunbury*, Goldsmith's metre was suggested by the cantering anapests of the *New Bath Guide*, and it is to be observed that "Little Comedy's" letter of invitation is to the same popular tune. But in annotating this edition, some enquiries as to the song of *Ally Croaker* mentioned in *She Stoops to Conquer*, elicited the fact that a line of that once popular lyric—

"Too dull for a wit, too grave for a joker"—

has a kind of echo in the—

"Too nice for a statesman, too proud for a wit"—

of Burke's portrait in *Retaliation*. What is still more remarkable is that Gray's *Sketch of his own Character*, the resemblance of which to Goldsmith has been pointed out by his editors, begins—

"Too poor for a bribe, and too proud to importune."

Whether Goldsmith was thinking of Anstey or *Ally Croaker*, it is at least worthy of passing notice that an Irish song of no particular literary merit should have succeeded in haunting the two foremost poets of their day.

III.

Poetry brought Goldsmith fame, but money only indirectly. Those Saturnian days of the subscription-edition, when Pope and Gay and Prior counted their gains by thousands, were over and gone. He had arrived, it has been well said, too late for the Patron, and too early for the Public. Of his lighter pieces the best were posthumous; the rest were either paid for at hack prices or not at all. For *The Deserted Village* Griffin gave him a hundred guineas, a sum so unexampled as to have prompted the pleasant legend that he returned it. For *The Traveller* the only payment that can be definitely traced is £21. "I cannot afford to court the draggle-tail Muses," he said laughingly to Lord Lisburn, "they would let me starve; but by my other labours I can make shift to eat, and drink, and have good clothes." It was in his "other labours" that his poems helped him. The booksellers who would not or could not remunerate him adequately for delayed production and minute revision, were willing enough to secure the sanction of his name for humbler journey-work. If he was ill-paid for *The Traveller*, he was not ill-paid for the *Beauties of English Poesy* or the *History of Animated Nature*.

Yet, notwithstanding his ready pen, and his skill

as a compiler, his life was a *métier de forçat.*
"While you are nibbling about elegant phrases, I
am obliged to write half a volume,"—he told his
friend Cradock ; and it was but natural that he
should desire to escape into walks where he might
accomplish something "for his own hand," by
which, at the same time, he might exist. Fiction
he had already essayed. Nearly two years before
The Traveller appeared, he had written a story
about the length of *Joseph Andrews*, for which he
had received little more than a third of the sum
paid by Andrew Millar to Fielding for his burlesque
of Richardson's *Pamela.* But obscure circumstances delayed the publication of the *Vicar of
Wakefield* for four years, and when at last it was
issued, its first burst of success—a success, as far
as can be ascertained, productive of no further
profit to its author—was followed by a long period
during which the sales were languid and uncertain.
There remained the stage, with its two-fold allurement of fame and fortune, both payable at sight,
added to which it was always possible that a
popular play, in those days when plays were
bought to read, might find a brisk market in book
form. The prospect was a tempting one, and it
is scarcely surprising that Goldsmith, weary of
the "dry drudgery at the desk's dead wood," and
conscious of better things within him, should engage in that most tantalizing of all enterprises, the
pursuit of dramatic success.

For acting and actors he had always shown a
decided partiality.[1] Vague stories, based, in all

---

[1] This is not inconsistent with the splenetic utterances in

probability, upon the references to strolling players in his writings, hinted that he himself had once worn the comic sock as "Scrub" in *The Beaux' Stratagem;* and it is clear that soon after he arrived in England, he had completed a tragedy, for he read it in manuscript to a friend. That he had been besides an acute and observant playgoer, is plain from his excellent account in *The Bee* of Mademoiselle Clairon, whom he had seen at Paris, and from his sensible notes in the same periodical on "gestic lore" as exhibited on the English stage. In his *Polite Learning in Europe*, he had followed up Ralph's *Case of Authors by Profession*, by protesting against the despotism of managers, and the unenlightened but economical policy of producing only the works of deceased playwrights ; and he was equally opposed to the growing tendency on the part of the public—a tendency dating from Richardson and the French *comédie larmoyante*—to substitute sham sensibility and superficial refinement for that humorous delineation of manners, which, with all their errors of morality and taste, had been the chief aim of Congreve and his contemporaries. To the fact that what was now known as "genteel comedy" had almost wholly supplanted this elder and better

---

the letters to Daniel Hodson, first made public in the "Great Writers" *Life of Goldsmith*, where he speaks of the stage as "an abominable resource which neither became a man of honour, nor a man of sense." Those letters were written when the production of *The Good-Natur'd Man* had supplied him with abundant practical evidence of the vexations and difficulties of theatrical ambition.

manner, must be attributed his deferred entry upon
a field so obviously adapted to his gifts.   But
when, in 1766, the *Clandestine Marriage* of Garrick
and Colman, with its evergreen "Lord Ogleby,"
seemed to herald a return to the side of laughter
as opposed to that of tears, he took heart of grace,
and, calling to mind something of the old incon-
siderate benevolence which had been the Goldsmith family-failing, set about his first comedy,
The Good-Natur'd Man.

Even without experiment, no one could have
known better than Goldsmith, upon what a sea of
troubles he had embarked.   Those obstacles which,
more than thirty years before, had been so graphi-
cally described in Fielding's *Pasquin*,—which
Goldsmith himself had indicated with equal accu-
racy in his earliest book, still lay in the way of all
dramatic purpose, and he was to avoid none of
them.   When he submitted his completed work
to Garrick, the all-powerful actor, who liked
neither piece nor author, blew hot and cold so
long, that Goldsmith at last, in despair, transferred
it to Colman.   But, as if fate was inexorable,
Colman, after accepting it effusively, also grew
dilatory, and ultimately entered into a tacit league
with Garrick not to produce it at Covent Garden
until his former rival had brought out at Drury
Lane a comedy by Goldsmith's countryman, Hugh
Kelly, a sentimentalist of the first water.   Upon
the heels of the enthusiastic reception which
Garrick's administrative tact secured for the
superfine *imbroglios* of *False Delicacy*, came limp-
ing *The Good-Natur'd Man* of Goldsmith, wet-

blanketed beforehand by a sententious prologue from Johnson. No *début* could have been less favourable. Until it was finally saved in the fourth act by the excellent art of Shuter, its fate hung trembling in the balance, and even then one of its scenes—not afterwards reckoned the worst —had to be withdrawn in deference to the delicate scruples of an audience which could not suffer such inferior beings as bailiffs to come between the wind and its gentility. Yet, in spite of all these disadvantages, *The Good-Natur'd Man* obtained a hearing, besides bringing its author about five hundred pounds, a sum far larger than anything he had ever made by poetry or fiction.

That the superior success of *False Delicacy*, with its mincing morality and jumble of inadequate motive, was wholly temporary and accidental, is evident from the fact that, to use a felicitous phrase, it has now to be disinterred in order to be discussed. But, notwithstanding one's instinctive sympathy for Goldsmith in his struggles with the managers, it is not equally clear that, everything considered, *The Good-Natur'd Man* was unfairly treated by the public. Because Kelly's play was praised too much, it by no means follows that Goldsmith's play was praised too little. With all the advantage of its author's reputation, it has never since passed into the *répertoire*, and, if it had something of the freshness of a first effort, it had also its inexperience. The chief character, Honeywood—the weak and amiable "good-natur'd man"—never stands very firmly on his feet, and the first actor, Garrick's promising young rival, Powell, failed, or disdained to make it a stage creation. On the other hand, "Croaker," an admitted elaboration of Johnson's sketch of "Suspirius" in the *Rambler*, is a first-rate comic character, and the charlatan "Lofty," a sort of "Beau-Tibbs-above-Stairs," is almost as good. But, as Garrick's keen eye saw, to have a second male figure of greater importance than the central personage was a serious error of judgment, added to which neither "Miss Richland" nor "Mrs. Croaker" ever establish any hold upon the audience. Last of all, the plot, such as it is, cannot be described as either particularly ingenious or particularly novel. In another way, the merit of the piece is, however, incontestable. It is written with all the perspicuous grace of Goldsmith's easy pen, and, in the absence of stage-craft, sparkles with neat and effective epigrams. One of these may be mentioned as illustrating the writer's curious (perhaps unconscious) habit of repeating ideas which had pleased him. He had quoted in his *Polite Learning* the exquisitely rhythmical close of Sir William Temple's prose essay on "Poetry," and in *The Bee* it still seems to haunt him. In *The Good-Natur'd Man* he has absorbed it altogether, for he places it, without inverted commas, in the lips of Croaker.

But, if its lack of constructive power and its errors of conception make it impossible to regard *The Good-Natur'd Man* as a substantial gain to humorous drama, it was undoubtedly a formidable attack upon that "mawkish drab of spurious breed," Sentimental Comedy, and its success was

amply sufficient to justify a second trial.   That
Goldsmith did not forthwith make this renewed
effort must be attributed partly to the recollection
of his difficulties in getting his first play produced,
partly to the fact that, his dramatic gains ex-
hausted, he was almost immediately involved in a
sequence of laborious taskwork.   Still, he had
never abandoned his ambition to restore humour
and character to the stage ; and as time went on,
the sense of his past discouragements grew fainter,
while the success of *The Deserted Village* increased
his importance as an author.   Sentimentalism, in
the meantime, had still a majority.   Kelly, it is
true, was now no longer to be feared.   His sudden
good fortune had swept him into the ranks of the
party-writers, with the result that the damning of
his next play, *A Word to the Wise*, had been
exaggerated into a political necessity.   But the
school which he represented had been recruited by
a much abler man, Richard Cumberland, and it
was probably the favourable reception of Cumberland's *West Indian* that stimulated Goldsmith
into striking one more blow for legitimate comedy.
At all events, in the autumn of the year in which
The West Indian was produced, he is hard at
work in the lanes at Hendon and Edgware,
"studying jests with a most tragical countenance"
for a successor to *The Good-Natur'd Man*.

To the modern spectator of *She Stoops to Conquer*, with its unflagging humour and bustling
action, it must seem almost inconceivable that its
stage qualities can ever have been questioned.   Yet
questioned they undoubtedly were, and Goldsmith

was spared none of his former humiliations. Even
from the outset, all was against him. His differences with Garrick had long been adjusted,
and the Drury Lane manager would now probably
have accepted a new play from his pen, especially
as that astute observer had already detected signs
of a reaction in the public taste. But Goldsmith
was morally bound to Colman and Covent
Garden; and Colman, in whose hands he placed
his manuscript, proved even more disheartening
and unmanageable than Garrick had been in the
past. Before he had come to his decision, the
close of 1772 had arrived. Early in the following
year, under the irritation of suspense and suggested
amendments combined, Goldsmith hastily transferred his proposal to Garrick; but, by Johnson's
advice, as hastily withdrew it. Only by the
express interposition of Johnson was Colman at
last induced to make a distinct promise to bring
out the play at a specific date. To believe in it,
he could not be persuaded, and his contagious
anticipations of its failure passed insensibly to the
actors, who, one after the other, shuffled out of
their parts. Even over the epilogue there were
vexatious disputes, and when at last, in March,
1773, *She Stoops to Conquer* was acted, its *jeune
premier* had previously held no more exalted
position than that of ground-harlequin, while one
of its most prominent characters had simply been
a post-boy in *The Good-Natur'd Man*. But once
fairly upon the boards neither lukewarm actors
nor an adverse manager had any further influence
over it, and the doubts of everyone vanished in

the uninterrupted applause of the audience. When, a few days later, it was printed with a brief and grateful dedication to its best friend, Johnson, the world already knew with certainty that a fresh masterpiece had been added to the roll of English Dramatic Literature, and that " genteel comedy " had received a decisive blow.

The effect of this blow, it must be admitted, had been aided not a little by the appearance, only a week or two earlier, of Foote's clever puppet-show of *The Handsome Housemaid ; or, Piety in Pattens*, which was openly directed at Kelly and his following. But ridicule by itself, without some sample of a worthier substitute, could not have sufficed to displace a persistent fashion. This timely antidote *She Stoops to Conquer*, in the most unmistakable way, afforded. From end to end of the piece there is not a sickly or a maudlin word. Even Sheridan, writing *The Rivals* two years later, thought it politic to insert " Faulkland " and " Julia " for the benefit of the sentimentalists. Goldsmith made no such concession, and his wholesome hearty merriment put to flight the Comedy of Tears, —even as the Coquecigrues vanished before the large-lunged laugh of Pantagruel. If, as Johnson feared, his plot bordered slightly upon farce— and of what good comedy may this not be said ?— at least it can be urged that its most farcical incident, the mistaking of a gentleman's house for an inn, had really happened, since it had happened to the writer himself. But the superfine objections of Walpole and his friends are now ancient

history,—history so ancient that it is scarcely
credited, while Goldsmith's manly assertion (after
Fielding) of the author's right "to stoop among
the low to copy nature," has been ratified by
successive generations of novelists and playwrights. What is beyond dispute is the healthy
atmosphere, the skilful setting, the lasting freshness and fidelity to human nature of the persons of
his drama. Not content with the finished portraits
of the Hardcastles (a Vicar and Mrs. Primrose
promoted to the squirearchy),—not content with the
incomparable and unapproachable Tony, the author
has managed to make attractive what is too often
insipid, his heroines and their lovers. Miss
Hardcastle and Miss Neville are not only charming young women, but charming characters, while
Marlow and Hastings are much more than stage
young men. And let it be remembered—it
cannot be too often remembered—that in returning to those Farquhars and Vanbrughs "of
the last age," who differed so widely from the
Kellys and Cumberlands of his own, Goldsmith has brought back no taint of their baser
part. Depending solely for its avowed intention to "make an audience merry," upon the
simple development of its humorous incident,
his play (wonderful to relate!) attains its end
without resorting to impure suggestion or equi-
vocal intrigue. Indeed, there is but one married
woman in the piece, and she traverses it without
a stain upon her character.

She Stoops to Conquer is Goldsmith's last
dramatic work, for the trifling sketch of *The
Grumbler* had never more than a grateful purpose.

When, only a year later, the little funeral pro-
cession from 2, Brick Court laid him in his unknown grave in the Temple burying-ground, the
new comedy of which he had written so hopefully
to Garrick was still non-existent. Would it have
been better than its last fortunate predecessor?—
would those early reserves of memory and experience have still proved inexhaustible? The
question cannot be answered. Through debt,
and drudgery, and depression, the writer's genius
had still advanced, and these might yet have
proved powerless to check his progress. But at
least it was given to him to end upon his best,
and not to outlive it. For, in that critical sense
which estimates the value of a work by its excellence at all points, it can scarcely be contested
that *She Stoops to Conquer* is his best production.
In spite of their beauty and humanity, the lasting
quality of *The Traveller* and *The Deserted Village*
is seriously prejudiced by his half-way attitude
between the poetry of convention and the poetry
of nature—between the gradus epithet of Pope
and the direct vocabulary of Wordsworth. With
The Vicar of Wakefield, again, immortal though it
be, it is less his art that holds us, than his charm,
his humour and his tenderness which tempt us to
forget his inconsistency and his errors of haste. In
She Stoops to Conquer, neither defect of art nor
defect of nature forbid us to give unqualified
admiration to a work which lapse of time has
shown to be still unrivalled in its kind.

AUSTIN DOBSON.

EALING, W.
February, 1889.

THE TRAVELLER;

OR,

A PROSPECT OF SOCIETY.

A POEM.

[*The Traveller, or a Prospect of Society. A Poem. Inscribed to the Rev. Mr. Henry Goldsmith. By Oliver Goldsmith, M.B.*—was first published by John Newbery of St. Paul's Church-yard, in a 4to. of thirty pages, on the 19th December, 1764. The title-page of the book (as given above) was dated 1765, and the price was 1*s*. 6*d*. Up to the sixth edition of 1770 numerous alterations were made in the text by the author. The poem is here reprinted from the ninth edition issued in 1774, the year of Goldsmith's death.]

DEDICATION.

TO THE REV. HENRY GOLDSMITH.[1]

DEAR SIR,

 AM sensible that the friendship between us can acquire no new force from the ceremonies of a Dedication; and perhaps it demands an excuse thus to prefix your name to my attempts, which you decline giving with your own. But as a part of this Poem was formerly written to you from Switzerland, the whole can now, with propriety, be only inscribed to you. It will also throw a light upon many parts of it, when the reader understands, that it is addressed to a man, who, despising Fame and Fortune, has retired early to Happiness and Obscurity, with an income of forty pounds a year.

I now perceive, my dear brother, the wisdom of your humble choice. You have entered upon a sacred office, where the harvest is great, and the labourers are but few; while you have left the

[1 Goldsmith's eldest brother. He died in May, 1768, being then curate of Kilkenny West.]

field of Ambition, where the labourers are many, and the harvest not worth carrying away. But of all kinds of ambition, what from the refinement of the times, from different systems of criticism, and from the divisions of party, that which pursues poetical fame is the wildest.

Poetry makes a principal amusement among unpolished nations; but in a country verging to the extremes of refinement, Painting and Music come in for a share. As these offer the feeble mind a less laborious entertainment, they at first rival Poetry, and at length supplant her; they engross all that favour once shown to her, and though but younger sisters, seize upon the elder's birthright.

Yet, however this art may be neglected by the powerful, it is still in greater danger from the mistaken efforts of the learned to improve it. What criticisms have we not heard of late in favour of blank verse, and Pindaric odes, choruses, anapests and iambics, alliterative care and happy negligence! Every absurdity has now a champion to defend it; and as he is generally much in the wrong, so he has always much to say; for error is ever talkative.

But there is an enemy to this art still more dangerous, I mean Party. Party entirely distorts the judgment, and destroys the taste. When the mind is once infected with this disease, it can only find pleasure in what contributes to increase the distemper. Like the tiger, that seldom desists from pursuing man after having once preyed upon human flesh, the reader, who has once gratified his appe-

tite with calumny, makes, ever after, the most
agreeable feast upon murdered reputation. Such
readers generally admire some half-witted thing,
who wants to be thought a bold man, having lost
the character of a wise one. Him they dignify
with the name of poet; his tawdry lampoons are
called satires, his turbulence is said to be force, and
his phrenzy fire.[1]

What reception a Poem may find, which has
neither abuse, party, nor blank verse to support
it, I cannot tell, nor am I solicitous to know. My
aims are right. Without espousing the cause of
any party, I have attempted to moderate the rage
of all. I have endeavoured to show, that there
may be equal happiness in states, that are differently governed from our own; that every state
has a particular principle of happiness, and that
this principle in each may be carried to a mischievous excess. There are few can judge, better
than yourself, how far these positions are illustrated
in this Poem.

I am, dear Sir,

Your most affectionate Brother,

OLIVER GOLDSMITH.

[1 Charles Churchill, the satirist (1731-64), is undoubtedly
intended here.]

THE TRAVELLER;

OR,

A PROSPECT OF SOCIETY.

EMOTE, unfriended, melancholy, slow,
Or by the lazy Scheldt, or wandering
Po ;
Or onward, where the rude Carinthian
boor,
Against the houseless stranger shuts the door ;
Or where Campania's plain forsaken lies,
A weary waste expanding to the skies :
Where'er I roam, whatever realms to see,
My heart untravell'd fondly turns to thee ;
Still to my Brother turns, with ceaseless pain,
And drags at each remove a lengthening chain.[1]

Eternal blessings crown my earliest friend,
And round his dwelling guardian saints attend :
Bless'd be that spot, where cheerful guests retire
To pause from toil, and trim their ev'ning fire ;
Bless'd that abode, where want and pain repair,

[1 Cf. *The Citizen of the World*, 1762, i. 5. (Letter iii.)]

And every stranger finds a ready chair ;
Bless'd be those feasts with simple plenty crown'd,
Where all the ruddy family around
Laugh at the jests or pranks that never fail,
Or sigh with pity at some mournful tale,
Or press the bashful stranger to his food,
And learn the luxury of doing good.

But me, not destin'd such delights to share,
My prime of life in wand'ring spent and care,
Impell'd, with steps unceasing, to pursue
Some fleeting good, that mocks me with the view ;
That, like the circle bounding earth and skies,
Allures from far, yet, as I follow, flies ; [1]
My fortune leads to traverse realms alone,
And find no spot of all the world my own.

Even now, where Alpine solitudes ascend,
I sit me down a pensive hour to spend ;
And, plac'd on high above the storm's career,
Look downward where an hundred realms appear ;
Lakes, forests, cities, plains, extending wide,
The pomp of kings, the shepherd's humbler pride.

When thus Creation's charms around combine,
Amidst the store, should thankless pride repine ?
Say, should the philosophic mind disdain
That good, which makes each humbler bosom vain ?
Let school-taught pride dissemble all it can,
These little things are great to little man ;
And wiser he, whose sympathetic mind

[1 Cf. *The Vicar of Wakefield*, 1766, ii. 160-1 (ch. x).]

Exults in all the good of all mankind.
Ye glitt'ring towns, with wealth and splendour
      crown'd,
Ye fields, where summer spreads profusion round,
Ye lakes, whose vessels catch the busy gale,
Ye bending swains, that dress the flow'ry vale,
For me your tributary stores combine ;
Creation's heir, the world, the world is mine !

As some lone miser visiting his store,
Bends at his treasure, counts, re-counts it o'er ;
Hoards after hoards his rising raptures fill,
Yet still he sighs, for hoards are wanting still :
Thus to my breast alternate passions rise,
Pleas'd with each good that heaven to man supplies :
Yet oft a sigh prevails, and sorrows fall,
To see the hoard of human bliss so small ;
And oft I wish, amidst the scene, to find
Some spot to real happiness consign'd,
Where my worn soul, each wand'ring hope at rest,
May gather bliss to see my fellows bless'd.

  But where to find that happiest spot below,
Who can direct, when all pretend to know ?
The shudd'ring tenant of the frigid zone
Boldly proclaims that happiest spot his own,
Extols the treasures of his stormy seas,
And his long nights of revelry and ease ;
The naked negro, panting at the line,
Boasts of his golden sands and palmy wine,
Basks in the glare, or stems the tepid wave,
And thanks his Gods for all the good they gave.
Such is the patriot's boast, where'er we roam,

His first, best country ever is, at home.
And yet, perhaps, if countries we compare,
And estimate the blessings which they share,
Though patriots flatter, still shall wisdom find
An equal portion dealt to all mankind,
As different good, by Art or Nature given,
To different nations makes their blessings even.

Nature, a mother kind alike to all,
Still grants her bliss at Labour's earnest call ;
With food as well the peasant is supplied
On Idra's [1] cliffs as Arno's shelvy side ;
And though the rocky-crested summits frown,
These rocks, by custom, turn to beds of down.
From Art more various are the blessings sent ;
Wealth, commerce, honour, liberty, content.
Yet these each other's power so strong contest,
That either seems destructive of the rest.
Where wealth and freedom reign contentment fails,
And honour sinks where commerce long prevails.
Hence every state to one lov'd blessing prone,
Conforms and models life to that alone.
Each to the favourite happiness attends,
And spurns the plan that aims at other ends ;
Till, carried to excess in each domain,
This favourite good begets peculiar pain.

But let us try these truths with closer eyes,
And trace them through the prospect as it lies :
Here for a while my proper cares resign'd,

[1 Bolton Corney thought Idria in Carniola intended
Birkbeck Hill suggests Lake Idro in North Italy which has
rocky shores.]

Here let me sit in sorrow for mankind,
Like yon neglected shrub at random cast,
That shades the steep, and sighs at every blast.

Far to the right where Apennine ascends,
Bright as the summer, Italy extends ;
Its uplands sloping deck the mountain's side,
Woods over woods in gay theatric pride ;
While oft some temple's mould'ring tops between
With venerable grandeur mark the scene.

Could Nature's bounty satisfy the breast,
The sons of Italy were surely blest.
Whatever fruits in different climes were found,
That proudly rise, or humbly court the ground ;
Whatever blooms in torrid tracts appear,
Whose bright succession decks the varied year ;
Whatever sweets salute the northern sky
With vernal lives that blossom but to die ;
These here disporting own the kindred soil,
Nor ask luxuriance from the planter's toil ;
While sea-born gales their gelid wings expand
To winnow fragrance round the smiling land.

But small the bliss that sense alone bestows,
And sensual bliss is all the nation knows.
In florid beauty groves and fields appear,
Man seems the only growth that dwindles here.
Contrasted faults through all his manners reign,
Though poor, luxurious, though submissive, vain,
Though grave, yet trifling, zealous, yet untrue ;
And e'en in penance planning sins anew.
All evils here contaminate the mind,

That opulence departed leaves behind ;
For wealth was theirs, not far remov'd the date,
When commerce proudly flourish'd through the
      state ;
At her command the palace learn'd to rise,
Again the long-fall'n column sought the skies ;
The canvas glow'd beyond e'en Nature warm,
The pregnant quarry teem'd with human form ;
Till, more unsteady than the southern gale,
Commerce on other shores display'd her sail ;
While nought remain'd of all that riches gave,
But towns unmann'd, and lords without a slave ;
And late the nation found with fruitless skill
Its former strength was but plethoric ill.[1]

   Yet still the loss of wealth is here supplied
By arts, the splendid wrecks of former pride ;
From these the feeble heart and long-fall'n mind
An easy compensation seem to find.
Here may be seen, in bloodless pomp array'd,
The paste-board triumph and the cavalcade ;
Processions form'd for piety and love,
A mistress or a saint in every grove.
By sports like these are all their cares beguil'd,
The sports of children satisfy the child ;[2]
Each nobler aim, represt by long control,
Now sinks at last, or feebly mans the soul ;
While low delights, succeeding fast behind,
In happier meanness occupy the mind :
As in those domes, where Caesars once bore sway,

[1 Cf. *The Citizen of the World*, 1762, i. 93. (Letter xxv.)]
[2 A pretty anecdote *a-propos* of this couplet is told in
Forster's *Life*, 1871, i. pp. 347-8.]

Defac'd by time and tottering in decay,
There in the ruin, heedless of the dead,
The shelter-seeking peasant builds his shed,
And, wond'ring man could want the larger pile,
Exults, and owns his cottage with a smile.

My soul, turn from them, turn we to survey
Where rougher climes a nobler race display,
Where the bleak Swiss their stormy mansions tread,
And force a churlish soil for scanty bread :
No product here the barren hills afford,
But man and steel, the soldier and his sword.
No vernal blooms their torpid rocks array,
But winter ling'ring chills the lap of May ;
No Zephyr fondly sues the mountain's breast,
But meteors glare, and stormy glooms invest.

Yet still, even here, content can spread a charm,
Redress the clime, and all its rage disarm.
Though poor the peasant's hut, his feasts though
    small,
He sees his little lot the lot of all ;
Sees no contiguous palace rear its head
To shame the meanness of his humble shed ;
No costly lord the sumptuous banquet deal,
To make him loathe his vegetable meal ;
But calm, and bred in ignorance and toil,
Each wish contracting, fits him to the soil.
Cheerful at morn he wakes from short repose,
Breasts the keen air, and carols as he goes ;
With patient angle trolls the finny deep,
Or drives his venturous ploughshare to the steep ;
Or seeks the den where snow-tracks mark the way,

And drags the struggling savage [1] into day.
At night returning, every labour sped,
He sits him down the monarch of a shed ;
Smiles by his cheerful fire, and round surveys
His children's looks, that brighten at the blaze ;
While his lov'd partner, boastful of her hoard,
Displays her cleanly platter on the board :
And haply too some pilgrim, thither led,
With many a tale repays the nightly bed.

Thus every good his native wilds impart,
Imprints the patriot passion on his heart,
And even those ills, that round his mansion rise,
Enhance the bliss his scanty fund supplies.
Dear is that shed to which his soul conforms,
And dear that hill which lifts him to the storms ;
And as a child, when scaring sounds molest,
Clings close and closer to the mother's breast,
So the loud torrent, and the whirlwind's roar,
But bind him to his native mountains more.

Such are the charms to barren states assign'd ;
Their wants but few, their wishes all confin'd.
Yet let them only share the praises due,
If few their wants, their pleasures are but few ;
For every want that stimulates the breast
Becomes a source of pleasure when redrest.
Whence from such lands each pleasing science flies,
That first excites desire, and then supplies ;
Unknown to them, when sensual pleasures cloy,

[1 *i.e.* wolf or bear.   Pope uses the word several times in
this sense.]

To fill the languid pause with finer joy ;
Unknown those powers that raise the soul to flame,
Catch every nerve, and vibrate through the frame.
Their level life is but a smould'ring fire,
Unquench'd by want, unfann'd by strong desire ;
Unfit for raptures, or, if raptures cheer
On some high festival of once a year,
In wild excess the vulgar breast takes fire,
Till, buried in debauch, the bliss expire.

But not their joys alone thus coarsely flow :
Their morals, like their pleasures, are but low,
For, as refinement stops, from sire to son
Unalter'd, unimprov'd, the manners run :
And love's and friendship's finely-pointed dart
Fall blunted from each indurated heart.
Some sterner virtues o'er the mountain's breast
May sit, like falcons cow'ring on the nest ;
But all the gentler morals, such as play
Through life's more cultur'd walks and charm the
   way,
These far dispers'd, on timorous pinions fly,
To sport and flutter in a kinder sky.

To kinder skies, where gentler manners reign,
I turn ; and France displays her bright domain.
Gay sprightly land of mirth and social ease,
Pleas'd with thyself, whom all the world can please,
How often have I led thy sportive choir,
With tuneless pipe, beside the murmuring Loire ?[1]

[1 *i.e.* in his pedestrian travels on the continent in 1755 6
Cf. *The Vicar of Wakefield*, 1766, ii., 24-5 (ch. i).]

Where shading elms along the margin grew,
And freshen'd from the wave the Zephyr flew ;
And haply, though my harsh touch faltering still,
But mock'd all tune, and marr'd the dancer's skill ;
Yet would the village praise my wondrous power,
And dance, forgetful of the noon-tide hour.
Alike all ages.   Dames of ancient days
Have led their children through the mirthful maze,
And the gay grandsire, skill'd in gestic lore,[1]
Has frisk'd beneath the burthen of threescore.

So bless'd a life these thoughtless realms display,
Thus idly busy rolls their world away :
Theirs are those arts that mind to mind endear,
For honour forms the social temper here :
Honour, that praise which real merit gains,
Or even imaginary worth obtains,
Here passes current ; paid from hand to hand,
It shifts in splendid traffic round the land :
From courts, to camps, to cottages it strays,
And all are taught an avarice of praise ;
They please, are pleas'd, they give to get esteem,
Till, seeming bless'd, they grow to what they seem.

But while this softer art their bliss supplies,
It gives their follies also room to rise ;
For praise too dearly lov'd, or warmly sought,
Enfeebles all internal strength of thought ;
And the weak soul, within itself unblest,
Leans for all pleasure on another's breast.
Hence ostentation here, with tawdry art,

[1 *i.e.* traditional gestures or action.]

Pants for the vulgar praise which fools impart;
Here vanity assumes her pert grimace,
And trims her robes of frieze with copper lace;
Here beggar pride defrauds her daily cheer,
To boast one splendid banquet once a year;
The mind still turns where shifting fashion draws,
Nor weighs the solid worth of self-applause.

. To men of other minds my fancy flies,
Embosom'd in the deep where Holland lies.
Methinks her patient sons before me stand,
Where the broad ocean leans against the land,
And, sedulous to stop the coming tide,
Lift the tall rampire's artificial pride.
Onward, methinks, and diligently slow,
The firm-connected bulwark seems to grow;
Spreads its long arms amidst the wat'ry roar,
Scoops out an empire, and usurps the shore.
While the pent ocean rising o'er the pile,
Sees an amphibious world beneath him smile;
The slow canal, the yellow-blossom'd vale,
The willow-tufted bank, the gliding sail,
The crowded mart, the cultivated plain,
A new creation rescu'd from his reign.

Thus, while around the wave-subjected soil
Impels the native to repeated toil,
Industrious habits in each bosom reign,
And industry begets a love of gain.
Hence all the good from opulence that springs,
With all those ills superfluous treasure brings,
Are here displayed. Their much-lov'd wealth
　　imparts

C

Convenience, plenty, elegance, and arts ;
But view them closer, craft and fraud appear,
Even liberty itself is barter'd here.
At gold's superior charms all freedom flies,
The needy sell it, and the rich man buys ;
A land of tyrants, and a den of slaves,[1]
Here wretches seek dishonourable graves,[2]
And calmly bent, to servitude conform,
Dull as their lakes that slumber in the storm.

Heavens ! how unlike their Belgic sires of old !
Rough, poor, content, ungovernably bold ;
War in each breast, and freedom on each brow ;
How much unlike the sons of Britain now !

Fir'd at the sound, my genius spreads her wing,
And flies where Britain courts the western spring ;
Where lawns extend that scorn Arcadian pride,
And brighter streams than fam'd Hydaspes[3] glide.
There all around the gentlest breezes stray,
There gentle music melts on every spray ;
Creation's mildest charms are there combin'd,
Extremes are only in the master's mind !
Stern o'er each bosom reason holds her state,
With daring aims irregularly great,
Pride in their port, defiance in their eye,
I see the lords of human kind pass by,
Intent on high designs, a thoughtful band,
By forms unfashion'd, fresh from Nature's hand ;

[1 This line occurs as prose in *The Citizen of the World*,
1762, i., 147.   (Letter xxxiv.)]

[2 *Julius Cæsar*, Act i., Sc. 2.]

[3 *Fabulosus Hydaspes*, Hor. Bk. i., Ode 22.]

Fierce in their native hardiness of soul,
True to imagin'd right, above control,
While even the peasant boasts these rights to scan,
And learns to venerate himself as man.

Thine, Freedom, thine the blessings pictur'd
here,
Thine are those charms that dazzle and endear ;
Too bless'd, indeed, were such without alloy,
But foster'd even by Freedom ills annoy :
That independence Britons prize too high,
Keeps man from man, and breaks the social tie ;
The self-dependent lordlings stand alone,
All claims that bind and sweeten life unknown ;
Here by the bonds of nature feebly held,
Minds combat minds, repelling and repell'd.
Ferments arise, imprison'd factions roar,
Repress'd ambition struggles round her shore
Till over-wrought, the general system feels
Its motions stop, or phrenzy fire the wheels.

Nor this the worst. As nature's ties decay,
As duty, love, and honour fail to sway,
Fictitious bonds, the bonds of wealth and law,
Still gather strength, and force unwilling awe.
Hence all obedience bows to these alone,
And talent sinks, and merit weeps unknown ;
Till time may come, when stripp'd of all her
charms,
The land of scholars, and the nurse of arms,
Where noble stems transmit the patriot flame,
Where kings have toil'd, and poets wrote for
fame,

One sink of level avarice shall lie,
And scholars, soldiers, kings, unhonour'd die.

Yet think not, thus when Freedom's ills I state,
I mean to flatter kings, or court the great ;
Ye powers of truth, that bid my soul aspire,
Far from my bosom drive the low desire ;
And thou, fair Freedom, taught alike to feel
The rabble's rage, and tyrant's angry steel ;
Thou transitory flower, alike undone
By proud contempt, or favour's fostering sun,
Still may thy blooms the changeful clime endure,
I only would repress them to secure :
For just experience tells, in every soil,
That those who think must govern those that toil ;
And all that freedom's highest aims can reach,
Is but to lay proportion'd loads on each.
Hence, should one order disproportion'd grow,
Its double weight must ruin all below.

O then how blind to all that truth requires,
Who think it freedom when a part aspires !
Calm is my soul, nor apt to rise in arms,
Except when fast-approaching danger warms :
But when contending chiefs blockade the throne,
Contracting regal power to stretch their own,[1]
When I behold a factious band agree
To call it freedom when themselves are free ;
Each wanton judge new penal statutes draw,
Laws grind the poor, and rich men rule the law ;[2]

[1 Cf. *The Vicar of Wakefield*, 1766, i., 202 (ch. xix).]
[2 *Ibid*, i., 206 (ch. xix).]

The wealth of climes, where savage nations roam,
Pillag'd from slaves to purchase slaves at home ;
Fear, pity, justice, indignation start,
Tear off reserve, and bare my swelling heart ;
Till half a patriot, half a coward grown,
I fly from petty tyrants to the throne.[1]

Yes, brother, curse with me that baleful hour,
When first ambition struck at regal power ;
And thus polluting honour in its source,
Gave wealth to sway the mind with double force.
Have we not seen, round Britain's peopled shore,[2]
Her useful sons exchanged for useless ore ?
Seen all her triumphs but destruction haste,
Like flaring tapers brightening as they waste ;
Seen opulence, her grandeur to maintain,
Lead stern depopulation in her train,
And over fields where scatter'd hamlets rose,
In barren solitary pomp repose?
Have we not seen at pleasure's lordly call,
The smiling long-frequented village fall ?
Beheld the duteous son, the sire decay'd,
The modest matron, and the blushing maid,
Forc'd from their homes, a melancholy train,
To traverse climes beyond the western main ;
Where wild Oswego spreads her swamps around,
And Niagara stuns with thund'ring sound ?

Even now, perhaps, as there some pilgrim strays

[1 Cf. *The Vicar of Wakefield*, 1766, i., 201 (ch. xix).]
[2 This and the lines that follow contain the germ of *The Deserted Village*.]

Through tangled forests, and through dangerous
    ways ;
Where beasts with man divided empire claim,
And the brown Indian marks with murderous
    aim ;
There, while above the giddy tempest flies,
And all around distressful yells arise,
The pensive exile, bending with his woe,
To stop too fearful, and too faint to go,[1]
Casts a long look where England's glories shine,
And bids his bosom sympathise with mine.

    Vain, very vain, my weary search to find
That bliss which only centres in the mind :
Why have I stray'd from pleasure and repose,
To seek a good each government bestows ?
In every government, though terrors reign,
Though tyrant kings, or tyrant laws restrain,
How small, of all that human hearts endure,[2]
That part which laws or kings can cause or cure.
Still to ourselves in every place consign'd,
Our own felicity we make or find :
With secret course, which no loud storms annoy,
Glides the smooth current of domestic joy.
The lifted axe, the agonising wheel,
Luke's iron crown,[3] and Damiens' bed of steel,[4]

[1 Johnson contributed this line. (Birkbeck Hill's *Boswell*,
1887, ii. 6.)]

[2 Johnson wrote these last lines, the penultimate couplet
excepted. (*Boswell, ut supra*.)]

[3 George (not Luke) Dosa, an Hungarian patriot, suffered
in 1514 the penalty of the red-hot iron crown.]

[4 Damiens was executed after horrible tortures for an

To men remote from power but rarely known,
Leave reason, faith, and conscience, all our own.

attempt to assassinate Louis XV. When in the Conciergerie
he was chained to an iron bed. (Smollett's *History of
England,* 1823, bk. iii., ch. 7, § xxv).]

THE DESERTED VILLAGE,

A POEM.

[*The Deserted Village, a Poem. By Dr. Goldsmith,* — was published by W. Griffin, at Garrick's Head, in Catherine-street, Strand, in a 4to. of thirty two pages, on the 26th May, 1770. The price was two shillings. It is here reprinted from the fourth edition, issued in the same year as the first, but considerably revised.]

DEDICATION.

TO SIR JOSHUA REYNOLDS.

DEAR SIR,

CAN have no expectations in an address of this kind, either to add to your reputation, or to establish my own. You can gain nothing from my admiration, as I am ignorant of that art in which you are said to excel; and I may lose much by the severity of your judgment, as few have a juster taste in poetry than you. Setting interest therefore aside, to which I never paid much attention, I must be indulged at present in following my affections. The only dedication I ever made was to my brother, because I loved him better than most other men. He is since dead.[1] Permit me to inscribe this Poem to you.

How far you may be pleased with the versification and mere mechanical parts of this attempt, I don't pretend to enquire; but I know you will object (and indeed several of our best and wisest

[1 See p. 3, and note.]

friends concur in the opinion) that the depopulation it deplores is no where to be seen, and the disorders it laments are only to be found in the poet's own imagination.   To this I can scarce make any other answer than that I sincerely believe what I have written ; that I have taken all possible pains, in my country excursions, for these four or five years past, to be certain of what I allege ; and that all my views and enquiries have led me to believe those miseries real, which I here attempt to display.   But this is not the place to enter into an enquiry, whether the country be depopulating, or not ; the discussion would take up much room, and I should prove myself, at best, an indifferent politician, to tire the reader with a long preface when I want his unfatigued attention to a long poem.

In regretting the depopulation of the country, I inveigh against the increase of our luxuries ; and here also I expect the shout of modern politicians against me.   For twenty or thirty years past, it has been the fashion to consider luxury as one of the greatest national advantages ; and all the wisdom of antiquity in that particular, as erroneous. Still however, I must remain a professed ancient on that head, and continue to think those luxuries prejudicial to states, by which so many vices are introduced, and so many kingdoms have been undone.[1]   Indeed so much has been poured out of late on the other side of the question, that, merely

[1 The increase of luxury was a favourite topic with Goldsmith. (Cf. Birkbeck Hill's *Boswell*, 1887, ii., 217-8.)]

for the sake of novelty and variety, one would sometimes wish to be in the right.

I am, Dear Sir,

Your sincere friend, and ardent admirer,

OLIVER GOLDSMITH.

THE DESERTED VILLAGE.

WEET Auburn ! loveliest village of the plain,
   Where health and plenty cheer'd the labouring swain,
Where smiling spring its earliest visit paid,
And parting summer's lingering blooms delay'd :
Dear lovely bowers of innocence and ease,
Seats of my youth,[1] when every sport could please,
How often have I loiter'd o'er thy green,
Where humble happiness endear'd each scene ;
How often have I paus'd on every charm,
The shelter'd cot, the cultivated farm,
The never-failing brook, the busy mill,
The decent church that topp'd the neighbouring hill,
The hawthorn bush, with seats beneath the shade,
For talking age and whispering lovers made ;
How often have I bless'd the coming day,
When toil remitting lent its turn to play,
And all the village train, from labour free,

[1 Some of the details of the picture are borrowed from Lissoy, the little hamlet in Westmeath where the author spent his younger days.]

Led up their sports beneath the spreading tree ;
While many a pastime circled in the shade,
The young contending as the old survey'd ;
And many a gambol frolick'd o'er the ground,
And sleights of art and feats of strength went
     round ;
And still as each repeated pleasure tir'd,
Succeeding sports the mirthful band inspir'd ;
The dancing pair that simply sought renown,
By holding out to tire each other down ;
The swain mistrustless of his smutted face,
While secret laughter titter'd round the place ;
The bashful virgin's side-long looks of love,
The matron's glance that would those looks re·
     prove :
These were thy charms, sweet village ; sports like
     these,
With sweet succession, taught even toil to please ;
These round thy bowers their cheerful influence
     shed,
These were thy charms—But all these charms are
     fled.

   Sweet smiling village, loveliest of the lawn,
Thy sports are fled, and all thy charms withdrawn ;
Amidst thy bowers the tyrant's hand is seen,
And desolation saddens all thy green :
One only master grasps the whole domain,
And half a tillage stints thy smiling plain :
No more thy glassy brook reflects the day,
But chok'd with sedges, works its weedy way.
Along thy glades, a solitary guest,

The hollow-sounding bittern guards its nest ; [1]
Amidst thy desert walks the lapwing flies,
And tires their echoes with unvaried cries.
Sunk are thy bowers, in shapeless ruin all,
And the long grass o'ertops the mouldering wall ;
And, trembling, shrinking from the spoiler's hand,
Far, far away, thy children leave the land.

Ill fares the land, to hastening ills a prey,
Where wealth accumulates, and men decay :
Princes and lords may flourish, or may fade ;
A breath can make them, as a breath has made ;
But a bold peasantry, their country's pride,
When once destroy'd, can never be supplied.

A time there was, ere England's griefs began,
When every rood of ground maintain'd its man ;
For him light labour spread her wholesome store,
Just gave what life requir'd, but gave no more :
His best companions, innocence and health ;
And his best riches, ignorance of wealth.

But times are alter'd ; trade's unfeeling train
Usurp the land and dispossess the swain ;
Along the lawn, where scatter'd hamlets rose,
Unwieldy wealth, and cumbrous pomp repose
And every want to opulence allied,
And every pang that folly pays to pride.
Those gentle hours that plenty bade to bloom,
Those calm desires that ask'd but little room,
Those healthful sports that grac'd the peaceful
    scene,
Liv'd in each look, and brighten'd all the green ;

[1 Cf. Bewick's *Water Birds*, 1847, p. 49.]

These, far departing, seek a kinder shore,
And rural mirth and manners are no more.

  Sweet AUBURN ! parent of the blissful hour,
Thy glades forlorn confess the tyrant's power.
Here as I take my solitary rounds,
Amidst thy tangling walks, and ruin'd grounds,
And, many a year elaps'd, return to view
Where once the cottage stood, the hawthorn grew,
Remembrance wakes with all her busy train,
Swells at my breast, and turns the past to pain.[1]

  In all my wanderings round this world of care,
In all my griefs—and GOD has given my share—
I still had hopes my latest hours to crown,
Amidst these humble bowers to lay me down ;
To husband out life's taper at the close,
And keep the flame from wasting by repose.
I still had hopes, for pride attends us still,
Amidst the swains to show my book-learn'd skill,
Around my fire an evening group to draw,
And tell of all I felt, and all I saw ;
And, as an hare, whom hounds and horns pursue,
Pants to the place from whence at first she flew,
I still had hopes, my long vexations pass'd,
Here to return—and die at home at last.[2]

  O blest retirement, friend to life's decline,
Retreats from care, that never must be mine,
How happy he who crowns in shades like these,

[1 There is no satisfactory evidence that Goldsmith ever
revisited Ireland after he left it in 1752.]
[2 Cf. *The Citizen of the World*, 1762, ii., 153. (Letter C.)]

A youth of labour with an age of ease ;
Who quits a world where strong temptations try,
And, since 'tis hard to combat, learns to fly !
For him no wretches, born to work and weep,
Explore the mine, or tempt the dangerous deep ;
No surly porter stands in guilty state
To spurn imploring famine from the gate ;
But on he moves to meet his latter end,
Angels around befriending Virtue's friend ;
Bends to the grave with unperceiv'd decay,
While Resignation gently slopes the way ;
And, all his prospects brightening to the last,
His Heaven commences ere the world be pass'd ! [1]

Sweet was the sound, when oft at evening's close
Up yonder hill the village murmur rose ;
There, as I pass'd with careless steps and slow,
The mingling notes came soften'd from below ;
The swain responsive as the milkmaid sung,
The sober herd that low'd to meet their young ;
The noisy geese that gabbled o'er the pool,
The playful children just let loose from school ;
The watchdog's voice that bay'd the whisp'ring
    wind,
And the loud laugh that spoke the vacant mind ;
These all in sweet confusion sought the shade,
And fill'd each pause the nightingale had made.
But now the sounds of population fail,
No cheerful murmurs fluctuate in the gale,
No busy steps the grass-grown footway tread,

[1 Under the title of *Resignation*, Reynolds in 1772 dedicated a print of an old man to Goldsmith as "expressing the character" sketched in this paragraph.]

For all the bloomy flush of life is fled.
All but yon widow'd, solitary thing,
That feebly bends beside the plashy spring ;
She, wretched matron, forc'd in age, for bread,
To strip the brook with mantling cresses spread,
To pick her wintry faggot from the thorn,
To seek her nightly shed, and weep till morn ;
She only left of all the harmless train,
The sad historian of the pensive plain.[1]

Near yonder copse, where once the garden
        smil'd,
And still where many a garden flower grows wild ;
There, where a few torn shrubs the place disclose,
The village preacher's modest mansion rose.[2]
A man he was to all the country dear,
And passing rich with forty pounds a year ;[3]
Remote from towns he ran his godly race,
Nor e'er had chang'd, nor wished to change his
        place ;
Unpractis'd he to fawn, or seek for power,
By doctrines fashion'd to the varying hour ;
Far other aims his heart had learn'd to prize,
More skill'd to raise the wretched than to rise.
His house was known to all the vagrant train,
He chid their wanderings, but reliev'd their pain ;
The long remember'd beggar was his guest,
Whose beard descending swept his aged breast ;

[1 This has been identified with Catherine Geraghty, a
familiar personage at Lissoy in Goldsmith's boyhood.]

[2 The character that follows is probably combined from
the author's father, his brother Henry, and his uncle
Contarine, all clergymen.]

[3 See p. 3.]

The ruin'd spendthrift, now no longer proud,
Claim'd kindred there, and had his claims allow'd ;
The broken soldier, kindly bade to stay,
Sat by his fire, and talk'd the night away ;
Wept o'er his wounds, or tales of sorrow done,
Shoulder'd his crutch, and show'd how fields were
    won.
Pleas'd with his guests, the good man learned to
    glow,
And quite forgot their vices in their woe ;
Careless their merits, or their faults to scan,
His pity gave ere charity began.

    Thus to relieve the wretched was his pride,
And e'en his failings lean'd to Virtue's side ;
But in his duty prompt at every call,
He watch'd and wept, he pray'd and felt, for all.
And, as a bird each fond endearment tries
To tempt its new-fledg'd offspring to the skies,
He tried each art, reprov'd each dull delay,
Allur'd to brighter worlds, and led the way.

    Beside the bed where parting life was laid,
And sorrow, guilt, and pain, by turns dismay'd,
The reverend champion stood. At his control
Despair and anguish fled the struggling soul ;
Comfort came down the trembling wretch to raise,
And his last faltering accents whisper'd praise.

    At church, with meek and unaffected grace,
His looks adorn'd the venerable place ;
Truth from his lips prevail'd with double sway,
And fools, who came to scoff, remain'd to pray.

The service pass'd, around the pious man,
With steady zeal, each honest rustic ran ;
Even children follow'd with endearing wile,
And pluck'd his gown, to share the good man's
       smile.
His ready smile a parent's warmth express'd,
Their welfare pleas'd him, and their cares dis-
       tress'd ;
To them his heart, his love, his griefs were given,
But all his serious thoughts had rest in Heaven.
As some tall cliff, that lifts its awful form,
Swells from the vale, and midway leaves the storm,
Though round its breast the rolling clouds are
       spread,
Eternal sunshine settles on its head.[1]

Beside yon straggling fence that skirts the way,
With blossom'd furze unprofitably gay,
There, in his noisy mansion, skill'd to rule,
The village master taught his little school ;[2]
A man severe he was, and stern to view ;
I knew him well, and every truant knew ;
Well had the boding tremblers learn'd to trace
The day's disasters in his morning face ;
Full well they laugh'd, with counterfeited glee,
At all his jokes, for many a joke had he ;
Full well the busy whisper, circling round,

[1 Chaulieu, Chapelain, and several "ancients" have been
credited with the suggestion of this simile. But perhaps
Goldsmith went no farther than the character of "Philander"
in Young's *Complaint* (*Night the Second*, 1742, p. 42).]

[2 Some of the traits of this portrait correspond with those
of Goldsmith's master at Lissoy, one Byrne.]

Convey'd the dismal tidings when he frown'd ;
Yet he was kind ; or if severe in aught,
The love he bore to learning was in fault ;
The village all declar'd how much he knew ;
'Twas certain he could write, and cypher too ;
Lands he could measure, terms and tides presage,
And even the story ran that he could gauge.
In arguing too, the parson own'd his skill,
For e'en though vanquish'd, he could argue still ;
While words of learned length and thundering
    sound
Amaz'd the gazing rustics rang'd around,
And still they gaz'd, and still the wonder grew,
That one small head could carry all he knew.

But past is all his fame. The very spot
Where many a time he triumph'd, is forgot.
Near yonder thorn, that lifts its head on high,
Where once the sign-post caught the passing eye,
Low lies that house where nut-brown draughts
    inspir'd,
Where grey-beard mirth and smiling toil retir'd,
Where village statesmen talk'd with looks pro-
    found,
And news much older than their ale went round.
Imagination fondly stoops to trace
The parlour splendours of that festive place ;
The white-wash'd wall, the nicely sanded floor,
The varnish'd clock that click'd behind the door ;
The chest contriv'd a double debt to pay,
A bed by night, a chest of drawers by day ;
The pictures plac'd for ornament and use,

The twelve good rules,[1] the royal game of goose ;[2]
The hearth, except when winter chill'd the day,
With aspen boughs, and flowers, and fennel gay ;
While broken tea-cups, wisely kept for show,
Rang'd o'er the chimney, glisten'd in a row.

Vain transitory splendours ! could not all
Reprieve the tottering mansion from its fall !
Obscure it sinks, nor shall it more impart
An hour's importance to the poor man's heart ;
Thither no more the peasant shall repair
To sweet oblivion of his daily care ;
No more the farmer's news, the barber's tale,
No more the wood-man's ballad shall prevail ;
No more the smith his dusky brow shall clear,
Relax his ponderous strength, and lean to hear ;
The host himself no longer shall be found
Careful to see the mantling bliss go round ;
Nor the coy maid, half willing to be press'd,
Shall kiss the cup to pass it to the rest.

Yes ! let the rich deride, the proud disdain,
These simple blessings of the lowly train ;
To me more dear, congenial to my heart,
One native charm, than all the gloss of art ;
Spontaneous joys, where Nature has its play,
The soul adopts, and owns their first-born sway;
Lightly they frolic o'er the vacant mind,
Unenvied, unmolested, unconfin'd :
But the long pomp, the midnight masquerade,

[1 The well-known maxims "found in the study of King Charles the First, of Blessed Memory," and common in Goldsmith's day as a broadside.]
[2 See Strutt's *Sports and Pastimes*, Bk. iv. ch. 2 (xxv).]

With all the freaks of wanton wealth array'd,
In these, ere triflers half their wish obtain,
The toiling pleasure sickens into pain ;
And, even while fashion's brightest arts decoy,
The heart distrusting asks, if this be joy.

Ye friends to truth, ye statesmen, who survey
The rich man's joys increase, the poor's decay,
'Tis yours to judge, how wide the limits stand
Between a splendid and a happy land.
Proud swells the tide with loads of freighted ore,
And shouting Folly hails them from her shore :
Hoards, even beyond the miser's wish abound,
And rich men flock from all the world around.
Yet count our gains. This wealth is but a name
That leaves our useful products still the same.
Not so the loss. The man of wealth and pride
Takes up a space that many poor supplied ;
Space for his lake, his park's extended bounds,
Space for his horses, equipage, and hounds ;
The robe that wraps his limbs in silken sloth
Has robb'd the neighbouring fields of half their
     growth,
His seat, where solitary sports are seen,
Indignant spurns the cottage from the green ;
Around the world each needful product flies,
For all the luxuries the world supplies :
While thus the land adorn'd for pleasure, all
In barren splendour feebly waits the fall.

As some fair female unadorn'd and plain,
Secure to please while youth confirms her reign,
Slights every borrow'd charm that dress supplies,

Nor shares with art the triumph of her eyes:
But when those charms are pass'd, for charms are
      frail,
When time advances and when lovers fail,
She then shines forth, solicitous to bless,
In all the glaring impotence of dress.
Thus fares the land, by luxury betray'd,
In nature's simplest charms at first array'd,
But verging to decline, its splendours rise,
Its vistas strike, its palaces surprise ;
While, scourg'd by famine, from the smiling land
The mournful peasant leads his humble band ;
And while he sinks, without one arm to save,
The country blooms—a garden, and a grave.

Where then, ah ! where, shall poverty reside,
To 'scape the pressure of contiguous pride?
If to some common's fenceless limits stray'd,
He drives his flock to pick the scanty blade,
Those fenceless fields the sons of wealth divide,
And even the bare-worn common is denied.

If to the city sped—What waits him there?
To see profusion that he must not share ;
To see ten thousand baneful arts combin'd
To pamper luxury, and thin mankind ;
To see those joys the sons of pleasure know
Extorted from his fellow creature's woe.
Here, while the courtier glitters in brocade,
There the pale artist plies the sickly trade ;
Here, while the proud their long-drawn pomps
      display,
There the black gibbet glooms beside the way.

The dome where Pleasure holds her midnight
    reign
Here, richly deck'd, admits the gorgeous train :
Tumultuous grandeur crowds the blazing square,
The rattling chariots clash, the torches glare.
Sure scenes like these no troubles e'er annoy!
Sure these denote one universal joy !
Are these thy serious thoughts?—Ah, turn thine
    eyes
Where the poor houseless shivering female lies.[1]
She once, perhaps, in village plenty bless'd,
Has wept at tales of innocence distress'd ;
Her modest looks the cottage might adorn,
Sweet as the primrose peeps beneath the thorn ;
Now lost to all ; her friends, her virtue fled,
Near her betrayer's door she lays her head,
And, pinch'd with cold, and shrinking from the
    shower,
With heavy heart deplores that luckless hour,
When idly first, ambitious of the town,
She left her wheel and robes of country brown.

    Do thine, sweet AUBURN, thine, the loveliest
    train,
Do thy fair tribes participate her pain ?
E'en now, perhaps, by cold and hunger led,
At proud men's doors they ask a little bread !

    Ah, no. To distant climes, a dreary scene,
Where half the convex world intrudes between.
Through torrid tracts with fainting steps they go,

[1 Cf. *The Bee*, 27 October, 1759 (*A City Night Piece*).]

Where wild Altama[1] murmurs to their woe.
Far different there from all that charm'd before,
The various terrors of that horrid shore ;
Those blazing suns that dart a downward ray,
And fiercely shed intolerable day ;
Those matted woods where birds forget to sing,
But silent bats in drowsy clusters cling ;
Those poisonous fields with rank luxuriance crown'd,
Where the dark scorpion gathers death around ;
Where at each step the stranger fears to wake
The rattling terrors of the vengeful snake :
Where crouching tigers wait their hapless prey,
And savage men more murderous still than they ;
While oft in whirls the mad tornado flies,
Mingling the ravag'd landscape with the skies.
Far different these from every former scene,
The cooling brook, the grassy-vested green,
The breezy covert of the warbling grove,
That only shelter'd thefts of harmless love.

Good Heaven! what sorrows gloom'd that
        parting day,
That call'd them from their native walks away ;
When the poor exiles, every pleasure pass'd,
Hung round their bowers, and fondly look'd their
        last,
And took a long farewell, and wish'd in vain
For seats like these beyond the western main ;
And shuddering still to face the distant deep,
Return'd and wept, and still return'd to weep.
The good old sire, the first prepar'd to go
To new-found worlds, and wept for others' woe ;

[1 Alatamaha, in Georgia, North America]

But for himself, in conscious virtue brave,
He only wish'd for worlds beyond the grave.
His lovely daughter, lovelier in her tears,
The fond companion of his helpless years,
Silent went next, neglectful of her charms,
And left a lover's for a father's arms.
With louder plaints the mother spoke her woes,
And bless'd the cot where every pleasure rose ;
And kiss'd her thoughtless babes with many a tear,
And clasp'd them close, in sorrow doubly dear ;
Whilst her fond husband strove to lend relief
In all the silent manliness of grief.

O luxury ! thou curs'd by Heaven's decree,
How ill exchang'd are things like these for thee !
How do thy potions, with insidious joy
Diffuse their pleasures only to destroy !
Kingdoms, by thee, to sickly greatness grown,
Boast of a florid vigour not their own ;
At every draught more large and large they grow,
A bloated mass of rank unwieldy woe ;
Till sapp'd their strength, and every part unsound,
Down, down they sink, and spread a ruin round.

Even now the devastation is begun,
And half the business of destruction done ;
Even now, methinks, as pondering here I stand,
I see the rural virtues leave the land :
Down where yon anchoring vessel spreads the sail,
That idly waiting flaps with every gale,
Downward they move, a melancholy band,
Pass from the shore, and darken all the strand.
Contented toil, and hospitable care,

And kind connubial tenderness, are there ;
And piety with wishes plac'd above,
And steady loyalty, and faithful love.
And thou, sweet Poetry, thou loveliest maid,
Still first to fly where sensual joys invade ;
Unfit in these degenerate times of shame,
To catch the heart, or strike for honest fame ;
Dear charming nymph, neglected and decried,
My shame in crowds, my solitary pride ;
Thou source of all my bliss, and all my woe,
That found'st me poor at first, and keep'st me so ;
Thou guide by which the nobler arts excel,
Thou nurse of every virtue, fare thee well !
Farewell, and Oh ! where'er thy voice be tried,
On Torno's [1] cliffs, or Pambamarca's [2] side,
Whether where equinoctial fervours glow,
Or winter wraps the polar world in snow,
Still let thy voice, prevailing over time,
Redress the rigours of th' inclement clime ;
Aid slighted truth ; with thy persuasive strain
Teach erring man to spurn the rage of gain ;
Teach him, that states of native strength possess'd,
Though very poor, may still be very bless'd ;
That trade's proud empire hastes to swift decay,
As ocean sweeps the labour'd mole away ;
While self-dependent power can time defy,
As rocks resist the billows and the sky. [3]

[1 Tornea, a river falling into the Gulf of Bothnia.]
[2 A mountain near Quito, South America.]
[3 Johnson wrote the last four lines. (Birkbeck Hill's
Boswell, 1837, ii. 7.)]

RETALIATION,

A POEM.

[*Retaliation: A Poem. By Dr. Goldsmith. Including Epitaphs on the Most Distinguished Wits of this Metropolis* —was first published on the 18th or 19th April, 1774, as a 4to. of twenty-four pages, by G. Kearsly of No. 46, Fleet Street. Under the title was a vignette-head of Goldsmith etched by Basire after Reynolds. To the second edition, which followed almost immediately, and the text of which is here printed, were added four pages of " Explanatory Notes, Observations, etc."

The poem originated in a contest of epitaphs which took place after a club dinner at the St. James's coffee house. Garrick led off with his well-known impromptu :—

" Here lies NOLLY Goldsmith, for shortness called Noll,
Who wrote like an angel, but talk'd like poor Poll,"

and several more were written by the company. Goldsmith reserved his " retaliation," and shortly afterwards set about the annexed poem, left incomplete at his death.]

RETALIATION.

A POEM.

F old, when Scarron[1] his companions
invited,
  Each guest brought his dish, and the
  feast was united ;
If our landlord supplies us with beef, and with fish,
Let each guest bring himself, and he brings the
  best dish :
Our Dean[2] shall be venison, just fresh from the
  plains ;
Our Burke[3] shall be tongue, with a garnish of
  brains ;
Our Will[4] shall be wild-fowl, of excellent flavour,
And Dick[5] with his pepper shall heighten their
  savour :

[1 Paul Scarron (1610-60), author of the *Roman Comique*,
to whose picnic dinners "*chacun apportait son plat.*"
(*Œuvres*, 1877, i., viii.)]

[2 Thomas Barnard, Dean of Derry, d. 1806.]

[3 Edmund Burke, 1729-97.]

[4 William Burke (his relation), d. 1798.]

[5 Richard Burke (Edmund Burke's brother), d. 1794.]

Our Cumberland's [1] sweet-bread its place shall
    obtain,
And Douglas [2] is pudding, substantial and plain :
Our Garrick's [3] a salad ; for in him we see
Oil, vinegar, sugar, and saltness agree :
To make out the dinner, full certain I am,
That Ridge [4] is anchovy, and Reynolds [5] is lamb ;
That Hickey's [6] a capon, and by the same rule,
Magnanimous Goldsmith a gooseberry fool.
At a dinner so various, at such a repast,
Who'd not be a glutton, and stick to the last ?
Here, waiter ! more wine, let me sit while I'm able,
Till all my companions sink under the table ;
Then, with chaos and blunders encircling my head,
Let me ponder, and tell what I think of the dead.

Here lies the good Dean, re-united to earth,
Who mix'd reason with pleasure, and wisdom with
    mirth :
If he had any faults, he has left us in doubt,
At least, in six weeks, I could not find 'em out ;
Yet some have declar'd, and it can't be denied 'em,
That sly-boots was cursedly cunning to hide 'em.

Here lies our good Edmund, whose genius was
    such,
We scarcely can praise it, or blame it too much ;

[1 Richard Cumberland the dramatist, 1732-1811.]
[2 Dr. Douglas, afterwards Bishop of Salisbury, d. 1807.]
[3 David Garrick, the actor, 1716-79.]
[4 John Ridge, an Irish Barrister.]
[5 Sir Joshua Reynolds, 1723-92.]
[6 Joseph Hickey, d. 1794, the legal adviser of Reynolds.]

Who, born for the Universe, narrow'd his mind,
And to party gave up what was meant for mankind.
Though fraught with all learning, yet straining his
	throat
To persuade Tommy Townshend [1] to lend him a
	vote ;
Who, too deep for his hearers, still went on refining,
And thought of convincing, while they thought of
	dining ;
Though equal to all things, for all things unfit,
Too nice for a statesman, too proud for a wit :
For a patriot, too cool ; for a drudge, disobedient ;
And too fond of the *right* to pursue the *expedient*.
In short, 'twas his fate, unemploy'd, or in place, Sir,
To eat mutton cold, and cut blocks with a razor.

Here lies honest William, whose heart was a
	mint,
While the owner ne'er knew half the good that was
	in't ;
The pupil of impulse, it forc'd him along,
His conduct still right, with his argument wrong ;
Still aiming at honour, yet fearing to roam,
The coachman was tipsy, the chariot drove home ;
Would you ask for his merits? alas ! he had none ;
What was good was spontaneous, his faults were
	his own.

Here lies honest Richard, whose fate I must sigh
	at ;
Alas, that such frolic should now be so quiet ;

[1 M.P. for Whitchurch, afterwards Ld. Sydney.]

What spirits were his ! what wit and what whim !
Now breaking a jest, and now breaking a limb ; [1]
Now wrangling and grumbling to keep up the
    ball,
Now teasing and vexing, yet laughing at all !
In short, so provoking a devil was Dick,
That we wish'd him full ten times a day at Old
    Nick ;
But, missing his mirth and agreeable vein,
As often we wish'd to have Dick back again.

  Here Cumberland lies, having acted his parts,
The Terence of England, the mender of hearts ;
A flattering painter, who made it his care
To draw men as they ought to be, not as they
    are.
His gallants are all faultless, his women divine,
And comedy wonders at being so fine ;
Like a tragedy queen he has dizen'd her out,
Or rather like tragedy giving a rout.
His fools have their follies so lost in a crowd
Of virtues and feelings, that folly grows proud ;
And coxcombs, alike in their failings alone,
Adopting his portraits, are pleas'd with their own.
Say, where has our poet this malady caught ?
Or, wherefore his characters thus without fault ?
Say, was it that vainly directing his view
To find out men's virtues, and finding them few,

[1 "The above Gentleman (Richard Burke) having slightly
fractured one of his arms and legs, at different times, the
Doctor (*i.e.* Goldsmith) has rallied him on those accidents, as
a kind of *retributive* justice for breaking his jests on other
people." (*Note to Second Edition.*)]

Quite sick of pursuing each troublesome elf,
He grew lazy at last, and drew from himself? [1]

Here Douglas retires, from his toils to relax,
The scourge of impostors, the terror of quacks : [2]
Come, all ye quack bards, and ye quacking divines,
Come, and dance on the spot where your tyrant
    reclines :
When Satire and Censure encircl'd his throne,
I fear'd for your safety, I fear'd for my own ;
But now he is gone, and we want a detector,
Our Dodds [3] shall be pious, our Kenricks [4] shall
    lecture ;
Macpherson [5] write bombast, and call it a style,
Our Townshend make speeches, and I shall com-
    pile ;
New Lauders and Bowers [6] the Tweed shall cross
    over,
No countryman living their tricks to discover ;
Detection her taper shall quench to a spark,
And Scotchmen meet Scotchmen, and cheat in the
    dark.

[1 Cumberland is said to have fancied that this epitaph
was *not* ironical.]

[2 Douglas exposed two literary impostors,—Archibald
Bower, author of a *History of the Popes*, and William
Lauder, who fabricated a charge of plagiarism against
Milton.]

[3 The Rev. William Dodd, executed for forgery in June,
1777.]

[4 Dr. Kenrick, who lectured on Shakespeare at the
Devil Tavern in 1774.]

[5 James Macpherson (1738-96) of *Ossian* notoriety. He
had recently (1773) published a prose translation of Homer.]

[6 *Vide* note 2 above.]

Here lies David Garrick, describe me, who can,
An abridgment of all that was pleasant in man ;
As an actor, confessed without rival to shine :
As a wit, if not first, in the very first line :
Yet, with talents like these, and an excellent heart,
The man had his failings, a dupe to his art.
Like an ill-judging beauty, his colours he spread,
And beplaster'd with rouge his own natural red.
On the stage he was natural, simple, affecting ;
'Twas only that when he was off he was acting.
With no reason on earth to go out of his way,
He turn'd and he varied full ten times a day.
Though secure of our hearts, yet confoundedly sick
If they were not his own by finessing and trick :
He cast off his friends, as a huntsman his pack,
For he knew when he pleas'd he could whistle them
     back.
Of praise a mere glutton, he swallowed what came,
And the puff of a dunce he mistook it for fame ;
Till his relish grown callous, almost to disease,
Who pepper'd the highest was surest to please.
But let us be candid, and speak out our mind,
If dunces applauded, he paid them in kind.
Ye Kenricks, ye Kellys,[1] and Woodfalls [2] so grave,
What a commerce was yours, while you got and
     you gave !
How did Grub-street re-echo the shouts that you
     rais'd,
While he was be-Roscius'd, and you were be-prais'd !

[1 Hugh Kelly, the dramatist (1739-77), author of *False
Delicacy*, *A Word to the Wise*, etc.

[2 William Woodfall, d. 1803, editor of *The Morning
Chronicle*.]

But peace to his spirit, wherever it flies,
To act as an angel, and mix with the skies :
Those poets, who owe their best fame to his skill,
Shall still be his flatterers, go where he will.
Old Shakespeare, receive him, with praise and
    with love,
And Beaumonts and Bens be his Kellys above.

    Here Hickey reclines, a most blunt, pleasant
    creature,
And slander itself must allow him good nature :
He cherish'd his friend, and he relish'd a bumper,
Yet one fault he had, and that one was a thumper.
Perhaps you may ask if the man was a miser ?
I answer, no, no, for he always was wiser :
Too courteous, perhaps, or obligingly flat ?
His very worst foe can't accuse him of that :
Perhaps he confided in men as they go,
And so was too foolishly honest ?   Ah no !
Then what was his failing ? come tell it, and burn
    ye !
He was, could he help it ?—a special attorney.

    Here Reynolds is laid, and to tell you my mind,
He has not left a better or wiser behind :
His pencil was striking, resistless, and grand ;
His manners were gentle, complying, and bland ;
Still born to improve us in every part,
His pencil our faces, his manners our heart :
To coxcombs averse, yet most civilly steering,
When they judg'd without skill he was still hard of
    hearing :

When they talked of their Raphaels, Correggios,
    and stuff,
He shifted his trumpet, and only took snuff . . .[1]

POSTSCRIPT.

[*First printed in the Fifth Edition,* 1774.]

After the Fourth Edition of this Poem was printed, the
Publisher received an Epitaph on Mr. Whitefoord, from a
friend of the late Doctor Goldsmith, inclosed in a letter, of
which the following is an abstract :

' I have in my possession a sheet of paper, containing
near forty lines in the Doctor's own hand-writing : there are
many scattered, broken verses, on Sir Jos. Reynolds, Coun-
sellor Ridge, Mr. Beauclerk, and Mr. Whitefoord. The
Epitaph on the last-mentioned gentleman is the only one
that is finished, and therefore I have copied it, that you may
add it to the next edition. It is a striking proof of Doctor
Goldsmith's good-nature. I saw this sheet of paper in the
Doctor's room, five or six days before he died ; and, as I had
got all the other Epitaphs, I asked him if I might take it.
" *In truth you may, my Boy,*" (replied he) "*for it will be
of no use to me where I am going.*" '

ERE Whitefoord[2] reclines, and deny it
    who can,
    Though he *merrily* liv'd, he is now a
      grave man ;
Rare compound of oddity, frolic, and fun !
Who relish'd a joke, and rejoic'd in a pun ;

[1 Prior (*Life of Goldsmith,* 1837, ii. 499) says half a line
more had been written. It was, " By flattery unspoiled "—
and remained unaltered in the MS.]

[2 Caleb Whitefoord, d. 1810, an inveterate punster, and
author of the once-popular " Cross Readings," for an account of which see Smith's *Life of Nollekens,* 1828, i. 336-7.]

Whose temper was generous, open, sincere ;
A stranger to flatt'ry, a stranger to fear ;
Who scatter'd around wit and humour at will ;
Whose daily *bon mots* half a column might fill :
A Scotchman, from pride and from prejudice free ;
A scholar, yet surely no pedant was he.
What pity, alas ! that so lib'ral a mind
Should so long be to news-paper essays confin'd ;
Who perhaps to the summit of science could soar,
Yet content 'if the table he set on a roar ;'
Whose talents to fill any station were fit,
Yet happy if Woodfall [1] confess'd him a wit.
Ye news-paper witlings ! ye pert scribbling folks !
Who copied his squibs, and re-echoed his jokes ;
Ye tame imitators, ye servile herd, come,
Still follow your master, and visit his tomb :
To deck it, bring with you festoons of the vine,
And copious libations bestow on his shrine :
Then strew all around it (you can do no less)
Cross-readings, Ship-news, and *Mistakes of the
        Press.*
Merry Whitefoord, farewell ! for *thy* sake I admit
That a Scot may have humour, I had almost said
        wit :
This debt to thy mem'ry I cannot refuse,
' Thou best humour'd man with the worst humour'd
        muse.' [2]

[1 H. S. Woodfall, d. 1805, printer of the *Public Advertiser,*
in which the " Cross Readings " appeared.]

[2 An adaptation of Rochester on Lord Buckhurst. It is
half suspected that Whitefoord wrote this " Postscript "
himself.]

THE HAUNCH OF VENISON.

A POETICAL EPISTLE TO

LORD CLARE.

[*The Haunch of Venison, a Poetical Epistle to Lord Clare.
By the late Dr. Goldsmith. With a Head of the Author,
Drawn by Henry Bunbury, Esq; and Etched by* [James]
Bretherton—was first published in 1776 by J. Ridley, in St.
James's Street and G. Kearsly, in Fleet Street. It is supposed to have been written early in 1771. The present version is printed from the second edition "taken from the
author's *last* Transcript," and issued in the same year as the
first.]

THE HAUNCH OF VENISON.

A POETICAL EPISTLE TO LORD CLARE.[1]

HANKS, my Lord, for your venison, for finer or fatter
    Never rang'd in a forest, or smok'd in
    a platter ;
The haunch was a picture for painters to study,
The fat was so white, and the lean was so ruddy.
Though my stomach was sharp, I could scarce help
    regretting
To spoil such a delicate picture by eating ;
I had thoughts, in my chambers, to place it in view,
To be shown to my friends as a piece of *virtù* ;
As in some Irish houses, where things are so so,
One gammon of bacon hangs up for a show :
But for eating a rasher of what they take pride in,
They'd as soon think of eating the pan it is fried in.
But hold—let me pause—Don't I hear you pro-
    nounce
This tale of the bacon a damnable bounce ?
Well, suppose it a bounce—sure a poet may try,
By a bounce now and then, to get courage to fly.

[1 Robert Nugent, of Carlanstown, Westmeath ; created
Viscount Clare in 1766 ; in 1776 Earl Nugent.]

But, my Lord, it's no bounce : I protest in my
    turn,
It's a truth—and your Lordship may ask Mr.
    Byrne.[1]
To go on with my tale—as I gaz'd on the haunch,
I thought of a friend that was trusty and staunch ;
So I cut it, and sent it to Reynolds undress'd,
To paint it, or eat it, just as he lik'd best.
Of the neck and the breast I had next to dispose ;
'Twas a neck and a breast—that might rival
    M[on]r[oe]'s :—[2]
But in parting with these I was puzzled again,
With the how, and the who, and the where, and
    the when.
There's H[owar]d, and C[ole]y, and H—rth, and
    H[i]ff,[3]
I think they love venison—I know they love beef ;
There's my countryman H[i]gg[i]ns—Oh ! let him
    alone,
For making a blunder, or picking a bone.
But hang it—to poets who seldom can eat,
Your very good mutton's a very good treat ;
Such dainties to them, their health it might hurt,
It's like sending them ruffles, when wanting a
    shirt.
While thus I debated, in reverie centred,
An acquaintance, a friend as he call'd himself,
    enter'd :
An under-bred, fine-spoken fellow was he,
And he smil'd as he look'd at the venison and me.

[1 Lord Clare's nephew.]
[2 Dorothy Monroe, a celebrated beauty.]
[3 Paul Hiffernan, M.D., a Grub-street writer.]

What have we got here?—Why this is good
    eating!
Your own, I suppose—or is it in waiting?'
' Why, whose should it be?' cried I with a flounce,
' I get these things often; '—but that was a bounce:
' Some lords, my acquaintance, that settle the
    nation,
Are pleas'd to be kind—but I hate ostentation.'

   ' If that be the case, then,' cried he, very gay,
' I'm glad I have taken this house in my way.
To-morrow you take a poor dinner with me;
No words—I insist on't—precisely at three:
We'll have Johnson, and Burke; all the wits will
    be there; [1]
My acquaintance is slight, or I'd ask my Lord
    Clare.
And now that I think on't, as I am a sinner!
We wanted this venison to make out the dinner.
What say you—a pasty? it shall, and it must,
And my wife, little Kitty, is famous for crust.
Here, porter!—this venison with me to Mile-end;
No stirring—I beg—my dear friend—my dear
    friend!'
Thus snatching his hat, he brush'd off like the wind,
And the porter and eatables follow'd behind.

   Left alone to reflect, having emptied my shelf,
' And nobody with me at sea but myself; ' [2]

[1 Cf. Boileau, *Sat.*, iii, ll. 25-6, which Goldsmith had in
mind.]
   [2 A textual quotation from the love letters of Henry
Frederick, Duke of Cumberland, to Lady Grosvenor.]

Though I could not help thinking my gentleman
      hasty,
Yet Johnson, and Burke, and a good venison pasty,
Were things that I never dislik'd in my life,
Though clogg'd with a coxcomb, and Kitty his wife.
So next day, in due splendour to make my approach,
I drove to his door in my own hackney coach.

   When come to the place where we all were to
      dine,
(A chair-lumber'd closet just twelve feet by nine :)
My friend bade me welcome, but struck me quite
      dumb,
With tidings that Johnson and Burke would not
      come ; [1]
' For I knew it,' he cried, ' both eternally fail,
The one with his speeches, and t'other with Thrale ;[2]
But no matter, I'll warrant we'll make up the party
With two full as clever, and ten times as hearty.
The one is a Scotchman, the other a Jew,
They['re] both of them merry and authors like you ;
The one writes the *Snarler*, the other the *Scourge* ;
Some think he writes *Cinna*—he owns to *Panurge*.'[3]
While thus he describ'd them by trade and by name,
They enter'd, and dinner was serv'd as they came.

   At the top a fried liver and bacon were seen,
At the bottom was tripe in a swingeing tureen ;

[1 Cf. Boileau, *ut supra*, ll. 31-4.]

[2 Henry Thrale, the Southwark brewer, Johnson's close
friend from 1765.]

[3 These were *noms de guerre* of Dr. W. Scott, Lord
Sandwich's chaplain, an active supporter of the Government.]

At the sides there was spinach and pudding made
    hot ;
In the middle a place where the pasty—was not.
Now, my Lord, as for tripe, it's my utter aversion,
And your bacon I hate like a Turk or a Persian ;
So there I sat stuck, like a horse in a pound,
While the bacon and liver went merrily round.
But what vex'd me most was that d—'d Scottish
    rogue,
With his long-winded speeches, his smiles and his
    brogue ;
And, 'Madam,' quoth he, 'may this bit be my
    poison,[1]
A prettier dinner I never set eyes on ;
Pray a slice of your liver, though may I be curs'd,
But I've eat of your tripe till I'm ready to burst.'
'The tripe,' quoth the Jew, with his chocolate
    cheek,
'I could dine on this tripe seven days in the week :
I like these here dinners so pretty and small ;
But your friend there, the Doctor, eats nothing
    at all.'
'O—Oh !' quoth my friend, 'he'll come on in a
    trice,
He's keeping a corner for something that's nice :
There's a pasty'—'A pasty !' repeated the Jew,
'I don't care if I keep a corner for't too.'
'What the de'il, mon, a pasty !' re-echoed the
    Scot,
'Though splitting, I'll still keep a corner for thot.'
'We'll all keep a corner,' the lady cried out ;
'We'll all keep a corner,' was echoed about.

[1 Cf. *She Stoops to Conquer*, Act i, Sc. 2.]

F

While thus we resolv'd, and the pasty delay'd,
With looks that quite petrified, enter'd the maid ;
A visage so sad, and so pale with affright,
Wak'd Priam in drawing his curtains by night.[1]
But we quickly found out, for who could mistake
    her ?
That she came with some terrible news from the
    baker :
And so it fell out, for that negligent sloven
Had shut out the pasty on shutting his oven.
Sad Philomel thus—but let similes drop—
And now that I think on't, the story may stop.
To be plain, my good Lord, it's but labour mis-
    plac'd
To send such good verses to one of your taste ;
You've got an odd something—a kind of dis-
    cerning—
A relish—a taste—sicken'd over by learning ;
At least it's your temper, as very well known,
That you think very slightly of all that's your own :
So, perhaps, in your habits of thinking amiss,
You may make a mistake, and think slightly of this.

[¹ Cf. 2 *Henry IV.* Act i, Sc. 1.]

MISCELLANEOUS PIECES.

PART OF A PROLOGUE WRITTEN AND SPOKEN BY THE POET LABERIUS,

A ROMAN KNIGHT, WHOM CAESAR FORCED UPON THE STAGE.

PRESERVED BY MACROBIUS.[1]

HAT ! no way left to shun th' inglorious
        stage,
    And save from infamy my sinking age !
    Scarce half alive, oppress'd with many
a year,
What in the name of dotage drives me here ?
A time there was, when glory was my guide,
Nor force nor fraud could turn my steps aside ;
Unaw'd by pow'r, and unappall'd by fear,
With honest thrift I held my honour dear :
But this vile hour disperses all my store,
And all my hoard of honour is no more.
For ah ! too partial to my life's decline,

[1 First printed at pp. 176-7 of Goldsmith's *Enquiry into
the Present State of Polite Learning*, 1759 (ch. xii.—' Of the
Stage'). The original lines are to be found in the *Satur-
nalia* of Macrobius, lib. ii. cap. vii. ed. Zeunii, pp. 565-70.]

Caesar persuades, submission must be mine;
Him I obey, whom heaven itself obeys,
Hopeless of pleasing, yet inclin'd to please.
Here then at once, I welcome every shame,
And cancel at threescore a life of fame ;
No more my titles shall my children tell,
The old buffoon will fit my name as well ;
This day beyond its term my fate extends,
For life is ended when our honour ends.

ON A BEAUTIFUL YOUTH STRUCK BLIND WITH LIGHTNING.[1]

(*Imitated from the Spanish.*)

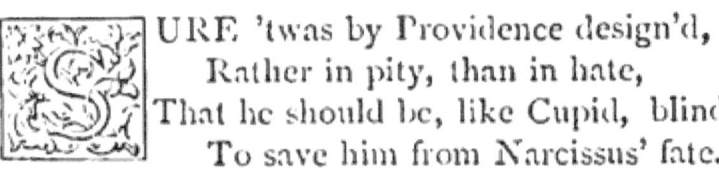

SURE 'twas by Providence design'd,
    Rather in pity, than in hate,
That he should be, like Cupid, blind,
    To save him from Narcissus' fate.

[1 First printed in *The Bee*, 6 October, 1759.]

THE GIFT.

TO IRIS, IN BOW-STREET, COVENT-GARDEN.[1]

AY, cruel IRIS, pretty rake,
 Dear mercenary beauty,
What annual offering shall I make,
 Expressive of my duty?

My heart, a victim to thine eyes,
 Should I at once deliver,
Say, would the angry fair one prize
 The gift, who slights the giver?

A bill, a jewel, watch, or toy,
 My rivals give—and let 'em :
If gems, or gold, impart a joy,
 I'll give them—when I get 'em

I'll give—but not the full-blown rose,
 Or rose-bud more in fashion ;
Such short-liv'd offerings but disclose
 A transitory passion.

[1 First printed in *The Bee*, 13 October, 1759. It is an adaptation of some lines headed *Etrene à Iris* in Part iii. of the *Ménagiana*.]

I'll give thee something yet unpaid,
  Not less sincere than civil :
I'll give thee—Ah ! too charming maid,
  I'll give thee—To the Devil.

THE LOGICIANS REFUTED.

IN IMITATION OF DEAN SWIFT.[1]

 OGICIANS have but ill defin'd
As rational the human kind;
Reason, they say, belongs to man,
But let them prove it if they can.
Wise Aristotle and Smiglecius,
By ratiocinations specious,
Have strove to prove with great precision,
With definition and division,
Homo est ratione praeditum,—
But for my soul I cannot credit 'em;
And must in spite of them maintain,
That man and all his ways are vain;
And that this boasted lord of nature
Is both a weak and erring creature;
That instinct is a surer guide
Than reason-boasting mortal's pride;
And that brute beasts are far before 'em
Deus est anima brutorum.
Who ever knew an honest brute

[1 First printed in *The Busy Body*, 18 October, 1759, with the heading :—"The following poem written by DR. SWIFT, is communicated to the Public by the BUSY BODY, to whom it was presented by a Nobleman of distinguished Learning and Taste." But tradition, and the early editors, ascribe the lines to Goldsmith.]

At law his neighbour prosecute,
Bring action for assault and battery,
Or friends beguile with lies and flattery?
O'er plains they ramble unconfin'd,
No politics disturb their mind;
They eat their meals, and take their sport,
Nor know who's in or out at court;
They never to the levee go
To treat as dearest friend, a foe;
They never importune his Grace,
Nor ever cringe to men in place;
Nor undertake a dirty job,
Nor draw the quill to write for B—b.[1]
Fraught with invective they ne'er go,
To folks at Paternoster Row;
No judges, fiddlers, dancing-masters,
No pickpockets, or poetasters,
Are known to honest quadrupeds;
No single brute his fellow leads.
Brutes never meet in bloody fray,
Nor cut each others' throats, for pay.
Of beasts, it is confess'd, the ape
Comes nearest us in human shape;
Like man he imitates each fashion,
And malice is his ruling passion;
But both in malice and grimaces
A courtier any ape surpasses.
Behold him humbly cringing wait
Upon a minister of state;
View him soon after to inferiors,
Aping the conduct of superiors;

[1 Sir Robert Walpole.]

He promises with equal air,
And to perform takes equal care.
He in his turn finds imitators ;
At court, the porters, lacqueys, waiters,
Their master's manners still contract,
And footmen, lords and dukes can act.
Thus at the court both great and small
Behave alike, for all ape all.

A SONNET.[1]

EEPING, murmuring, complaining,
   Lost to every gay delight ;
MYRA, too sincere for feigning,
   Fears th' approaching bridal night.

Yet, why impair thy bright perfection?
   Or dim thy beauty with a tear?
Had MYRA follow'd my direction,
   She long had wanted cause of fear.

[1 First printed in *The Bee*, 20 October, 1759. It is said
to be an imitation of Denis Sanguin de St.-Pavin, d. 1670.]

STANZAS,

ON THE TAKING OF QUEBEC, AND DEATH OF GENERAL WOLFE.[1]

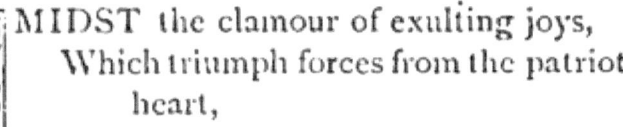 MIDST the clamour of exulting joys,
    Which triumph forces from the patriot
        heart,
  Grief dares to mingle her soul-piercing
      voice,
And quells the raptures which from pleasures
    start.

O Wolfe ! to thee a streaming flood of woe,
  Sighing we pay, and think e'en conquest dear ;
Quebec in vain shall teach our breast to glow,
  Whilst thy sad fate extorts the heart-wrung tear.

Alive, the foe thy dreadful vigour fled,
  And saw thee fall with joy-pronouncing eyes :
Yet they shall know thou conquerest, though
    dead—
  Since from thy tomb a thousand heroes rise !

[1 First printed in *The Busy Body*, 22 October, 1759, a week after the news of Wolfe's death (on 13 September previous) had reached England.]

AN ELEGY ON THAT GLORY OF HER SEX, MRS. MARY BLAIZE.[1]

OOD people all, with one accord,
  Lament for Madam BLAIZE,
Who never wanted a good word—
  From those who spoke her praise.

The needy seldom pass'd her door,
  And always found her kind ;
She freely lent to all the poor,—
  Who left a pledge behind.

She strove the neighbourhood to please,
  With manners wond'rous winning,
And never followed wicked ways,—
  Unless when she was sinning.

At church, in silks and satins new,
  With hoop of monstrous size,
She never slumber'd in her pew,—
  But when she shut her eyes.

Her love was sought, I do aver,
  By twenty beaux and more ;
The king himself has follow'd her,—
  When she has walk'd before.

[1 First printed in *The Bee*, 27 October, 1759. It is
modelled on the old song of M. de la Palice, a version of
which is to be found in Part iii. of the *Menagiana.*]

But now her wealth and finery fled,
   Her hangers-on cut short all ;
The doctors found, when she was dead, —
   Her last disorder mortal.

Let us lament, in sorrow sore,
   For Kent-street well may say,
That had she lived a twelve-month more, —
   She had not died to-day.

DESCRIPTION OF AN AUTHOR'S BEDCHAMBER.[1]

WHERE the Red Lion flaring o'er the way,
  Invites each passing stranger that can pay ;
Where Calvert's butt, and Parsons' black champagne,[2]
Regale the drabs and bloods of Drury-lane ;
There in a lonely room, from bailiffs snug,
The Muse found Scroggen stretch'd beneath a rug ;
A window, patch'd with paper, lent a ray,
That dimly show'd the state in which he lay ;
The sanded floor that grits beneath the tread ;
The humid wall with paltry pictures spread :
The royal game of goose was there in view,
And the twelve rules the royal martyr drew ;[3]
The seasons, fram'd with listing, found a place,
And brave prince William show'd his lamp-black face ;[4]

[1 First printed in a Chinese Letter in *The Public Ledger*, 2 May, 1760, afterwards Letter xxix. of *The Citizen of the World*, 1762, i. 121.]

[2 *i.e.*, "Entire butt beer" or porter.]

[3 See notes, p. 40.]

[4 William Augustus, Duke of Cumberland, 1721-65,— probably a silhouette.]

The morn was cold, he views with keen desire
The rusty grate unconscious of a fire ;
With beer and milk arrears the frieze was scor'd,
And five crack'd teacups dress'd the chimney board ;
A nightcap deck'd his brows instead of bay,
A cap by night—a stocking all the day ![1]

[1 Cf. *The Deserted Village*, p. 39 :—
    " A bed by night, a chest of drawers by day."]

ON SEEING MRS. * * PERFORM IN THE CHARACTER OF * * * *.[1]

OR you, bright fair, the Nine address
their lays,
And tune my feeble voice to sing thy
praise.
The heartfelt power of every charm divine,
Who can withstand their all commanding shine?
See how she moves along with every grace,
While soul-brought tears steal down each shining
face.
She speaks ! 'tis rapture all, and nameless bliss,
Ye gods ! what transport e'er compared to this?
As when in Paphian groves the Queen of Love
With fond complaint address'd the listening Jove ;
'Twas joy and endless blisses all around,
And rocks forgot their hardness at the sound.
Then first, at last even Jove was taken in,
And felt her charms, without disguise, within.

[1 From Letter lxxxii. of *The Citizen of the World*, 1762,
ii. 87, first printed in *The Public Ledger*, 21 October, 1760.
The verses are intended as a specimen of the newspaper
muse.]

OF THE DEATH OF THE RIGHT
HON. * * *.[1]

E muses, pour the pitying tear
    For Pollio snatch'd away ;
O ! had he liv'd another year !
    He had not died to-day.

O ! were he born to bless mankind
    In virtuous times of yore,
Heroes themselves had fallen behind
    Whene'er he went before.

How sad the groves and plains appear,
    And sympathetic sheep ;
Even pitying hills would drop a tear
    If hills could learn to weep.

His bounty in exalted strain
    Each bard might well display :
Since none implor'd relief in vain
    That went reliev'd away.

[1 From Letter ciii. of *The Citizen of the World,* 1762, ii.
164, first printed in *The Public Ledger,* 4 March, 1761.
The verses are given as "a specimen of a poem on the
decease of a great man." Cf. the *Elegy on Mrs. Mary
Blaize,* p. 77.]

And hark ! I hear the tuneful throng
   His obsequies forbid,
He still shall live, shall live as long
   As ever dead man did.

AN EPIGRAM.

ADDRESSED TO THE GENTLEMEN REFLECTED ON IN THE ROSCIAD, A POEM, BY THE AUTHOR.[1]

> Worried with debts, and past all hopes of bail,
> His pen he prostitutes t'avoid a gaol.
>
> ROSCOM.

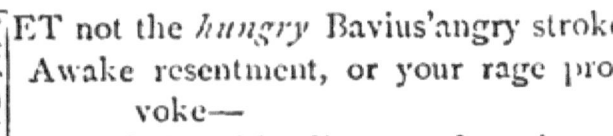ET not the *hungry* Bavius'angry stroke
Awake resentment, or your rage pro-
      voke—
But pitying his distress, let virtue[2]
      shine,
And giving each your bounty,[3] *let him dine.*
For thus retain'd, as learned counsel can,
Each case, however bad, he'll new japan ;
And by a quick transition, plainly show
'Twas no defect of yours, but *pocket low,*
That caus'd his *putrid kennel* to o'erflow.

[1 From Letter ex. of *The Citizen of the World,* 1762, ii. 193, first printed in *The Public Ledger,* 14th April, 1761. The epigram, however, had been printed in the *Ledger* for 4th April, and so was only revived in the letter of ten days later. It is one of Goldsmith's doubtful pieces, but his animosity to Churchill is unquestioned.]

[2] Charity *(Author's note).*

[3] Settled at one shilling, the price of the poem *(Author's note).*

TO G. C. AND R. L.[1]

'WAS you, or I, or he, or all together,
    'Twas one, both, three of them, they
        know not whether;
    This, I believe, between us great or
        small,
You, I, he, wrote it not—'twas Churchill's all.

TRANSLATION OF A SOUTH AMERICAN ODE.[2]

IN all my Enna's beauties blest,
    Amidst profusion still I pine;
For though she gives me up her breast,
    Its panting tenant is not mine.

[1 From the same letter as the preceding epigram; but not a reprint. George Colman (G. C.), and Robert Lloyd (R. L.), were supposed to have assisted Churchill in the *Rosciad*, the "it" of the epigram.]

[2 From Letter cxiii. of *The Citizen of the World*, 1762, ii. 209, first printed in *The Public Ledger*, 13th May, 1761.]

THE DOUBLE TRANSFORMATION.

A TALE.[1]

ECLUDED from domestic strife,
Jack Book-worm led a college life;
A fellowship at twenty-five
Made him the happiest man alive;
He drank his glass and cracked his joke,
And Freshmen wondered as he spoke.

Such pleasures unalloy'd with care,
Could any accident impair?
Could Cupid's shaft at length transfix
Our swain, arriv'd at thirty-six?
O had the archer ne'er come down
To ravage in a country town!
Or Flavia been content to stop
At triumphs in a Fleet-street shop.
O had her eyes forgot to blaze!
Or Jack had wanted eyes to gaze.
O!——But let exclamation cease,
Her presence banish'd all his peace.
So with decorum all things carried;
Miss frown'd, and blush'd, and then was—married.

[1 First printed in *Essays, by Mr. Goldsmith*, 1765, p. 229.
The version here followed is that of the second edition of
1766, which was revised.]

Need we expose to vulgar sight
The raptures of the bridal night?
Need we intrude on hallow'd ground,
Or draw the curtains clos'd around?
Let it suffice, that each had charms;
He clasp'd a goddess in his arms;
And, though she felt his usage rough,
Yet in a man 'twas well enough.

The honey-moon like lightning flew,
The second brought its transports too.
A third, a fourth, were not amiss,
The fifth was friendship mix'd with bliss:
But, when a twelvemonth pass'd away,
Jack found his goddess made of clay;
Found half the charms that deck'd her face
Arose from powder, shreds, or lace;
But still the worst remain'd behind,
That very face had robb'd her mind.

Skill'd in no other arts was she,
But dressing, patching, repartee;
And, just as humour rose or fell,
By turns a slattern or a belle:
'Tis true she dress'd with modern grace,
Half naked at a ball or race;
But when at home, at board or bed,
Five greasy nightcaps wrapp'd her head.
Could so much beauty condescend
To be a dull domestic friend?
Could any curtain-lectures bring
To decency so fine a thing?
In short, by night, 'twas fits or fretting;

By day, 'twas gadding or coquetting.
Fond to be seen, she kept a bevy
Of powder'd coxcombs at her levy;
The 'squire and captain took their stations,
And twenty other near relations;
Jack suck'd his pipe, and often broke
A sigh in suffocating smoke;
While all their hours were pass'd between
Insulting repartee or spleen.

Thus as her faults each day were known,
He thinks her features coarser grown;
He fancies every vice she shows,
Or thins her lip, or points her nose:
Whenever rage or envy rise,
How wide her mouth, how wild her eyes!
He knows not how, but so it is,
Her face is grown a knowing phiz;
And, though her fops are wond'rous civil,
He thinks her ugly as the devil.

Now, to perplex the ravell'd noose,
As each a different way pursues,
While sullen or loquacious strife,
Promis'd to hold them on for life,
That dire disease, whose ruthless power
Withers the beauty's transient flower:
Lo! the small-pox, whose horrid glare
Levell'd its terrors at the fair:
And, rifling ev'ry youthful grace,
Left but the remnant of a face.

The glass, grown hateful to her sight,
Reflected now a perfect fright:

Each former art she vainly tries
To bring back lustre to her eyes.
In vain she tries her paste and creams,
To smooth her skin, or hide its seams;
Her country beaux and city cousins,
Lovers no more, flew off by dozens:
The 'squire himself was seen to yield,
And even the captain quit the field.

Poor Madam, now condemn'd to hack
The rest of life with anxious Jack,
Perceiving others fairly flown,
Attempted pleasing him alone.
Jack soon was dazzl'd to behold
Her present face surpass the old;
With modesty her cheeks are dy'd,
Humility displaces pride;
For tawdry finery is seen
A person ever neatly clean:
No more presuming on her sway,
She learns good-nature every day;
Serenely gay, and strict in duty,
Jack finds his wife a perfect beauty.

A NEW SIMILE.

IN THE MANNER OF SWIFT.[1]

LONG had I sought in vain to find
A likeness for the scribbling kind ;
The modern scribbling kind, who write
In wit, and sense, and nature's spite :
Till reading, I forgot what day on,
A chapter out of Tooke's Pantheon,
I think I met with something there,
To suit my purpose to a hair ;
But let us not proceed too furious,
First please to turn to god Mercurius ;
You'll find him pictur'd at full length
In book the second, page the tenth :
The stress of all my proofs on him I lay,
And now proceed we to our simile.

Imprimis, pray observe his hat,
Wings upon either side—mark that.
Well ! what is it from thence we gather ?
Why these denote a brain of feather.
A brain of feather ! very right,
With wit that's flighty, learning light ;
Such as to modern bard's decreed :
A just comparison,— proceed.

[1 First printed in *Essays, by Mr. Goldsmith*, 1765, p. 234.
The version here followed is that of the second edition of
1766, which was slightly revised.]

In the next place, his feet peruse,
Wings grow again from both his shoes;
Design'd, no doubt, their part to bear,
And waft his godship through the air;
And here my simile unites,
For in a modern poet's flights,
I'm sure it may be justly said,
His feet are useful as his head.

Lastly, vouchsafe t' observe his hand,
Filled with a snake-encircl'd wand;
By classic authors term'd caduceus,
And highly fam'd for several uses.
To wit—most wond'rously endu'd,
No poppy water [1] half so good;
For let folks only get a touch,
Its soporific virtue's such,
Though ne'er so much awake before,
That quickly they begin to snore.
Add too, what certain writers tell,
With this he drives men's souls to hell.

Now to apply, begin we then;
His wand's a modern author's pen;
The serpents round about it twin'd
Denote him of the reptile kind;
Denote the rage with which he writes,
His frothy slaver, venom'd bites;
An equal semblance still to keep,
Alike too both conduce to sleep.

[1 A favourite sleeping-draught. "Juno shall give her peacock *poppy-water*." (Congreve's *Love for Love*, 1695, Act IV., sc. 3.)]

This diff'rence only, as the god
Drove souls to Tart'rus with his rod,
With his goosequill the scribbling elf,
Instead of others, damns himself.

   And here my simile almost tript,
Yet grant a word by way of postscript.
Moreover, Merc'ry had a failing :
Well ! what of that ? out with it—stealing ;
In which all modern bards agree,
Being each as great a thief as he :
But ev'n this deity's existence
Shall lend my simile assistance.
Our modern bards ! why what a pox
Are they but senseless stones and blocks ?

EDWIN AND ANGELINA.

A BALLAD.[1]

'TURN, gentle Hermit of the dale,
   And guide my lonely way,
To where yon taper cheers the vale,
   With hospitable ray.

'For here, forlorn and lost I tread,
   With fainting steps and slow;
Where wilds, immeasurably spread,
   Seem lengthening as I go.'

'Forbear, my son,' the Hermit cries,
   'To tempt the dangerous gloom;
For yonder faithless phantom[2] flies
   To lure thee to thy doom.

'Here to the houseless child of want
   My door is open still;

[1 Written in or before 1765, when it was printed privately
"for the amusement of the Countess of Northumberland,"
under the title of *Edwin and Angelina. A Ballad. By
Mr. Goldsmith*. A copy in this rare form was sold at
Heber's sale for 3s. It was first published in *The Vicar of
Wakefield*, 1766, i. 70 (ch. viii.); and again in *Poems for
Young Ladies*, 1767, p. 91. The version here followed is
that in the fifth edition of the *Vicar*, 1773 [4], pp. 78-85.]

[2 *i.e.*, Will o' the Wisp.]

And though my portion is but scant,
  I give it with good will.

'Then turn to-night, and freely share
  Whate'er my cell bestows ;
My rushy couch, and frugal fare,
  My blessing and repose.

No flocks that range the valley free
  To slaughter I condemn :
Taught by that Power that pities me,
  I learn to pity them.

'But from the mountain's grassy side
  A guiltless feast I bring ;
A scrip with herbs and fruits supplied,
  And water from the spring.

'Then, pilgrim, turn, thy cares forego ;
  All earth-born cares are wrong :
Man wants but little here below,
  Nor wants that little long.'[1]

Soft as the dew from heav'n descends,
  His gentle accents fell :
The modest stranger lowly bends,
  And follows to the cell.

Far in a wilderness obscure
  The lonely mansion lay ;
A refuge to the neighbouring poor
  And strangers led astray.

[1 A quotation from Young's *Complaint, Night* iv., 1743,
p. 9.]

No stores beneath its humble thatch
    Requir'd a master's care ;
The wicket, opening with a latch,
    Receiv'd the harmless pair.

And now, when busy crowds retire
    To take their evening rest,
The Hermit trimm'd his little fire,
    And cheer'd his pensive guest :

And spread his vegetable store,
    And gaily press'd, and smil'd ;
And, skill'd in legendary lore,
    The lingering hours beguil'd.

Around in sympathetic mirth
    Its tricks the kitten tries ;
The cricket chirrups in the hearth ;
    The crackling faggot flies.

But nothing could a charm impart
    To soothe the stranger's woe ;
For grief was heavy at his heart,
    And tears began to flow.

His rising cares the Hermit spied,
    With answering care oppress'd ;
' And whence, unhappy youth,' he cried,
    ' The sorrows of thy breast ?

' From better habitations spurn'd,
    Reluctant dost thou rove ;
Or grieve for friendship unreturn'd,
    Or unregarded love ?

' Alas ! the joys that fortune brings
    Are trifling and decay ;
And those who prize the paltry things,
    More trifling still than they.

' And what is friendship but a name,
    A charm that lulls to sleep ;
A shade that follows wealth or fame,
    But leaves the wretch to weep ?

' And love is still an emptier sound,
    The modern fair one's jest :
On earth unseen, or only found
    To warm the turtle's nest.

' For shame, fond youth, thy sorrows hush,
    And spurn the sex,' he said :
But, while he spoke, a rising blush
    His love-lorn guest betray'd.

Surpris'd, he sees new beauties rise,
    Swift mantling to the view ;
Like colours o'er the morning skies,
    As bright, as transient too.

The bashful look, the rising breast,
    Alternate spread alarms :
The lovely stranger stands confess'd
    A maid in all her charms.

' And, ah ! forgive a stranger rude,
    A wretch forlorn,' she cried ;
' Whose feet unhallow'd thus intrude
    Where heaven and you reside.

'But let a maid thy pity share,
  Whom love has taught to stray;
Who seeks for rest, but finds despair
  Companion of her way.

'My father liv'd beside the Tyne,
  A wealthy lord was he;
And all his wealth was mark'd as mine,
  He had but only me.

'To win me from his tender arms
  Unnumber'd suitors came;
Who prais'd me for imputed charms,
  And felt or feign'd a flame.

'Each hour a mercenary crowd
  With richest proffers strove:
Amongst the rest young Edwin bow'd,
  But never talk'd of love.

'In humble, simplest habit clad,
  No wealth nor power had he;
Wisdom and worth were all he had,
  But these were all to me.

['And when beside me in the dale
  He caroll'd lays of love;
His breath lent fragrance to the gale,
  And music to the grove.']

[¹ This stanza, which is not in the contemporary versions,
was given to Bishop Percy, for his edition of the *Works*
(1801), by Richard Archdal, Esq., who had received it from
the author.]

H

'The blossom opening to the day,
  The dews of heaven refin'd,
Could nought of purity display,
  To emulate his mind.

'The dew, the blossom on the tree,
  With charms inconstant shine ;
Their charms were his, but woe to me !
  Their constancy was mine.

'For still I tried each fickle art,
  Importunate and vain :
And while his passion touch'd my heart,
  I triumph'd in his pain.

'Till quite dejected with my scorn,
  He left me to my pride ;
And sought a solitude forlorn,
  In secret, where he died.

'But mine the sorrow, mine the fault,
  And well my life shall pay ;
I'll seek the solitude he sought,
  And stretch me where he lay.

'And there forlorn, despairing, hid,
  I'll lay me down and die ;
'Twas so for me that Edwin did,
  And so for him will I.'

'Forbid it, Heaven !' the Hermit cried,
  And clasp'd her to his breast :
The wondering fair one turned to chide,
  'Twas Edwin's self that prest.

'Turn, Angelina, ever dear,
 My charmer, turn to see
Thy own, thy long-lost Edwin here,
 Restor'd to love and thee.

'Thus let me hold thee to my heart,
 And ev'ry care resign ;
And shall we never, never part,
 My life—my all that's mine ?

'No, never from this hour to part,
 We'll live and love so true ;
The sigh that rends thy constant heart
 Shall break thy Edwin's too.'

ELEGY ON THE DEATH OF A MAD DOG.[1]

OOD people all, of every sort,
　　Give ear unto my song ;
And if you find it wond'rous short,
　　It cannot hold you long.

In Islington there was a man,
　　Of whom the world might say,
That still a godly race he ran,
　　Whene'er he went to pray.[2]

A kind and gentle heart he had,
　　To comfort friends and foes ;
The naked every day he clad,
　　When he put on his clothes.[2]

And in that town a dog was found,
　　As many dogs there be,
Both mongrel, puppy, whelp, and hound,
　　And curs of low degree.

This dog and man at first were friends ;
　　But when a pique began,
The dog, to gain some private ends,
　　Went mad and bit the man.

[1 First printed in *The Vicar of Wakefield*, 1766, i. 175.]
[2 Cf. *An Elegy on Mrs. Mary Blaize*, p. 77 ante.]

Around from all the neighbouring streets
    The wond'ring neighbours ran,
And swore the dog had lost his wits,
    To bite so good a man.

The wound it seem'd both sore and sad
    To every Christian eye ;
And while they swore the dog was mad,
    They swore the man would die.

But soon a wonder came to light,
    That show'd the rogues they lied :
The man recover'd of the bite,
    The dog it was that died.[1]

[1 This termination is based upon an epigram in the *Greek Anthology*, or perhaps upon an adaptation by Voltaire :
    "L'autre jour, au fond d'un vallon
    Un serpent mordit Jean Fréron.
    Devinez ce qu'il arriva ?
    Ce fut le serpent qui creva."]

SONG,

FROM 'THE VICAR OF WAKEFIELD.'[1]

HEN lovely Woman stoops to folly,
    And finds too late that men betray,
What charm can soothe her melancholy,
    What art can wash her guilt away?

The only art her guilt to cover,
    To hide her shame from every eye,
To give repentance to her lover,
    And wring his bosom, is—to die.

[1 Sung by Olivia in chap. v. of *The Vicar of Wakefield*, 1766, ii. 78, where it was first printed.]

EPILOGUE TO 'THE SISTER.'

HAT ! five long acts—and all to make
us wiser !
Our authoress sure has wanted an
adviser.

Had she consulted *me*, she should have made
Her moral play a speaking masquerade ;
Warm'd up each bustling scene, and in her rage
Have emptied all the green-room on the stage.
My life on't, this had kept her play from sinking ;
Have pleas'd our eyes, and sav'd the pain of
thinking.
Well ! since she thus has shown her want of skill,
What if I give a masquerade ?—I will.
But how ? ay, there's the rub ! [*pausing*]—I've got
my cue :
The world's a masquerade ! the maskers, you, you,
you.   (*To Boxes, Pit, and Gallery.*)
Lud ! what a group the motley scene discloses !
False wits, false wives, false virgins, and false
spouses !
Statesmen with bridles on ; and, close beside 'em,
Patriots, in party-coloured suits, that ride 'em.
There Hebes, turn'd of fifty, try once more
To raise a flame in Cupids of threescore.

[¹ *The Sister*, 1769, in which this epilogue was first printed,
was a comedy by Mrs. Charlotte Lennox (1720-1804), produced at Covent Garden, 18 February, 1769.]

These in their turn, with appetites as keen,
Deserting fifty, fasten on fifteen,
Miss, not yet full fifteen, with fire uncommon,
Flings down her sampler, and takes up the woman :
The little urchin smiles, and spreads her lure,
And tries to kill, ere she's got power to cure.
Thus 'tis with all—their chief and constant care
Is to seem everything but what they are.
Yon broad, bold, angry spark, I fix my eye on,
Who seems to have robb'd his vizor from the lion ;
Who frowns, and talks, and swears, with round
   parade,
Looking, as who should say, Dam'me ! who's
   afraid ?   (*mimicking.*)
Strip but his vizor off, and sure I am
You'll find his lionship a very lamb.
Yon politician, famous in debate,
Perhaps, to vulgar eyes, bestrides the state ;
Yet, when he deigns his real shape t' assume,
He turns old woman, and bestrides a broom.
Yon patriot, too, who presses on your sight,
And seems to every gazer all in white,
If with a bribe his candour you attack,
He bows, turns round, and whip—the man's a
   black !
Yon critic, too—but whither do I run ?
If I proceed, our bard will be undone !
Well then a truce, since she requests it too :
Do you spare her, and I'll for once spare you.

PROLOGUE TO 'ZOBEIDE.'[1]

SPOKEN BY QUICK IN THE CHARACTER OF A SAILOR.

IN these bold times,[2] when Learning's
    sons explore
The distant climate and the savage
    shore;
When wise Astronomers to India steer,
And quit for Venus, many a brighter here;
While Botanists, all cold to smiles and dimpling,
Forsake the fair, and patiently—go simpling;
When every bosom swells with wond'rous scenes,
Priests, cannibals, and hoity-toity queens:
Our bard into the general spirit enters,
And fits his little frigate for adventures:
With Scythian stores, and trinkets deeply laden,
He this way steers his course, in hopes of trading—
Yet ere he lands he'as ordered me before,
To make an observation on the shore.
Where are we driven? our reck'ning sure is lost!
This seems a barren and a dangerous coast.

[1 *Zobeide* was a play by Joseph Cradock of Gumley, in
Leicestershire, a friend of Goldsmith's latter days. It was
translated from *Les Scythes* of Voltaire, and produced at
Covent Garden, 11 December, 1771. Goldsmith's prologue
is here printed from Cradock's *Memoirs*, 1828, iii. 8.]

[2 A reference to Cook's just concluded voyage to Otaheite
to observe the transit of Venus.]

Lord, what a sultry climate am I under !
Yon ill foreboding cloud seems big with thunder.
                              (*Upper Gallery.*)
There Mangroves spread, and larger than I've seen
          'em—   (*Pit.*)
Here trees of stately size—and turtles in 'em—
                                    (*Balconies.*)
Here ill-condition'd oranges abound——
                                        (*Stage.*)
And apples (*takes up one and tastes it*), bitter apples
          strew the ground.
The place is uninhabited, I fear !
I heard a hissing—there are serpents here !
O there the natives are—a dreadful race !
The men have tails, the women paint the face !
No doubt they're all barbarians.—Yes, 'tis so ;
I'll try to make palaver [1] with them though ;
                              (*making signs.*)
'Tis best, however, keeping at a distance.
Good Savages, our Captain craves assistance ;
Our ship's well stor'd ;—in yonder creek we've
          laid her ;
His honour is no mercenary trader ; [2]
This is his first adventure ; lend him aid,
Or you may chance to spoil a thriving trade.
His goods, he hopes, are prime, and brought from
          far,
Equally fit for gallantry and war.
What ! no reply to promises so ample ?
I'd best step back—and order up a sample.

[1 *i.e.* to hold a parley.]
[2 Cradock gave his profits to his "Zobeide,"—Mrs. Yates,
the actress.]

THRENODIA AUGUSTALIS:

SACRED TO THE MEMORY OF HER LATE ROYAL HIGHNESS THE PRINCESS DOWAGER OF WALES.[1]

ADVERTISEMENT.

THE following may more properly be termed a compilation than a poem. It was prepared for the composer in little more than two days: and may therefore rather be considered as an industrious effort of gratitude than of genius.

In justice to the composer it may likewise be right to inform the public, that the music was adapted in a period of time equally short.

SPEAKERS.
Mr. Lee and Mrs. Bellamy.

SINGERS.

Mr. Champnes, Mr. Dine, and Miss Jameson.
The music prepared and adapted by Signor Vento.

[1 Augusta, mother of George the Third, who died at Carlton House, 8 February, 1772. This piece was spoken and sung in Mrs. Teresa Cornelys' Great Room in Soho Square on Thursday, the 20th following, being sold at the doors as a 4to. pamphlet. The publisher was W. Woodfall. The author's name was not given; but the advertisement here reproduced preceded the verses, with the list of performers.]

THRENODIA AUGUSTALIS.

OVERTURE—A SOLEMN DIRGE.   AIR—TRIO.

RISE, ye sons of worth, arise,
   And waken every note of woe ;
   When truth and virtue reach the skies,
   'Tis ours to weep the want below !

CHORUS.

When truth and virtue, &c.

MAN SPEAKER.

The praise attending pomp and power,
The incense given to kings,
Are but the trappings of an hour,
Mere transitory things.
The base bestow them : but the good agree
To spurn the venal gifts as flattery.
But when to pomp and power are joined
An equal dignity of mind ;
When titles are the smallest claim :
When wealth, and rank, and noble blood,
But aid the power of doing good,
Then all their trophies last,—and flattery turns
    to fame.
  Blest spirit thou, whose fame, just born to bloom,
Shall spread and flourish from the tomb,
How hast thou left mankind for Heaven !

Even now reproach and faction mourn,
And, wondering how their rage was born,
Request to be forgiven !
Alas ! they never had thy hate :
Unmov'd in conscious rectitude,
Thy towering mind self-centred stood,
Nor wanted man's opinion to be great.
In vain, to charm thy ravish'd sight,
A thousand gifts would fortune send ;
In vain, to drive thee from the right,
A thousand sorrows urg'd thy end :
Like some well-fashion'd arch thy patience stood,
And purchas'd strength from its increasing load.
Pain met thee like a friend to set thee free,
Affliction still is virtue's opportunity !
Virtue, on herself relying,
Every passion hushed to rest,
Loses every pain of dying
In the hopes of being blest.
Every added pang she suffers
Some increasing good bestows,
And every shock that malice offers
Only rocks her to repose.

SONG. BY A MAN.—AFFETTUOSO.

Virtue, on herself relying,
Every passion hushed to rest,
Loses every pain of dying
In the hopes of being blest.
Every added pang she suffers
Some increasing good bestows,
And every shock that malice offers
Only rocks her to repose.

WOMAN SPEAKER.

Yet ah ! what terrors frowned upon her fate,
Death with its formidable band,
Fever, and pain, and pale consumptive care,
Determin'd took their stand.
Nor did the cruel ravagers design
To finish all their efforts at a blow :
But, mischievously slow,
They robb'd the relic and defac'd the shrine.
With unavailing grief,
Despairing of relief,
Her weeping children round,
Beheld each hour
Death's growing power,
And trembled as he frown'd.

As helpless friends who view from shore
The labouring ship, and hear the tempest roar,
While winds and waves their wishes cross :
They stood, while hope and comfort fail,
Not to assist, but to bewail
The inevitable loss.
Relentless tyrant, at thy call
How do the good, the virtuous fall !
Truth, beauty, worth, and all that most engage,
But wake thy vengeance and provoke thy rage.

SONG.   BY A MAN—BASSO, STACCATO, SPIRITOSO.
When vice my dart and scythe supply
How great a king of terrors I !
If folly, fraud, your hearts engage,
Tremble, ye mortals, at my rage !
Fall, round me fall, ye little things,

Ye statesmen, warriors, poets, kings !
If virtue fail her counsel sage,
Tremble, ye mortals, at my rage !

MAN SPEAKER.

Yet let that wisdom, urged by her example,
Teach us to estimate what all must suffer ;
Let us prize death as the best gift of nature,
As a safe inn, where weary travellers,
When they have journey'd through a world of cares,
May put off life and be at rest for ever.
Groans, weeping friends, indeed, and gloomy
      sables,
May oft distract us with their sad solemnity.
The preparation is the executioner.
Death, when unmask'd, shows me a friendly face,
And is a terror only at a distance :
For as the line of life conducts me on
To death's great court, the prospect seems more
      fair,
'Tis nature's kind retreat, that's always open
To take us in when we have drained the cup
Of life, or worn our days to wretchedness.
In that secure, serene retreat,
Where all the humble, all the great,
Promiscuously recline :
Where wildly huddled to the eye,
The beggar's pouch and prince's purple lie,
May every bliss be thine.
And ah ! blest spirit, wheresoe'er thy flight,
Through rolling worlds, or fields of liquid light,
May cherubs welcome their expected guest,
May saints with songs receive thee to their rest,

May peace that claim'd while here thy warmest
    love,
May blissful endless peace be thine above !

SONG. BY A WOMAN— AMOROSO.

Lovely lasting Peace below,
Comforter of every woe,
Heavenly born and bred on high,
To crown the favourites of the sky ;
Lovely lasting Peace, appear,
This world itself, if thou art here,
Is once again with Eden blest,
And man contains it in his breast.

WOMAN SPEAKER.

Our vows are heard ! Long, long to mortal eyes,
Her soul was fitting to its kindred skies :
Celestial-like her bounty fell,
Where modest want and patient sorrow dwell,
Want pass'd for merit at her door,
Unseen the modest were supplied,
Her constant pity fed the poor,
Then only poor, indeed, the day she died.
And oh ! for this ! while sculpture decks thy shrine,
And art exhausts profusion round,
The tribute of a tear be mine,
A simple song, a sigh profound.
There Faith shall come, a pilgrim gray,[1]
To bless the tomb that wraps thy clay :
And calm Religion shall repair
To dwell a weeping hermit there.

[1 Thesef our lines, with some alteration, are taken from
Collins's *Ode written in the year* 1746.]

Truth, Fortitude, and Friendship, shall agree
To blend their virtues while they think of thee.

AIR. CHORUS—POMPOSO.

Let us, let all the world agree,
To profit by resembling thee.

PART II.

OVERTURE.—PASTORALE.

MAN SPEAKER.

AST by that shore where Thames'
    translucent stream
Reflects new glories on his breast,
Where, splendid as the youthful poet's
    dream,
He forms a scene beyond Elysium blest:
Where sculptur'd elegance and native grace
Unite to stamp the beauties of the place:
While, sweetly blending, still are seen
The wavy lawn, the sloping green:
While novelty, with cautious cunning,
Through every maze of fancy running,
From China borrows aid to deck the scene:
There sorrowing by the river's glassy bed,
Forlorn, a rural band complain'd,
All whom Augusta's bounty fed,
All whom her clemency sustain'd;
The good old sire, unconscious of decay,
The modest matron, clad in homespun gray,
The military boy, the orphan'd maid,
The shatter'd veteran, now first dismay'd;
These sadly join beside the murmuring deep,
And as they view

The towers of Kew,[1]
Call on their mistress, now no more, and weep.

CHORUS.—AFFETTUOSO, LARGO.

Ye shady walks, ye waving greens,
Ye nodding towers, ye fairy scenes,
Let all your echoes now deplore,
That she who form'd your beauties is no more.

MAN SPEAKER.

First of the train the patient rustic came,
Whose callous hand had form'd the scene,
Bending at once with sorrow and with age,
With many a tear, and many a sigh between,
'And where,' he cried, 'shall now my babes
        have bread,
Or how shall age support its feeble fire?
No lord will take me now, my vigour fled,
Nor can my strength perform what they require:
Each grudging master keeps the labourer bare,
A sleek and idle race is all their care:
My noble mistress thought not so!
Her bounty, like the morning dew,
Unseen, though constant, used to flow,
And as my strength decay'd, her bounty grew.'

WOMAN SPEAKER.

In decent dress, and coarsely clean,
The pious matron next was seen,

[1 "The embellishment of Kew Palace and gardens, under the direction of [Sir William] Chambers and others, was the favourite object of her [Royal Highness's] widowhood." (Bolton Corney.)]

Clasp'd in her hand a godly book was borne,
By use and daily meditation worn ;
That decent dress, this holy guide,
Augusta's care had well supplied.
' And ah !' she cries, all woe-begone,
' What now remains for me ?
Oh ! where shall weeping want repair,
To ask for charity ?
Too late in life for me to ask,
And shame prevents the deed,
And tardy, tardy are the times
To succour, should I need.
But all my wants, before I spoke,
Were to my Mistress known ;
She still reliev'd, nor sought my praise,
Contented with her own.
But every day her name I'll bless,
My morning prayer, my evening song,
I'll praise her while my life shall last,
A life that cannot last me long."

SONG. BY A WOMAN.

Each day, each hour, her name I'll bless,
My morning and my evening song,
And when in death my vows shall cease,
My children shall the note prolong.

MAN SPEAKER.

The hardy veteran after struck the sight,
Scarr'd, mangled, maim'd in every part,
Lopp'd of his limbs in many a gallant fight,
In nought entire—except his heart :
Mute for a while, and sullenly distress'd,

At last the impetuous sorrow fired his breast.
' Wild is the whirlwind rolling
O'er Afric's sandy plain,
And wild the tempest howling
Along the billowed main :[1]
But every danger felt before,
The raging deep, the whirlwind's roar,
Less dreadful struck me with dismay,
Than what I feel this fatal day.
Oh, let me fly a land that spurns the brave,
Oswego's dreary shores shall be my grave ;[2]
I'll seek that less inhospitable coast,
And lay my body where my limbs were lost.'

SONG. BY A MAN.—BASSO, SPIRITOSO.

Old Edward's sons, unknown to yield,
Shall crowd from Cressy's laurell'd field,
To do thy memory right :
For thine and Britain's wrongs they feel,
Again they snatch the gleamy steel,
And wish the avenging fight.[3]

WOMAN SPEAKER.

In innocence and youth complaining,
Next appear'd a lovely maid,
Affliction o'er each feature reigning,
Kindly came in beauty's aid ;
Every grace that grief dispenses,

[1 Cf. *The Captivity*, p. 139.]
[2 Cf. *The Traveller*, p. 21.]
[3 Varied from Collins's *Ode on the Death of Colonel Charles Ross at Fontenoy*.]

Every glance that warms the soul,
In sweet succession charm'd the senses,
While pity harmoniz'd the whole.
' The garland of beauty' ('tis thus she would say,)
' No more shall my crook or my temples adorn,
I'll not wear a garland, Augusta's away,
I'll not wear a garland until she return :
But alas ! that return I never shall see :
The echoes of Thames shall my sorrows proclaim,
There promis'd a lover to come, but, Oh me !
'Twas death,—'twas the death of my mistress that
    came.
But ever, for ever, her image shall last,
I'll strip all the spring of its earliest bloom ;
On her grave shall the cowslip and primrose be
    cast,
And the new-blossom'd thorn shall whiten her
    tomb.'

SONG.   BY A WOMAN.— PASTORALE.

With garlands of beauty the queen of the May
No more will her crook or her temples adorn ;
For who'd wear a garland when she is away,
When she is remov'd, and shall never return.

On the grave of Augusta these garlands be plac'd,
We'll rifle the spring of its earliest bloom,[1]
And there shall the cowslip and primrose be cast,
And the new-blossom'd thorn shall whiten her
    tomb.

[1 Cf. Collins's *Dirge in Cymbeline.*]

CHORUS.—ALTRO MODO.

On the grave of Augusta this garland be plac'd,
We'll rifle the spring of its earliest bloom ;
And there shall the cowslip and primrose be cast,
And the tears of her country shall water her tomb.

SONG.

INTENDED TO HAVE BEEN SUNG IN 'SHE STOOPS TO CONQUER.'[1]

AH, me ! when shall I marry me ?
 Lovers are plenty ; but fail to relieve
  me :
 He, fond youth, that could carry me,
Offers to love, but means to deceive me.

But I will rally, and combat the ruiner :
 Not a look, not a smile shall my passion discover :
She that gives all to the false one pursuing her,
 Makes but a penitent, loses a lover.

[1 This was first printed by Boswell in the *London Maga-zine* for June, 1774. It had been intended for the part of "Miss Hardcastle," but Mrs. Bulkley, who played that part, was no vocalist. Goldsmith himself sang it very agreeably to an Irish air, *The Humours of Balamagairy*. (See Birkbeck Hill's *Boswell*, 1887, ii. 219.)]

TRANSLATION.[1]

Addison, in some beautiful Latin lines inserted in the Spectator, is entirely of opinion that birds observe a strict chastity of manners, and never admit the caresses of a different tribe.—(*v. Spectator*, No. 412.)

CHASTE are their instincts, faithful is their fire,
No foreign beauty tempts to false desire ;
The snow-white vesture, and the glittering crown,
The simple plumage, or the glossy down
Prompt not their love :—the patriot bird pursues
His well acquainted tints, and kindred hues.
Hence through their tribes no mix'd polluted flame,
No monster-breed to mark the groves with shame;
But the chaste blackbird, to its partner true,
Thinks black alone is beauty's favourite hue.
The nightingale, with mutual passion blest,
Sings to its mate, and nightly charms the nest :
While the dark owl to court its partner flies,
And owns its offspring in their yellow eyes.

[1 From Goldsmith's *History of the Earth and Animated Nature*, 1774, v., 312.]

EPITAPH ON THOMAS PARNELL.[1]

THIS tomb, inscrib'd to gentle Parnell's name,
   May speak our gratitude, but not his fame.
What heart but feels his sweetly-moral lay,
That leads to truth through pleasure's flowery way !
Celestial themes confess'd his tuneful aid ;
And Heaven, that lent him genius, was repaid.
Needless to him the tribute we bestow—
The transitory breath of fame below :
More lasting rapture from his works shall rise,
While converts thank their poet in the skies.

[1 This epitaph was first printed with *The Haunch of Venison,* 1776. Parnell died in 1718. In 1770 Goldsmith wrote his life.]

THE CLOWN'S REPLY.[1]

JOHN TROTT was desired by two witty peers
　To tell them the reason why asses had
　　ears.
'An't please you,' quoth John, 'I'm not given
　to letters,
Nor dare I pretend to know more than my betters;
Howe'er from this time I shall ne'er see your
　graces,
As I hope to be saved! without thinking on
　asses.'

EPITAPH ON EDWARD
PURDON.[2]

HERE lies poor Ned Purdon, from misery
　freed,
　Who long was a bookseller's hack;
　He led such a damnable life in this
　　world,—
I don't think he'll wish to come back.

[1 First printed at p. 79 of *Poems and Plays.* *By Oliver
Goldsmith,* *M.B.* Dublin, 1777. It is there dated "Edin-
burgh, 1753."]

[2 First printed as Goldsmith's in *Poems and Plays,*
1777, p. 79. Purdon had been at Trinity College, Dublin,
with Goldsmith. Swift wrote a somewhat similar epigram;
but Goldsmith's model was probably *La Mort du Sieur
Etienne.* (Forster's *Life,* 1871, ii., 5).)]

EPILOGUE FOR MR. LEE LEWES.[1]

OLD! Prompter, hold! a word before
    your nonsense;
    I'd speak a word or two, to ease my
    conscience.
My pride forbids it ever should be said,
My heels eclips'd the honours of my head;
That I found humour in a piebald vest,
Or ever thought that jumping was a jest.
               (*Takes off his mask.*)
Whence, and what art thou, visionary birth?
Nature disowns, and reason scorns thy mirth,
In thy black aspect every passion sleeps,
The joy that dimples, and the woe that weeps.
How hast thou fill'd the scene with all thy brood,
Of fools pursuing, and of fools pursu'd!
Whose ins and outs no ray of sense discloses,
Whose only plot it is to break our noses;
Whilst from below the trap-door Demons rise,
And from above the dangling deities;
And shall I mix in this unhallow'd crew?
May rosin'd lightning blast me, if I do!
No—I will act, I'll vindicate the stage:

[1 Charles Lee Lewes (1740-1803) was the original "Young
Marlow" of *She Stoops to Conquer.* He had previously
been harlequin of the theatre, but he thoroughly succeeded
in his new part, and the grateful author wrote him this *Epilogue* for his Benefit, May 7, 1773.]

Shakespeare himself shall feel my tragic rage.
Off! off! vile trappings! a new passion reigns!
The madd'ning monarch revels in my veins.
Oh! for a Richard's voice to catch the theme:
'Give me another horse! bind up my wounds!—
    soft—'twas but a dream.'
Ay, 'twas but a dream, for now there's no retreating:
If I cease Harlequin, I cease from eating.
'Twas thus that Aesop's stag, a creature blameless,
Yet something vain, like one that shall be nameless,
Once on the margin of a fountain stood,
And cavill'd at his image in the flood.
'The deuce confound,' he cries, 'these drumstick
    shanks,
They never have my gratitude nor thanks;
They're perfectly disgraceful! strike me dead!
But for a head, yes, yes, I have a head.
How piercing is that eye! how sleek that brow!
My horns! I'm told horns are the fashion now.'
Whilst thus he spoke, astonish'd, to his view,
Near, and more near, the hounds and huntsmen
    drew.
'Hoicks! hark forward!' came thund'ring from
    behind,
He bounds aloft, outstrips the fleeting wind:
He quits the woods, and tries the beaten ways;
He starts, he pants, he takes the circling maze.
At length his silly head, so priz'd before,
Is taught his former folly to deplore;
Whilst his strong limbs conspire to set him free,
And at one bound he saves himself,—like me.
       (*Taking a jump through the stage door.*)

EPILOGUE.

INTENDED TO HAVE BEEN SPOKEN FOR 'SHE STOOPS TO CONQUER.'[1]

Enter MRS. BULKLEY, *who curtsies very low as beginning to speak. Then enter* MISS CATLEY, *who stands full before her, and curtsies to the audience.*

MRS. BULKLEY.

OLD, Ma'am, your pardon. What's your business here?

MISS CATLEY.

The Epilogue.

MRS. BULKLEY.
The Epilogue?

MISS CATLEY.
Yes, the Epilogue, my dear.

MRS. BULKLEY.
Sure you mistake, Ma'am. The Epilogue, *I* bring it.

[1 This Epilogue, given to Bishop Percy by Goldsmith, was first printed at p. 82, vol. ii, of the *Miscellaneous Works* of 1801. It was written with intent to conciliate the rival claims of Mrs. Bulkley and Miss Catley, the former of whom wished to speak, the latter to sing the Epilogue. (See Cradock's *Memoirs*, 1826, i., 225.)]

MISS CATLEY.

Excuse me, Ma'am. The Author bid *me* sing it.

Recitative.

Ye beaux and belles, that form this splendid ring,
Suspend your conversation while I sing.

MRS. BULKLEY.

Why, sure the girl's beside herself: an Epilogue
    of singing,
A hopeful end indeed to such a blest beginning.
Besides, a singer in a comic set !—
Excuse me, Ma'am, I know the etiquette.

MISS CATLEY.

What if we leave it to the House?

MRS. BULKLEY.

        The House !—Agreed

MISS CATLEY.

            Agreed.

MRS. BULKLEY.

And she, whose party's largest, shall proceed.
And first, I hope you'll readily agree
I've all the critics and the wits for me.
They, I am sure, will answer my commands ;
Ye candid judging few, hold up your hands.
What ! no return ? I find too late, I fear,
That modern judges seldom enter here.

MISS CATLEY.

I'm for a different set.—Old men, whose trade is
Still to gallant and dangle with the ladies ;—

Recitative.

Who mump their passion, and who, grimly smiling,
Still thus address the fair with voice beguiling :—

Air— Cotillon.

Turn, my fairest, turn, if ever
   Strephon caught thy ravish'd eye ;
Pity take on your swain so clever,
   Who without your aid must die.
      Yes, I shall die, hu, hu, hu, hu !
      Yes, I must die, ho, ho, ho, ho !
                (*Da capo.*)

MRS. BULKLEY.

Let all the old pay homage to your merit ;
Give me the young, the gay, the men of spirit.
Ye travell'd tribe, ye macaroni [1] train,
Of French friseurs, and nosegays, justly vain,
Who take a trip to Paris once a year
To dress, and look like awkward Frenchmen here,
Lend me your hands.—Oh ! fatal news to tell :
Their hands are only lent to the Heinel. [2]

[1 A name derived from the Italian dish first patronized by
the " Macaroni Club," and afterwards extended to "the
younger and gayer part of our nobility and gentry, who, at
the same time that they gave in to the luxuries of eating,
went equally into the extravagancies of dress." (*Macaroni
and Theatrical Magazine*, October, 1772.) See note to
the *Pallissimo Macaroni* in *She Stoops to Conquer.*]

[2 Mademoiselle Anna-Frederica Heinel, a beautiful Prus-
sian *danseuse* at this time in London, afterwards the wife of
the elder Vestris.]

MISS CATLEY.

Ay, take your travellers, travellers indeed !
Give me my bonny Scot, that travels from the
      Tweed.
Where are the chiels? Ah ! Ah, I well discern
The smiling looks of each bewitching bairn.

Air—A bonny young lad is my Jockey.
I'll sing to amuse you by night and by day,
And be unco merry when you are but gay ;
When you with your bagpipes are ready to play,
My voice shall be ready to carol away
      With Sandy, and Sawney, and Jockey,
      With Sawney, and Jarvie, and Jockey.

MRS. BULKLEY.

Ye gamesters, who, so eager in pursuit,
Make but of all your fortune one *va toute :*
Ye jockey tribe, whose stock of words are few,
' I hold the odds.—Done, done, with you, with
      you.'
Ye barristers, so fluent with grimace,
' My Lord,—your Lordship misconceives the case.'
Doctors, who cough and answer every misfortuner,
' I wish I'd been call'd in a little sooner,'
Assist my cause with hands and voices hearty,
Come end the contest here, and aid my party.

MISS CATLEY.
Air—Ballinamony.
Ye brave Irish lads, hark away to the crack,
Assist me, I pray, in this woful attack ;
For sure I don't wrong you, you seldom are slack,

K

When the ladies are calling, to blush, and hang
    back.
    For you're always polite and attentive,
    Still to amuse us inventive,
    And death is your only preventive :
        Your hands and your voices for me.

MRS. BULKLEY.

Well, Madam, what if, after all this sparring,
We both agree, like friends, to end our jarring?

MISS CATLEY.

And that our friendship may remain unbroken,
What if we leave the Epilogue unspoken?

MRS. BULKLEY.

Agreed.

MISS CATLEY.

    Agreed.

MRS. BULKLEY.

    And now with late repentance,
Un-epilogued the Poet waits his sentence.
Condemn the stubborn fool who can't submit
To thrive by flattery, though he starves by wit.
                (*Exeunt.*)

EPILOGUE

INTENDED TO HAVE BEEN SPOKEN BY MRS. BULKLEY FOR 'SHE STOOPS TO CONQUER.'[1]

HERE is a place, so Ariosto sings,[2]
A treasury for lost and missing things;
Lost human wits have places there as-
    sign'd them,
And they, who lose their senses, there may find
    them.
But where's this place, this storehouse of the age?
The Moon, says he :—but *I* affirm the Stage :
At least in many things, I think, I see
His lunar, and our mimic world agree.
Both shine at night, for, but at Foote's alone,[3]
We scarce exhibit till the sun goes down.
Both prone to change, no settled limits fix,
And sure the folks of both are lunatics.
But in this parallel my best pretence is,
That mortals visit both to find their senses.
To this strange spot, Rakes, Macaronies, Cits,
Come thronging to collect their scatter'd wits.

[1 This epilogue, also given to Bishop Percy by Goldsmith in MS., was first printed in the *Miscellaneous Works* of 1801, ii, 87. Colman, the Manager, thought it "too bad to be spoken," and the author accordingly wrote that printed with *She Stoops to Conquer* in vol. ii. (See Cradock's *Memoirs*, 1826, i, 225.)]

[2 *Orlando Furioso.* Canto xxxiv.]

[3 Foote gave *matinées* at the Haymarket.]

The gay coquette, who ogles all the day,
Comes here at night, and goes a prude away.
Hither the affected city dame advancing,
Who sighs for operas, and dotes on dancing,
Taught by our art her ridicule to pause on,
Quits the *Ballet*, and calls for *Nancy Dawson*.[1]
The Gamester too, whose wit's all high or low,
Oft risks his fortune on one desperate throw,
Comes here to saunter, having made his bets,
Finds his lost senses out, and pay his debts.
The Mohawk too, with angry phrases stored,
As 'Dam'me, Sir,' and 'Sir, I wear a sword ;'
Here lesson'd for a while, and hence retreating,
Goes out, affronts his man, and takes a beating.
Here come the sons of scandal and of news,
But find no sense—for they had none to lose.
Of all the tribe here wanting an adviser
Our Author's the least likely to grow wiser ;
Has he not seen how you your favour place,
On sentimental Queens and Lords in lace?
Without a star, a coronet or garter,
How can the piece expect or hope for quarter?
No high-life scenes, no sentiment :—the creature
Still stoops among the low to copy nature.[2]
Yes, he's far gone :—and yet some pity fix,
The English laws forbid to punish lunatics.

[1 A popular song bearing the name of a famous hornpipe
dancer and "toast" who died at Hampstead in 1767.]
[2 An obvious reference to the title of the play.]

THE CAPTIVITY: AN ORATORIO.[1]

[THE PERSONS.

First Jewish Prophet.   *First Chaldean Priest.*
Second Jewish Prophet.   *Second Chaldean Priest.*
Israelitish Woman.   *Chaldean Woman.*
Chorus of Youths and Virgins.
SCENE.—*The banks of the River Euphrates, near Babylon.*]

ACT I.

SCENE.—*Israelites sitting on the banks of the
Euphrates.*

FIRST PROPHET.

RECITATIVE.

E captive tribes, that hourly work and
weep
Where flows Euphrates murmuring to
the deep,
Suspend awhile the task, the tear suspend,
And turn to God, your Father and your Friend.
Insulted, chain'd, and all the world a foe, ·
Our God alone is all we boast below.

[1 *The Captivity* was set to music, but never performed.
It was first printed in the *Miscellaneous Works* (trade
edition), 1820. In 1837, Prior printed it again from another
MS. (*Miscellaneous Works*, 1837). It is here given mainly as
reproduced by Mr. Bolton Corney from the second version,
Author's MS. Two of the songs, with variations, were published with *The Haunch of Venison*, 1776.]

CHORUS OF ISRAELITES.

Our God is all we boast below,
　　To Him we turn our eyes;
And every added weight of woe
　　Shall make our homage rise.

And though no temple richly drest,
　　Nor sacrifice is here;
We'll make His temple in our breast,
　　And offer up a tear.

SECOND PROPHET.

RECITATIVE.

That strain once more; it bids remembrance rise,
And calls my long-lost country to mine eyes.
Ye fields of Sharon, drest in flowery pride,
Ye plains where Jordan rolls its glassy tide,
Ye hills of Lebanon, with cedars crown'd,
Ye Gilead groves, that fling perfumes around,
These hills how sweet, those plains how wondrous
　　　　fair,
But sweeter still when Heaven was with us there!

AIR.

O Memory! thou fond deceiver,
　　Still importunate and vain;
To former joys recurring ever,
　　And turning all the past to pain:

Hence, deceiver most distressing!
　　Seek the happy and the free:
The wretch who wants each other blessing,
　　Ever wants a friend in thee.

FIRST PROPHET.

RECITATIVE.

Yet why repine? What though by bonds confin'd,
Should bonds enslave the vigour of the mind?
Have we not cause for triumph when we see
Ourselves alone from idol-worship free?
Are not this very day those rites begun
Where prostrate folly hails the rising sun?
Do not our tyrant lords this day ordain
For superstitious rites and mirth profane?
And should we mourn? should coward virtue fly,
When impious folly rears her front on high?
No; rather let us triumph still the more,
And as our fortune sinks, our wishes soar.

AIR.

The triumphs that on vice attend
Shall ever in confusion end;
The good man suffers but to gain,
And every virtue springs from pain:

As aromatic plants bestow
No spicy fragrance while they grow;
But crush'd, or trodden to the ground,
Diffuse their balmy sweets around.

SECOND PROPHET.

RECITATIVE.

But hush, my sons, our tyrant lords are near,
The sound of barbarous mirth offends mine ear;
Triumphant music floats along the vale,
Near, nearer still, it gathers on the gale;

The growing note their near approach declares !
Desist, my sons, nor mix the strain with theirs.

Enter Chaldean Priests attended.

FIRST PRIEST.

AIR.

Come on, my companions, the triumph display,
   Let rapture the minutes employ ;
The sun calls us out on this festival day,
   And our monarch partakes of our joy.

Like the sun, our great monarch all pleasure sup-
      plies,
   Both similar blessings bestow ;
The sun with his splendour illumines the skies,
   And our monarch enlivens below.

AIR.

CHALDEAN WOMAN.

Haste, ye sprightly sons of pleasure,
Love presents its brightest treasure,
   Leave all other sports for me.

A CHALDEAN ATTENDANT.

Or rather, love's delights despising,
Haste to raptures ever rising,
   Wine shall bless the brave and free.

SECOND PRIEST.

Wine and beauty thus inviting,
Each to different joys exciting,
   Whither shall my choice incline ?

FIRST PRIEST.

I'll waste no longer thought in choosing,
But, neither love nor wine refusing,
   I'll make them both together mine.

RECITATIVE.

But whence, when joys should brighten o'er the
    land,
This sullen gloom in Judah's captive band?
Ye sons of Judah, why the lute unstrung?
Or why those harps on yonder willows hung?
Come, leave your griefs, and join our tuneful choir,
For who like you can wake the sleeping lyre?

SECOND PROPHET.

Bow'd down with chains, the scorn of all mankind,
To want, to toil, and every ill consign'd,
Is this a time to bid us raise the strain,
And mix in rites that Heaven regards with pain?
No, never. May this hand forget each art
That speeds the powers of music to the heart,
Ere I forget the land that gave me birth,
Or join with sounds profane its sacred mirth!

FIRST PRIEST.

Insulting slaves! if gentler methods fail,
The whip and angry tortures shall prevail.
                [*Exeunt Chaldeans.*

FIRST PROPHET.

Why, let them come, one good remains to cheer—
We fear the Lord, and know no other fear.

CHORUS.

Can whips or tortures hurt the mind
On God's supporting breast reclin'd?
Stand fast, and let our tyrants see
That fortitude is victory.

End of the First Act.

ACT II.

SCENE.—*As before.*

CHORUS OF ISRAELITES.

 PEACE of mind, thou lovely guest !
Thou softest soother of the breast !
 Dispense thy balmy store !
Wing all our thoughts to reach the skies,
Till earth, diminish'd to our eyes,
 Shall vanish as we soar.

FIRST PRIEST.

RECITATIVE.

No more ! Too long has justice been delay'd,
The king's commands must fully be obey'd ;
Compliance with his will your peace secures,
Praise but our gods, and every good is yours.
But if, rebellious to his high command,
You spurn the favours offer'd at his hand,
Think, timely think, what ills remain behind ;
Reflect, nor tempt to rage the royal mind.

SECOND PRIEST.

AIR.

Fierce is the whirlwind howling
 O'er Afric's sandy plain,
And fierce the tempest rolling
 Along the furrow'd main.

But storms that fly,
To rend the sky,
Every ill presaging,
Less dreadful show
To worlds below,
Than angry monarch's raging.

ISRAELITISH WOMAN.

RECITATIVE.

Ah me ! what angry terrors round us grow,
How shrinks my soul to meet the threaten'd blow !
Ye prophets, skill'd in Heaven's eternal truth,
Forgive my sex's fears, forgive my youth !
If shrinking thus, when frowning power appears
I wish for life, and yield me to my fears :
Let us one hour, one little hour obey ;
To-morrow's tears may wash our stains away.

AIR.

To the last moment of his breath
On hope the wretch relies ;
And e'en the pang preceding death
Bids expectation rise.

Hope, like the gleaming taper's light,
Adorns and cheers our way ;
And still, as darker grows the night,
Emits a brighter ray.

SECOND PRIEST.

RECITATIVE.

Why this delay ? at length for joy prepare.

I read your looks, and see compliance there.
Come, raise the strain, and grasp the full-ton'd
    lyre—
The time, the theme, the place, and all conspire.

CHALDEAN WOMAN.

AIR.

See the ruddy morning smiling,
Hear the grove to bliss beguiling;
Zephyrs through the valley playing,
Streams along the meadow straying.

FIRST PRIEST.

While these a constant revel keep,
Shall reason only bid me weep?
Hence, intruder! we'll pursue
Nature, a better guide than you.

SECOND PRIEST.

Every moment, as it flows,
Some peculiar pleasure owes;
Then let us providently wise,
Seize the debtor as it flies.

Think not to-morrow can repay
The pleasures that we lose to-day;
To-morrow's most unbounded store
Can but pay its proper score.

FIRST PRIEST.

RECITATIVE.

But hush! see, foremost of the captive choir,
The master-prophet grasps his full-toned lyre.

Mark where he sits with executing art,
Feels for each tone and speeds it to the heart ;
See inspiration fills his rising form,
Awful as clouds that nurse the growing storm.
And now his voice, accordant to the string,
Prepares our monarch's victories to sing.

FIRST PROPHET.

AIR.

From north, from south, from east, from west,
    Conspiring foes shall come ;
Tremble, thou vice-polluted breast ;
    Blasphemers, all be dumb.

The tempest gathers all around,
    On Babylon it lies ;
Down with her ! down, down to the ground ;
    She sinks, she groans, she dies.

SECOND PROPHET.

Down with her, Lord, to lick the dust,
    Ere yonder setting sun ;
Serve her as she hath serv'd the just !
    'Tis fix'd—It shall be done.

FIRST PRIEST.

RECITATIVE.

Enough ! when slaves thus insolent presume,
The king himself shall judge, and fix their doom.
Short-sighted wretches ! have not you, and all,
Beheld our power in Zedekiah's fall?
To yonder gloomy dungeon turn your eyes ;
Mark where dethron'd your captive monarch lies,

Depriv'd of sight, and rankling in his chain ;
He calls on death to terminate his pain.
Yet know, ye slaves, that still remain behind
More ponderous chains, and dungeons more con-
  fined.

CHORUS.

Arise, All-potent Ruler, rise,
  And vindicate thy people's cause ;
Till every tongue in every land
  Shall offer up unfeign'd applause.

End of the Second Act.

ACT III.

FIRST PRIEST.

RECITATIVE.

ES, my companions, Heaven's decrees
are past,
And our fix'd empire shall for ever last :
In vain the madd'ning prophet threatens
woe,
In vain rebellion aims her secret blow ;
Still shall our fame and growing power be spread,
And still our vengeance crush the guilty head.

AIR.

Coeval with man
Our empire began,
And never shall fall
Till ruin shakes all.
With the ruin of all,
Shall Babylon fall.

SECOND [FIRST] PROPHET.

RECITATIVE.

'Tis thus that pride triumphant rears the head,
A little while, and all their power is fled.
But ha ! what means yon sadly plaintive train,
That this way slowly bends along the plain ?
And now, methinks, a pallid corse they bear
To yonder bank, and rest the body there.

Alas! too well mine eyes observant trace
The last remains of Judah's royal race.
Our monarch falls, and now our fears are o'er,
The wretched Zedekiah is no more.

AIR.

Ye wretches who by fortune's hate
    In want and sorrow groan,
Come ponder his severer fate
    And learn to bless your own.

Ye sons, from fortune's lap supplied,
    Awhile the bliss suspend ;
Like yours, his life began in pride,
    Like his, your lives may end.

SECOND PROPHET.

RECITATIVE.

Behold his squalid corse with sorrow worn,
His wretched limbs with ponderous fetters torn ;
Those eyeless orbs that shock with ghastly glare
These ill-becoming robes, and matted hair !
And shall not Heaven for this its terrors show,
And deal its angry vengeance on the foe ?
How long, how long, Almighty Lord of all,
Shall wrath vindictive threaten ere it fall !

ISRAELITISH WOMAN.

AIR.

As panting flies the hunted hind,
    Where brooks refreshing stray ;

L

And rivers through the valley wind,
    That stop the hunter's way ;

Thus we, O Lord, alike distress'd,
    For streams of mercy long ;
Those streams that cheer the sore oppress'd,
    And overwhelm the strong.

FIRST PROPHET.

RECITATIVE.

But whence that shout? Good heavens ! amaze
       ment all !
See yonder tower just nodding to the fall :
See where an army covers all the ground,
Saps the strong wall and pours destruction round ; –
The ruin smokes, destruction pours along—
How low the great, how feeble are the strong !
The foe prevails, the lofty walls recline—
Oh, God of hosts, the victory is Thine !

CHORUS OF ISRAELITES.

Down with her, Lord, to lick the dust ;
    Let vengeance be begun ;
Serve her as she hath serv'd the just,
    And let Thy Will be done.

FIRST PRIEST.

RECITATIVE.

All, all is lost.   The Syrian army fails,
Cyrus, the conqueror of the world, prevails !
Save us, O Lord ! to Thee, though late, we pray ;
And give repentance but an hour's delay.

SECOND PRIEST.

AIR.

Thrice happy, who in happy hour
 To Heaven their praise bestow,
And own His all-consuming power
 Before they feel the blow !

FIRST PROPHET.

RECITATIVE.

Now, now's our time ! ye wretches bold and
  blind,
Brave but to God, and cowards to mankind,
Too late you seek that power unsought before,
Your wealth, your pride, your empire, are no more.

AIR.

O Lucifer ! thou son of morn,
 Alike of Heaven and man the foe ;
  Heaven, men, and all,
  Now press thy fall,
And sink thee lowest of the low.

SECOND PRIEST [PROPHET ?]

O Babylon, how art thou fallen—
Thy fall more dreadful from delay ;
 Thy streets forlorn
 To wilds shall turn,
Where toads shall pant, and vultures prey !

FIRST PROPHET.

RECITATIVE.

Such be their fate. But listen ! from afar

The clarion's note proclaims the finish'd war !
Cyrus, our great restorer, is at hand,
And this way leads his formidable band.
Now give your songs of Zion to the wind,
And hail the benefactor of mankind :
He comes pursuant to divine decree,
To chain the strong, and set the captive free.

CHORUS OF YOUTHS.

Rise to raptures past expressing,
　　Sweeter from remember'd woes ;
Cyrus comes, our wrongs redressing,
　　Comes to give the world repose.

CHORUS OF VIRGINS.

Cyrus comes, the world redressing,
　　Love and pleasure in his train ;
Comes to heighten every blessing,
　　Comes to soften every pain.

CHORUS OF YOUTHS AND VIRGINS.

Hail to him with mercy reigning,
　　Skill'd in every peaceful art ;
Who, from bonds our limbs unchaining,
　　Only binds the willing heart.

LAST CHORUS.

But chief to Thee, our God, our Father, Friend,
　　Let praise be given to all eternity ;
O Thou, without beginning, without end—
　　Let us, and all, begin and end in Thee !

VERSES IN REPLY TO AN INVITATION TO DINNER AT DR. BAKER'S.[1]

'This *is* a poem ! This *is* a copy of verses !

OUR mandate I got,
   You may all go to pot ;
   Had your senses been right,
   You'd have sent before night ;
As I hope to be saved,
I put off being shaved ;
For I could not make bold,
While the matter was cold,
To meddle in suds,
Or to put on my duds :
So tell Horneck[2] and Nesbitt,[3]
And Baker[4] and his bit,
And Kauffman[5] beside,
And the Jessamy Bride,[6]

[1 Prior first printed this in the *Miscellaneous Works* of 1837, iv, 132, having obtained it from Major-General Sir H. E. Bunbury, Bart., son of H. W. Bunbury, the artist. (See note 1 to p. 152.)]

[2 Mrs. Horneck, widow of Captain Kane Horneck.]

[3 Mr. Thrale's brother-in-law.]

[4 Dr. (afterwards Sir) George Baker, Reynolds's doctor.]

[5 Angelica Kauffman, the artist, 1740-1807.]

[6 Mrs. Horneck's younger daughter, Mary.]

With the rest of the crew,
The Reynoldses two,[1]
Little Comedy's face,[2]
And the Captain in lace,[3]
(By-the-bye you may tell him,
I have something to sell him ;
Of use I insist,
When he comes to enlist.
Your worships must know
That a few days ago,
An order went out,
For the foot-guards so stout
To wear tails in high taste,
Twelve inches at least :
Now I've got him a scale
To measure each tail,
To lengthen a short tail,
And a long one to curtail.)—
   Yet how can I when vext,
Thus stray from my text ?
Tell each other to rue
Your Devonshire crew,
For sending so late
To one of my state.
But 'tis Reynolds's way
From wisdom to stray,
And Angelica's whim
To be frolick like him,

[1 Sir Joshua and his sister.]
[2 Mrs. Horneck's elder daughter, Catherine. (See notes p. 152.)]
[3 Captain Charles Horneck, Mrs. Horneck's son.]

But alas ! your good worships, how could they be
    wiser,
When both have been spoil'd in to-day's *Adver-
    tiser?* [1]

OLIVER GOLDSMITH.

[[1] An allusion to some complimentary verses which appeared in that paper.]

LETTER IN PROSE AND VERSE
TO MRS. BUNBURY.[1]

MADAM,

 READ your letter with all that allow-
ance which critical candour could
require, but after all find so much to
object to, and so much to raise my indignation, that I cannot help giving it a serious
answer.

I am not so ignorant, Madam, as not to see
there are many sarcasms contained in it, and solecisms also. (Solecism is a word that comes from
the town of Soleis in Attica, among the Greeks,
built by Solon, and applied as we use the word
Kidderminster for curtains from a town also of
that name ;—but this is learning you have no taste
for !)—I say, Madam, there are sarcasms in it, and
solecisms also. But, not to seem an ill-natured
critic, I'll take leave to quote your own words,
and give you my remarks upon them as they
occur. You begin as follows :—

'I hope, my good Doctor, you soon will be here,
And your spring-velvet coat very smart will appear,
To open our ball the first day of the year.'[2]

[1 This letter, "probably written in 1773 or 1774," was first
printed by Prior in the *Miscellaneous Works*, 1837, iv. 148.
It was addressed to the "Little Comedy" of p. 150, by this
time married to H. W. Bunbury, the artist.]

[2 Mrs. Bunbury had apparently invited the poet (in rhyme)
to spend Christmas at the family seat of Great Barton in
Suffolk.]

Pray, Madam, where did you ever find the epithet 'good,' applied to the title of Doctor? Had you called me 'learned Doctor,' or 'grave Doctor,' or 'noble Doctor,' it might be allowable, because they belong to the profession. But, not to cavil at trifles, you talk of my 'spring-velvet coat,' and advise me to wear it the first day in the year,—that is, in the middle of winter!—a spring-velvet in the middle of winter!!! That would be a solecism indeed! and yet, to increase the inconsistence, in another part of your letter you call me a beau. Now, on one side or other, you must be wrong. If I am a beau, I can never think of wearing a spring-velvet in winter: and if I am not a beau, why then, that explains itself. But let me go on to your two next strange lines :—

'And bring with you a wig, that is modish and gay,
To dance with the girls that are makers of hay.'

The absurdity of making hay at Christmas you yourself seem sensible of: you say your sister will laugh; and so indeed she well may! The Latins have an expression for a contemptuous sort of laughter, 'Naso contemnere adunco'; that is, to laugh with a crooked nose. She may laugh at you in the manner of the ancients if she thinks fit. But now I come to the most extraordinary of all extraordinary propositions, which is, to take your and your sister's advice in playing at loo. The presumption of the offer raises my indignation beyond the bounds of prose: it inspires me at once with verse and resentment. I take advice! and from whom? You shall hear.

First let me suppose, what may shortly be true,
The company set, and the word to be, Loo ;
All smirking, and pleasant, and big with adventure,
And ogling the stake which is fix'd in the centre.
Round and round go the cards, while I inwardly
        damn
At never once finding a visit from Pam.
I lay down my stake, apparently cool,
While the harpies about me all pocket the pool.
I fret in my gizzard, yet, cautious and sly,
I wish all my friends may be bolder than I :
Yet still they sit snug, not a creature will aim
By losing their money to venture at fame.
'Tis in vain that at niggardly caution I scold,
'Tis in vain that I flatter the brave and the bold :
All play their own way, and they think me an ass,—
' What does Mrs. Bunbury ?' ' I, Sir? I pass.'
' Pray what does Miss Horneck ?' take courage,
        come do,'—
' Who, I? let me see, Sir, why I must pass too.'
Mr. Bunbury frets, and I fret like the devil,
To see them so cowardly, lucky, and civil.
Yet still I sit snug, and continue to sigh on,
Till made by my losses as bold as a lion,
I venture at all,—while my avarice regards
The whole pool as my own—' Come, give me five
        cards.'
' Well done !' cry the ladies ; ' Ah, Doctor, that's
        good !
The pool's very rich—ah ! the Doctor is loo'd !'

[1 Mary Horneck, *see* p. 149 and note. She ultimately
married Colonel Gwyn, and survived until 1840. Reynolds
and Hoppner both painted her.]

Thus foil'd in my courage, on all sides perplex'd,
I ask for advice from the lady that's next:
'Pray, Ma'am, be so good as to give your advice;
Don't you think the best way is to venture for't
    twice?'
'I advise,' cries the lady, 'to try it, I own.—
Ah! the Doctor is loo'd! Come, Doctor, put
    down.'
Thus, playing, and playing, I still grow more
    eager,
And so bold, and so bold, I'm at last a bold
    beggar.
Now, ladies, I ask, if law-matters you're skill'd in,
Whether crimes such as yours should not come
    before Fielding?[1]
For giving advice that is not worth a straw,
May well be call'd picking of pockets in law;
And picking of pockets, with which I now charge
    ye,
Is, by quinto Elizabeth, Death without Clergy.
What justice, when both to the Old Bailey brought!
By the gods, I'll enjoy it; though 'tis but in
    thought!
Both are plac'd at the bar, with all proper de-
    corum,
With bunches of fennel, and nosegays before 'em;[2]
Both cover their faces with mobs and all that;
But the judge bids them, angrily, take off their
    hat.
When uncover'd, a buzz of enquiry runs round,—

[1 Sir John Fielding, d. 1780, Henry Fielding's blind half-
brother and successor at Bow Street.]
[2 A practice dating from the goal-fever of 1750.]

'Pray what are their crimes?'—'They've been
    pilfering found.'
'But, pray, whom have they pilfer'd?'—'A
    Doctor, I hear.'
'What, yon solemn-faced, odd-looking man that
    stands near!'
'The same.'—'What a pity! how does it sur-
    prise one!
Two handsomer culprits I never set eyes on!'
Then their friends all come round me with cring-
    ing and leering,
To melt me to pity, and soften my swearing.
First Sir Charles[1] advances with phrases well
    strung,
'Consider, dear Doctor, the girls are but young.'
'The younger the worse,' I return him again,
'It shows that their habits are all dyed in grain.'
'But then they're so handsome, one's bosom it
    grieves.'
'What signifies *handsome*, when people are
    thieves?'
'But where is your justice? their cases are hard.'
'What signifies *justice?* I want the *reward*.

There's the parish of Edmonton offers forty
pounds; there's the parish of St. Leonard, Shore-
ditch, offers forty pounds; there's the parish of
Tyburn, from the Hog-in-the-Pound to St. Giles's
watchhouse, offers forty pounds,—I shall have all
that if I convict them!'—

[1 Sir Charles Bunbury, Henry Bunbury's elder brother,
died s.p. 1821.]

'But consider their case,—it may yet be your
    own !
And see how they kneel ! Is your heart made of
    stone ? '
This moves :—so at last I agree to relent,
For ten pounds in hand, and ten pounds to be
    spent.

I challenge you all to answer this : I tell you, you
cannot. It cuts deep ;—but now for the rest of
the letter : and next—but I want room—so I
believe I shall battle the rest out at Barton some
day next week.

I don't value you all !

O. G.

VIDA'S GAME OF CHESS.

TRANSLATED.[1]

RMIES of box that sportively engage
　　And mimic real battles in their rage,
　　Pleas'd I recount ; how, smit with
　　　　glory's charms,
Two mighty Monarchs met in adverse arms,
Sable and white ; assist me to explore,
Ye Serian Nymphs, what ne'er was sung before.
No path appears : yet resolute I stray
Where youth undaunted bids me force my way.
O'er rocks and cliffs while I the task pursue,
Guide me, ye Nymphs, with your unerring clue.
For you the rise of this diversion know,
You first were pleas'd in Italy to show
This studious sport ; from Scacchis was its name,
The pleasing record of your Sister's fame.

　　When Jove through Ethiopia's parch'd extent
To grace the nuptials of old Ocean went,
Each god was there ; and mirth and joy around
To shores remote diffus'd their happy sound.
Then when their hunger and their thirst no more
Claim'd their attention, and the feast was o'er ;

[1 This translation of Marco Vida's *Scacchia Ludus* was
first printed by Mr. Peter Cunningham in 1854, from a
manuscript in Goldsmith's hand-writing then in the possession of Mr. Bolton Corney, who, with Mr. Forster, believed
it to be by Goldsmith.]

Ocean, with pastime to divert the thought,
Commands a painted table to be brought.
Sixty-four spaces fill the chequer'd square ;
Eight in each rank eight equal limits share.
Alike their form, but different are their dyes,
They fade alternate, and alternate rise,
White after black ; such various stains as those
The shelving backs of tortoises disclose.
Then to the Gods that mute and wondering sate,
You see (says he) the field prepared for fate.
Here will the little armies please your sight,
With adverse colours hurrying to the fight :
On which so oft, with silent sweet surprise,
The Nymphs and Nereids used to feast their eyes,
And all the neighbours of the hoary deep,
When calm the sea, and winds were lull'd asleep.
But see, the mimic heroes tread the board ;
He said, and straightway from an urn he pour'd
The sculptur'd box, that neatly seem'd to ape
The graceful figure of a human shape :—
Equal the strength and number of each foe,
Sixteen appear'd like jet, sixteen like snow.
As their shape varies various is the name,
Different their posts, nor is their strength the
    same.
There might you see two Kings with equal pride
Gird on their arms, their Consorts by their side ;
Here the Foot-warriors glowing after fame,
There prancing Knights and dexterous Archers
    came
And Elephants, that on their backs sustain
Vast towers of war, and fill and shake the plain.
  And now both hosts, preparing for the storm

Of adverse battle, their encampments form.
In the fourth space, and on the farthest line,
Directly opposite the Monarchs shine ;
The swarthy on white ground, on sable stands
The silver King ; and thence they send commands.
Nearest to these the Queens exert their might ;
One the left side, and t'other guards the right :
Where each, by her respective armour known,
Chooses the colour that is like her own.
Then the young Archers, two that snowy-white
Bend the tough yew, and two as black as night ;
(Greece called them Mars's favourites heretofore,
From their delight in war, and thirst of gore).
These on each side the Monarch and his Queen
Surround obedient ; next to these are seen
The crested Knights in golden armour gay ;
Their steeds by turns curvet, or snort or neigh.
In either army on each distant wing
Two mighty Elephants their castles bring,
Bulwarks immense ! and then at last combine
Eight of the Foot to form the second line,
The vanguard to the King and Queen ; from far
Prepared to open all the fate of war.
So moved the boxen hosts, each double-lined,
Their different colours floating in the wind :
As if an army of the Gauls should go,
With their white standards, o'er the Alpine snow
To meet in rigid fight on scorching sands
The sun-burnt Moors and Memnon's swarthy bands.
    Then Father Ocean thus ; you see them here,
Celestial Powers, what troops, what camps appear.
Learn now the sev'ral orders of the fray,
For ev'n these arms their stated laws obey.

To lead the fight, the Kings from all their bands
Choose whom they please to bear their great com-
    mands.
Should a black hero first to battle go,   )
Instant a white one guards against the blow ; }
But only one at once can charge or shun the foe.)
Their gen'ral purpose on one scheme is bent,
So to besiege the King within the tent,
That there remains no place by subtle flight
From danger free ; and that decides the fight.
Meanwhile, howe'er, the sooner to destroy
Th' imperial Prince, remorseless they employ
Their swords in blood ; and whosoever dare
Oppose their vengeance, in the ruin share.
Fate thins their camp ; the parti-colour'd field
Widens apace, as they o'ercome or yield,
But the proud victor takes the captive's post ;
There fronts the fury of th' avenging host
One single shock : and (should he ward the blow),
May then retire at pleasure from the foe.
The Foot alone (so their harsh laws ordain)
When they proceed can ne'er return again.
   But neither all rush on alike to prove
The terror of their arms : the Foot must move
Directly on, and but a single square ;
Yet may these heroes, when they first prepare
To mix in combat on the bloody mead,
Double their sally, and two steps proceed ;
But when they wound, their swords they subtly
    guide
With aim oblique, and slanting pierce his side.
But the great Indian beasts, whose backs sustain
Vast turrets arm'd, when on the redd'ning plain

They join in all the terror of the fight,
Forward or backward, to the left or right,
Run furious, and impatient of confine
Scour through the field, and threat the farthest
    line.
Yet must they ne'er obliquely aim their blows ;
That only manner is allow'd to those
Whom Mars has favour'd most, who bend the
    stubborn bows.
These glancing sideways in a straight career,
Yet each confin'd to their respective sphere,
Or white or black, can send th' unerring dart
Wing'd with swift death to pierce through ev'ry
    part.
The fiery steed, regardless of the reins,
Comes prancing on ; but sullenly disdains
The path direct, and boldly wheeling round,
Leaps o'er a double space at ev'ry bound :
And shifts from white or black to diff'rent
    colour'd ground.
But the fierce Queen, whom dangers ne'er dismay,
The strength and terror of the bloody day,
In a straight line spreads her destruction wide,
To left or right, before, behind, aside.
Yet may she never with a circling course
Sweep to the battle like the fretful Horse ;
But unconfin'd may at her pleasure stray,
If neither friend nor foe block up the way ;
For to o'erleap a warrior, 'tis decreed
Those only dare who curb the snorting steed.
With greater caution and majestic state
The warlike Monarchs in the scene of fate
Direct their motions, since for these appear

Zealous each hope, and anxious ev'ry fear.
While the King's safe, with resolution stern
They clasp their arms ; but should a sudden turn
Make him a captive, instantly they yield,
Resolv'd to share his fortune in the field.
He moves on slow ; with reverence profound
His faithful troops encompass him around,
And oft, to break some instant fatal scheme,
Rush to their fates, their sov'reign to redeem ;
While he, unanxious where to wound the foe,
Need only shift and guard against a blow.
But none, however, can presume t' appear
Within his reach, but must his vengeance fear ;
For he on ev'ry side his terror throws ;
But when he changes from his first repose,
Moves but one step, most awfully sedate,
Or idly roving, or intent on fate.
These are the sev'ral and establish'd laws:
Now see how each maintains his bloody cause.
   Here paused the God, but (since whene'er they
      wage
War here on earth the Gods themselves engage
In mutual battle as they hate or love,
And the most stubborn war is oft above)
Almighty Jove commands the circling train
Of Gods from fav'ring either to abstain,
And let the fight be silently survey'd ;
And added solemn threats if disobey'd.
Then call'd he Phœbus from among the Powers
And subtle Hermes, whom in softer hours
Fair Maia bore : youth wanton'd in their face ;
Both in life's bloom, both shone with equal grace.
Hermes as yet had never wing'd his feet ;

As yet Apollo in his radiant seat
Had never driv'n his chariot through the air,
Known by his bow alone and golden hair.
These Jove commission'd to attempt the fray,
And rule the sportive military day ;
Bid them agree which party each maintains,
And promis'd a reward that's worth their pains.
The greater took their seats ; on either hand
Respectful the less Gods in order stand,
But careful not to interrupt their play,
By hinting when t' advance or run away.
    Then they examine, who shall first proceed
To try their courage, and their army lead.
Chance gave it for the White, that he should go
First with a brave defiance to the foe.
Awhile he ponder'd which of all his train
Should bear his first commission o'er the plain ;
And then determin'd to begin the scene
With him that stood before to guard the Queen.
He took a double step : with instant care
Does the black Monarch in his turn prepare
The adverse champion, and with stern command
Bid him repel the charge with equal hand.
There front to front, the midst of all the field,
With furious threats their shining arms they wield ;
Yet vain the conflict, neither can prevail
While in one path each other they assail.
On ev'ry side to their assistance fly
Their fellow soldiers, and with strong supply
Crowd to the battle, but no bloody stain
Tinctures their armour ; sportive in the plain
Mars plays awhile, and in excursion slight
Harmless they sally forth, or wait the fight.

But now the swarthy Foot, that first appear'd
To front the foe, his pond'rous jav'lin rear'd
Leftward aslant, and a pale warrior slays,
Spurns him aside, and boldly takes his place.
Unhappy youth, his danger not to spy !
Instant he fell, and triumph'd but to die.
At this the sable King with prudent care
Remov'd his station from the middle square,
And slow retiring to the farthest ground,
There safely lurk'd, with troops entrench'd around.
Then from each quarter to the war advance
The furious Knights, and poise the trembling lance :
By turns they rush, by turns the victors yield,
Heaps of dead Foot choke up the crimson'd field :
They fall unable to retreat ; around
The clang of arms and iron hoofs resound.

But while young Phœbus pleas'd himself to view
His furious Knight destroy the vulgar crew,
Sly Hermes long'd t' attempt with secret aim
Some noble act of more exalted fame.
For this, he inoffensive pass'd along
Through ranks of Foot, and midst the trembling
       throng
Sent his left Horse, that free without confine
Rov'd o'er the plain, upon some great design
Against the King himself. At length he stood,
And having fix'd his station as he would,
Threaten'd at once with instant fate the King
And th' Indian beast that guarded the right wing.
Apollo sigh'd, and hast'ning to relieve
The straiten'd Monarch, griev'd that he must leave
His martial Elephant exposed to fate,
And view'd with pitying eyes his dang'rous state.

First in his thoughts however was his care
To save his King, whom to the neighbouring square
On the right hand, he snatch'd with trembling
  flight ;
At this with fury springs the sable Knight,
Drew his keen sword, and rising to the blow,
Sent the great Indian brute to shades below.
O fatal loss ! for none except the Queen
Spreads such a terror through the bloody scene.
Yet shall you ne'er unpunish'd boast your prize,
The Delian God with stern resentment cries ;
And wedg'd him round with foot, and pour'd in
  fresh supplies.
Thus close besieg'd trembling he cast his eye
Around the plain, but saw no shelter nigh,
No way for flight ; for here the Queen oppos'd,
The Foot in phalanx there the passage clos'd :
At length he fell ; yet not unpleas'd with fate,
Since victim to a Queen's vindictive hate.
With grief and fury burns the whiten'd host,
One of their Tow'rs thus immaturely lost.
As when a bull has in contention stern
Lost his right horn, with double vengeance burn
His thoughts for war, with blood he's cover'd o'er,
And the woods echo to his dismal roar,
So look'd the flaxen host, when angry fate
O'erturn'd the Indian bulwark of their state.
Fir'd at this great success, with double rage
Apollo hurries on his troops t' engage,
For blood and havoc wild ; and, while he leads
His troops thus careless, loses both his steeds :
For if some adverse warriors were o'erthrown,
He little thought what dangers threat his own.

But slyer Hermes with observant eyes
March'd slowly cautious, and at distance spies
What moves must next succeed, what dangers
      next arise.

Often would he, the stately Queen to snare,
The slender Foot to front her arms prepare,
And to conceal his scheme he sighs and feigns
Such a wrong step would frustrate all his pains.
Just then an Archer, from the right-hand view,
At the pale Queen his arrow boldly drew,
Unseen by Phœbus, who, with studious thought,
From the left side a vulgar hero brought.
But tender Venus, with a pitying eye,
Viewing the sad destruction that was nigh,
Wink'd upon Phœbus (for the Goddess sat
By chance directly opposite) ; at that
Rous'd in an instant, young Apollo threw
His eyes around the field his troops to view ;
Perceiv'd the danger, and with sudden fright
Withdrew the Foot that he had sent to fight,
And sav'd his trembling Queen by seasonable
      flight.

But Maia's son with shouts fill'd all the coast :
The Queen, he cried, the important Queen is lost.
Phœbus, howe'er, resolving to maintain
What he had done, bespoke the heavenly train.

   What mighty harm, in sportive mimic fight,
Is it to set a little blunder right,
When no preliminary rule debarr'd ?
If you henceforward, Mercury, would guard
Against such practice, let us make the law :
And whosoe'er shall first to battle draw,
Or white, or black, remorseless let him go

At all events, and dare the angry foe.
  He said, and this opinion pleas'd around :
Jove turn'd aside, and on his daughter frown'd,
Unmark'd by Hermes, who, with strange surprise,
Fretted and foam'd, and roll'd his ferret eyes,
And but with great reluctance could refrain
From dashing at a blow all off the plain.
Then he resolv'd to interweave deceits, —
To carry on the war by tricks and cheats.
Instant he call'd an Archer from the throng,
And bid him like the courser wheel along :
Bounding he springs, and threats the pallid Queen.
The fraud, however, was by Phœbus seen ;
He smil'd, and, turning to the Gods, he said :
Though, Hermes, you are perfect in your trade,
And you can trick and cheat to great surprise, ⎫
These little sleights no more shall blind my eyes : ⎬
Correct them if you please, the more you thus ⎪
　　　disguise. ⎭
The circle laugh'd aloud ; and Maia's son
(As if it had but by mistake been done)
Recall'd his Archer, and with motion due,
Bid him advance, the combat to renew.
But Phœbus watch'd him with a jealous eye,
Fearing some trick was ever lurking nigh,
For he would oft, with sudden sly design,
Send forth at once two combatants to join
His warring troops, against the law of arms,
Unless the wary foe was ever in alarms.
  Now the white Archer with his utmost force
Bent the tough bow against the sable Horse,
And drove him from the Queen, where he had
　　　stood

Hoping to glut his vengeance with her blood.
Then the right Elephant with martial pride
Rov'd here and there, and spread his terrors wide :
Glittering in arms from far a courser came,
Threaten'd at once the King and Royal Dame ;
Thought himself safe when he the post had seiz'd,
And with the future spoils his fancy pleas'd.
Fir'd at the danger a young Archer came,
Rush'd on the foe, and levell'd sure his aim ;
(And though a Pawn his sword in vengeance
draws,
Gladly he'd lose his life in glory's cause).
The whistling arrow to his bowels flew,
And the sharp steel his blood profusely drew ;
He drops the reins, he totters to the ground,
And his life issu'd murm'ring through the wound.
Pierc'd by the Foot, this Archer bit the plain ;
The Foot himself was by another slain ;
And with inflam'd revenge, the battle burns
again.
Towers, Archers, Knights, meet on the crimson
ground,
And the field echoes to the martial sound.
Their thoughts are heated, and their courage
fir'd,
Thick they rush on with double zeal inspir'd ;
Generals and Foot, with different colour'd mien,
Confus'dly warring in the camps are seen,—
Valour and Fortune meet in one promiscuous
scene.
Now these victorious, lord it o'er the field ;
Now the foe rallies, the triumphant yield :
Just as the tide of battle ebbs or flows.

As when the conflict more tempestuous grows
Between the winds, with strong and boisterous
    sweep
They plough th' Ionian or Atlantic deep !
By turns prevails the mutual blustering roar,
And the big waves alternate lash the shore.
  But in the midst of all the battle rag'd
The snowy Queen, with troops at once engag'd ;
She fell'd an Archer as she sought the plain,—
As she retir'd an Elephant was slain :
To right and left her fatal spears she sent,
Burst through the ranks, and triumph'd as she
    went ;
Through arms and blood she seeks a glorious fate,
Pierces the farthest lines, and nobly great
Leads on her army with a gallant show,
Breaks the battalions, and cuts through the foe.
At length the sable King his fears betray'd,
And begg'd his military consort's aid :
With cheerful speed she flew to his relief,
And met in equal arms the female chief.
  Who first, great Queen, and who at last did
    bleed ?
How many Whites lay gasping on the mead?
Half dead, and floating in a bloody tide,
Foot, Knights, and Archer lie on every side.
Who can recount the slaughter of the day?
How many leaders threw their lives away?
The chequer'd plain is fill'd with dying box,
Havoc ensues, and with tumultuous shocks
The different colour'd ranks in blood engage,
And Foot and Horse promiscuously rage.
With nobler courage and superior might

The dreadful Amazons sustain the fight,
Resolv'd alike to mix in glorious strife,
Till to imperious fate they yield their life.
   Meanwhile each Monarch, in a neighbouring
      cell,
Confin'd the warriors that in battle fell,
There watch'd the captives with a jealous eye,
Lest, slipping out again, to arms they fly.
But Thracian Mars, in steadfast friendship join'd
To Hermes, as near Phœbus he reclin'd,
Observ'd each chance, how all their motions bend,
Resolv'd if possible to serve his friend.
He a Foot-soldier and a Knight purloin'd
Out from the prison that the dead confin'd ;
And slyly push'd 'em forward on the plain ;
Th' enliven'd combatants their arms regain,
Mix in the bloody scene, and boldly war again.
   So the foul hag, in screaming wild alarms,
O'er a dead carcase muttering her charms
(And with her frequent and tremendous yell
Forcing great Hecate from out of hell),
Shoots in the corpse a new fictitious soul ;
With instant glare the supple eyeballs roll,
Again it moves and speaks, and life informs the
      whole.
   Vulcan alone discern'd the subtle cheat ;
And wisely scorning such a base deceit,
Call'd out to Phœbus. Grief and rage assail
Phœbus by turns ; detected Mars turns pale.
Then awful Jove with sullen eye reprov'd
Mars, and the captives order'd to be mov'd
To their dark caves ; bid each fictitious spear
Be straight recall'd, and all be as they were.

And now both Monarchs with redoubl'd rage
Led on their Queens, the mutual war to wage.
O'er all the field their thirsty spears they send,
Then front to front their Monarchs they defend.
But lo ! the female White rush'd in unseen,
And slew with fatal haste the swarthy Queen ;
Yet, soon, alas ! resign'd her royal spoils,
Snatch'd by a shaft from her successful toils.
Struck at the sight, both hosts in wild surprise
Pour'd forth their tears, and fill'd the air with cries ;
They wept and sigh'd, as pass'd the fun'ral train,
As if both armies had at once been slain.

    And now each troop surrounds its mourning chief,
To guard his person, or assuage his grief.
One is their common fear ; one stormy blast
Has equally made havoc as it pass'd.
Not all, however, of their youth are slain ;
Some champions yet the vig'rous war maintain.
Three Foot, an Archer, and a stately Tower,
For Phœbus still exert their utmost power.
Just the same number Mercury can boast,
Except the Tower, who lately in his post
Unarm'd inglorious fell, in peace profound,
Pierced by an Archer with a distant wound ;
But his right Horse retain'd its mettled pride,—
The rest were swept away by war's strong tide.
    But fretful Hermes, with despairing moan,
Griev'd that so many champions were o'erthrown,
Yet reassumes the fight ; and summons round
The little straggling army that he found,—
All that had 'scap'd from fierce Apollo's rage,—
Resolv'd with greater caution to engage
In future strife, by subtle wiles (if fate

Should give him leave) to save his sinking state.
The sable troops advance with prudence slow,
Bent on all hazards to distress the foe.
More cheerful Phœbus, with unequal pace,
Rallies his arms to lessen his disgrace.
But what strange havoc everywhere has been !
A straggling champion here and there is seen ;
And many are the tents, yet few are left within.

Th' afflicted Kings bewail their consorts dead,
And loathe the thoughts of a deserted bed ;
And though each monarch studies to improve
The tender mem'ry of his former love,
Their state requires a second nuptial tie.
Hence the pale ruler with a love-sick eye
Surveys th' attendants of his former wife,
And offers one of them a royal life.
These, when their martial mistress had been slain,
Weak and despairing tried their arms in vain ;
Willing, howe'er, amidst the Black to go,
They thirst for speedy vengeance on the foe.
Then he resolves to see who merits best,
By strength and courage, the imperial vest ;
Points out the foe, bids each with bold design
Pierce through the ranks, and reach the deepest
        line :
For none must hope with monarchs to repose
But who can first, through thick surrounding foes,
Through arms and wiles, with hazardous essay,
Safe to the farthest quarters force their way.
Fir'd at the thought, with sudden, joyful pace
They hurry on ; but first of all the race
Runs the third right-hand warrior for the prize,—
The glitt'ring crown already charms her eyes.

Her dear associates cheerfully give o'er
The nuptial chase; and swift she flies before,
And Glory lent her wings, and the reward in store.
Nor would the sable King her hopes prevent,
For he himself was on a Queen intent,
Alternate, therefore, through the field they go.
Hermes led on, but by a step too slow,
His fourth left Pawn : and now th' advent'rous
     White
Had march'd through all, and gain'd the wish'd-
    for site.
Then the pleas'd King gives orders to prepare
The crown, the sceptre, and the royal chair,
And owns her for his Queen : around exult
The snowy troops, and o'er the Black insult.
   Hermes burst into tears,—with fretful roar
Fill'd the wide air, and his gay vesture tore.
The swarthy Foot had only to advance
One single step ; but oh ! malignant chance !
A tower'd Elephant, with fatal aim,
Stood ready to destroy her when she came :
He keeps a watchful eye upon the whole,
Threatens her entrance, and protects the goal.
Meanwhile the royal new-created bride,
Pleas'd with her pomp, spread death and terror wide ;
Like lightning through the sable troops she flies,
Clashes her arms, and seems to threat the skies.
The sable troops are sunk in wild affright,
And wish th' earth op'ning snatch'd 'em from her
    sight.
In burst the Queen, with vast impetuous swing :
The trembling foes come swarming round the
    King,

Where in the midst he stood, and form a valiant }
    ring. }
So the poor cows, straggling o'er pasture land,
When they perceive the prowling wolf at hand,
Crowd close together in a circle full,
And beg the succour of the lordly bull ;
They clash their horns, they low with dreadful
    sound,
And the remotest groves re-echo round.
    But the bold Queen, victorious, from behind
Pierces the foe ; yet chiefly she design'd
Against the King himself some fatal aim,
And full of war to his pavilion came.
Now here she rush'd, now there ; and had she been
But duly prudent, she had slipp'd between,
With course oblique, into the fourth white square,
And the long toil of war had ended there,
The King had fall'n, and all his sable state ;
And vanquish'd Hermes curs'd his partial fate.
For thence with ease the championess might go,
Murder the King, and none could ward the blow,
    With silence, Hermes, and with panting heart,
Perceiv'd the danger, but with subtle art
(Lest he should see the place) spurs on the foe,
Confounds his thoughts, and blames his being slow.
For shame ! move on ; would you for ever stay ?
What sloth is this, what strange perverse delay ?—
How could you e'er my little pausing blame ?—
What ! you would wait till night shall end the game?
Phœbus, thus nettled, with imprudence slew
A vulgar Pawn, but lost his nobler view.
Young Hermes leap'd, with sudden joy elate ;
And then, to save the monarch from his fate,

Led on his martial Knight, who stepp'd between,
Pleas'd that his charge was to oppose the Queen—
Then, pondering how the Indian beast to slay,
That stopp'd the Foot from making farther way,--
From being made a Queen ; with slanting aim
An Archer struck him ; down the monster came,
And dying shook the earth : while Phœbus tries
Without success the monarch to surprise.
The Foot, then uncontroll'd with instant pride,
Seiz'd the last spot, and mov'd a royal bride.
And now with equal strength both war again,
And bring their second wives upon the plain ;
Then, though with equal views each hop'd and
      fear'd,
Yet, as if every doubt had disappear'd,
As if he had the palm, young Hermes flies
Into excess of joy ; with deep disguise,
Extols his own Black troops, with frequent spite
And with invective taunts disdains the White.
Whom Phœbus thus reprov'd with quick return—
As yet we cannot the decision learn
Of this dispute, and do you triumph now ?
Then your big words and vauntings I'll allow,
When you the battle shall completely gain ;
At present I shall make your boasting vain.
He said, and forward led the daring Queen ;
Instant the fury of the bloody scene
Rises tumultuous, swift the warriors fly
From either side to conquer or to die.
They front the storm of war ; around 'em Fear,
Terror, and Death, perpetually appear.
All meet in arms, and man to man oppose,
Each from their camp attempts to drive their foes ;

Each tries by turns to force the hostile lines ;
Chance and impatience blast their best designs.
The sable Queen spread terror as she went
Through the mid ranks: with more reserv'd intent
The adverse dame declin'd the open fray,
And to the King in private stole away :
Then took the royal guard, and bursting in,
With fatal menace close besieg'd the King.
Alarm'd at this, the swarthy Queen, in haste,
From all her havoc and destructive waste
Broke off, and her contempt of death to show, ⎫
Leap'd in between the monarch and the foe, ⎬
To save the King and state from this impending ⎭
    blow.
But Phœbus met a worse misfortune here :
For Hermes now led forward, void of fear,
His furious Horse into the open plain,
That onward chaf'd, and pranc'd, and paw'd
    amain.
Nor ceas'd from his attempts until he stood
On the long-wish'd-for spot, from whence he could
Slay King or Queen. O'erwhelm'd with sudden
    fears,
Apollo saw, and could not keep from tears.
Now all seem'd ready to be overthrown ;
His strength was wither'd, ev'ry hope was flown.
Hermes, exulting at this great surprise,
Shouted for joy, and fill'd the air with cries ;
Instant he sent the Queen to shades below,
And of her spoils made a triumphant show.
But in return, and in his mid career,
Fell his brave Knight, beneath the Monarch's spear.
    Phœbus, however, did not yet despair,

But still fought on with courage and with care.
He had but two poor common men to show,
And Mars's favourite with his iv'ry bow.
The thoughts of ruin made 'em dare their best
To save their King, so fatally distress'd.
But the sad hour requir'd not such an aid ;
And Hermes breath'd revenge where'er he stray'd.
Fierce comes the sable Queen with fatal threat,
Surrounds the monarch in his royal seat :
Rush'd here and there, nor rested till she slew
The last remainder of the whiten'd crew.
Sole stood the King, the midst of all the plain,
Weak and defenceless, his companions slain,
As when the ruddy morn ascending high
Has chas'd the twinkling stars from all the sky,
Your star, fair Venus, still retains its light,
And, loveliest, goes the latest out of sight.
No safety's left, no gleams of hope remain ;
Yet did he not as vanquish'd quit the plain,
But tried to shut himself between the foe,—⎫
Unhurt through swords and spears he hoped to go, ⎬
Until no room was left to shun the fatal blow ⎭
For if none threaten'd his immediate fate,
And his next move must ruin all his state,
All their past toil and labour is in vain, ⎫
Vain all the bloody carnage of the plain,— ⎪
Neither would triumph then, the laurel neither ⎬
     gain. ⎭
Therefore through each void space and desert ten t,
By different moves his various course he bent :
The Black King watch'd him with observant eye,
Follow'd him close, but left him room to fly.
Then when he saw him take the farthest line,

He sent the Queen his motions to confine,
And guard the second rank, that he could go
No farther now than to that distant row.
The sable monarch then with cheerful mien
Approach'd, but always with one space between.
But as the King stood o'er against him there,
Helpless, forlorn, and sunk in his despair,
The martial Queen her lucky moment knew,
Seized on the farthest seat with fatal view,
Nor left th' unhappy King a place to flee unto.
At length in vengeance her keen sword she draws,
Slew him, and ended thus the bloody cause :
And all the gods around approv'd it with
  applause.

  The victor could not from his insults keep,
But laugh'd and sneer'd to see Apollo weep.
Jove call'd him near, and gave him in his hand
The powerful, happy, and mysterious wand
By which the Shades are call'd to purer day,
When penal fire has purged their sins away ;
By which the guilty are condemn'd to dwell
In the dark mansions of the deepest hell ;
By which he gives us sleep, or sleep denies,
And closes at the last the dying eyes.
Soon after this, the heavenly victor brought
The game on earth, and first th' Italians taught.

  For (as they say) fair Scacchis he espied
Feeding her cygnets in the silver tide
(Scacchis, the loveliest Seriad of the place),
And as she stray'd, took her to his embrace.
Then, to reward her for her virtue lost,
Gave her the men and chequer'd board, emboss'd
With gold and silver curiously inlay'd ;

And taught her how the game was to be play'd.
Ev'n now 'tis honour'd with her happy name ;
And Rome and all the world admire the game.
All which the Seriads told me heretofore,
When my boy-notes amus'd the Serian shore.

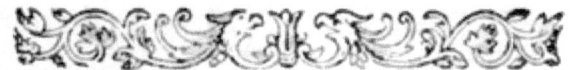

THE GOOD-NATUR'D MAN:

A COMEDY.

[*The Good-Natur'd Man* was produced on Friday, the 20th January, 1768. It was played for ten nights in succession, the fifth representation being "commanded by Their Majesties." On the 5th February it was published in *octavo* by W. Griffin, of Catherine-Street, Strand, with the following title :—*The Good Natur'd Man : A Comedy. As Performed at the Theatre-Royal in Covent-Garden. By Mr. Goldsmith.* The price was one shilling and sixpence. The present reprint is from the fifth edition which appeared in the same year as the first.]

PREFACE.

WHEN I undertook to write a comedy, I confess I was strongly prepossessed in favour of the poets of the last age, and strove to imitate them. The term, *genteel comedy*, was then unknown amongst us, and little more was desired by an audience, than nature and humour, in whatever walks of life they were most conspicuous. The author of the following scenes never imagined that more would be expected of him, and therefore to delineate character has been his principal aim. Those who know anything of composition, are sensible, that in pursuing humour, it will sometimes lead us into the recesses of the mean; I was even tempted to look for it in the master of a spunging-house : but in deference to the public taste, grown of late, perhaps, too delicate, the scene of the bailiffs was retrenched in the representation.[1] In deference also to the judgment of a few friends, who think in a particular way, the scene is here restored.

[1 *Vide* Act iii, pp. 47-55.]

The author submits it to the reader in his closet; and hopes that too much refinement will not banish humour and character from ours, as it has already done from the French theatre. Indeed the French comedy is now become so very elevated and sentimental, that it has not only banished humour and *Molière* from the stage, but it has banished all spectators too.

Upon the whole, the author returns his thanks to the public for the favourable reception which the " Good-Natur'd Man " has met with : and to Mr. Colman in particular, for his kindness to it.[1] It may not also be improper to assure any, who shall hereafter write for the theatre, that merit, or supposed merit, will ever be a sufficient passport to his protection.

[1 This was the gratitude of success. Colman had not been particularly kind to *The Good-Natur'd Man.*]

PROLOGUE

WRITTEN BY DR. JOHNSON:

SPOKEN BY MR. BENSLEY.

REST by the load of life, the weary mind
Surveys the general toil of human kind;
With cool submission joins the labouring train,
And social sorrow loses half its pain:
Our anxious Bard,[1] without complaint, may share
This bustling season's epidemic care,
Like Cæsar's pilot, dignified by fate,
Tost in one common storm with all the great;
Distrest alike, the statesman and the wit,
When one a Borough courts, and one the Pit.
The busy candidates for power and fame,
Have hopes, and fears, and wishes, just the same;
Disabled both to combat, or to fly,

[1 This Prologue, as spoken, and as published in the *Public Advertiser* for February 3, 1768, differs somewhat from the version here printed. In particular "Our anxious Bard" was originally "Our *little* Bard"—an epithet which could scarcely have gratified the author of the Play.]

Must hear all taunts, and hear without reply.
Uncheck'd on both, loud rabbles vent their rage,
As mongrels bay the lion in a cage.
Th' offended burgess hoards his angry tale,
For that blest year when all that vote may rail ;
Their schemes of spite the poet's foes dismiss,
Till that glad night, when all that hate may hiss.
This day the powder'd curls and golden coat,
Says swelling Crispin, begg'd a cobbler's vote.
This night, our wit, the pert apprentice cries,
Lies at my feet, I hiss him, and he dies.
The great, 'tis true, can charm th' electing tribe ;
The bard may supplicate, but cannot bribe.
Yet judg'd by those, whose voices ne'er were sold,
He feels no want of ill-persuading gold ;
But, confident of praise, if praise be due,
Trusts without fear, to merit, and to you.

DRAMATIS PERSONÆ.[1]

MEN.

Mr. Honeywood,	Mr. Powell.
Croaker,	Mr. Shuter.
Lofty,	Mr. Woodward.
Sir William Honeywood,	Mr. Clarke.
Leontine,	Mr. Bensley.
Jarvis,	Mr. Dunstall.
Butler,	Mr. Cushing.
Bailiff,	Mr. R. Smith.
Dubardieu,	Mr. Holton.
Postboy,	Mr. Quick.

WOMEN.

Miss Richland,	Mrs. Bulkley.
Olivia,	Mrs. Mattocks.
Mrs. Croaker,	Mrs. Pitt.
Garnet,	Mrs. Green.
Landlady,	Mrs. White.

Scene.—LONDON.

[1 The cast given is that of the piece as first acted.]

THE GOOD-NATUR'D MAN.[1]

ACT THE FIRST.

SCENE, *An Apartment in* YOUNG HONEYWOOD'S *House.*

Enter SIR WILLIAM HONEYWOOD, JARVIS.

Sir William.

GOOD Jarvis, make no apologies for this honest bluntness. Fidelity, like yours, is the best excuse for every freedom.

Jarvis. I can't help being blunt, and being very angry too, when I hear you talk of disinheriting so good, so worthy a young gentleman as your nephew, my master. All the world loves him.

Sir Will. Say rather, that he loves all the world; that is his fault.

Jarvis. I'm sure there is no part of it more dear to him than you are, though he has not seen you since he was a child.

[1 A personage known as "the good-natured man" is described at p. 85 of Goldsmith's *Life of Richard Nash, Esq.*, 1762, and may have suggested this title.]

Sir Will. What signifies his affection to me, or how can I be proud of a place in a heart where every sharper and coxcomb find an easy entrance?

Jarvis. I grant you that he's rather too good-natured; that he's too much every man's man; that he laughs this minute with one, and cries the next with another; but whose instructions may he thank for all this?

Sir Will. Not mine, sure? My letters to him during my employment in Italy, taught him only that philosophy which might prevent, not defend his errors.

Jarvis. Faith, begging your honour's pardon, I'm sorry they taught him any philosophy at all; it has only served to spoil him. This same philosophy is a good horse in the stable, but an arrant jade on a journey. For my own part, whenever I hear him mention the name on't, I'm always sure he's going to play the fool.

Sir Will. Don't let us ascribe his faults to his philosophy, I entreat you. No, Jarvis, his good nature arises rather from his fears of offending the importunate, than his desire of making the deserving happy.

Jarvis. What it rises from, I don't know. But, to be sure, everybody has it, that asks it.

Sir Will. Ay, or that does not ask it. I have been now for some time a concealed spectator of his follies, and find them as boundless as his dissipation.

Jarvis. And yet, faith, he has some fine name or other for them all. He calls his extravagance, generosity; and his trusting everybody, universal benevolence. It was but last week he went security for a fellow whose face he scarce knew, and that he called an act of exalted mu—mu—munificence ; ay, that was the name he gave it.

Sir Will. And upon that I proceed, as my last effort, though with very little hopes to reclaim him. That very fellow has just absconded, and I have taken up the security. Now, my intention is to involve him in fictitious distress, before he has plunged himself into real calamity. To arrest him for that very debt, to clap an officer upon him, and then let him see which of his friends will come to his relief.

Jarvis. Well, if I could but any way see him thoroughly vexed, every groan of his would be music to me ; yet, faith, I believe it impossible. I have tried to fret him myself every morning these three years ; but, instead of being angry, he sits as calmly to hear me scold, as he does to his hairdresser.

Sir Will. We must try him once more, however, and I'll go this instant to put my scheme into execution ; and I don't despair of succeeding, as, by your means, I can have frequent opportunities of being about him, without being known. What a pity it is, Jarvis, that any man's good-will to others should produce so much neglect of himself, as to require correction. Yet, we must touch his weaknesses with a delicate hand. There are some faults so nearly allied to excellence, that we can scarce weed out the vice without eradicating the virtue. [*Exit.*

Jarvis. Well, go thy ways, Sir William Honeywood. It is not without reason that the world allows thee to be the best of men. But here comes his hopeful nephew; the strange good-natur'd, foolish, open-hearted—And yet, all his faults were such that one loves him still the better for them.

Enter HONEYWOOD.

Honeyw. Well, Jarvis, what messages from my friends this morning?

Jarvis. You have no friends.

Honeyw. Well; from my acquaintance then?

Jarvis. (*Pulling out bills.*) A few of our usual cards of compliment, that's all. This bill from your tailor; this from your mercer; and this from the little broker in Crooked-lane.[1] He says he has been at a great deal of trouble to get back the money you borrowed.

Honeyw. That I don't know; but I'm sure we were at a great deal of trouble in getting him to lend it.

Jarvis. He has lost all patience.

Honeyw. Then he has lost a very good thing.

Jarvis. There's that ten guineas you were send-ing to the poor gentleman and his children in the Fleet. I believe that would stop his mouth, for a while at least.

Honeyw. Ay, Jarvis, but what will fill their mouths in the mean time? Must I be cruel be-cause he happens to be importunate; and, to relieve his avarice, leave them to insupportable distress?

[1 Perhaps, but not necessarily, Crooked-lane, Cannon-street, City.]

Jarvis. 'Sdeath ! Sir, the question now is how
to relieve yourself. Yourself—Haven't I reason to
be out of my senses, when I see things going on
at sixes and sevens ?

Honeyw. Whatever reason you may have for
being out of your senses, I hope you'll allow that
I'm not quite unreasonable for continuing in
mine.

Jarvis. You're the only man alive in your
present situation that could do so—Everything
upon the waste. There's Miss Richland and her
fine fortune gone already, and upon the point of
being given to your rival.

Honeyw. I'm no man's rival.

Jarvis. Your uncle in Italy preparing to disin-
herit you ; your own fortune almost spent ; and
nothing but pressing creditors, false friends, and a
pack of drunken servants that your kindness has
made unfit for any other family.

Honeyw. Then they have the more occasion for
being in mine.

Jarvis. Soh ! What will you have done with
him that I caught stealing your plate in the pantry ?
In the fact ; I caught him in the fact.

Honeyw. In the fact ! If so, I really think that
we should pay him his wages, and turn him off.

Jarvis. He shall be turn'd off at Tyburn, the
dog ; we'll hang him, if it be only to frighten the
rest of the family.

Honeyw. No, Jarvis : it's enough that we have lost
what he has stolen, let us not add to it the loss of
a fellow-creature !

Jarvis. Very fine ; well, here was the footman

O

just now, to complain of the butler; he says he does most work, and ought to have most wages.

Honeyw. That's but just; though perhaps, here comes the butler to complain of the footman.

Jarvis. Ay, it's the way with them all, from the scullion to the privy-counsellor. If they have a bad master, they keep quarrelling with him; if they have a good master, they keep quarrelling with one another.

Enter BUTLER, *drunk.*

Butler. Sir, I'll not stay in the family with Jonathan; you must part with him, or part with me, that's the ex-ex-exposition of the matter, sir.

Honeyw. Full and explicit enough. But what's his fault, good Philip?

Butler. Sir, he's given to drinking, sir, and I shall have my morals corrupted, by keeping such company.

Honeyw. Ha! Ha! He has such a diverting way—

Jarvis. O quite amusing!

Butler. I find my wines a-going, sir; and liquors don't go without mouths, sir; I hate a drunkard, sir!

Honeyw. Well, well, Philip, I'll hear you upon that another time, so go to bed now.

Jarvis. To bed! Let him go to the devil!

Butler. Begging your honour's pardon, and begging your pardon master Jarvis, I'll not go to bed, nor to the devil neither. I have enough to do to mind my cellar. I forgot, your honour, Mr. Croaker is below. I came on purpose to tell you.

Honeyw. Why didn't you show him up, block-head?

Butler. Show him up, sir? With all my heart, sir. Up or down, all's one to me. [*Exit.*

Jarvis. Ay, we have one or other of that family in this house from morning till night. He comes on the old affair, I suppose. The match between his son, that's just returned from Paris, and Miss Richland, the young lady he's guardian to.

Honeyw. Perhaps so. Mr. Croaker, knowing my friendship for the young lady, has got it into his head that I can persuade her to what I please.

Jarvis. Ah! If you loved yourself but half as well as she loves you, we should soon see a marriage that would set all things to rights again.

Honeyw. Love me! Sure, Jarvis, you dream. No, no; her intimacy with me never amounted to more than friendship—mere friendship. That she is the most lovely woman that ever warmed the human heart with desire, I own. But never let me harbour a thought of making her unhappy, by a connection with one so unworthy her merits as I am. No, Jarvis, it shall be my study to serve her, even in spite of my wishes; and to secure her happiness, though it destroys my own.

Jarvis. Was ever the like! I want patience.

Honeyw. Besides, Jarvis, though I could obtain Miss Richland's consent, do you think I could succeed with her guardian, or Mrs. Croaker his wife; who, though both very fine in their way, are yet a little opposite in their dispositions, you know.

Jarvis. Opposite enough, Heaven knows; the very reverse of each other; she all laugh and no

joke ; he always complaining, and never sorrowful ;
a fretful poor soul that has a new distress for every
hour in the four-and-twenty—

Honeyw. Hush, hush, he's coming up, he'll
hear you.

Jarvis. One whose voice is a passing bell—

Honeyw. Well, well, go, do.

Jarvis. A raven that bodes nothing but mischief;
a coffin and cross bones ; a bundle of rue ; a sprig
of deadly night shade ; a—(*Honeywood stopping his
mouth at last, pushes him off.*)   [*Exit* JARVIS.

Honeyw. I must own my old monitor is not
entirely wrong.   There is something in my friend
Croaker's conversation that quite depresses me.
His very mirth is an antidote to all gaiety, and his
appearance has a stronger effect on my spirits than
an undertaker's shop.—Mr. Croaker, this is such a
satisfaction—

Enter CROAKER.[1]

Croaker. A pleasant morning to Mr. Honeywood, and many of them.   How is this ! You look
most shockingly to-day, my dear friend.   I hope
this weather does not affect your spirits.   To be
sure, if this weather continues—I say nothing—
But God send we be all better this day three
months.

Honeyw. I heartily concur in the wish, though
I own not in your apprehensions.

Croaker. May be not ! Indeed what signifies
what weather we have in a country going to ruin

[1 The character of Croaker is said to have been based on
Johnson's " Suspirius," *Rambler*, No. 59.]

like ours? Taxes rising and trade falling. Money
flying out of the kingdom and Jesuits swarming
into it. I know at this time no less than a hundred and twenty-seven Jesuits between Charing-
cross and Temple-bar.

Honeyw. The Jesuits will scarce pervert you or
me, I should hope.

Croaker. May be not. Indeed what signifies
whom they pervert in a country that has scarce any
religion to lose? I'm only afraid for our wives and
daughters.

Honeyw. I have no apprehensions for the ladies,
I assure you.

Croaker. May be not. Indeed what signifies
whether they be perverted or no? The women in
my time were good for something. I have seen a
lady dressed from top to toe in her own manufactures formerly. But now-a-days, the devil a thing
of their own manufactures about them, except their
faces.

Honeyw. But, however these faults may be
practised abroad, you don't find them at home,
either with Mrs. Croaker, Olivia or Miss Richland.

Croaker. The best of them will never be
canoniz'd for a saint when she's dead. By the bye,
my dear friend, I don't find this match between
Miss Richland and my son much relish'd, either
by one side or t'other.

Honeyw. I thought otherwise.

Croaker. Ah, Mr. Honeywood, a little of your
fine serious advice to the young lady might go far:
I know she has a very exalted opinion of your
understanding.

Honeyw. But would not that be usurping an authority that more properly belongs to yourself?

Croaker. My dear friend, you know but little of my authority at home. People think, indeed, because they see me come out in a morning thus, with a pleasant face, and to make my friends merry, that all's well within. But I have cares that would break a heart of stone. My wife has so encroach'd upon every one of my privileges, that I'm now no more than a mere lodger in my own house !

Honeyw. But a little spirit exerted on your side might perhaps restore your authority.

Croaker. No, though I had the spirit of a lion ! I do rouse sometimes. But what then ! Always haggling and haggling. A man is tired of getting the better before his wife is tired of losing the victory.

Honeyw. It's a melancholy consideration indeed, that our chief comforts often produce our greatest anxieties, and that an increase of our possessions is but an inlet to new disquietudes.

Croaker. Ah, my dear friend, these were the very words of poor Dick Doleful to me not a week before he made away with himself. Indeed, Mr. Honeywood, I never see you but you put me in mind of poor--Dick. Ah, there was merit neglected for you ! and so true a friend ! we lov'd each other for thirty years, and yet he never asked me to lend him a single farthing !

Honeyw. Pray what could induce him to commit so rash an action at last ?

Croaker. I don't know, some people were

malicious enough to say it was keeping company
with me; because we used to meet now and then
and open our hearts to each other. To be sure I
lov'd to hear him talk, and he lov'd to hear me talk;
poor dear Dick. He used to say that Croaker
rhymed to joker; and so we used to laugh—Poor
Dick. (*Going to cry.*)

Honeyw. His fate affects me.

Croaker. Ay, he grew sick of this miserable life,
where we do nothing but eat and grow hungry,
dress and undress, get up and lie down; while
reason, that should watch like a nurse by our side,
falls as fast asleep as we do.

Honeyw. To say truth, if we compare that part
of life which is to come, by that which we have
past, the prospect is hideous.

Croaker. Life at the greatest and best is but a
froward child, that must be humour'd and coax'd
a little till it falls asleep, and then all the care is
over.[1]

Honeyw. Very true, sir, nothing can exceed the
vanity of our existence, but the folly of our pursuits.
We wept when we came into the world, and every
day tells us why.

Croaker. Ah, my dear friend, it is a perfect
satisfaction to be miserable with you. My son
Leontine shan't lose the benefit of such fine conversation. I'll just step home for him. I am
willing to shew him so much seriousness in one

[1 An unacknowledged quotation from Sir William
Temple's essay on Poetry (*Works*, 1720, i, 249.). Goldsmith
had already used it in the *Enquiry into the Present State
of Polite Learning*, 1759, p. 196.]

scarce older than himself—And what if I bring my
last letter to the Gazetteer on the increase and
progress of earthquakes? It will amuse us, I
promise you. I there prove how the late earthquake is coming round to pay us another visit from
London to Lisbon, from Lisbon to the Canary
Islands, from the Canary Islands to Palmyra, from
Palmyra to Constantinople, and so from Constantinople back to London again. [*Exit.*

Honeyw. Poor Croaker! His situation deserves
the utmost pity. I shall scarce recover my spirits
these three days. Sure, to live upon such terms is
worse than death itself. And yet, when I consider
my own situation, a broken fortune, a hopeless
passion, friends in distress; the wish but not the
power to serve them——(*pausing and sighing.*)

Enter BUTLER.

Butler. More company below, sir; Mrs.
Croaker and Miss Richland; shall I show them
up? But they're showing up themselves. [*Exit.*

Enter Mrs. CROAKER *and Miss* RICHLAND.

Miss Rich. You're always in such spirits.

Mrs. Croaker. We have just come, my dear
Honeywood, from the auction. There was the old
deaf dowager, as usual, bidding like a fury against
herself. And then so curious in antiques! Herself
the most genuine piece of antiquity in the whole
collection!

Honeyw. Excuse me, ladies, if some uneasiness
from friendship makes me unfit to share in this
good humour; I know you'll pardon me.

Mrs. Croaker. I vow he seems as melancholy as if he had taken a dose of my husband this morning. Well, if Richland here can pardon you, I must.

Miss Rich. You would seem to insinuate, madam, that I have particular reasons for being dispos'd to refuse it.

Mrs. Croaker. Whatever I insinuate, my dear, don't be so ready to wish an explanation.

Miss Rich. I own I should be sorry Mr. Honeywood's long friendship and mine should be misunderstood.

Honeyw. There's no answering for others, madam. But I hope you'll never find me presuming to offer more than the most delicate friendship may readily allow.

Miss Rich. And I shall be prouder of such a tribute from you than the most passionate professions from others.

Honeyw. My own sentiments, madam: friendship is a disinterested commerce between equals; love, an abject intercourse between tyrants and slaves.

Miss Rich. And, without a compliment, I know none more disinterested or more capable of friendship than Mr. Honeywood.

Mrs. Croaker. And indeed I know nobody that has more friends, at least among the ladies. Miss Fruzz, Miss Oddbody and Miss Winterbottom, praise him in all companies. As for Miss Biddy Bundle, she's his professed admirer.

Miss Rich. Indeed! an admirer! I did not know, sir, you were such a favourite there. But is she seriously so handsome? Is she the mighty thing talk'd of?

Honeyw. The town, madam, seldom begins to praise a lady's beauty, till she's beginning to lose it! (*Smiling.*)

Mrs. Croaker. But she's resolved never to lose it, it seems. For as her natural face decays, her skill improves in making the artificial one. Well, nothing diverts me more than one of those fine old dressy things, who thinks to conceal her age, by everywhere exposing her person; sticking herself up in the front of a side-box;[1] trailing through a minuet at Almack's; and then, in the public gardens; looking for all the world like one of the painted ruins of the place.[2]

Honeyw. Every age has its admirers, ladies. While you, perhaps, are trading among the warmer climates of youth, there ought to be some to carry on a useful commerce in the frozen latitudes beyond fifty.

Miss Rich. But then the mortifications they must suffer before they can be fitted out for traffic. I have seen one of them fret a whole morning at her hair-dresser, when all the fault was her face.

Honeyw. And yet I'll engage has carried that face at last to a very good market. This good-natur'd town, madam, has husbands, like spectacles, to fit every age, from fifteen to fourscore.

[1 In Pope's time the gentlemen sat in the *side*-boxes. But by this date things must have altered, as Johnson and his friends occupied a *front*-box on the first night of *She Stoops to Conquer.*]

[2 *E.g.* the Ruins of Palmyra and other painted scenes in the walks at old Vauxhall Gardens.]

Mrs. Croaker. Well, you're a dear good-natur'd creature. But you know you're engaged with us this morning upon a strolling party. I want to shew Olivia the town, and the things; I believe I shall have business for you for the whole day.

Honeyw. I am sorry, madam, I have an appointment with Mr. Croaker, which it is impossible to put off.

Mrs. Croaker. What! with my husband! Then I'm resolved to take no refusal. Nay, I protest you must. You know I never laugh so much as with you.

Honeyw. Why, if I must, I must. I'll swear you have put me into such spirits. Well, do you find jest, and I'll find laugh, I promise you. We'll wait for the chariot in the next room.

[*Exeunt.*

Enter LEONTINE *and* OLIVIA.

Leont. There they go, thoughtless and happy. My dearest Olivia, what would I give to see you capable of sharing in their amusements, and as cheerful as they are.

Olivia. How, my Leontine, how can I be cheerful, when I have so many terrors to oppress me? The fear of being detected by this family, and the apprehensions of a censuring world, when I must be detected—

Leont. The world! my love, what can it say? At worst it can only say that, being compelled by a mercenary guardian to embrace a life you disliked, you formed a resolution of flying with the man of your choice; that you confided in his honour, and took refuge in my father's house; the only one where your's could remain without censure.

Olivia. But consider, Leontine, your disobedience and my indiscretion: your being sent to France to bring home a sister; and, instead of a sister, bringing home——

Leont. One dearer than a thousand sisters. One that I am convinc'd will be equally dear to the rest of the family, when she comes to be known.

Olivia. And that, I fear, will shortly be.

Leont. Impossible, till we ourselves think proper to make the discovery. My sister, you know, has been with her aunt, at Lyons, since she was a child, and you find every creature in the family takes you for her.

Olivia. But mayn't she write, mayn't her aunt write?

Leont. Her aunt scarce ever writes, and all my sister's letters are directed to me.

Olivia. But won't your refusing Miss Richland, for whom you know the old gentleman intends you, create a suspicion?

Leont. There, there's my master-stroke. I have resolved not to refuse her; nay, an hour hence I have consented to go with my father, to make her an offer of my heart and fortune.

Olivia. Your heart and fortune!

Leont. Don't be alarm'd, my dearest. Can Olivia think so meanly of my honour, or my love, as to suppose I could ever hope for happiness from any but her? No, my Olivia, neither the force, nor, permit me to add, the delicacy of my passion, leave any room to suspect me. I only offer Miss Richland a heart I am convinced she will refuse; as I am confidant that, without knowing it, her affections are fixed upon Mr. Honeywood.

Olivia. Mr. Honeywood! You'll excuse my apprehensions; but when your merits come to be put in the balance—

Leont. You view them with too much partiality. However, by making this offer, I show a seeming compliance with my father's commands; and perhaps, upon her refusal, I may have his consent to choose for myself.

Olivia. Well, I submit. And yet, my Leontine, I own, I shall envy her even your pretended addresses. I consider every look, every expression of your esteem, as due only to me. This is folly, perhaps: I allow it; but it is natural to suppose, that merit which has made an impression on one's own heart, may be powerful over that of another.

Leont. Don't, my life's treasure, don't let us make imaginary evils, when you know we have so many real ones to encounter. At worst, you know, if Miss Richland should consent, or my father refuse his pardon, it can but end in a trip to Scotland; and—— ——

Enter CROAKER.

Croaker. Where have you been, boy? I have been seeking you. My friend Honeywood here, has been saying such comfortable things. Ah! he's an example indeed. Where is he? I left him here.

Leont. Sir, I believe you may see him, and hear him, too, in the next room: he's preparing to go out with the ladies

Croaker. Good gracious, can I believe my eyes or my ears! I'm struck dumb with his vivacity, and stunn'd with the loudness of his laugh. Was there ever such a transformation! (*A laugh behind the scenes, Croaker mimics it.*) Ha! ha! ha! there it goes: a plague take their balderdash; yet I could expect nothing less, when my precious wife was of the party. On my conscience, I believe she could spread a horse-laugh through the pews of a tabernacle.

Leont. Since you find so many objections to a wife, sir, how can you be so earnest in recommending one to me?

Croaker. I have told you, and tell you again, boy, that Miss Richland's fortune must not go out of the family; one may find comfort in the money, whatever one does in the wife.

Leont. But, sir, though, in obedience to your desire, I am ready to marry her, it may be possible she has no inclination to me.

Croaker. I'll tell you once for all how it stands. A good part of Miss Richland's large fortune consists in a claim upon government, which my good friend Mr. Lofty, assures me the Treasury will allow. One half of this she is to forfeit, by her father's will, in case she refuses to marry you. So, if she rejects you, we seize half her fortune; if she accepts you, we seize the whole, and a fine girl into the bargain.

Leont. But, sir, if you will but listen to reason—

Croaker. Come, then, produce your reasons. I tell you I'm fixed, determined, so now produce your reasons. When I'm determined, I always listen to reason, because it can then do no harm.

Leont. You have alleged that a mutual choice was the first requisite in matrimonial happiness.

Croaker. Well, and you have both of you a mutual choice. She has her choice—to marry you, or lose half her fortune ; and you have your choice—to marry her, or pack out of doors without any fortune at all.

Leont. An only son, sir, might expect more indulgence.

Croaker. An only father, sir, might expect more obedience ; besides, has not your sister here, that never disobliged me in her life, as good a right as you? He's a sad dog, Livy, my dear, and would take all from you. But he shan't, I tell you he shan't, for you shall have your share.

Olivia. Dear sir, I wish you'd be convinced that I can never be happy in any addition to my fortune, which is taken from his.

Croaker. Well, well, it's a good child, so say no more, but come with me, and we shall see something that will give us a great deal of pleasure, I promise you ; old Ruggins, the curry-comb-maker, lying in state ;[1] I'm told he makes a very handsome corpse, and becomes his coffin prodigiously. He was an intimate friend of mine, and these are friendly things we ought to do for each other.

[*Exeunt.*

[1 Lying in state for several days, with a "fitting environment" of wax candles and velvet hangings, was a common practice in the last century, even among merchants and tradesmen. Cf. *The Citizen of the World*, 1762, i. 39.]

END OF THE FIRST ACT.

ACT THE SECOND.

SCENE.—*Croaker's House.*

Miss RICHLAND, GARNET.

Miss Rich.

OLIVIA not his sister? Olivia not Leontine's sister? You amaze me!

Gar. No more his sister than I am; I had it all from his own servant; I can get anything from that quarter.

Miss Rich. But how? Tell me again, Garnet.

Gar. Why, madam, as I told you before, instead of going to Lyons to bring home his sister, who has been there with her aunt these ten years, he never went further than Paris; there he saw and fell in love with this young lady; by the bye, of a prodigious family.

Miss Rich. And brought her home to my guardian, as his daughter?

Gar. Yes, and daughter she will be. If he don't consent to their marriage, they talk of trying what a Scotch parson can do.

Miss Rich. Well, I own they have deceived me —And so demurely as Olivia carried it, too!— Would you believe it, Garnet, I told her all my secrets; and yet the sly cheat concealed all this from me?

Gar. And, upon my word, Madam, I don't

much blame her; she was loath to trust one with her secrets, that was so very bad at keeping her own.

Miss Rich. But, to add to their deceit, the young gentleman, it seems, pretends to make me serious proposals. My guardian and he are to be here presently, to open the affair in form. You know I am to lose half my fortune if I refuse him.

Gar. Yet, what can you do? For being, as you are, in love with Mr. Honeywood, madam—

Miss Rich. How! idiot! what do you mean? In love with Mr. Honeywood! Is this to provoke me?

Gar. That is, madam, in friendship with him; I meant nothing more than friendship, as I hope to be married; nothing more.

Miss Rich. Well, no more of this! As to my guardian, and his son, they shall find me prepared to receive them; I'm resolved to accept their proposal with seeming pleasure, to mortify them by compliance, and so throw the refusal at last upon them.

Gar. Delicious! and that will secure your whole fortune to yourself. Well, who could have thought so innocent a face could cover so much cuteness!

Miss Rich. Why, girl, I only oppose my prudence to their cunning, and practise a lesson they have taught me against themselves.

Gar. Then you're likely not long to want employment, for here they come, and in close conference!

Enter CROAKER, LEONTINE.

Leont. Excuse me, sir, if I seem to hesitate upon the point of putting the lady so important a question.

Croaker. Lord! good sir, moderate your fears; you're so plaguy shy, that one would think you had changed sexes. I tell you we must have the half or the whole. Come, let me see with what spirit you begin? Well, why don't you? Eh! What? Well then—I must, it seems—Miss Richland, my dear, I believe you guess at our business; an affair which my son here comes to open, that nearly concerns your happiness.

Miss Rich. Sir, I should be ungrateful not to be pleased with anything that comes recommended by you.

Croaker. How, boy, could you desire a finer opening? Why don't you begin, I say?

(*To Leont.*)

Leont. 'Tis true, madam, my father, madam, has some intentions—hem—of explaining an affair— which—himself—can best explain, madam.

Croaker. Yes, my dear; it comes entirely from my son; it's all a request of his own, madam. And I will permit him to make the best of it.

Leont. The whole affair is only this, madam; my father has a proposal to make, which he insists none but himself shall deliver.

Croaker. My mind misgives me, the fellow will never be brought on. (*Aside.*)—In short, madam, you see before you one that loves you; one whose whole happiness is all in you.

Miss Rich. I never had any doubts of your

regard, sir, and I hope you can have none of my duty.

Croaker. That's not the thing, my little sweeting, my love! No, no, another guess lover than I ; there he stands, madam ; his very looks declare the force of his passion !—Call up a look, you dog —But then, had you seen him, as I have, weeping, speaking soliloquies and blank verse, sometimes melancholy, and sometimes absent—

Miss Rich. I fear, sir, he's absent now ; or such a declaration would have come most properly from himself.

Croaker. Himself! madam ! he would die before he could make such a confession ; and if he had not a channel for his passion through me, it would ere now have drowned his understanding.

Miss Rich. I must grant, sir, there are attractions in modest diffidence, above the force of words. A silent address is the genuine eloquence of sincerity.

Croaker. Madam, he has forgot to speak any other language ; silence is become his mother tongue.

Miss Rich. And it must be confessed, sir, it speaks very powerfully in his favour. And yet, I shall be thought too forward in making such a confession ; shan't I, Mr. Leontine ?

Leont. Confusion! my reserve will undo me. But, if modesty attracts her, impudence may disgust her. I'll try. (*Aside.*)—Don't imagine from my silence, madam, that I want a due sense of the

---

[¹ *Another guess* = of another fashion, guise.]

honour and happiness intended me. My father, madam, tells me your humble servant is not totally indifferent to you. He admires you ; I adore you ; and when we come together, upon my soul I believe we shall be the happiest couple in all St. James's !

Miss Rich. If I could flatter myself you thought as you speak, sir——

Leont. Doubt my sincerity, madam ? By your dear self I swear. Ask the brave if they desire glory ; ask cowards if they covet safety——

Croaker. Well, well, no more questions about it.

Leont. Ask the sick if they long for health, ask misers if they love money, ask——

Croaker. Ask a fool if he can talk nonsense ! What's come over the boy ? What signifies asking, when there's not a soul to give you an answer ? If you would ask to the purpose, ask this lady's consent to make you happy.

Miss Rich. Why, indeed, sir, his uncommon ardour almost compels me, forces me, to comply. And yet I'm afraid he'll despise a conquest gained with too much ease ; won't you, Mr. Leontine ?

Leont. Confusion ! (*Aside.*)—O, by no means, madam, by no means. And yet, madam, you talked of force. There is nothing I would avoid so much as compulsion in a thing of this kind. No, madam, I will still be generous, and leave you at liberty to refuse.

Croaker. But I tell you, sir, the lady is not at liberty. It's a match. You see she says nothing. Silence gives consent.

Leont. But, sir, she talked of force. Consider,

sir, the cruelty of constraining her inclinations.

Croaker. But I say there's no cruelty. Don't you know, blockhead, that girls have always a roundabout way of saying yes before company? So get you both gone together into the next room, and hang him that interrupts the tender explanation. Get you gone, I say; I'll not hear a word.

Leont. But, sir, I must beg leave to insist——

Croaker. Get off, you puppy, or I'll beg leave to insist upon knocking you down. Stupid whelp! But I don't wonder, the boy takes entirely after his mother! [*Exeunt Miss* RICH. *and* LEONT.

Enter Mrs. CROAKER.

Mrs. Croaker. Mr. Croaker, I bring you something, my dear, that I believe will make you smile.

Croaker. I'll hold you a guinea of that, my dear.

Mrs. Croaker. A letter; and, as I knew the hand, I ventured to open it!

Croaker. And how can you expect your breaking open my letters should give me pleasure?

Mrs. Croaker. Poo, it's from your sister at Lyons, and contains good news: read it.

Croaker. What a Frenchified cover is here! That sister of mine has some good qualities, but I could never teach her to fold a letter.

Mrs. Croaker. Fold a fiddlestick! Read what it contains.

Croaker, (*reading.*)

DEAR NICK,

An English gentleman, of large fortune, has for some time made private, though honourable proposals

to your daughter Olivia. *They love each other
tenderly, and I find she has consented, without
letting any of the family know, to crown his
addresses. As such good offers don't come every day,
your own good sense, his large fortune, and family
considerations, will induce you to forgive her.*

Yours ever,

RACHEL CROAKER.

My daughter, Olivia, privately contracted to a
man of large fortune ! This is good news indeed !
My heart never foretold me of this. And yet, how
slily the little baggage has carried it since she came
home. Not a word on't to the old ones for the
world. Yet, I thought I saw something she
wanted to conceal.

Mrs. Croaker. Well, if they have concealed
their amour, they shan't conceal their wedding ;
that shall be public, I'm resolved.

Croaker. I tell thee, woman, the wedding is the
most foolish part of the ceremony. I can never
get this woman to think of the more serious part
of the nuptial engagement.

Mrs. Croaker. What, would you have me think
of their funeral? But come, tell me, my dear,
don't you owe more to me than you care to confess? Would you have ever been known to Mr.
Lofty, who has undertaken Miss Richland's claim
at the Treasury, but for me? Who was it first
made him an acquaintance at Lady Shabbaroon's
rout? Who got him to promise us his interest?
Is not he a backstairs favourite, one that can do
what he pleases with those that do what they

please? Isn't he an acquaintance that all your groaning and lamentations could never have got us?

Croaker. He is a man of importance, I grant you. And yet, what amazes me is, that while he is giving away places to all the world, he can't get one for himself.

Mrs. Croaker. That perhaps may be owing to his nicety. Great men are not easily satisfied!

Enter FRENCH SERVANT.

Servant. An expresse from Monsieur Lofty. He vil be vait upon your honours instammant. He be only giving four five instruction, read two tree memorial, call upon von ambassadeur! He vil be vid you in one tree minutes.

Mrs. Croaker. You see now, my dear. What an extensive department! Well, friend, let your master know, that we are extremely honoured by this honour. Was there anything ever in a higher style of breeding! All messages among the great are now done by express.

Croaker. To be sure, no man does little things with more solemnity, or claims more respect than he. But he's in the right on't. In our bad world, respect is given, where respect is claimed.

Mrs. Croaker. Never mind the world, my dear; you were never in a pleasanter place in your life. Let us now think of receiving him with proper respect (*a loud rapping at the door*) and there he is, by the thundering rap.

Croaker. Ay, verily, there he is; as close upon the heels of his own express, as an endorsement upon the back of a bill. Well, I'll leave you to

receive him, whilst I go to chide my little Olivia
for intending to steal a marriage without mine or
her aunt's consent. I must seem to be angry, or
she, too, may begin to despise my authority.

[*Exit.*

Enter LOFTY,[1] *speaking to his servant.*

Lofty. And if the Venetian Ambassador, or that
teasing creature the Marquis, should call, I'm
not at home. Dam'me, I'll be pack-horse to
none of them! My dear madam, I have just
snatched a moment—And if the expresses to his
Grace be ready, let them be sent off; they're of
importance. Madam, I ask a thousand pardons!

Mrs. Croaker. Sir, this honour——

Lofty. And, Dubardieu! If the person calls
about the commission, let him know that it is
made out. As for Lord Cumbercourt's stale request, it can keep cold: you understand me.
Madam, I ask ten thousand pardons!

Mrs. Croaker. Sir, this honour——

Lofty. And, Dubardieu! If the man comes
from the Cornish borough, you must do him;
you must do him, I say! Madam, I ask ten
thousand pardons! And if the Russian—Ambassador calls: but he will scarce call to-day, I
believe. And now, madam, I have just got time
to express my happiness in having the honour of
being permitted to profess myself your most obedient humble servant!

Mrs. Croaker. Sir, the happiness and honour

[1 Lofty, in some respects, is a variation upon " Beau
Tibbs' in the *Citizen of the World.*]

are all mine; and yet, I'm only robbing the public while I detain you.

Lofty. Sink the public, madam, when the fair are to be attended. Ah, could all my hours be so charmingly devoted! Sincerely, don't you pity us poor creatures in affairs? Thus it is eternally; solicited for places here, teased for pensions there, and courted everywhere. I know you pity me. Yes, I see you do!

Mrs. Croaker. Excuse me, sir. Toils of empires pleasures are, as Waller says.

Lofty. Waller, Waller; is he of the House?

Mrs. Croaker. The modern poet of that name, sir.

Lofty. Oh, a modern! We men of business despise the moderns; and as for the ancients, we have no time to read them. Poetry is a pretty thing enough for our wives and daughters; but not for us. Why now, here I stand that know nothing of books. I say, madam, I know nothing of books; and yet, I believe, upon a land carriage fishery, a stamp act, or a jag-hire, I can talk my two hours without feeling the want of them!

Mrs. Croaker. The world is no stranger to Mr. Lofty's eminence in every capacity!

Lofty. I vow to Gad, madam, you make me blush. I'm nothing, nothing, nothing in the world; a mere obscure gentleman! To be sure, indeed, one or two of the present ministers are pleased to represent me as a formidable man. I know they are pleased to bespatter me at all their little dirty levées. Yet, upon my soul, I wonder what they see in me to treat me so! Measures,

not men,[1] have always been my mark ; and I vow,
by all that's honourable, my resentment has never
done the men, as mere men, any manner of harm—
That is, as mere men.

Mrs. Croaker. What importance, and yet what
modesty !

Lofty. Oh, if you talk of modesty, madam !
There, I own, I'm accessible to praise : modesty is
my foible : it was so the Duke of Brentford used to
say of me. I love Jack Lofty, he used to say : no
man has a finer knowledge of things ; quite a man
of information ; and when he speaks upon his legs,
by the lord, he's prodigious, he scouts them ; and
yet all men have their faults ; too much modesty is
his, says his Grace.

Mrs. Croaker. And yet, I dare say, you don't
want assurance when you come to solicit for your
friends.

Lofty. O, there indeed I'm in bronze. A-propos,
I have just been mentioning Miss Richland's case
to a certain personage ; we must name no names.
When I ask, I am not to be put off, madam ! No,
no, I take my friend by the button. A fine girl,
sir ; great justice in her case. A friend of mine.
Borough interest. Business must be done, Mr.
Secretary. I say, Mr. Secretary, her business must
be done, sir. That's my way, madam !

Mrs. Croaker. Bless me ! you said all this to
the Secretary of State, did you ?

[1 Goldsmith is generally credited with this sentiment;
but from a sentence in Burke's *Thoughts on the Present
Discontents* it would seem to have been a cant political
phrase.]

Lofty. I did not say the Secretary, did I ? Well, curse it, since you have found me out, I will not deny it. It was to the Secretary !

Mrs. Croaker. This was going to the fountain-head at once, not applying to the understrappers, as Mr. Honeywood would have had us.

Lofty. Honeywood! he ! he ! He was, indeed, a fine solicitor. I suppose you have heard what has just happened to him ?

Mrs. Croaker. Poor dear man ! no accident, I hope !

Lofty. Undone, madam, that's all. His creditors have taken him into custody. A prisoner in his own house !

Mrs. Croaker. A prisoner in his own house ! How ! At this very time ! I'm quite unhappy for him.

Lofty. Why, so am I ! The man, to be sure, was immensely good-natur'd. But then, I could never find that he had anything in him.

Mrs. Croaker. His manner, to be sure, was excessive harmless ; some, indeed, thought it a little dull. For my part, I always concealed my opinion.

Lofty. It can't be concealed, madam ; the man was dull, dull as the last new comedy ![1] A poor impracticable creature ! I tried once or twice to know if he was fit for business ; but he had scarce talents to be groom-porter to an orange barrow !

[1 The " last new comedy " was the *False Delicacy* of Goldsmith's rival, Hugh Kelly, just produced at Drury Lane. But Goldsmith could scarcely have intended this " palpable hit."]

Mrs. Croaker. How differently does Miss Richland think of him! For, I believe, with all his faults, she loves him.

Lofty. Loves him! Does she? You should cure her of that, by all means. Let me see, what if she were sent to him this instant, in his present doleful situation? My life for it, that works her cure! Distress is a perfect antidote to love. Suppose we join her in the next room? Miss Richland is a fine girl, has a fine fortune, and must not be thrown away. Upon my honour, madam, I have a regard for Miss Richland; and, rather than she should be thrown away, I should think it no indignity to marry her myself!

[*Exeunt.*

Enter OLIVIA *and* LEONTINE.

Leont. And yet, trust me, Olivia, I had every reason to expect Miss Richland's refusal, as I did everything in my power to deserve it. Her indelicacy surprises me!

Olivia. Sure, Leontine, there's nothing so indelicate in being sensible of your merit. If so, I fear, I shall be the most guilty thing alive!

Leont. But you mistake, my dear. The same attention I used to advance my merit with you, I practised to lessen it with her. What more could I do?

Olivia. Let us now rather consider what's to be done. We have both dissembled too long—I have always been asham'd—I am now quite weary of it. Sure, I could never have undergone so much for any other but you.

Leont. And you shall find my gratitude equal to your kindest compliance. Though our friends should totally forsake us, Olivia, we can draw upon content for the deficiencies of fortune.

Olivia. Then why should we defer our scheme of humble happiness, when it is now in our power? I may be the favourite of your father, it is true; but can it ever be thought, that his present kindness to a supposed child, will continue to a known deceiver?

Leont. I have many reasons to believe it will. As his attachments are but few, they are lasting. His own marriage was a private one, as ours may be. Besides, I have sounded him already at a distance, and find all his answers exactly to our wish. Nay, by an expression or two that dropped from him, I am induced to think he knows of this affair.

Olivia. Indeed! But that would be an happiness too great to be expected.

Leont. However it be, I'm certain you have power over him; and am persuaded, if you informed him of our situation, that he would be disposed to pardon it.

Olivia. You had equal expectations, Leontine, from your last scheme with Miss Richland, which you find has succeeded most wretchedly.

Leont. And that's the best reason for trying another.

Olivia. If it must be so, I submit.

Leont. As we could wish, he comes this way. Now, my dearest Olivia, be resolute. I'll just retire within hearing, to come in at a proper time, either to share your danger, or confirm your victory. [*Exit.*

Enter CROAKER.

Croaker. Yes, I must forgive her; and yet not too easily, neither. It will be proper to keep up the decorums of resentment a little, if it be only to impress her with an idea of my authority.

Olivia. How I tremble to approach him!— Might I presume, sir—if I interrupt you—

Croaker. No, child, where I have an affection, it is not a little thing can interrupt me. Affection gets over little things.

Olivia. Sir, you're too kind! I'm sensible how ill I deserve this partiality. Yet, Heaven knows, there is nothing I would not do to gain it.

Croaker. And you have but too well succeeded, you little hussy, you! With those endearing ways of yours, on my conscience, I could be brought to forgive anything, unless it were a very great offence indeed.

Olivia. But mine is such an offence—when you know my guilt—yes, you shall know it, though I feel the greatest pain in the confession.

Croaker. Why, then, if it be so very great a pain, you may spare yourself the trouble, for I know every syllable of the matter before you begin.

Olivia. Indeed! Then I'm undone!

Croaker. Ay, miss, you wanted to steal a match, without letting me know it, did you! But I'm not worth being consulted, I suppose, when there's to be a marriage in my own family! No, I'm to have no hand in the disposal of my own children! No, I'm nobody! I'm to be a mere article of family lumber; a piece of cracked china to be stuck up in a corner!

Olivia. Dear sir, nothing but the dread of your authority could induce us to conceal it from you.

Croaker. No, no, my consequence is no more; I'm as little minded as a dead Russian in winter, just stuck up with a pipe in his mouth till there comes a thaw—it goes to my heart to vex her.

Olivia. I was prepared, sir, for your anger, and despaired of pardon, even while I presumed to ask it. But your severity shall never abate my affection, as my punishment is but justice.

Croaker. And yet you should not despair neither, Livy. We ought to hope all for the best.

Olivia. And do you permit me to hope, sir! Can I ever expect to be forgiven? But hope has too long deceived me!

Croaker. Why then, child, it shan't deceive you now, for I forgive you this very moment. I forgive you all; and now you are indeed my daughter.

Olivia. O transport! This kindness overpowers me!

Croaker. I was always against severity to our children. We have been young and giddy ourselves, and we can't expect boys and girls to be old before their time.

Olivia. What generosity! But can you forget the many falsehoods, the dissimulation——

Croaker. You did indeed dissemble, you urchin, you; but where's the girl that won't dissemble for a husband! My wife and I had never been married, if we had not dissembled a little beforehand!

Olivia. It shall be my future care never to put such generosity to a second trial. And as for the partner of my offence and folly, from his native

honour, and the just sense he has of his duty, I
can answer for him that ——

Enter LEONTINE.

Leont. Permit him thus to answer for himself.
(*Kneeling.*) Thus, sir, let me speak my gratitude
for this unmerited forgiveness. Yes, sir, this even
exceeds all your former tenderness : I now can
boast the most indulgent of fathers. The life, he
gave, compared to this, was but a trifling blessing !

Croaker. And, good sir, who sent for you, with
that fine tragedy face, and flourishing manner? I
don't know what we have to do with your gratitude
upon this occasion !

Leont. How, sir ! is it possible to be silent when
so much obliged? Would you refuse me the pleasure
of being grateful? Of adding my thanks to my
Olivia's ! Of sharing in the transports that you have
thus occasioned?

Croaker. Lord, sir, we can be happy enough,
without your coming in to make up the party. I
don't know what's the matter with the boy all this
day ; he has got into such a rhodomontade manner
all the morning !

Leont. But, sir, I that have so large a part in the
benefit, is it not my duty to show my joy? Is the
being admitted to your favour so slight an
obligation? Is the happiness of marrying my
Olivia so small a blessing ?

Croaker. Marrying Olivia ! marrying Olivia !
marrying his own sister ! Sure the boy is out of
his senses. His own sister !

Leont. My sister !

Olivia. Sister! How have I been mistaken! (*aside.*)

Leont. Some cursed mistake in this I find. (*aside.*)

Croaker. What does the booby mean, or has he any meaning. Eh, what do you mean, you block-head, you?

Leont. Mean, sir—why, sir—only when my sister is to be married, that I have the pleasure of marrying her, sir; that is, of giving her away, sir—I have made a point of it.

Croaker. O, is that all? Give her away. You have made a point of it. Then you had as good make a point of first giving away yourself, as I'm going to prepare the writings between you and Miss Richland this very minute. What a fuss is here about nothing! Why, what's the matter now? I thought I had made you at least as happy as you could wish.

Olivia. O! yes, sir, very happy.

Croaker. Do you foresee anything, child? You look as if you did. I think if anything was to be foreseen, I have as sharp a look out as another: and yet I foresee nothing. [*Exit.*

LEONTINE, OLIVIA.

Olivia. What can it mean?

Leont. He knows something, and yet for my life, I can't tell what.

Olivia. It can't be the connection between us, I'm pretty certain.

Leont. Whatever it be, my dearest, I'm resolved to put it out of fortune's power to repeat our mor-

Q

tification. I'll haste, and prepare for our journey to Scotland this very evening. My friend Honeywood has promised me his advice and assistance. I'll go to him, and repose our distresses on his friendly bosom: and I know so much of his honest heart, that if he can't relieve our uneasinesses, he will at least share them. [*Exeunt.*

END OF THE SECOND ACT.

ACT THE THIRD.

SCENE.—*Young Honeywood's House.*

BAILIFF, HONEYWOOD, FOLLOWER.

Bailiff.

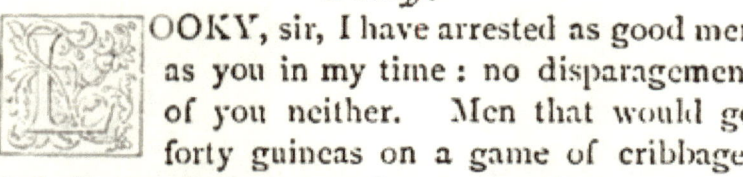

OOKY, sir, I have arrested as good men as you in my time : no disparagement of you neither. Men that would go forty guineas on a game of cribbage. I challenge the town to shew a man in more genteeler practice than myself !

Honeyw. Without all question, Mr.——I forget your name, sir?

Bailiff. How can you forget what you never knew ? he, he, he !

Honeyw. May I beg leave to ask your name?

Bailiff. Yes, you may.

Honeyw. Then, pray, sir, what is your name, sir?

Bailiff. That I didn't promise to tell you. He, he, he ! A joke breaks no bones, as we say among us that practice the law.

Honeyw. You may have reason for keeping it a secret, perhaps?

Bailiff. The law does nothing without reason. I'm ashamed to tell my name to no man, sir. If you can shew cause, as why, upon a special capus, that I should prove my name—But, come, Timothy Twitch is my name. And, now you know my name, what have you to say to that ?

Honeyw. Nothing in the world, good Mr.
Twitch, but that I have a favour to ask, that's all.

Bailiff. Ay, favours are more easily asked than
granted, as we say among us that practice the law.
I have taken an oath against granting favours.
Would you have me perjure myself?

Honeyw. But my request will come recommended
in so strong a manner, as I believe you'll have no
scruple (*pulling out his purse*). The thing is only
this : I believe I shall be able to discharge this
trifle in two or three days at farthest ; but as I
would not have the affair known for the world, I
have thoughts of keeping you, and your good
friend here, about me, till the debt is discharged ;
for which I shall be properly grateful.[1]

Bailiff. Oh ! that's another maxum, and altogether within my oath. For certain, if an honest
man is to get anything by a thing, there's no reason
why all things should not be done in civility.

Honeyw. Doubtless, all trades must live, Mr.
Twitch ; and yours is a necessary one.

                    [*Gives him money.*

Bailiff. Oh ! your honour ; I hope your honour
takes nothing amiss as I does, as I does nothing
but my duty in so doing. I'm sure no man can say
I ever give a gentleman, that was a gentleman, ill
usage. If I saw that a gentleman was a gentleman,
I have taken money not to see him for ten weeks
together.

Honeyw. Tenderness is a virtue, Mr. Twitch.

[1 The elaboration of this expedient was perhaps suggested
by an anecdote of Steele, who is said to have put his bailiffs
into livery. See *Steele,* (*English Worthies*), 1886, p. 222.]

Bailiff. Ay, sir, it's a perfect treasure. I love to see a gentleman with a tender heart. I don't know, but I think I have a tender heart myself. If all that I have lost by my heart was put together, it would make a—but no matter for that.

Honeyw. Don't account it lost, Mr. Twitch. The ingratitude of the world can never deprive us of the conscious happiness of having acted with humanity ourselves.

Bailiff. Humanity, sir, is a jewel. It's better than gold. I love humanity. People may say that we in our way have no humanity; but I'll show you my humanity this moment. There's my follower here, little Flanigan, with a wife and four children, a guinea or two would be more to him, than twice as much to another. Now, as I can't shew him any humanity myself, I must beg leave you'll do it for me.

Honeyw. I assure you, Mr. Twitch, yours is a most powerful recommendation.

[Giving money to the follower.

Bailiff. Sir, you're a gentleman. I see you know what to do with your money. But, to business: we are to be with you here as your friends, I suppose. But set in case company comes.— Little Flanigan here, to be sure, has a good face, a very good face: but then, he is a little seedy, as we say among us that practice the law. Not well in clothes. Smoke [1] the pocket holes.

Honeyw. Well, that shall be remedied without delay.

[1 " Smoke "—here = " observe." Now-a-days Mr. Twitch would say " twig."]

Enter SERVANT.

Servant. Sir, Miss Richland is below.

Honeyw. How unlucky! Detain her a moment. We must improve, my good friend, little Mr. Flanigan's appearance first. Here, let Mr. Flanigan have a suit of my clothes—quick—the brown and silver—Do you hear?

Servant. That your honour gave away to the begging gentleman that makes verses, because it was as good as new.

Honeyw. The white and gold, then.

Servant. That, your honour, I made bold to sell, because it was good for nothing.

Honeyw. Well, the first that comes to hand, then. The blue and gold. I believe Mr. Flanigan will look best in blue.   [*Exit* FLANIGAN.

Bailiff. Rabbit me, but little Flanigan will look well in anything. Ah, if your honour knew that bit of flesh as well as I do, you'd be perfectly in love with him. There's not a prettier scout in the four counties after a shy-cock than he. Scents like a hound; sticks like a weazel. He was master of the ceremonies to the black queen of Morocco when I took him to follow me. (*Re-enter* FLANIGAN.) Heh, ecod, I think he looks so well, that I don't care if I have a suit from the same place for myself.

Honeyw. Well, well, I hear the lady coming. Dear Mr. Twitch, I beg you'll give your friend directions not to speak. As for yourself, I know you will say nothing without being directed.

Bailiff. Never you fear me, I'll shew the lady

that I have something to say for myself as well as another. One man has one way of talking, and another man has another, that's all the difference between them.

Enter Miss RICHLAND *and her* MAID.

Miss Rich. You'll be surprised, sir, with this visit. But you know I'm yet to thank you for choosing my little library.

Honeyw. Thanks, madam, are unnecessary, as it was I that was obliged by your commands. Chairs here. Two of my very good friends, Mr. Twitch and Mr. Flanigan. Pray, gentlemen, sit without ceremony.

Miss Rich. (*aside.*) Who can these odd-looking men be? I fear it is as I was informed. It must be so.

Bailiff (*after a pause*). Pretty weather, very pretty weather for the time of the year, madam.

Follower. Very good circuit weather in the country.

Honeyw. You officers are generally favourites among the ladies. My friends, madam, have been upon very disagreeable duty, I assure you. The fair should, in some measure, recompense the toils of the brave.

Miss Rich. Our officers do indeed deserve every favour. The gentlemen are in the marine service, I presume, sir?

Honeyw. Why, madam, they do—occasionally serve in the Fleet, madam! A dangerous service!

Miss Rich. I'm told so. And I own, it has often surprised me, that, while we have had so

many instances of bravery there, we have had so
few of wit at home to praise it.

Honeyw. I grant, madam, that our poets have
not written as our soldiers have fought ; but they
have done all they could, and Hawke or Amherst
could do no more.

Miss Rich. I'm quite displeased when I see a
fine subject spoiled by a dull writer.

Honeyw. We should not be so severe against
dull writers, madam. It is ten to one, but the
dullest writer exceeds the most rigid French critic
who presumes to despise him.

Follower. Damn the French, the parle-vous, and
all that belongs to them !

Miss Rich. Sir !

Honeyw. Ha, ha, ha, honest Mr. Flanigan ! A
true English officer, madam ; he's not contented
with beating the French, but he will scold them
too.

Miss Rich. Yet, Mr. Honeywood, this does not
convince me but that severity in criticism is necessary. It was our first adopting the severity of
French taste, that has brought them in turn to
taste us.

Bailiff. Taste us ! By the Lord, madam, they
devour us ! Give Monseers but a taste, and I'll
be damned, but they come in for a bellyful !

Miss Rich. Very extraordinary, this !

Follower. But very true. What makes the bread
rising : the parle-vous that devour us. What
makes the mutton fivepence a pound : the parle-
vous that eat it up. What makes the beer three
pence half-penny a pot——

Honeyw. Ah! the vulgar rogues, all will be out! Right, gentlemen, very right, upon my word, and quite to the purpose. They draw a parallel, madam, between the mental taste, and that of our senses. We are injured as much by French severity in the one, as by French rapacity in the other. That's their meaning.

Miss Rich. Though I don't see the force of the parallel, yet, I'll own, that we should sometimes pardon books, as we do our friends, that have now and then agreeable absurdities to recommend them.

Bailiff. That's all my eye! The King only can pardon, as the law says; for set in case——

Honeyw. I'm quite of your opinion, sir! I see the whole drift of your argument. Yes, certainly, our presuming to pardon any work, is arrogating a power that belongs to another. If all have power to condemn, what writer can be free?

Bailiff. By his habus corpus. His habus corpus can set him free at any time. For set in case——

Honeyw. I'm obliged to you, sir, for the hint. If, madam, as my friend observes, our laws are so careful of a gentleman's person, sure we ought to be equally careful of his dearer part, his fame.

Follower. Ay, but if so be a man's nabbed, you know——

Honeyw. Mr. Flanigan, if you spoke for ever, you could not improve the last observation. For my own part, I think it conclusive.

Bailiff. As for the matter of that, mayhap——

Honeyw. Nay, sir, give me leave in this instance to be positive. For where is the necessity of cen-

suring works without genius, which must shortly
sink of themselves : what is it, but aiming our unnecessary blow against a victim already under the
hands of justice ?

Bailiff. Justice ! O, by the elevens, if you talk
about justice, I think I am at home there ; for, in
a course of law——

Honeyw. My dear Mr. Twitch, I discern what
you'd be at perfectly, and I believe the lady must
be sensible of the art with which it is introduced.
I suppose you perceive the meaning, madam, of
his course of law ?

Miss Rich. I protest, sir, I do not. I perceive
only that you answer one gentleman before he
has finished, and the other before he has well
begun !

Bailiff. Madam, you are a gentlewoman, and I
will make the matter out. This here question is
about severity and justice, and pardon, and the like
of they. Now, to explain the thing——

Honeyw. (*aside.*) O ! curse your explanations.

Enter SERVANT.

Servant. Mr. Leontine, sir, below, desires to
speak with you upon earnest business.

Honeyw. That's lucky (*Aside*).—Dear madam,
you'll excuse me, and my good friends here, for a
few minutes. There are books, madam, to amuse
you. Come, gentlemen, you know I make no
ceremony with such friends. After you, sir. Excuse me. Well, if I must. But I know your
natural politeness !

Bailiff. Before and behind, you know.

Follower. Ay, ay, before and behind, before and behind !

[*Exeunt* HONEYWOOD, BAILIFF, *and* FOLLOWER.

Miss Rich. What can all this mean, Garnet ?

Gar. Mean, madam? why, what should it mean, but what Mr. Lofty sent you here to see? These people he calls officers, are officers sure enough : sheriff's officers ; bailiffs, madam !

Miss Rich. Ay, it is certainly so. Well, though his perplexities are far from giving me pleasure, yet, I own, there's something very ridiculous in them, and a just punishment for his dissimulation.

Gar. And so they are. But I wonder, madam, that the lawyer you just employed to pay his debts, and set him free, has not done it by this time. He ought at least to have been here before now. But lawyers are always more ready to get a man into troubles, than out of them!

Enter SIR WILLIAM.

Sir Will. For Miss Richland to undertake setting him free, I own, was quite unexpected. It has totally unhinged my schemes to reclaim him. Yet, it gives me pleasure to find, that, among a number of worthless friendships, he has made one acquisition of real value ; for there must be some softer passion on her side that prompts this generosity. Ha ! here before me : I'll endeavour to sound her affections. Madam, as I am the person that have had some demands upon the gentleman of this house, I hope you'll excuse me, if, before I enlarged him, I wanted to see yourself !

Miss Rich. The precaution was very unnecessary, sir! I suppose your wants were only such as
my agent had power to satisfy.

Sir Will. Partly, madam. But I was also
willing you should be fully apprized of the character of the gentleman you intended to serve.

Miss Rich. It must come, sir, with a very ill
grace from you. To censure it, after what you
have done, would look like malice; and to speak
favourably of a character you have oppressed,
would be impeaching your own. And, sure, his
tenderness, his humanity, his universal friendship,
may atone for many faults!

Sir Will. That friendship, madam, which is
exerted in too wide a sphere, becomes totally
useless. Our bounty, like a drop of water, dis-
appears when diffused too widely. They, who
pretend most to this universal benevolence, are
either deceivers, or dupes. Men who desire to
cover their private ill-nature, by a pretended regard
for all; or, men who, reasoning themselves into
false feelings, are more earnest in pursuit of splendid, than of useful virtues.

Miss Rich. I am surprised, sir, to hear one who
has probably been a gainer by the folly of others,
so severe in his censure of it.

Sir Will. Whatever I may have gained by folly,
madam, you see I am willing to prevent your losing
by it.

Miss Rich. Your cares for me, sir, are unnecessary! I always suspect those services which are
denied where they are wanted, and offered, perhaps
in hopes of a refusal. No, sir, my directions have

been given, and I insist upon their being complied with.

Sir Will. Thou amiable woman! I can no longer contain the expressions of my gratitude: my pleasure. You see before you, one who has been equally careful of his interest: one who has for some time been a concealed spectator of his follies, and only punished in hopes to reclaim them —His uncle!

Miss Rich. Sir William Honeywood! You amaze me. How shall I conceal my confusion? I fear, sir, you'll think I have been too forward in my services, I confess I——

Sir Will. Don't make any apologies, madam. I only find myself unable to repay the obligation. And yet, I have been trying my interest of late to serve you. Having learnt, madam, that you had some demands upon government, I have, though unasked, been your solicitor there.

Miss Rich. Sir, I'm infinitely obliged to your intentions. But my guardian has employed another gentleman who assures him of success.

Sir Will. Who, the important little man that visits here! Trust me, madam, he's quite contemptible among men in power, and utterly unable to serve you. Mr. Lofty's promises are much better known to people of fashion than his person, I assure you.

Miss Rich. How have we been deceived! As sure as can be, here he comes.

Sir Will. Does he? Remember I'm to continue unknown. My return to England has not as yet been made public. With what impudence he enters!

Enter LOFTY.

Lofty. Let the chariot—let my chariot drive off,
I'll visit to his Grace's in a chair.   Miss Richland
here before me !   Punctual, as usual, to the calls of
humanity.   I'm very sorry, madam, things of this
kind should happen, especially to a man I have
shewn everywhere, and carried amongst us as a
particular acquaintance.

Miss Rich. I find, sir, you have the art of making
the misfortunes of others your own.

Lofty. My dear madam, what can a private man
like me, do?   One man can't do everything; and
then, I do so much in this way every day: Let
me see, something considerable might be done for
him by subscription; it could not fail if I carried
the list.   I'll undertake to set down a brace of
dukes, two dozen lords, and half the lower house,
at my own peril !

Sir Will. And after all, it's more than probable,
sir, he might reject the offer of such powerful
patronage.

Lofty. Then, madam, what can we do?   You
know I never make promises.   In truth, I once or
twice tried to do something with him in the way
of business; but, as I often told his uncle, Sir
William Honeywood, the man was utterly impracticable.

Sir Will. His uncle !   Then that gentleman, I
suppose, is a particular friend of yours.

Lofty. Meaning me, sir?—Yes, madam, as I
often said, my dear Sir William, you are sensible
I would do anything as far as my poor interest

goes, to serve your family; but what can be done? there's no procuring first-rate places for ninth-rate abilities.

Miss Rich. I have heard of Sir William Honeywood; he's abroad in employment; he confided in your judgment, I suppose.

Lofty. Why, yes, madam; I believe Sir William has some reason to confide in my judgment; one little reason, perhaps.

Miss Rich. Pray, sir, what was it?

Lofty. Why, madam—but let it go no further— it was I procured him his place.

Sir Will. Did you, sir?

Lofty. Either you or I, sir.

Miss Rich. This, Mr. Lofty, was very kind, indeed.

Lofty. I did love him, to be sure; he had some amusing qualities; no man was fitter to be toast-master to a club, or had a better head.

Miss Rich. A better head?

Lofty. Ay, at a bottle. To be sure, he was as dull as a choice spirit; but hang it, he was grateful, very grateful; and gratitude hides a multitude of faults!

Sir Will. He might have reason, perhaps. His place is pretty considerable, I'm told.

Lofty. A trifle, a mere trifle, among us men of business. The truth is, he wanted dignity to fill up a greater.

Sir Will. Dignity of person, do you mean, sir? I'm told he's much about my size and figure, sir.

Lofty. Ay, tall enough for a marching regiment; but then he wanted a something—a consequence of form—a kind of a—I believe the lady perceives my meaning.

Miss Rich. O perfectly ! you courtiers can do anything, I see !

Lofty. My dear madam, all this is but a mere exchange ; we do greater things for one another every day. Why, as thus, now : let me suppose you the first lord of the Treasury, you have an employment in you that I want ; I have a place in me that you want ; do me here, do you there : interest of both sides, few words, flat, done and done, and its over.

Sir Will. A thought strikes me. (*Aside.*)—Now you mention Sir William Honeywood, madam ; and as he seems, sir, an acquaintance of yours ; you'll be glad to hear he's arrived from Italy ; I had it from a friend who knows him as well as he does me, and you may depend on my information.

Lofty. The devil he is !—If I had known that, we should not have been quite so well acquainted. (*Aside.*)

Sir Will. He is certainly returned ; and as this gentleman is a friend of yours, he can be of signal service to us, by introducing me to him ; there are some papers relative to your affairs, that require dispatch and his inspection.

Miss Rich. This gentleman, Mr. Lofty, is a person employed in my affairs : I know you'll serve us !

Lofty. My dear madam, I live but to serve you. Sir William shall even wait upon him, if you think proper to command it.

Sir Will. That would be quite unnecessary.

Lofty. Well, we must introduce you, then. Call upon me—let me see—ay, in two days.

Sir Will. Now, or the opportunity will be lost for ever.

Lofty. Well, if it must be now, now let it be. But, damn it, that's unfortunate; my lord Grig's cursed Pensacola business comes on this very hour, and I'm engaged to attend—another time—

Sir Will. A short letter to Sir William will do.

Lofty. You shall have it; yet, in my opinion, a letter is a very bad way of going to work; face to face, that's my way.

Sir Will. The letter, sir, will do quite as well.

Lofty. Zounds, sir, do you pretend to direct me; direct me in the business of office? Do you know me, sir? who am I?

Miss Rich. Dear Mr. Lofty, this request is not so much his as mine; if my commands—but you despise my power.

Lofty. Delicate creature! your commands could even control a debate at midnight; to a power so constitutional, I am all obedience and tranquillity. He shall have a letter; where is my secretary? Dubardieu! And yet I protest I don't like this way of doing business. I think if I spoke first to Sir William—But you will have it so.

[*Exit with Miss* RICH.

Sir WILLIAM *alone.*

Sir Will. Ha, ha, ha! This, too, is one of my nephew's hopeful associates. O vanity, thou constant deceiver, how do all thy efforts to exalt, serve but to sink us. Thy false colourings, like those em-

R

ployed to heighten beauty, only seem to mend that
bloom which they contribute to destroy.   I'm not
displeased at this interview ; exposing this fellow's
impudence to the contempt it deserves, may be of
use to my design ; at least, if he can reflect, it
will be of use to himself.

Enter JARVIS.

Sir Will. How now, Jarvis, where's your master, my nephew ?

Jarvis. At his wit's end, I believe ; he's scarce
gotten out of one scrape, but he's running his head
into another.

Sir Will. How so?

Jarvis. The house has but just been cleared of
the bailiffs, and now he's again engaging tooth and
nail in assisting old Croaker's son to patch up a
clandestine match with the young lady that passes in
the house for his sister !

Sir Will. Ever busy to serve others.

Jarvis. Ay, anybody but himself.   The young
couple, it seems, are just setting out for Scotland,
and he supplies them with money for the journey.

Sir Will. Money ! how is he able to supply
others, who has scarce any for himself ?

Jarvis. Why, there it is ; he has no money, that's
true ; but then, as he never said no to any request
in his life, he has given them a bill drawn by a
friend of his upon a merchant in the city, which I
am to get changed ; for you must know that I am
to go with them to Scotland myself.

Sir Will. How !

Jarvis. It seems the young gentleman is obliged

to take a different road from his mistress, as he is to call upon an uncle of his that lives out of the way, in order to prepare a place for their reception, when they return ; so they have borrowed me from my master, as the properest person to attend the young lady down.

Sir Will. To the land of matrimony ! A pleasant journey, Jarvis.

Jarvis. Ay, but I'm only to have all the fatigues on't.

Sir Will. Well, it may be shorter, and less fatiguing than you imagine. I know but too much of the young lady's family and connexions, whom I have seen abroad. I have also discovered that Miss Richland is not indifferent to my thoughtless nephew : and will endeavour, though I fear, in vain, to establish that connexion. But, come, the letter I wait for must be almost finished ; I'll let you further into my intentions, in the next room.

[*Exeunt.*

END OF THE THIRD ACT.

ACT THE FOURTH.

SCENE.—*Croaker's House.*

LOFTY.

Lofty.

ELL, sure the devil's in me of late, for running my head into such defiles, as nothing but a genius like my own could draw me from. I was formerly contented to husband out my places and pensions with some degree of frugality; but, curse it, of late I have given away the whole Court Register in less time than they could print the title page; yet, hang it, why scruple a lie or two to come at a fine girl, when I every day tell a thousand for nothing. Ha! Honeywood here before me. Could Miss Richland have set him at liberty?

Enter HONEYWOOD.

Mr. Honeywood, I'm glad to see you abroad again. I find my concurrence was not necessary in your unfortunate affairs. I had put things in a train to do your business; but it is not for me to say what I intended doing.

Honeyw. It was unfortunate, indeed, sir. But what adds to my uneasiness is, that while you seem to be acquainted with my misfortune, I, myself, continue still a stranger to my benefactor.

Lofty. How! not know the friend that served you?

Honeyw. Can't guess at the person.

Lofty. Enquire.

Honeyw. I have, but all I can learn is, that he chooses to remain concealed, and that all enquiry must be fruitless.

Lofty. Must be fruitless?

Honeyw. Absolutely fruitless.

Lofty. Sure of that?

Honeyw. Very sure.

Lofty. Then I'll be damned if you shall ever know it from me.

Honeyw. How, sir!

Lofty. I suppose, now, Mr. Honeywood, you think my rent-roll very considerable, and that I have vast sums of money to throw away; I know you do. The world, to be sure, says such things of me.

Honeyw. The world, by what I learn, is no stranger to your generosity. But where does this tend?

Lofty. To nothing; nothing in the world. The town, to be sure, when it makes such a thing as me the subject of conversation, has asserted, that I never yet patronized a man of merit.

Honeyw. I have heard instances to the contrary, even from yourself.

Lofty. Yes, Honeywood, and there are instances to the contrary that you shall never hear from myself.

Honeyw. Ha, dear sir, permit me to ask you but one question.

Lofty. Sir, ask me no questions: I say, sir, ask me no questions; I'll be damned if I answer them!

Honeyw. I will ask no further. My friend, my benefactor, it is, it must be here, that I am indebted for freedom, for honour. Yes, thou worthiest of men, from the beginning I suspected it, but was afraid to return thanks; which, if undeserved, might seem reproaches.

Lofty. I protest I don't understand all this, Mr. Honeywood! You treat me very cavalierly. I do assure you, sir.—Blood, sir, can't a man be permitted to enjoy the luxury of his own feelings without all this parade?

Honeyw. Nay, do not attempt to conceal an action that adds to your honour. Your looks, your air, your manner, all confess it.

Lofty. Confess it, sir! Torture itself, sir, shall never bring me to confess it. Mr. Honeywood, I have admitted you upon terms of friendship. Don't let us fall out; make me happy, and let this be buried in oblivion. You know I hate ostentation; you know I do. Come, come, Honeywood, you know I always loved to be a friend, and not a patron. I beg this may make no kind of distance between us. Come, come, you and I must be more familiar—Indeed we must.

Honeyw. Heavens! Can I ever repay such friendship! Is there any way! Thou best of men, can I ever return the obligation?

Lofty. A bagatelle, a mere bagatelle. But I see your heart is labouring to be grateful. You shall be grateful. It would be cruel to disappoint you.

Honeyw. How! Teach me the manner. Is there any way?

Lofty. From this moment you're mine. Yes, my friend, you shall know it—I'm in love!

Honeyw. And can I assist you?

Lofty. Nobody so well.

Honeyw. In what manner? I'm all impatience.

Lofty. You shall make love for me.

Honeyw. And to whom shall I speak in your favour?

Lofty. To a lady with whom you have great interest, I assure you. Miss Richland!

Honeyw. Miss Richland!

Lofty. Yes, Miss Richland. She has struck the blow up to the hilt in my bosom, by Jupiter!

Honeyw. Heavens! was ever anything more unfortunate! It is too much to be endured.

Lofty. Unfortunate, indeed! And yet I can endure it, till you have opened the affair to her for me. Between ourselves, I think she likes me. I'm not apt to boast, but I think she does.

Honeyw. Indeed! But do you know the person you apply to?

Lofty. Yes, I know you are her friend and mine: that's enough. To you, therefore, I commit the success of my passion. I'll say no more, let friendship do the rest. I have only to add, that if at any time my little interest can be of service—but, hang it, I'll make no promises—you know my interest is yours at any time. No apologies, my friend, I'll not be answered, it shall be so.   [*Exit.*

Honeyw. Open, generous, unsuspecting man! He little thinks that I love her too; and with such an ardent passion!—But then it was ever but a vain and hopeless one; my torment, my persecution ! What shall I do ! Love, friendship, a hopeless passion, a deserving friend ! Love, that has been my tormentor; a friend, that has, perhaps, distressed himself to serve me. It shall be so. Yes, I will discard the fondling hope from my bosom, and exert all my influence in his favour. And yet to see her in the possession of another !— Insupportable. But then to betray a generous, trusting friend !—Worse, worse. Yes, I'm resolved. Let me but be the instrument of their happiness, and then quit a country, where I must for ever despair of finding my own.   [*Exit.*

Enter OLIVIA *and* GARNET, *who carries a Milliner's Box.*

Olivia. Dear me, I wish this journey were over. No news of Jarvis yet ? I believe the old peevish creature delays purely to vex me.

Gar. Why, to be sure, madam, I did hear him say a little snubbing before marriage would teach you to bear it the better afterwards.

Olivia. To be gone a full hour, though he had only to get a bill changed in the city ! How provoking !

Gar. I'll lay my life, Mr. **Leontine**, that had twice as much to do, is setting off by this time from his inn : and here you are left behind.

Olivia. Well, let us be prepared for his coming, however. Are you sure you have omitted nothing, Garnet ?

Gar. Not a stick, madam—all's here. Yet I wish you could take the white and silver to be married in. It's the worst luck in the world, in

anything but white. I knew one Bet Stubbs, of
our town, that was married in red ; and, as sure
as eggs is eggs, the bridegroom and she had a miff
before morning.

Olivia. No matter. I'm all impatience till we
are out of the house.

Gar. Bless me, madam, I had almost forgot
the wedding-ring !—The sweet little thing—I don't
think it would go on my little finger. And what
if I put in a gentleman's night-cap, in case of
necessity, madam ? But here's Jarvis.

Enter JARVIS.

Olivia. O, Jarvis, are you come at last ? We
have been ready this half hour. Now let's be
going. Let us fly !

Jarvis. Aye, to Jericho ! for we shall have no
going to Scotland this bout, I fancy.

Olivia. How ! What's the matter ?

Jarvis. Money, money, is the matter, madam.
We have got no money. What the plague do you
send me of your fool's errand for ? My master's
bill upon the city is not worth a rush. Here it is;
Mrs. Garnet may pin up her hair with it.

Olivia. Undone ! How could Honeywood serve
us so ! What shall we do ? Can't we go without it?

Jarvis. Go to Scotland without money ! To
Scotland without money ! Lord how some people
understand geography ! We might as well set
sail for Patagonia upon a cork jacket.

Olivia. Such a disappointment ! What a base
insincere man was your master, to serve us in this
manner. Is this his good nature ?

Jarvis. Nay, don't talk ill of my master, madam. I won't bear to hear anybody talk ill of him but myself.

Gar. Bless us! now I think on't, madam, you need not be under any uneasiness: I saw Mr. Leontine receive forty guineas from his father just before he set out, and he can't yet have left the inn. A short letter will reach him there.

Olivia. Well remembered, Garnet; I'll write immediately. How's this! Bless me, my hand trembles so, I can't write a word. Do you write, Garnet; and, upon second thought, it will be better from you.

Gar. Truly, madam, I write and indite but poorly. I never was kute in my larning. But I'll do what I can to please you. Let me see. All out of my own head, I suppose?

Olivia. Whatever you please.

Gar. (*Writing.*) Muster Croaker—Twenty guineas, madam?

Olivia. Ay, twenty will do.

Gar. At the bar of the Talbot till called for. Expedition—will be blown up—all of a flame— Quick, dispatch—Cupid, the little God of Love— I conclude it, madam, with Cupid; I love to see a love-letter end like poetry.[1]

Olivia. Well, well, what you please, anything. But how shall we send it? I can trust none of the servants of this family.

Gar. Odso, madam, Mr. Honeywood's butler is in the next room; he's a dear, sweet man; he'll do anything for me.

[1 Sam Weller's opinion. Cf. *Pickwick Papers*, ch. xxxiii.]

Jarvis. He! the dog, he'll certainly commit some blunder. He's drunk and sober ten times a day!

Olivia. No matter. Fly, Garnet; anybody we can trust will do. [*Exit* GARNET.] Well, Jarvis, now we can have nothing more to interrupt us. You may take up the things, and carry them on to the inn. Have you no hands, Jarvis?

Jarvis. Soft and fair, young lady. You, that are going to be married, think things can never be done too fast: but we that are old, and know what we are about, must elope methodically, madam.

Olivia. Well, sure, if my indiscretions were to be done over again——

Jarvis. My life for it you would do them ten times over.

Olivia. Why will you talk so? If you knew how unhappy they make me——

Jarvis. Very unhappy, no doubt: I was once just as unhappy when I was going to be married myself. I'll tell you a story about that——

Olivia. A story! when I'm all impatience to be away. Was there ever such a dilatory creature!——

Jarvis. Well, madam, if we must march, why we will march; that's all. Though, odds bobs we have still forgot one thing we should never travel without—a case of good razors, and a box of shaving-powder. But no matter, I believe we shall be pretty well shaved by the way. [*Going.*

Enter GARNET.

Garnet. Undone, undone, madam! Ah, Mr. Jarvis, you said right enough. As sure as death

Mr. Honeywood's rogue of a drunken butler dropped the letter before he went ten yards from the door. There's old Croaker has just picked it up, and is this moment reading it to himself in the hall !

Olivia. Unfortunate ! We shall be discovered !

Gar. No, madam ; don't be uneasy, he can make neither head nor tail of it. To be sure he looks as if he was broke loose from Bedlam about it, but he can't find what it means for all that. O Lud, he is coming this way all in the horrors !

Olivia. Then let us leave the house this instant, for fear he should ask further questions. In the mean time, Garnet, do you write and send off just such another.   [*Exeunt.*

Enter CROAKER.

Croaker. Death and destruction ! Are all the horrors of air, fire and water to be levelled only at me ! Am I only to be singled out for gunpowder-plots, combustibles, and conflagration ! Here it is —An incendiary letter dropped at my door. *To Muster Croaker, these, with speed.* Ay, ay, plain enough the direction : all in the genuine incendiary spelling, and as cramp as the devil. *With speed.* O, confound your speed. But let me read it once more. (*Reads.*)

Mustar Croakar as sone as yoew see this leve twenty gunnes at the bar of the Talboot tell caled for or yowe and yower experetion will be al blown up ! Ah, but too plain ! Blood and gunpowder in every line of it. Blown up ! murderous dog ! All blown up ! Heavens ! what have I and my poor family

done, to be all blown up? (*Reads.*) *Our pockets
are low, and money we must have.* Ay, there's the
reason ; they'll blow us up, because they have got
low pockets. (*Reads.*) *It is but a short time you
have to consider : for if this takes wind, the house
will quickly be all of a flame.* Inhuman monsters !
blow us up, and then burn us. The earthquake at
Lisbon was but a bonfire to it ! (*Reads.*) *Make
quick dispatch, and so no more at present. But
may Cupid, the little God of Love, go with you
wherever you go.* The little God of Love ! Cupid,
the little God of Love go with me ! Go you to the
devil, you and your little Cupid together ; I'm so
frightened, I scarce know whether I sit, stand, or
go. Perhaps this moment I'm treading on lighted
matches, blazing brimstone and barrels of gunpowder. They are preparing to blow me up into
the clouds. Murder ! We shall be all burnt in
our beds ; we shall be all burnt in our beds.[1]

Enter MISS RICHLAND.

Miss Rich. Lord, sir, what's the matter ?

Croaker. Murder's the matter. We shall be all
blown up in our beds before morning !

Miss Rich. I hope not, sir.

Croaker. What signifies what you hope, madam,
when I have a certificate of it here in my hand ?
Will nothing alarm my family ? Sleeping and
eating, sleeping and eating is the only work from
morning till night in my house. My insensible

[1 Shuter's reading of this letter is said to have decided the
success of the play.]

crew could sleep, though rocked by an earthquake, and fry beef steaks at a volcano!

Miss Rich. But, sir, you have alarmed them so often already, we have nothing but earthquakes, famines, plagues, and mad dogs from year's end to year's end. You remember, sir, it is not above a month ago, that you assured us of a conspiracy among the bakers, to poison us in our bread ; and so kept the whole family a week upon potatoes.

Croaker. And potatoes were too good for them. But why do I stand talking here with a girl, when I should be facing the enemy without ? Here, John, Nicodemus, search the house. Look into the cellars, to see if there be any combustibles below ; and above, in the apartments, that no matches be thrown in at the windows. Let all the fires be put out, and let the engine be drawn out in the yard, to play upon the house in case of necessity. [*Exit.*

MISS RICHLAND *alone.*

Miss Rich. What can he mean by all this? Yet, why should I enquire, when he alarms us in this manner almost every day? But Honeywood has desired an interview with me in private. What can he mean ; or, rather, what means this palpitation at his approach? It is the first time he ever shewed anything in his conduct that seemed particular. Sure he cannot mean to —— but he's here.

Enter HONEYWOOD.

Honeyw. I presumed to solicit this interview, madam, before I left town, to be permitted—

Miss Rich. Indeed ! Leaving town, sir ?—

Honeyw. Yes, madam ; perhaps the kingdom. I have presumed, I say, to desire the favour of this interview—in order to disclose something which our long friendship prompts. And yet my fears—

Miss Rich. His fears ! What are his fears to mine ? (*Aside.*)—We have indeed been long acquainted, sir ; very long. If I remember, our first meeting was at the French Ambassador's.— Do you recollect how you were pleased to rally me upon my complexion there ?

Honeyw. Perfectly, madam ; I presumed to reprove you for painting : but your warmer blushes soon convinced the company that the colouring was all from nature.

Miss Rich. And yet you only meant it, in your good-natur'd way, to make me pay a compliment to myself. In the same manner you danced that night with the most awkward woman in company, because you saw nobody else would take her out.

Honeyw. Yes ; and was rewarded the next night, by dancing with the finest woman in company, whom everybody wished to take out.

Miss Rich. Well, sir, if you thought so then, I fear your judgment has since corrected the errors of a first impression. We generally show to most advantage at first. Our sex are like poor tradesmen, that put all their best goods to be seen at the windows.

Honeyw. The first impression, madam, did indeed deceive me. I expected to find a woman with all the faults of conscious flattered beauty.

I expected to find her vain and insolent. But every day has since taught me that it is possible to possess sense without pride, and beauty without affectation.

Miss Rich. This, sir, is a style unusual with Mr. Honeywood; and I should be glad to know why he thus attempts to increase that vanity, which his own lessons have taught me to despise.

Honeyw. I ask pardon, madam. Yet, from our long friendship, I presumed I might have some right to offer, without offence, what you may refuse without offending.

Miss Rich. Sir! I beg you'd reflect; though, I fear, I shall scarce have any power to refuse a request of yours; yet, you may be precipitate: consider, sir.

Honeyw. I own my rashness; but, as I plead the cause of friendship, of one who loves—Don't be alarmed, madam—Who loves you with the most ardent passion; whose whole happiness is placed in you—

Miss Rich. I fear, sir, I shall never find whom you mean, by this description of him.

Honeyw. Ah, madam, it but too plainly points him out; though he should be too humble himself to urge his pretensions, or you too modest to understand them.

Miss Rich. Well; it would be affectation any longer to pretend ignorance; and, I will own, sir, I have long been prejudiced in his favour. It was but natural to wish to make his heart mine, as he seemed himself ignorant of its value.

Honeyw. I see she always loved him! (*Aside*).—

I find, madam, you're already sensible of his worth, his passion. How happy is my friend, to be the favourite of one with such sense to distinguish merit, and such beauty to reward it!

Miss Rich. Your friend! sir. What friend?

Honeyw. My best friend—My friend Mr. Lofty, madam.

Miss Rich. He, sir!

Honeyw. Yes, he, madam! He is, indeed, what your warmest wishes might have formed him. And to his other qualities, he adds that of the most passionate regard for you.

Miss Rich. Amazement!—No more of this, I beg you, sir.

Honeyw. I see your confusion, madam, and know how to interpret it. And since I so plainly read the language of your heart, shall I make my friend happy, by communicating your sentiments?

Miss Rich. By no means.

Honeyw. Excuse me; I must; I know you desire it.

Miss Rich. Mr. Honeywood, let me tell you, that you wrong my sentiments and yourself. When I first applied to your friendship, I expected advice and assistance; but now, sir, I see that it is vain to expect happiness from him, who has been so bad an economist of his own; and that I must disclaim his friendship, who ceases to be a friend to himself.   [*Exit.*

Honeyw. How is this! she has confessed she loved him, and yet she seemed to part in displeasure. Can I have done anything to reproach myself with? No; I believe not; yet, after all,

S

these things should not be done by a third person;
I should have spared her confusion.   My friendship carried me a little too far.

Enter CROAKER, *with the Letter in his Hand,*
and MRS. CROAKER.

Mrs. Croaker. Ha, ha, ha! And so, my dear,
it's your supreme wish that I should be quite
wretched upon this occasion? Ha, ha.

Croaker. (*Mimicking*) Ha, ha, ha! and so, my
dear, it's your supreme pleasure to give me no
better consolation?

Mrs. Croaker. Positively, my dear, what is this
incendiary stuff and trumpery to me? Our house
may travel through the air like the house of
Loretto,[1] for ought I care, if I'm to be miserable
in it.

Croaker. Would to Heaven it were converted
into a house of correction for your benefit. Have
we not everything to alarm us? Perhaps, this
very moment, the tragedy is beginning.

Mrs. Croaker. Then let us reserve our distress
till the rising of the curtain, or give them the
money they want, and have done with them.

Croaker. Give them my money!—And pray,
what right have they to my money?

Mrs. Croaker. And pray, what right then have
you to my good humour?

Croaker. And so your good humour advises me
to part with my money? Why, then, to tell your

[1 The Santa Casa, or House of the Virgin, is said to have
been miraculously transported into various towns until it
settled finally at Loretto.]

good humour a piece of my mind, I'd sooner part with my wife! Here's Mr. Honeywood, see what he'll say to it. My dear Honeywood, look at this incendiary letter dropped at my door. It will freeze you with terror; and yet lovey here can read it—can read it, and laugh!

Mrs. Croaker. Yes, and so will Mr. Honeywood.

Croaker. If he does, I'll suffer to be hanged the next minute in the rogue's place, that's all!

Mrs. Croaker. Speak, Mr. Honeywood! is there anything more foolish than my husband's fright upon this occasion?

Honeyw. It would not become me to decide, madam; but doubtless, the greatness of his terrors now, will but invite them to renew their villainy another time.

Mrs. Croaker. I told you, he'd be of my opinion.

Croaker. How, sir! do you maintain that I should lie down under such an injury, and show, neither by my tears, or complaints, that I have something of the spirit of a man in me?

Honeyw. Pardon me, sir. You ought to make the loudest complaints, if you desire redress. The surest way to have redress, is to be earnest in the pursuit of it.

Croaker. Ay, whose opinion is he of now?

Mrs. Croaker. But don't you think that laughing off our fears is the best way?

Honeyw. What is the best, madam, few can say; but I'll maintain it to be a very wise way.

Croaker. But we're talking of the best. Surely the best way is to face the enemy in the field, and not wait till he plunders us in our very bed chamber.

Honeyw. Why, sir, as to the best, that—that's a very wise way too.

Mrs. Croaker. But can anything be more absurd, than to double our distresses by our apprehensions, and put it in the power of every low fellow, that can scrawl ten words of wretched spelling, to torment us?

Honeyw. Without doubt, nothing more absurd.

Croaker. How! would it not be more absurd to despise the rattle till we are bit by the snake?

Honeyw. Without doubt, perfectly absurd.

Croaker. Then you are of my opinion?

Honeyw. Entirely.

Mrs. Croaker. And you reject mine?

Honeyw. Heaven forbid, madam. No, sure, no reasoning can be more just than yours. We ought certainly to despise malice if we cannot oppose it, and not make the incendiary's pen as fatal to our repose as the highwayman's pistol.

Mrs. Croaker. O! then you think I'm quite right?

Honeyw. Perfectly right!

Croaker. A plague of plagues, we can't be both right. I ought to be sorry, or I ought to be glad. My hat must be on my head, or my hat must be off.

Mrs. Croaker. Certainly, in two opposite opinions, if one be perfectly reasonable, the other can't be perfectly right.

Honeyw. And why may not both be right, madam? Mr. Croaker in earnestly seeking redress, and you in waiting the event with good humour? Pray let me see the letter again. I have it. This letter requires twenty guineas to be left at the bar of the Talbot inn. If it be indeed an incendiary letter, what if you and I, sir, go there ; and, when the writer comes to be paid his expected booty, seize him?

Croaker. My dear friend, it's the very thing ; the very thing. While I walk by the door, you shall plant yourself in ambush near the bar ; burst out upon the miscreant like a masked battery ; extort a confession at once, and so hang him up by surprise.

Honeyw. Yes; but I would not choose to exercise too much severity. It is my maxim, sir, that crimes generally punish themselves.

Croaker. Well, but we may upbraid him a little, I suppose? (*Ironically.*)

Honeyw. Ay, but not punish him too rigidly.

Croaker. Well, well, leave that to my own benevolence.

Honeyw. Well, I do : but remember that universal benevolence is the first law of nature.

[*Exeunt* HONEYWOOD *and Mrs.* CROAKER.

Croaker. Yes; and my universal benevolence will hang the dog, if he had as many necks as a hydra !

END OF THE FOURTH ACT.

ACT THE FIFTH.

SCENE.—*An Inn.*

Enter OLIVIA, JARVIS.

Olivia.

WELL, we have got safe to the inn, how-ever. Now, if the post-chaise were ready—

Jarvis. The horses are just finishing their oats; and, as they are not going to be married, they choose to take their own time.

Olivia. You are for ever giving wrong motives to my impatience.

Jarvis. Be as impatient as you will, the horses must take their own time; besides, you don't consider, we have got no answer from our fellow-traveller yet. If we hear nothing from Mr. Leontine, we have only one way left us.

Olivia. What way?

Jarvis. The way home again.

Olivia. Not so. I have made a resolution to go, and nothing shall induce me to break it.

Jarvis. Ay; resolutions are well kept when they jump with inclination. However, I'll go hasten things without. And I'll call too at the bar to see if anything should be left for us there.

Don't be in such a plaguy hurry, madam, and we shall go the faster, I promise you. [*Exit* JARVIS.

Enter LANDLADY.

Landlady. What! Solomon; why don't you move? Pipes and tobacco for the Lamb there.— Will nobody answer? To the Dolphin; quick. The Angel has been outrageous this half hour. Did your ladyship call, madam?

Olivia. No, madam.

Landlady. I find, as you're for Scotland, madam —But, that's no business of mine; married, or not married, I ask no questions. To be sure, we had a sweet little couple set off from this two days ago for the same place. The gentleman, for a tailor, was, to be sure, as fine a spoken tailor, as ever blew froth from a full pot. And the young lady so bashful, it was near half an hour before we could get her to finish a pint of raspberry between us.

Olivia. But this gentleman and I are not going to be married, I assure you.

Landlady. May be not. That's no business of mine; for certain, Scotch marriages seldom turn out. There was, of my own knowledge, Miss Macfag, that married her father's footman.— Alack-a-day, she and her husband soon parted, and now keep separate cellars in Hedge Lane.[1]

[1 *Cf.* Goldsmith's essay entitled *A Register of Scotch Marriages*, in the *Westminster Magazine*, February, 1773.]

Olivia. (*aside.*) A very pretty picture of what lies before me.

Enter LEONTINE.

Leont. My dear Olivia, my anxiety till you were out of danger, was too great to be resisted. I could not help coming to see you set out, though it exposes us to a discovery.

Olivia. May everything you do prove as fortunate. Indeed, Leontine, we have been most cruelly disappointed. Mr. Honeywood's bill upon the city, has, it seems, been protested, and we have been utterly at a loss how to proceed.

Leont. How! An offer of his own too. Sure, he could not mean to deceive us.

Olivia. Depend upon his sincerity; he only mistook the desire for the power of serving us. But let us think no more of it. I believe the post-chaise is ready by this.

Landlady. Not quite yet: and, begging your ladyship's pardon, I don't think your ladyship quite ready for the post-chaise. The north road is a cold place, madam. I have a drop in the house of as pretty raspberry as ever was tipt over tongue. Just a thimbleful to keep the wind off your stomach. To be sure, the last couple we had here, they said it was a perfect nosegay. Ecod, I sent them both away as good-natur'd— Up went the blinds, round went the wheels, and drive away post-boy, was the word.

Enter CROAKER.

Croaker. Well, while my friend Honeywood is

upon the post of danger at the bar, it must be my business to have an eye about me here. I think I know an incendiary's look; for, wherever the devil makes a purchase, he never fails to set his mark. Ha! who have we here? My son and daughter! What can they be doing here?

Landlady. I tell you, madam, it will do you good; I think I know by this time what's good for the north road. It's a raw night, madam—sir—

Leont. Not a drop more, good madam. I should now take it as a greater favour, if you hasten the horses, for I am afraid to be seen myself.

Landlady. That shall be done. Wha, Solomon! are you all dead there? Wha, Solomon, I say.

[*Exit bawling.*

Olivia. Well; I dread lest an expedition begun in fear should end in repentance.—Every moment we stay increases our danger, and adds to my apprehensions.

Leont. There's no danger, trust me, my dear; there can be none: if Honeywood has acted with honour, and kept my father, as he promised, in employment, till we are out of danger, nothing can interrupt our journey.

Olivia. I have no doubt of Mr. Honeywood's sincerity, and even his desires to serve us. My fears are from your father's suspicions. A mind so disposed to be alarmed without a cause, will be but too ready when there's a reason.

Leont. Why, let him, when we are out of his power. But, believe me, Olivia, you have no

great reason to dread his resentment. His re-
pining temper, as it does no manner of injury to
himself, so will it never do harm to others. He
only frets to keep himself employed, and scolds
for his private amusement.

Olivia. I don't know that; but, I'm sure, on
some occasions, it makes him look most shockingly.

Croaker. (*Discovering himself.*) How does he
look now?—How does he look now?

Olivia. Ah!

Leont. Undone!

Croaker. How do I look now? Sir, I am your
very humble servant. Madam, I am yours. What,
you are going off, are you? Then, first, if you
please, take a word or two from me with you
before you go. Tell me first where you are going,
and when you have told me that, perhaps I shall
know as little as I did before.

Leont. If that be so, our answer might but
increase your displeasure, without adding to your
information.

Croaker. I want no information from you,
puppy; and you, too, good madam, what answer
have you got? Eh! (*A cry without, stop him.*) I
think I heard a noise. My friend, Honeywood,
without—has he seized the incendiary? Ah, no,
for now I hear no more on't.

Leont. Honeywood, without! Then, sir, it was
Mr. Honeywood that directed you hither.

Croaker. No, sir, it was Mr. Honeywood con-
ducted me hither.

Leont. Is it possible?

Croaker. Possible! Why, he's in the house

now, sir. More anxious about me, than my own son, sir.

Leont. Then, sir, he's a villain!

Croaker. How, sirrah! a villain, because he takes most care of your father? I'll not bear it. I tell you I'll not bear it. Honeywood is a friend to the family, and I'll have him treated as such.

Leont. I shall study to repay his friendship as it deserves.

Croaker. Ah, rogue, if you knew how earnestly he entered into my griefs, and pointed out the means to detect them, you would love him as I do. (*A cry without, stop him.*) Fire and fury! they have seized the incendiary : they have the villain, the incendiary in view. Stop him, stop an incendiary, a murderer ; stop him ! [*Exit.*

Olivia. Oh, my terrors! What can this new tumult mean?

Leont. Some new mark, I suppose, of Mr. Honeywood's sincerity. But we shall have satisfaction : he shall give me instant satisfaction.

Olivia. It must not be, my Leontine, if you value my esteem, or my happiness. Whatever be our fate, let us not add guilt to our misfortunes— Consider that our innocence will shortly be all we have left us. You must forgive him.

Leont. Forgive him! Has he not in every instance betrayed us? Forced me to borrow money from him, which appears a mere trick to delay us: promised to keep my father engaged till we were out of danger, and here brought him to the very scene of our escape?

Olivia. Don't be precipitate. We may yet be mistaken.

Enter POSTBOY, *dragging in* JARVIS : HONEY-
WOOD *entering soon after.*

Postboy. Ay, master, we have him fast enough.
Here is the incendiary dog. I'm entitled to the
reward ; I'll take my oath I saw him ask for the
money at the bar, and then run for it.

Honeyw. Come, bring him along. Let us see
him. Let him learn to blush for his crimes.
(*Discovering his mistake.*) Death ! what's here !
Jarvis, Leontine, Olivia ! What can all this
mean ?

Jarvis. Why, I'll tell you what it means : that
I was an old fool, and that you are my master—
that's all.

Honeyw. Confusion !

Leont. Yes, sir, I find you have kept your word
with me. After such baseness, I wonder how you
can venture to see the man you have injured.

Honeyw. My dear Leontine, by my life, my
honour—

Leont. Peace, peace, for shame ; and do not
continue to aggravate baseness by hypocrisy. I
know you, sir, I know you.

Honeyw. Why, won't you hear me ! By all
that's just, I knew not—

Leont. Hear you, sir ! to what purpose ? I now
see through all your low arts ; your ever complying
with every opinion ; your never refusing any request ; your friendship as common as a prostitute's
favours, and as fallacious ; all these, sir, have long
been contemptible to the world, and are now
perfectly so to me.

Honeyw. (*aside.*) Ha! contemptible to the world! That reaches me.

Leont. All the seeming sincerity of your professions I now find were only allurements to betray; and all your seeming regret for their consequences, only calculated to cover the cowardice of your heart. Draw, villain!

Enter CROAKER *out of Breath.*

Croaker. Where is the villain? Where is the incendiary? (*Seizing the post-boy.*) Hold him fast, the dog; he has the gallows in his face. Come, you dog, confess; confess all, and hang yourself.

Post-Boy. Zounds! master, what do you throttle me for?

Croaker. (*Beating him.*) Dog, do you resist; do you resist?

Post-Boy. Zounds! master, I'm not he; there's the man that we thought was the rogue, and turns out to be one of the company.

Croaker. How!

Honeyw. Mr. Croaker, we have all been under a strange mistake here; I find there is nobody guilty; it was all an error; entirely an error of our own.

Croaker. And I say, sir, that you're in an error: for there's guilt and double guilt, a plot, a damn'd Jesuitical pestilential plot, and I must have proof of it.

Honeyw. Do but hear me.

Croaker. What, you intend to bring 'em off, I suppose; I'll hear nothing.

Honeyw. Madam, you seem at least calm enougn to hear reason.

Olivia. Excuse me.

Honeyw. Good Jarvis, let me then explain it to you.

Jarvis. What signifies explanation, when the thing is done?

Honeyw. Will nobody hear me? Was there ever such a set, so blinded by passion and prejudice! (*To the Post-Boy.*) My good friend, I believe you'll be surprised when I assure you—

Post-Boy. Sure me nothing—I'm sure of nothing but a good beating.

Croaker. Come then, you, madam, if you ever hope for any favour or forgiveness, tell me sincerely all you know of this affair.

Olivia. Unhappily, sir, I'm but too much the cause of your suspicions: you see before you, sir, one that with false pretences has stept into your family to betray it: not your daughter—

Croaker. Not my daughter!

Olivia. Not your daughter—but a mean deceiver —who—support me, I cannot—

Honeyw. Help, she's going, give her air.

Croaker. Ay, ay, take the young woman to the air; I would not hurt a hair of her head, whose ever daughter she may be—not so bad as that neither.   [*Exeunt all but* CROAKER.

Croaker. Yes, yes, all's out; I now see the whole affair: my son is either married, or going to be so, to this lady, whom he imposed upon me as his sister. Ay, certainly so; and yet I don't find it afflicts me so much as one might think. There's the advantage of fretting away our misfortunes beforehand, we never feel them when they come.

Enter Miss RICHLAND *and Sir* WILLIAM.

Sir Will. But how do you know, madam, that my nephew intends setting off from this place ?

Miss Rich. My maid assured me he was come to this inn, and my own knowledge of his intending to leave the kingdom, suggested the rest. But what do I see, my guardian here before us ! Who, my dear sir, could have expected meeting you here ; to what accident do we owe this pleasure ?

Croaker. To a fool, I believe.

Miss Rich. But to what purpose did you come ?

Croaker. To play the fool.

Miss Rich. But with whom ?

Croaker. With greater fools than myself.

Miss Rich. Explain.

Croaker. Why, Mr. Honeywood brought me here, to do nothing now I am here ; and my son is going to be married to I don't know who that is here ; so now you are as wise as I am.

Miss Rich. Married ! to whom, sir ?

Croaker. To Olivia ; my daughter, as I took her to be ; but who the devil she is, or whose daughter she is, I know no more than the man in the moon.

Sir Will. Then, sir, I can inform you ; and, though a stranger, yet you shall find me a friend to your family : it will be enough at present, to assure you, that, both in point of birth and fortune, the young lady is at least your son's equal. Being left by her father, Sir James Woodville—

Croaker. Sir James Woodville ! What, of the West ?

Sir Will. Being left by him, I say, to the care of a mercenary wretch, whose only aim was to secure her fortune to himself, she was sent into France, under pretence of education ; and there every art was tried to fix her for life in a convent, contrary to her inclinations. Of this I was informed upon my arrival in Paris ; and, as I had been once her father's friend, I did all in my power to frustrate her guardian's base intentions. I had even meditated to rescue her from his authority, when your son stept in with more pleasing violence, gave her liberty, and you a daughter.

Croaker. But I intend to have a daughter of my own choosing, sir. A young lady, sir, whose fortune, by my interest with those that have interest, will be double what my son has a right to expect ! Do you know Mr. Lofty, sir ?

Sir Will. Yes, sir ; and know that you are deceived in him. But step this way, and I'll convince you.

[CROAKER *and Sir* WILLIAM *seem to confer.*

Enter HONEYWOOD.

Honeyw. Obstinate man, still to persist in his outrage ! Insulted by him, despised by all, I now begin to grow contemptible, even to myself. How have I sunk by too great an assiduity to please ! How have I overtaxed all my abilities, lest the approbation of a single fool should escape me ! But all is now over ; I have survived my reputation,

my fortune, my friendships, and nothing remains
henceforward for me but solitude and repentance.

Miss Rich. Is it true, Mr. Honeywood, that
you are setting off, without taking leave of your
friends? The report is, that you are quitting
England. Can it be?

Honeyw. Yes, madam; and though I am so unhappy as to have fallen under your displeasure,
yet, thank Heaven, I leave you to happiness; to
one who loves you, and deserves your love; to one
who has power to procure you affluence, and generosity to improve your enjoyment of it.

Miss Rich. And are you sure, sir, that the
gentleman you mean is what you describe him?

Honeyw. I have the best assurances of it, his
serving me. He does indeed deserve the highest
happiness, and that is in your power to confer.
As for me, weak and wavering as I have been,
obliged by all, and incapable of serving any, what
happiness can I find but in solitude? What hope
but in being forgotten?

Miss Rich. A thousand! to live among friends
that esteem you, whose happiness it will be to be
permitted to oblige you.

Honeyw. No, madam; my resolution is fixed.
Inferiority among strangers is easy; but among
those that once were equals, insupportable. Nay,
to show you how far my resolution can go, I can
now speak with calmness of my former follies, my
vanity, my dissipation, my weakness. I will even
confess, that, among the number of my other pre-
sumptions, I had the insolence to think of loving
you. Yes, madam, while I was pleading the

T

passion of another, my heart was tortured with its
own. But it is over, it was unworthy our friendship, and let it be forgotten.

Miss Rich. You amaze me !

Honeyw. But you'll forgive it, I know you will ;
since the confession should not have come from
me even now, but to convince you of the sincerity
of my intention of—never mentioning it more.

[*Going.*

Miss Rich. Stay, sir, one moment—Ha ! he
here—

Enter LOFTY.

Lofty. Is the coast clear ? None but friends.
I have followed you here with a trifling piece of
intelligence : but it goes no farther, things are not
yet ripe for a discovery. I have spirits working at
a certain board ; your affair at the Treasury will
be done in less than—a thousand years. Mum !

Miss Rich. Sooner, sir, I should hope !

Lofty. Why, yes, I believe it may, if it falls into
proper hands, that know where to push and where
to parry ; that know how the land lies—eh,
Honeywood?

Miss Rich. It is fallen into yours.

Lofty. Well, to keep you no longer in suspense,
your thing is done. It is done, I say—that's all.
I have just had assurances from Lord Neverout,
that the claim has been examined, and found ad-
missible. *Quietus* is the word, madam.

Honeyw. But how ! his lordship has been at
Newmarket these ten days !

Lofty. Indeed ! Then Sir Gilbert Goose must

have been most damnably mistaken. I had it of him.

Miss Rich. He! why Sir Gilbert and his family have been in the country this month!

Lofty. This month! It must certainly be so—Sir Gilbert's letter did come to me from Newmarket, so that he must have met his lordship there; and so it came about. I have his letter about me, I'll read it to you. (*Taking out a large bundle.*) That's from Paoli of Corsica,[1] that from the Marquis of Squilachi.—Have you a mind to see a letter from Count Poniatowski, now King of Poland—Honest Pon—— [*Searching.* O, sir, what are you here too? I'll tell you what, honest friend, if you have not absolutely delivered my letter to Sir William Honeywood, you may return it. The thing will do without him.

Sir Will. Sir, I have delivered it, and must inform you it was received with the most mortifying contempt.

Croaker. Contempt! Mr. Lofty, what can that mean?

Lofty. Let him go on, let him go on, I say. You'll find it come to something presently.

Sir Will. Yes, sir, I believe you'll be amazed, if, after waiting some time in the ante-chamber, after being surveyed with insolent curiosity by the passing servants, I was at last assured, that Sir William Honeywood knew no such person, and I must certainly have been imposed upon.

Lofty. Good; let me die, very good. Ha! ha! ha!

[1 Pascal Paoli, the Corsican patriot. He came to England in 1769. Squillaci, an Italian, was Prime Minister at Madrid.]

Croaker. Now, for my life, I can't find out half the goodness of it.

Lofty. You can't? Ha ! ha !

Croaker. No, for the soul of me ; I think it was as confounded a bad answer as ever was sent from one private gentleman to another.

Lofty. And so you can't find out the force of the message? Why I was in the house at that very time. Ha ! ha ! It was I that sent that very answer to my own letter. Ha ! ha !

Croaker. Indeed ! How ! why !

Lofty. In one word, things between Sir William and me must be behind the curtain. A party has many eyes. He sides with Lord Buzzard, I side with Sir Gilbert Goose. So that unriddles the mystery.

Croaker. And so it does indeed, and all my suspicions are over.

Lofty. Your suspicions ! What then, you have been suspecting, you have been suspecting, have you ? Mr. Croaker, you and I were friends, we are friends no longer. Never talk to me. It's over ; I say, it's over !

Croaker. As I hope for your favour, I did not mean to offend. It escaped me. Don't be discomposed.

Lofty. Zounds, sir, but I am discomposed, and will be discomposed. To be treated thus ! Who am I ? Was it for this I have been dreaded both by ins and outs? Have I been libelled in the Gazetteer, and praised in the St. James's ;[1] have I been chaired at Wildman's, and a speaker at Mer-

[1 The *St. James's Chronicle.*]

chant Tailor's Hall; have I had my hand to addresses, and my head in the print-shops, and talk to me of suspects!

Croaker. My dear sir, be pacified. What can you have but asking pardon?

Lofty. Sir, I will not be pacified—Suspects! Who am I? To be used thus, have I paid court to men in favour to serve my friends, the Lords of the Treasury. Sir William Honeywood, and the rest of the gang, and talk to me of suspects! Who am I, I say, who am I?

Sir Will. Since, sir, you're so pressing for an answer, I'll tell you who you are. A gentleman, as well acquainted with politics, as with men in power; as well acquainted with persons of fashion, as with modesty; with Lords of the Treasury, as with truth; and with all, as you are with Sir William Honeywood. I am Sir William Honeywood! [*Discovering his ensigns of the Bath.*

Croaker. Sir William Honeywood!

Honeyw. Astonishment! my uncle! (*aside.*)

Lofty. So then my confounded genius has been all this time only leading me up to the garret, in order to fling me out of the window.

Croaker. What, Mr. Importance, and are these your works? Suspect you! You, who have been dreaded by the ins and outs: you, who have had your hand to addresses, and your head stuck up in print-shops. If you were served right, you should have your head stuck up in the pillory.

Lofty. Ay, stick it where you will, for, by the Lord, it cuts but a very poor figure where it sticks at present.

Sir Will. Well, Mr. Croaker, I hope you now see how incapable this gentleman is of serving you, and how little Miss Richland has to expect from his influence.

Croaker. Ay, sir, too well I see it, and I can't but say I have had some boding of it these ten days. So I'm resolved, since my son has placed his affections on a lady of moderate fortune to be satisfied with his choice, and not run the hazard of another Mr. Lofty, in helping him to a better.

Sir Will. I approve your resolution, and here they come, to receive a confirmation of your pardon and consent.

Enter Mrs. CROAKER, JARVIS, LEONTINE, OLIVIA.

Mrs. Croaker. Where's my husband? Come, come, lovey, you must forgive them. Jarvis here has been to tell me the whole affair; and, I say, you must forgive them. Our own was a stolen match, you know, my dear; and we never had any reason to repent of it.

Croaker. I wish we could both say so; however, this gentleman, Sir William Honeywood, has been beforehand with you, in obtaining their pardon. So, if the two poor fools have a mind to marry, I think we can tack them together without crossing the Tweed for it. [*Joining their hands.*

Leont. How blest, and unexpected! What, what can we say to such goodness! But our future obedience shall be the best reply. And, as for this gentleman, to whom we owe—

Sir Will. Excuse me, sir, if I interrupt your

thanks, as I have here an interest that calls me. (*Turning to Honeywood.*) Yes, sir, you are surprised to see me; and I own that a desire of correcting your follies led me hither. I saw, with indignation, the errors of a mind that only sought applause from others; that easiness of disposition, which, though inclined to the right, had not courage to condemn the wrong. I saw with regret those splendid errors, that still took name from some neighbouring duty. Your charity, that was but injustice; your benevolence, that was but weakness; and your friendship but credulity. I saw, with regret, great talents and extensive learning only employed to add sprightliness to error, and increase your perplexities. I saw your mind with a thousand natural charms; but the greatness of its beauty served only to heighten my pity for its prostitution.

Honeyw. Cease to upbraid me, sir; I have for some time but too strongly felt the justice of your reproaches. But there is one way still left me. Yes, sir, I have determined, this very hour, to quit forever a place where I have made myself the voluntary slave of all; and to seek among strangers that fortitude which may give strength to the mind, and marshal all its dissipated virtues. Yet, ere I depart, permit me to solicit favour for this gentleman; who, notwithstanding what has happened, has laid me under the most signal obligations. Mr. Lofty—

Lofty. Mr. Honeywood, I'm resolved upon a reformation, as well as you. I now begin to find that the man who first invented the art of speaking

truth was a much cunninger fellow than I thought
him. And to prove that I design to speak truth
for the future, I must now assure you that you owe
your late enlargement to another; as, upon my
soul, I had no hand in the matter. So now, if
any of the company has a mind for preferment, he
may take my place. I'm determined to resign.

[*Exit.*

Honeyw. How have I been deceived!

Sir Will. No, sir, you have been obliged to a
kinder, fairer friend for that favour. To Miss
Richland. Would she complete our joy, and
make the man she has honoured by her friendship happy in her love, I should then forget all,
and be as blest as the welfare of my dearest kins-
man can make me.

Miss Rich. After what is past, it would be but
affectation to pretend to indifference. Yes, I will
own an attachment, which, I find, was more than
friendship. And if my entreaties cannot alter his
resolution to quit the country, I will even try if my
hand has not power to detain him.

[*Giving her hand.*

Honeyw. Heavens! how can I have deserved all
this? How express my happiness, my gratitude?
A moment like this over-pays an age of apprehension!

Croaker. Well, now I see content in every face;
but Heaven send we be all better this day three
months.

Sir Will. Henceforth, nephew, learn to respect
yourself. He who seeks only for applause from
without, has all his happiness in another's keeping.

Honeyw. Yes, sir, I now too plainly perceive my errors. My vanity, in attempting to please all, by fearing to offend any. My meanness in approving folly, lest fools should disapprove. Henceforth, therefore, it shall be my study to reserve my pity for real distress ; my friendship for true merit, and my love for her, who first taught me what it is to be happy.

EPILOGUE [1]

SPOKEN BY MRS. BULKLEY.

S puffing quacks some caitiff wretch pro-
   cure
  To swear the pill, or drop, has wrought
   a cure:
Thus on the stage, our playwrights still depend
For Epilogues and Prologues on some friend,
Who knows each art of coaxing up the town,
And makes full many a bitter pill go down.
Conscious of this, our bard has gone about,
And teas'd each rhyming friend to help him out.
An Epilogue, things can't go on without it;
It could not fail, would you but set about it.
Young man, cries one (a bard laid up in clover)
Alas, young man, my writing days are over;
Let boys play tricks, and kick the straw, not I;
Your brother Doctor there, perhaps may try.
What I! dear sir, the Doctor interposes,

---

1 The Author, in expectation of an Epilogue from a
Friend at Oxford, deferred writing one himself till the very
last hour. What is here offered, owes all its success to the
graceful manner of the Actress who spoke it.

What, plant my thistle, sir, among his roses?
No, no, I've other contests to maintain;
To-night I head our troops at Warwick Lane.[1]
Go, ask your manager [2]—Who, me? your pardon;
Those things are not our forte at Covent Garden.
Our Author's friends, thus plac'd at happy dis-
     tance,
Give him good words indeed, but no assistance.
As some unhappy wight, at some new play,
At the Pit door stands elbowing away,
While oft, with many a smile, and many a shrug,
He eyes the centre, where his friends sit snug,
His simpering friends with pleasure in their eyes,
Sink as he sinks, and as he rises rise:
He nods, they nod; he cringes, they grimace;
But not a soul will budge to give him place.
Since then, unhelp'd, our bard must now conform
To 'bide the pelting of this pitiless storm,[3]
Blame where you must, be candid where you can,
And be each critic the Good-Natur'd Man.

[1 A reference to the pending quarrel between the Fellows
and Licentiates of the College of Physicians in Warwick
Lane, respecting the exclusion of some of the Licentiates
from Fellowships.]
  [2 George Colman, the Elder.]
  [3 *King Lear*, Act III. sc. 4.]

SHE STOOPS TO CONQUER

OR,

THE MISTAKES OF A NIGHT.

A COMEDY.

[*She Stoops to Conquer* was produced at Covent Garden on
Monday, the 15th March, 1773. It was played twelve times
before the conclusion of the season (31st May), the tenth
representation (5th May) being commande! by the King
and Queen. On the 26th March it was published in *octavo*
by Francis Newbery, at the corner of St. Paul's Churchyard,
with the following title :—*She Stoops to Conquer : or, The
Mistakes of a Night. A Comedy. As it is acted at the
Theatre-Royal in Covent-Garden. Written by Doctor
Goldsmith.* The price was one shilling and sixpence. The
present reprint is from the fourth edition which appeared in
the same year as the first.]

TO SAMUEL JOHNSON, LL.D.

DEAR SIR,

BY inscribing this slight performance to you, I do not mean so much to compliment you as myself. It may do me some honour to inform the public, that I have lived many years in intimacy with you. It may serve the interests of mankind also to inform them, that the greatest wit may be found in a character, without impairing the most unaffected piety.

I have, particularly, reason to thank you for your partiality to this performance.[1] The undertaking a comedy, not merely sentimental, was very dangerous[2]; and Mr. Colman, who saw this piece in its various stages, always thought it so. However, I ventured to trust it to the public; and,

[1 Johnson had throughout befriended the play, and had been mainly instrumental in inducing Colman to produce it.]

[2 See *Introduction*, vol. i, p. xxv.]

though it was necessarily delayed till late in the season,[1] I have every reason to be grateful.

      I am, dear sir,

        Your most sincere friend

         And admirer,

           OLIVER GOLDSMITH.

[1 *I.e.*—When, owing to holidays and actors' benefits, there could not be many representations.]

PROLOGUE.

BY DAVID GARRICK, ESQ.

Enter Mr. WOODWARD,[1] dressed in black, and holding a Handkerchief to his Eyes.

XCUSE me, sirs, I pray—I can't yet speak—
    I'm crying now—and have been all the week !
'Tis not alone this mourning suit, good masters ;[2]
I've that within—for which there are no plasters !
Pray would you know the reason why I'm crying ?
The Comic muse, long sick, is now a-dying !
And if she goes, my tears will never stop ;
For as a player, I can't squeeze out one drop :
I am undone, that's all—shall lose my bread—
I'd rather, but that's nothing—lose my head.
When the sweet maid is laid upon the bier,

[1 Woodward had no part in the piece. He refused "Tony Lumpkin," which fell to Quick, who had played the "Post-boy" in the *Good-Natur'd Man.*]
[2 *Hamlet*, Act 1. sc. 2.]

Shuter and *I* shall be chief mourners here.
To *her* a mawkish drab of spurious breed,
Who deals in *sentimentals* will succeed !
Poor *Ned* and *I* are dead to all intents,
We can as soon speak *Greek* as *sentiments !*
Both nervous grown, to keep our spirits up,
We now and then take down a hearty cup.
What shall we do?—If Comedy forsake us !
They'll turn us out, and no one else will take
       us,
But why can't I be moral?—Let me try—
My heart thus pressing—fix'd my face and eye—
With a sententious look, that nothing means
(Faces are blocks, in sentimental scenes),
Thus I begin—*All is not gold that glitters,*
Pleasure seems sweet, but proves a glass of bitters.
When ignorance enters, folly is at hand ;
Learning is better far than house and land.
Let not your virtue trip, who trips may stumble,
And virtue is not virtue, if she tumble.
    I give it up—morals won't do for me ;
To make you laugh I must play tragedy.
One hope remains—hearing the maid was ill,
A *doctor* comes this night to show his skill.
To cheer her heart, and give your muscles
       motion,
He in *five draughts* prepar'd, presents a potion :
A kind of magic charm—for he assur'd,
If you will *swallow* it, the maid is cur'd.
But desperate the Doctor, and her case is,
If you reject the dose, and make wry faces !
This truth he boasts, will boast it while he lives,
No *poisonous drugs* are mix'd in what he gives ;

Should he succeed, you'll give him his degree ;
If not, within he will receive no fee !
The college *you*, must his pretentions back,
Pronounce him *regular*, or dub him *quack.*

DRAMATIS PERSONÆ.[1]

MEN.

Sir Charles Marlow,	Mr. Gardner.
Young Marlow (his Son)	Mr. Lewes.
Hardcastle,	Mr. Shuter.
Hastings,	Mr. Dubellamy.
Tony Lumpkin,	Mr. Quick.
Diggory,	Mr. Saunders.

WOMEN.

Mrs. Hardcastle,	Mrs. Green.
Miss Hardcastle,	Mrs. Bulkley.
Miss Neville,	Mrs. Kniveton.
Maid,	Miss Willems.

Landlords, Servants, &c., &c.

[1 The cast given is that of the piece as first acted.]

SHE STOOPS TO CONQUER:

OR,

THE MISTAKES OF A NIGHT.[1]

ACT I.

SCENE.—*A Chamber in an old-fashioned House.*
Enter Mrs. HARDCASTLE *and*
Mr. HARDCASTLE.

Mrs. Hardcastle.

 VOW, Mr. Hardcastle, you're very particular. Is there a creature in the whole country, but ourselves, that does not take a trip to town now and then, to rub off the rust a little? There's the two Miss Hoggs, and our neighbour, Mrs. Grigsby, go to take a month's polishing every winter.

[1 Mitford suggested to Mr. Forster that the first title originated in Dryden's—

"But kneels to conquer, and but stoops to rise."

The second title was originally the only one; but was rejected as undignified. Reynolds wanted to christen the play *The Belle's Stratagem*, a name afterwards used by Mrs. Cowley. *The Old House a New Inn* was also debated.]

Hard. Ay, and bring back vanity and affectation to last them the whole year. I wonder why London cannot keep its own fools at home. In my time, the follies of the town crept slowly among us, but now they travel faster than a stage-coach. Its fopperies come down, not only as inside passengers, but in the very basket.[1]

Mrs. Hard. Ay, *your* times were fine times, indeed; you have been telling us of *them* for many a long year. Here we live in an old rumbling mansion, that looks for all the world like an inn, but that we never see company. Our best visitors are old Mrs. Oddfish, the curate's wife, and little Cripplegate, the lame dancing-master: And all our entertainment your old stories of Prince Eugene and the Duke of Marlborough. I hate such old-fashioned trumpery.

Hard. And I love it. I love everything that's old: old friends, old times, old manners, old books, old wine; and, I believe, Dorothy (*taking her hand*), you'll own I have been pretty fond of an old wife.

Mrs. Hard. Lord, Mr. Hardcastle, you're for ever at your Dorothys and your old wifes. You may be a Darby, but I'll be no Joan, I promise you. I'm not so old as you'd make me, by more than one good year. Add twenty to twenty, and make money of that.

[1] A large wicker receptacle fixed on the hind axle-tree, sometimes used for luggage, sometimes for passengers, occasionally for both. See Hogarth's *Country Inn-Yard*, 1747.]

Hard. Let me see ; twenty added to twenty, makes just fifty and seven !

Mrs. Hard. It's false, Mr. Hardcastle : I was but twenty when I was brought to bed of Tony, that I had by Mr. Lumpkin, my first husband ; and he's not come to years of discretion yet.

Hard. Nor ever will, I dare answer for him. Ay, you have taught *him* finely !

Mrs. Hard. No matter, Tony Lumpkin has a good fortune. My son is not to live by his learning. I don't think a boy wants much learning to spend fifteen hundred a year.

Hard. Learning, quotha ! A mere composition of tricks and mischief !

Mrs. Hard. Humour, my dear : nothing but humour. Come, Mr. Hardcastle, you must allow the boy a little humour.

Hard. I'd sooner allow him a horse-pond ! If burning the footmen's shoes, frightening the maids, and worrying the kittens, be humour, he has it. It was but yesterday he fastened my wig to the back of my chair, and when I went to make a bow, I popped my bald head in Mrs. Frizzle's face ! [1]

Mrs. Hard. And am I to blame ? The poor boy was always too sickly to do any good. A school would be his death. When he comes to be a little stronger, who knows what a year or two's Latin may do for him ?

Hard. Latin for him ! A cat and fiddle ! No, no, the ale-house and the stable are the only schools he'll ever go to !

[1 A trick played on Goldsmith himself by Lord Clare's daughter. (Forster's *Life of Goldsmith*, Bk. iv., ch. 15, n.)]

Mrs. Hard. Well, we must not snub the poor
boy now, for I believe we shan't have him long
among us. Anybody that looks in his face may
see he's consumptive.

Hard. Ay, if growing too fat be one of the
symptoms.

Mrs. Hard. He coughs sometimes.

Hard. Yes, when his liquor goes the wrong way.

Mrs. Hard. I'm actually afraid of his lungs.

Hard. And truly, so am I; for he sometimes
whoops like a speaking-trumpet—(TONY *hallooing
behind the Scenes.*)—O, there he goes—A very
consumptive figure, truly!

Enter TONY, *crossing the stage.*

Mrs. Hard. Tony, where are going, my charmer?
Won't you give papa and I a little of your company, lovey?

Tony. I'm in haste, mother, I cannot stay.

Mrs. Hard. You shan't venture out this raw
evening, my dear: You look most shockingly.

Tony. I can't stay, I tell you. The Three
Pigeons expects me down every moment. There's
some fun going forward.

Hard. Ay; the ale-house, the old place: I
thought so.

Mrs. Hard. A low, paltry set of fellows.

Tony. Not so low, neither. There's Dick
Muggins the exciseman, Jack Slang the horse
doctor, Little Aminadab that grinds the music
box, and Tom Twist that spins the pewter platter.

Mrs. Hard. Pray, my dear, disappoint them
for one night, at least.

Tony. As for disappointing *them*, I should not much mind; but I can't abide to disappoint *myself!*

Mrs. Hard. (*Detaining him.*) You shan't go.

Tony. I will, I tell you.

Mrs. Hard. I say you shan't.

Tony. We'll see which is strongest, you or I.

[*Exit hauling her out.*

HARDCASTLE *solus.*

Hard. Ay, there goes a pair that only spoil each other. But is not the whole age in a combination to drive sense and discretion out of doors? There's my pretty darling Kate; the fashions of the times have almost infected her too. By living a year or two in town, she is as fond of gauze, and French frippery, as the best of them.

Enter Miss HARDCASTLE.

Hard. Blessings on my pretty innocence! Dressed out as my usual, my Kate! Goodness! What a quantity of superfluous silk hast thou got about thee, girl! I could never teach the fools of this age, that the indigent world could be clothed out of the trimmings of the vain.

Miss Hard. You know our agreement, sir. You allow me the morning to receive and pay visits, and to dress in my own manner; and in the evening, I put on my housewife's dress, to please you.

Hard. Well, remember, I insist on the terms of our agreement; and, by-the-bye, I believe I shall have occasion to try your obedience this very evening.

Miss Hard. I protest, sir, I don't comprehend your meaning.

Hard. Then, to be plain with you, Kate, I expect the young gentleman I have chosen to be your husband from town this very day. I have his father's letter, in which he informs me his son is set out, and that he intends to follow himself shortly after.

Miss Hard. Indeed! I wish I had known something of this before. Bless me, how shall I behave? It's a thousand to one I shan't like him; our meeting will be so formal, and so like a thing of business, that I shall find no room for friendship or esteem.

Hard. Depend upon it, child, I'll never control your choice; but Mr. Marlow, whom I have pitched upon, is the son of my old friend, Sir Charles Marlow, of whom you have heard me talk so often. The young gentleman has been bred a scholar, and is designed for an employment in the service of his country. I am told he's a man of an excellent understanding.

Miss Hard. Is he?

Hard. Very generous.

Miss Hard. I believe I shall like him.

Hard. Young and brave.

Miss Hard. I'm sure I shall like him.

Hard. And very handsome.

Miss Hard. My dear papa, say no more (*kissing his hand*), he's mine, I'll have him!

Hard. And, to crown all, Kate, he's one of the most bashful and reserved young fellows in all the world.

Miss Hard. Eh! you have frozen me to death again. That word reserved has undone all the rest of his accomplishments. A reserved lover, it is said, always makes a suspicious husband.

Hard. On the contrary, modesty seldom resides in a breast that is not enriched with nobler virtues. It was the very feature in his character that first struck me.

Miss Hard. He must have more striking features to catch me, I promise you. However, if he be so young, so handsome, and so everything, as you mention, I believe he'll do still. I think I'll have him.

Hard. Ay, Kate, but there is still an obstacle. It is more than an even wager, he may not have *you.*

Miss Hard. My dear papa, why will you mortify one so?—Well, if he refuses, instead of breaking my heart at his indifference, I'll only break my glass for its flattery. Set my cap to some newer fashion, and look out for some less difficult admirer.

Hard. Bravely resolved! In the meantime I'll go prepare the servants for his reception; as we seldom see company, they want as much training as a company of recruits the first day's muster.

[*Exit.*

Miss HARDCASTLE *sola.*

Miss Hard. Lud, this news of papa's puts me all in a flutter. Young, handsome; these he put last; but I put them foremost. Sensible, goodnatur'd; I like all that. But then reserved, and sheepish, that's much against him. Yet can't he be cured of his timidity, by being taught to be proud of his wife? Yes, and can't I—But I vow I'm disposing of the husband before I have secured the lover!

Enter Miss NEVILLE.

Miss Hard. I'm glad you're come, Neville, my dear. Tell me, Constance, how do I look this evening? Is there anything whimsical about me? Is it one of my well-looking days, child? Am I in face to-day?

Miss Neville. Perfectly, my dear. Yet, now I look again—bless me!—sure no accident has happened among the canary birds or the goldfishes? Has your brother or the cat been meddling? Or has the last novel been too moving?

Miss Hard. No; nothing of all this. I have been threatened—I can scarce get it out—I have been threatened with a lover!

Miss Neville. And his name——

Miss Hard. Is Marlow.

Miss Neville. Indeed!

Miss Hard. The son of Sir Charles Marlow.

Miss Neville. As I live, the most intimate friend of Mr. Hastings, *my* admirer. They are never asunder. I believe you must have seen him when we lived in town.

Miss Hard. Never.

Miss Neville. He's a very singular character, I assure you. Among women of reputation and virtue, he is the modestest man alive; but his acquaintance give him a very different character among creatures of another stamp : you understand me ?

Miss Hard. An odd character, indeed! I shall never be able to manage him. What shall I do? Pshaw, think no more of him, but trust to occurrences for success. But how goes on your own affair, my dear? Has my mother been courting you for my brother Tony, as usual?

Miss Neville. I have just come from one of our agreeable *tête-a-têtes.* She has been saying a hundred tender things, and setting off her pretty monster as the very pink of perfection.

Miss Hard. And her partiality is such, that she actually thinks him so. A fortune like yours is no small temptation. Besides, as she has the sole management of it, I'm not surprised to see her unwilling to let it go out of the family.

Miss Neville. A fortune like mine, which chiefly consists in jewels, is no such mighty temptation. But, at any rate, if my dear Hastings be but constant, I make no doubt to be too hard for her at last. However, I let her suppose that I am in love with her son, and she never once dreams that my affections are fixed upon another.

Miss Hard. My good brother holds out stoutly. I could almost love him for hating you so.

Miss Neville. It is a good-natur'd creature at bottom, and I'm sure would wish to see me married to anybody but himself. But my aunt's bell rings for our afternoon's walk through the improvements. *Allons.* Courage is necessary, as our affairs are critical.

Miss Hard. Would it were bed-time and all were well.[1]   [*Exeunt.*

SCENE.—*An Alehouse Room. Several shabby fellows, with punch and tobacco.* TONY *at the head of the table, a little higher than the rest: a mallet in his hand.*

Omnes. Hurrea, hurrea, hurrea, bravo!

First Fellow. Now, gentlemen, silence for a song. The 'Squire is going to knock himself down for a song.

Omnes. Ay, a song, a song.

Tony. Then I'll sing you, gentlemen, a song I made upon this ale-house, the Three Pigeons.

SONG.

Let school-masters puzzle their brain,
  With grammar, and nonsense, and learning;
Good liquor, I stoutly maintain,
  Gives genus *a better discerning,*
Let them brag of their Heathenish Gods,
  Their Lethes, their Styxes, and Stygians;
Their Quis, and their Quæs, and their Quods,
  They're all but a parcel of Pigeons.
                    Toroddle, toroddle, toroll!

When Methodist preachers come down,
  A-preaching that drinking is sinful,

[1 I *Henry* IV. Act v. Sc. 1.]

I'll wager the rascals a crown,
   They always preach best with a skinful.
But when you come down with your pence,
   For a slice of their scurvy religion,
I'll leave it to all men of sense,
   But you, my good friend, are the pigeon.
                    Toroddle, toroddle, toroll !

Then come, put the jorum about,
   And let us be merry and clever,
Our hearts and our liquors are stout,
   Here's the Three Jolly Pigeons for ever.
Let some cry up woodcock or hare,
   Your bustards, your ducks, and your widgeons
But of all the birds in the air,
   Here's a health to the Three Jolly Pigeons.
                    Toroddle, toroddle, toroll !

Omnes. Bravo, bravo !

First Fellow. The 'Squire has got spunk in him.

Second Fellow. I loves to hear him sing, bekeays he never gives us nothing that's *low*.[1]

Third Fellow. O damn anything that's *low*, I cannot bear it !

Fourth Fellow. The genteel thing is the genteel thing at any time. If so be that a gentleman bees in a concatenation accordingly.

Third Fellow. I like the maxum of it, Master

---

[1] Goldsmith, Fielding, and other contemporary humourists much objected to this particular form of depreciation on the part of the sentimentalists. In the whole of this discussion, the author, no doubt, had in mind the rejection of the Bailiff scene in the *Good-Natur'd Man.*]

Muggins. What, though I am obligated to dance a bear, a man may be a gentleman for all that. May this be my poison if my bear ever dances but to the very genteelest of tunes. Water Parted,[1] or the minuet in Ariadne.[2]

Second Fellow. What a pity it is the 'Squire is not come to his own. It would be well for all the publicans within ten miles round of him.

Tony. Ecod, and so it would, Master Slang. I'd then show what it was to keep choice of company.

Second Fellow. O, he takes after his own father for that. To be sure, old 'Squire Lumpkin was the finest gentleman I ever set my eyes on. For winding the straight horn, or beating a thicket for a hare, or a wench, he never had his fellow. It was a saying in the place, that he kept the best horses, dogs, and girls in the whole county.

Tony. Ecod, and when I'm of age I'll be no bastard, I promise you. I have been thinking of Bet Bouncer and the miller's grey mare to begin with. But come, my boys, drink about and be merry, for you pay no reckoning. Well, Stingo, what's the matter?

Enter LANDLORD.

Landlord. There be two gentlemen in a post-chaise at the door. They have lost their way upo' the forest; and they are talking something about Mr. Hardcastle.

Tony. As sure as can be, one of them must be

[1 The song of Arbaces in Arne's *Artaxerxes*, 1762.]

[2 By Handel. The minuet came at the end of the over-ture, and is said to have been the best thing in the opera.]

the gentleman that's coming down to court my sister. Do they seem to be Londoners?

Landlord. I believe they may. They look woundily like Frenchmen.

Tony. Then desire them to step this way, and I'll set them right in a twinkling. (*Exit Landlord.*) Gentlemen, as they mayn't be good enough company for you, step down for a moment, and I'll be with you in the squeezing of a lemon.

[*Exeunt Mob.*

TONY *solus.*

Tony. Father-in-law has been calling me whelp, and hound, this half year. Now, if I pleased, I could be so revenged upon the old grumbletonian. But then I'm afraid—afraid of what? I shall soon be worth fifteen hundred a year, and let him frighten me out of *that* if he can!

Enter LANDLORD, *conducting* MARLOW *and* HASTINGS.

Marlow. What a tedious uncomfortable day have we had of it! We were told it was but forty miles across the country, and we have come above threescore!

Hastings. And all, Marlow, from that unaccountable reserve of yours, that would not let us enquire more frequently on the way.

Marlow. I own, Hastings, I am unwilling to lay myself under an obligation to every one I meet; and often stand the chance of an unmannerly answer.

Hastings. At present, however, we are not likely to receive any answer.

Tony. No offence, gentlemen. But I'm told you have been enquiring for one Mr. Hardcastle, in these parts. Do you know what part of the country you are in?

Hastings. Not in the least, sir, but should thank you for information.

Tony. Nor the way you came?

Hastings. No, sir, but if you can inform us——

Tony. Why, gentlemen, if you know neither the road you are going, nor where you are, nor the road you came, the first thing I have to inform is, that—you have lost your way.

Marlow. We wanted no ghost to tell us that.[1]

Tony. Pray, gentlemen, may I be so bold as to ask the place from whence you came?

Marlow. That's not necessary towards directing us where we are to go.

Tony. No offence; but question for question is all fair, you know. Pray, gentlemen, is not this same Hardcastle a cross-grained, old-fashioned, whimsical fellow with an ugly face; a daughter, and a pretty son?

Hastings. We have not seen the gentleman, but he has the family you mention.

Tony. The daughter, a tall, trapesing, trolloping, talkative maypole——The son, a pretty, well-bred, agreeable youth, that everybody is fond of!

Marlow. Our information differs in this. The daughter is said to be well-bred and beautiful; the son, an awkward booby, reared up and spoiled at his mother's apron-string.

Tony. He-he-hem—then gentlemen, all I have

[1 *Hamlet*, Act 1., Sc. 5.]

to tell you is, that you won't reach Mr. Hardcastle's house this night, I believe.

Hastings. Unfortunate!

Tony. It's a damned long, dark, boggy, dirty,
dangerous way. Stingo, tell the gentlemen the
way to Mr. Hardcastle's. (*Winking upon the
Landlord.*) Mr. Hardcastle's of Quagmire Marsh,
you understand me.

Landlord. Master Hardcastle's! Lack-a-daisy,
my masters, you're come a deadly deal wrong!
When you came to the bottom of the hill, you
should have crossed down Squash Lane.

Marlow. Cross down Squash Lane!

Landlord. Then you were to keep straight forward, until you came to four roads.

Marlow. Come to where four roads meet!

Tony. Ay, but you must be sure to take only
one of them.

Marlow. O, sir, you're facetious!

Tony. Then, keeping to the right, you are to go
sideways till you come upon Crack-skull common:
there you must look sharp for the track of the
wheel, and go forward, till you come to farmer
Murrain's barn. Coming to the farmer's barn,
you are to turn to the right, and then to the left,
and then to the right about again, till you find out
the old mill——

Marlow. Zounds, man! we could as soon find
out the longitude![1]

---

[1] This was a popular inquiry in the last century, owing
to the reward of £20,000 offered by Parliament in 1714 for
the discovery of a means of accurately ascertaining the
longitude at sea. The father of Johnson's friend Miss

Hastings. What's to be done, Marlow?

Marlow. This house promises but a poor reception, though, perhaps, the landlord can accommodate us.

Landlord. Alack, master, we have but one spare bed in the whole house.

Tony. And to my knowledge, that's taken up by three lodgers already. (*After a pause, in which the rest seem disconcerted.*) I have hit it. Don't you think, Stingo, our landlady could accommodate the gentlemen by the fire-side, with——three chairs and a bolster?

Hastings. I hate sleeping by the fire-side.

Marlow. And I detest your three chairs and a bolster.

Tony. You do, do you?—then let me see— what—if you go on a mile further, to the Buck's Head; the old Buck's Head on the hill, one of the best inns in the whole county?

Hastings. Oh, oh! so we have escaped an adventure for this night, however.

Landlord (*apart to Tony*). Sure, you ben't sending them to your father's as an inn, be you?[1]

Tony. Mum, you fool, you. Let *them* find that out. (*To them.*) You have only to keep on straight forward, till you come to a large old house

Williams, is said by Boswell to have made " many ingenious advances" in this direction; but the reward was finally gained by John Harrison.]

[1 This was the recollection of a trick played upon Goldsmith himself in his youth. Enquiring at Ardagh, with boyish importance, for the "best house" (*i.e.* inn), he was directed by a practical joker to the residence of the local magnate, Squire Featherston.]

by the roadside. You'll see a pair of large horns over the door. That's the sign. Drive up the yard, and call stoutly about you.

Hastings. Sir, we are obliged to you. The servants can't miss the way?

Tony. No, no: But I tell you though, the landlord is rich, and going to leave off business; so he wants to be thought a gentleman, saving your presence, he! he! he! He'll be for giving you his company, and, ecod, if you mind him, he'll persuade you that his mother was an alderman, and his aunt a justice of the peace!

Landlord. A troublesome old blade, to be sure; but 'a keeps as good wines and beds as any in the whole country.

Marlow. Well, if he supplies us with these, we shall want no further connection. We are to turn to the right, did you say?

Tony. No, no; straight forward. I'll just step myself, and show you a piece of the way. (*To the Landlord.*) Mum.

Landlord. Ah, bless your heart, for a sweet, pleasant——damned mischievous son of a whore
[*Exeunt.*

END OF THE FIRST ACT.

ACT II.

Scene.—*An old-fashioned House.*

Enter Hardcastle, *followed by three or four awkward Servants.*

Hardcastle.

WELL, I hope you're perfect in the table exercise I have been teaching you these three days. You all know your posts and your places, and can show that you have been used to good company, without ever stirring from home.

Omnes. Ay, ay.

Hard. When company comes, you are not to pop out and stare, and then run in again, like frightened rabbits in a warren.

Omnes. No, no.

Hard. You, Diggory, whom I have taken from the barn are to make a show at the side-table; and you, Roger, whom I have advanced from the plough, are to place yourself behind *my* chair. But you're not to stand so, with your hands in your pockets. Take your hands from your pockets, Roger; and from your head, you blockhead, you. See how Diggory carries his hands. They're a little too stiff, indeed, but that's no great matter.

Diggory. Ay, mind how I hold them. I learned

to hold my hands this way, when I was upon drill for the militia. And so being upon drill——

Hard. You must not be so talkative, Diggory. You must be all attention to the guests. You must hear us talk, and not think of talking; you must see us drink, and not think of drinking; you must see us eat, and not think of eating.

Diggory. By the laws, your worship, that's parfectly unpossible. Whenever Diggory sees yeating going forward, ecod, he's always wishing for a mouthful himself.

Hard. Blockhead! Is not a bellyful in the kitchen as good as a bellyful in the parlour? Stay your stomach with that reflection.

Diggory. Ecod, I thank your worship, I'll make a shift to stay my stomach with a slice of cold beef in the pantry.

Hard. Diggory, you are too talkative. Then, if I happen to say a good thing, or tell a good story at table, you must not all burst out a-laughing, as if you made part of the company.

Diggory. Then, ecod, your worship must not tell the story of Ould Grouse in the gun-room:[1] I can't help laughing at that—he! he! he!—for the soul of me! We have laughed at that these twenty years—ha! ha! ha!

Hard. Ha! ha! ha! The story is a good one. Well, honest Diggory, you may laugh at that— but still remember to be attentive. Suppose one of the company should call for a glass of wine

---

[1] This story has escaped identification, like "Taffy in the Sedan Chair" in the *Citizen of the World.*

how will you behave? A glass of wine, sir, if you please (*to* DIGGORY)—Eh, why don't you move?

Diggory. Ecod, your worship, I never have courage till I see the eatables and drinkables brought upo' the table, and then I'm as bauld as a lion.

Hard. What, will nobody move?

First Servant. I'm not to leave this pleace.

Second Servant. I'm sure it's no pleace of mine.

Third Servant. Nor mine, for sartain.

Diggory. Wauns, and I'm sure it canna be mine.

Hard. You numskulls! and so while, like your betters, you are quarrelling for places, the guests must be starved. O, you dunces! I find I must begin all over again.—But don't I hear a coach drive into the yard? To your posts, you blockheads! I'll go in the meantime and give my old friend's son a hearty reception at the gate.

[*Exit* HARDCASTLE.

Diggory. By the elevens, my pleace is gone quite out of my head!

Roger. I know that my pleace is to be everywhere!

First Servant. Where the devil is mine?

Second Servant. My pleace is to be nowhere at all; and so I ze go about my business!

[*Exeunt Servants, running about as
if frighted, different ways.*

Enter SERVANT *with Candles, showing in*
MARLOW *and* HASTINGS.

Servant. Welcome, gentlemen, very welcome. This way.

Hastings. After the disappointments of the day, welcome once more, Charles, to the comforts of a clean room and a good fire. Upon my word, a very well-looking house; antique but creditable.

Marlow. The usual fate of a large mansion. Having first ruined the master by good housekeeping, it at last comes to levy contributions as an inn.

Hastings. As you say, we passengers are to be taxed to pay all these fineries. I have often seen a good sideboard, or a marble chimney-piece, though not actually put in the bill, inflame a reckoning confoundedly.

Marlow. Travellers, George, must pay in all places. The only difference is, that in good inns, you pay dearly for luxuries; in bad inns, you are fleeced and starved.

Hastings. You have lived pretty much among them. In truth, I have been often surprised, that you who have seen so much of the world, with your natural good sense, and your many opportunities, could never yet acquire a requisite share of assurance.

Marlow. The Englishman's malady. But tell me, George, where could I have learned that assurance you talk of? My life has been chiefly spent in a college, or an inn, in seclusion from that lovely part of the creation that chiefly teach men confidence. I don't know that I was ever familiarly acquainted with a single modest woman —except my mother—But among females of another class, you know—

Hastings. Ay, among them you are impudent enough of all conscience !

Marlow. They are of *us*, you know.

Hastings. But in the company of women of reputation I never saw such an idiot, such a trembler; you look for all the world as if you wanted an opportunity of stealing out of the room.

Marlow. Why, man, that's because I *do* want to steal out of the room. Faith, I have often formed a resolution to break the ice, and rattle away at any rate. But I don't know how, a single glance from a pair of fine eyes has totally overset my resolution. An impudent fellow may counterfeit modesty, but I'll be hanged it a modest man can ever counterfeit impudence.

Hastings. If you could but say half the fine things to them that I have heard you lavish upon the barmaid of an inn, or even a college bed-maker—

Marlow. Why, George, I can't say fine things to them. They freeze, they petrify me. They may talk of a comet, or a burning mountain, or some such bagatelle. But to me, a modest woman, dressed out in all her finery, is the most tremendous object of the whole creation.

Hastings. Ha! ha! ha! At this rate, man, how can you ever expect to marry !

Marlow. Never, unless, as among kings and princes, my bride were to be courted by proxy. If, indeed, like an Eastern bridegroom, one were to be introduced to a wife he never saw before, it might be endured. But to go through all the terrors of a formal courtship, together with the episode of aunts, grandmothers and cousins, and at last to blurt out the broad staring question of, *madam, will you marry me?* No, no, that's a strain much above me, I assure you!

Hastings. I pity you. But how do you intend behaving to the lady you are come down to visit at the request of your father?

Marlow. As I behave to all other ladies. Bow very low. Answer yes, or no, to all her demands —But for the rest, I don't think I shall venture to look in her face, till I see my father's again.

Hastings. I'm surprised that one who is so warm a friend can be so cool a lover.

Marlow. To be explicit, my dear Hastings, my chief inducement down was to be instrumental in forwarding your happiness, not my own. Miss Neville loves you, the family don't know you, as my friend you are sure of a reception, and let honour do the rest.

Hastings. My dear Marlow! But I'll suppress the emotion. Were I a wretch, meanly seeking to carry off a fortune, you should be the last man in the world I would apply to for assistance. But Miss Neville's person is all I ask, and that is mine, both from her deceased father's consent, and her own inclination.

Marlow. Happy man! You have talents and art to captivate any woman. I'm doomed to adore the sex, and yet to converse with the only part of it I despise. This stammer in my address, and this awkward prepossessing visage of mine, can never permit me to soar above the reach of a milliner's apprentice, or one of the duchesses of

Drury-lane. Pshaw! this fellow here to interrupt us.

Enter HARDCASTLE.

Hard. Gentlemen, once more you are heartily welcome. Which is Mr. Marlow? Sir, you're heartily welcome. It's not my way, you see, to receive my friends with my back to the fire. I like to give them a hearty reception in the old style at my gate. I like to see their horses and trunks taken care of.

Marlow. (*aside.*) He has got our names from the servants already. (*To him.*) We approve your caution and hospitality, sir. (*To* HASTINGS.) I have been thinking, George, of changing our travelling dresses in the morning. I am grown confoundedly ashamed of mine.

Hard. I beg, Mr. Marlow, you'll use no ceremony in this house.

Hastings. I fancy, George, you're right: the first blow is half the battle. I intend opening the campaign with the white and gold.

Hard. Mr. Marlow—Mr. Hastings—gentlemen —pray be under no constraint in this house. This is Liberty Hall, gentlemen. You may do just as you please here.

Marlow. Yet, George, if we open the campaign too fiercely at first, we may want ammunition before it is over. I think to reserve the embroidery to secure a retreat.

Hard. Your talking of a retreat, Mr. Marlow, puts me in mind of the Duke of Marlborough, when we went to besiege Denain. He first summoned the garrison——

Marlow. Don't you think the *ventre d'or* waist-coat will do with the plain brown?

Hard. He first summoned the garrison, which might consist of about five thousand men——

Hastings. I think not : brown and yellow mix but very poorly.

Hard. I say, gentlemen, as I was telling you, he summoned the garrison, which might consist of about five thousand men——

Marlow. The girls like finery.

Hard. Which might consist of about five thousand men, well appointed with stores, ammunition, and other implements of war. "Now," says the Duke of Marlborough to George Brooks, that stood next to him — you must have heard of George Brooks ; "I'll pawn my Dukedom," says he, "but I take that garrison without spilling a drop of blood !" So——

Marlow. What, my good friend, if you gave us a glass of punch in the meantime, it would help us to carry on the siege with vigour.

Hard. Punch, sir !——(*Aside.*) This is the most unaccountable kind of modesty I ever met with !

Marlow. Yes, sir, punch ! A glass of warm punch, after our journey, will be comfortable. This is Liberty Hall, you know.

Hard. Here's cup, sir.

Marlow (*aside*). So this fellow, in his Liberty Hall, will only let us have just what he pleases.

Hard. (*taking the cup.*) I hope you'll find it to your mind. I have prepared it with my own hands, and I believe you'll own the ingredients are tole-

rable.   Will you be so good as to pledge me, sir ?
Here, Mr. Marlow, here is our better acquaintance !

[*Drinks.*

Marlow (*aside*). A very impudent fellow this !
but he's a character, and I'll humour him a little.
Sir, my service to you.   [*Drinks.*

Hastings (*aside*). I see this fellow wants to give
us his company, and forgets that he's an innkeeper,
before he has learned to be a gentleman.

Marlow. From the excellence of your cup, my
old friend, I suppose you have a good deal of business in this part of the country.   Warm work, now
and then, at elections, I suppose ?

Hard. No, sir, I have long given that work
over.   Since our betters have hit upon the expedient of electing each other, there's no business
for us that sell ale.

Hastings. So, then you have no turn for politics, I find.

Hard. Not in the least.   There was a time,
indeed, I fretted myself about the mistakes of
government, like other people ; but, finding myself every day grow more angry, and the government growing no better, I left it to mend itself.
Since that, I no more trouble my head about
Hyder Ally,[1] or *Ally Cawn,*[2] than about *Ally
Croaker.*[3]   Sir, my service to you.

[1 The famous Sultan of Mysore, 1717-82.]
[2 Cossim Ali Cawn, Subah of Bengal.]
[3 "Ally Croaker" is the Irish ditty beginning—

> " There lived a man in Ballinacrasy
> Who wanted a wife to make him unasy."

It was described as "a new Song " in 1753.]

Hastings. So that, with eating above stairs, and drinking below, with receiving your friends within, and amusing them without, you lead a good pleasant bustling life of it.

Hard. I do stir about a great deal, that's certain. Half the differences of the parish are adjusted in this very parlour.

Marlow (*After drinking*). And you have an argument in your cup, old gentleman, better than any in Westminster Hall.

Hard. Ay, young gentleman, that, and a little philosophy.

Marlow (*aside*). Well, this is the first time I ever heard of an innkeeper's philosophy.

Hastings. So then, like an experienced general, you attack them on every quarter. If you find their reason manageable, you attack it with your philosophy; if you find they have no reason, you attack them with this. Here's your health, my philosopher. [*Drinks.*

Hard. Good, very good, thank you; ha! ha! Your generalship puts me in mind of Prince Eugene, when he fought the Turks at the battle of Belgrade. You shall hear.

Marlow. Instead of the battle of Belgrade, I believe it's almost time to talk about supper. What has your philosophy got in the house for supper?

Hard. For supper, sir!——(*Aside.*) Was ever such a request to a man in his own house!

Marlow. Yes, sir, supper, sir; I begin to feel an appetite. I shall make devilish work to-night in the larder, I promise you.

Hard. (*aside.*) Such a brazen dog sure never my eyes beheld. (*To him.*) Why, really, sir, as for supper I can't well tell. My Dorothy, and the cook maid, settle these things between them. I leave these kind of things entirely to them.

Marlow. You do, do you?

Hard. Entirely. By-the-bye, I believe they are in actual consultation upon what's for supper this moment in the kitchen.

Marlow. Then I beg they'll admit *me* as one of their privy council. It's a way I have got. When I travel, I always choose to regulate my own supper. Let the cook be called. No offence, I hope, sir.

Hard. O, no, sir, none in the least ; yet, I don't know how : our Bridget, the cook maid, is not very communicative upon these occasions. Should we send for her, she might scold us all out of the house.

Hastings. Let's see your list of the larder, then. I ask it as a favour. I always match my appetite to my bill of fare.

Marlow (*To* HARDCASTLE, *who looks at them with surprise*). Sir, he's very right, and it's my way, too.

Hard. Sir, you have a right to command here. Here, Roger, bring us the bill of fare for to-night's supper. I believe it's drawn out. Your manner, Mr. Hastings, puts me in mind of my uncle, Colonel Wallop. It was a saying of his, that no man was sure of his supper till he had eaten it.

Hastings (*aside*). All upon the high ropes ! His uncle a colonel ! We shall soon hear of his mother being a justice of peace. But let's hear the bill of fare.

Marlow (*Perusing*). What's here? For the first course; for the second course; for the desert. The devil, sir, do you think we have brought down the whole Joiners' Company, or the Corporation of Bedford, to eat up such a supper? Two or three little things, clean and comfortable, will do.

Hastings. But let's hear it.

Marlow (*Reading*). For the first course at the top, a pig, and prune sauce.

Hastings. Damn your pig, I say!

Marlow. And damn your prune sauce, say I!

Hard. And yet, gentlemen, to men that are hungry, pig, with prune sauce, is very good eating.

Marlow. At the bottom, a calf's tongue and brains.

Hastings. Let your brains be knocked out, my good sir; I don't like them.

Marlow. Or you may clap them on a plate by themselves, I do.

Hard. (*aside.*) Their impudence confounds me. (*To them.*) Gentlemen, you are my guests, make what alterations you please. Is there anything else you wish to retrench or alter, gentlemen?

Marlow. Item. A pork pie, a boiled rabbit and sausages, a florentine, a shaking pudding, and a dish of tiff—taff—taffety cream!

Hastings. Confound your made dishes, I shall be as much at a loss in this house as at a green and yellow dinner at the French ambassador's table, I'm for plain eating.

Hard. I'm sorry, gentlemen, that I have nothing you like, but if there be anything you have a particular fancy to——

Marlow. Why, really, sir, your bill of fare is so exquisite, that any one part of it is full as good as another. Send us what you please. So much for supper. And now to see that our beds are aired, and properly taken care of.

Hard. I entreat you'll leave all that to me. You shall not stir a step.

Marlow. Leave that to you! I protest, sir, you must excuse me, I always look to these things myself.

Hard. I must insist, sir, you'll make yourself easy on that head.

Marlow. You see I'm resolved on it.—(*Aside.*) A very troublesome fellow this, as ever I met with.

Hard. Well, sir, I'm resolved at least to attend you.—(*Aside.*) This may be modern modesty, but I never saw anything look so like old-fashioned impudence. [*Exeunt* MARLOW *and* HARDCASTLE.

HASTINGS *solus.*

Hastings. So I find this fellow's civilities begin to grow troublesome. But who can be angry at those assiduities which are meant to please him? Ha! what do I see! Miss Neville, by all that's happy!

Enter Miss NEVILLE.

Miss Neville. My dear Hastings! To what unexpected good fortune? to what accident am I to ascribe this happy meeting?

Hastings. Rather let me ask the same question, as I could never have hoped to meet my dearest Constance at an inn.

Miss Neville. An inn ! sure you mistake ! my aunt, my guardian, lives here. What could induce you to think this house an inn ?

Hastings. My friend, Mr. Marlow, with whom I came down, and I, have been sent here as to an inn, I assure you. A young fellow whom we accidentally met at a house hard by directed us hither.

Miss Neville. Certainly it must be one of my hopeful cousin's tricks, of whom you have heard me talk so often, ha ! ha ! ha ! ha !

Hastings. He whom your aunt intends for you? He of whom I have such just apprehensions?

Miss Neville. You have nothing to fear from him, I assure you. You'd adore him if you knew how heartily he despises me. My aunt knows it too, and has undertaken to court me for him, and actually begins to think she has made a conquest.

Hastings. Thou dear dissembler ! You must know, my Constance, I have just seized this happy opportunity of my friend's visit here to get admittance into the family. The horses that carried us down are now fatigued with their journey, but they'll soon be refreshed ; and then, if my dearest girl will trust in her faithful Hastings, we shall soon be landed in France, where even among slaves the laws of marriage are respected.[1]

Miss Neville. I have often told you, that though

[1 This was regarded as an oblique allusion to the marriage of the Duke of Gloucester with Lady Waldegrave, which was one of the causes of the restrictive "Royal Marriage Act" of 1772.]

ready to obey you, I yet should leave my little
fortune behind with reluctance. The greatest part
of it was left me by my uncle, the India Director,
and chiefly consists in jewels. I have been for
some time persuading my aunt to let me wear
them. I fancy I'm very near succeeding. The
instant they are put into my possession you shall
find me ready to make them and myself yours.

Hastings. Perish the baubles! Your person is
all I desire. In the meantime, my friend Marlow
must not be let into his mistake. I know the
strange reserve of his temper is such, that if
abruptly informed of it, he would instantly quit
the house before our plan was ripe for execution.

Miss Neville. But how shall we keep him in the
deception? Miss Hardcastle is just returned from
walking; what if we still continue to deceive him?
—This, this way—— [*They confer.*

Enter MARLOW.

Marlow. The assiduities of these good people
tease me beyond bearing. My host seems to think
it ill manners to leave me alone, and so he claps
not only himself, but his old-fashioned wife on my
back. They talk of coming to sup with us, too;
and then, I suppose, we are to run the gauntlet
through all the rest of the family.—What have we
got here?—

Hastings. My dear Charles! Let me congratu-
late you!—The most fortunate accident!—Who
do you think is just alighted?

Marlow. Cannot guess.

Hastings. Our mistresses, boy, Miss Hardcastle

and Miss Neville. Give me leave to introduce Miss Constance Neville to your acquaintance. Happening to dine in the neighbourhood, they called, on their return to take fresh horses, here. Miss Hardcastle has just stept into the next room, and will be back in an instant. Wasn't it lucky? eh!

Marlow (*aside*). I have just been mortified enough of all conscience, and here comes something to complete my embarrassment.

Hastings. Well! but wasn't it the most fortunate thing in the world?

Marlow. Oh! yes. Very fortunate—a most joyful encounter——But our dresses, George, you know, are in disorder——What if we should postpone the happiness till to-morrow?——To morrow at her own house——It will be every bit as convenient——And rather more respectful——To-morrow let it be. [*Offering to go.*

Miss Neville. By no means, sir. Your ceremony will displease her. The disorder of your dress will shew the ardour of your impatience. Besides, she knows you are in the house, and will permit you to see her.

Marlow. O! the devil! how shall I support it? Hem! hem! Hastings, you must not go. You are to assist me, you know. I shall be confoundedly ridiculous. Yet, hang it! I'll take courage. Hem!

Hastings. Pshaw, man! it's but the first plunge, and all's over. She's but a woman, you know.

Marlow. And of all women, she that I dread most to encounter!

Enter Miss HARDCASTLE, *as returned from walking, a Bonnet, &c.*

Hastings (*introducing them*). Miss Hardcastle, Mr. Marlow, I'm proud of bringing two persons of such merit together, that only want to know, to esteem each other.

Miss Hard. (*aside.*) Now, for meeting my modest gentleman with a demure face, and quite in his own manner. (*After a pause, in which he appears very uneasy and disconcerted.*) I'm glad of your safe arrival, sir——I'm told you had some accidents by the way.

Marlow. Only a few, madam. Yes, we had some. Yes, madam, a good many accidents, but should be sorry—madam—or rather glad of any accidents — that are so agreeably concluded. Hem !

Hastings (*To him*). You never spoke better in your whole life. Keep it up, and I'll insure you the victory.

Miss Hard. I'm afraid you flatter, sir. You that have seen so much of the finest company can find little entertainment in an obscure corner of the country.

Marlow (*Gathering courage*). I have lived, indeed, in the world, madam ; but I have kept very little company. I have been but an observer upon life, madam, while others were enjoying it.

Miss Neville. But that, I am told, is the way to enjoy it at last.

Hastings (*To him*). Cicero never spoke better,

Once more, and you are confirmed in assurance for ever.

Marlow (*To him*). Hem! Stand by me, then, and when I'm down, throw in a word or two to set me up again.

Miss Hard. An observer, like you, upon life, were, I fear, disagreeably employed, since you must have had much more to censure than to approve.

Marlow. Pardon me, madam. I was always willing to be amused. The folly of most people is rather an object of mirth than uneasiness.

Hastings (*To him*). Bravo, bravo. Never spoke so well in your whole life. Well, Miss Hardcastle, I see that you and Mr. Marlow are going to be very good company. I believe our being here will but embarrass the interview.

Marlow. Not in the least, Mr. Hastings. We like your company of all things. (*To him.*) Zounds! George, sure you won't go? How can you leave us?

Hastings. Our presence will but spoil conversation, so we'll retire to the next room. (*To him.*) You don't consider, man, that we are to manage a little *tête-à-tête* of our own. [*Exeunt.*

Miss Hard. (*After a pause.*) But you have not been wholly an observer, I presume, sir. The ladies, I should hope, have employed some part of your addresses.

Marlow (*Relapsing into timidity*). Pardon me, madam, I—I—I--as yet have studied—only—to —deserve them.

Miss Hard. And that some say is the very worst way to obtain them.

Marlow. Perhaps so, madam. But I love to converse only with the more grave and sensible part of the sex.——But I'm afraid I grow tiresome.

Miss Hard. Not at all, sir ; there is nothing I like so much as grave conversation myself : I could hear it for ever. Indeed, I have often been surprised how a man of *sentiment* could ever admire those light airy pleasures, where nothing reaches the heart.

Marlow. It's—a disease—of the mind, madam. In the variety of tastes there must be some who, wanting a relish for—um-a-um.

Miss Hard. I understand you, sir. There must be some, who, wanting a relish for refined pleasures, pretend to despise what they are incapable of tasting.

Marlow. My meaning, madam, but infinitely better expressed. And I can't help observing—a——

Miss Hard. (*aside.*) Who could ever suppose this fellow impudent upon some occasions. (*To him.*) You were going to observe, sir——

Marlow. I was observing, madam——I protest, madam, I forget what I was going to observe.

Miss Hard. (*aside.*) I vow and so do I. (*To him.*) You were observing, sir, that in this age of hypocrisy—something about hypocrisy, sir.

Marlow. Yes, madam. In this age of hypocrisy, there are few who upon strict enquiry do not—a—a—a——

Miss Hard. I understand you perfectly, sir.

Marlow (*aside*). Egad ! and that's more than I do myself !

Miss Hard. You mean that in this hypocritical age there are few that do not condemn in public what they practise in private, and think they pay every debt to virtue when they praise it.

Marlow. True, madam; those who have most virtue in their mouths, have least of it in their bosoms. But I'm sure I tire you, madam.

Miss Hard. Not in the least, sir; there's something so agreeable and spirited in your manner, such life and force——pray, sir, go on.

Marlow. Yes, madam. I was saying——that there are some occasions——when a total want of courage, madam, destroys all the——and puts us——upon a——a——a——

Miss Hard. I agree with you entirely, a want of courage upon some occasions assumes the appearance of ignorance, and betrays us when we most want to excel. I beg you'll proceed.

Marlow. Yes, ma'am. Morally speaking, madam——But I see Miss Neville expecting us in the next room. I would not intrude for the world.

Miss Hard. I protest, sir, I never was more agreeably entertained in all my life. Pray go on.

Marlow. Yes, madam. I was——But she beckons us to join her. Madam, shall I do myself the honour to attend you?

Miss Hard. Well then, I'll follow.

Marlow (aside). This pretty smooth dialogue has done for me. [*Exit.*

Miss HARDCASTLE *sola.*

Miss Hard. Ha! ha! ha! Was there ever such a sober sentimental interview? I'm certain he scarce looked in my face the whole time. Yet the fellow, but for his unacccountable bashfulness, is pretty well, too.   He has good sense, but then so buried in his fears, that it fatigues one more than ignorance.   If I could teach him a little confidence, it would be doing somebody that I know of a piece of service.   But who is that somebody?—that, faith, is a question I can scarce answer.   [*Exit.*

Enter TONY *and Miss* NEVILLE, *followed by Mrs.* HARDCASTLE *and* HASTINGS.

Tony. What do you follow me for, cousin Con? I wonder you're not ashamed to be so very engaging.

Miss Neville. I hope, cousin, one may speak to one's own relations, and not be to blame.

Tony. Ay, but I know what sort of a relation you want to make me, though; but it won't do. I tell you, cousin Con, it won't do, so I beg you'll keep your distance, I want no nearer relationship.
        [*She follows coquetting him to the back scene.*

Mrs. Hard. Well! I vow, Mr. Hastings, you are very entertaining.   There's nothing in the world I love to talk of so much as London, and the fashions, though I was never there myself.

Hastings. Never there! You amaze me! From your air and manner, I concluded you had been bred all your life either at Ranelagh, St. James's, or Tower Wharf.

Mrs. Hard. O! sir, you're only pleased to say so.   We country persons can have no manner at all.   I'm in love with the town, and that serves to raise me above some of our neighbouring rustics; but who can have a manner, that has never seen the Pantheon, the Grotto Gardens, the Borough, and such places where the nobility chiefly resort? All I can do is to enjoy London at second-hand. I take care to know every *tête-à-tête* from the Scandalous Magazine,[1] and have all the fashions as they come out, in a letter from the two Miss Rickets of Crooked Lane. Pray how do you like this head, Mr. Hastings?

Hastings. Extremely elegant and *dégagé*, upon my word, madam. Your friseur is a Frenchman, I suppose?

Mrs. Hard. I protest, I dressed it myself from a print in the Ladies' Memorandum-book for the last year.

Hastings. Indeed. Such a head in a side-box, at the Play-house, would draw as many gazers as my Lady Mayoress at a City Ball.

Mrs. Hard. I vow, since inoculation began, there is no such thing to be seen as a plain woman; so one must dress a little particular or one may escape in the crowd.

Hastings. But that can never be your case, madam, in any dress! (*Bowing.*)

Mrs. Hard. Yet, what signifies *my* dressing when I have such a piece of antiquity by my side as Mr. Hardcastle: all I can say will never argue down a single button from his clothes. I have often wanted him to throw off his great flaxen wig, and where he was bald, to plaster it over like my Lord Pately, with powder.

[1 An allusion to the bust-portraits called "Tête-à-Têtes," published, with satirical biographies, in the *Town and Country Magazine.* Lady Waldegrave and the Duke of Gloucester came early in the series.]

Hastings. You are right, madam ; for, as among the ladies there are none ugly, so among the men there are none old.

Mrs. Hard. But what do you think his answer was ? Why, with his usual Gothic vivacity, he said I only wanted him to throw off his wig to convert it into a *téte* for my own wearing !

Hastings. Intolerable ! At your age you may wear what you please, and it must become you.

Mrs. Hard. Pray, Mr. Hastings, what do you take to be the most fashionable age about town ?

Hastings. Some time ago forty was all the mode ; but I'm told the ladies intend to bring up fifty for the ensuing winter.

Mrs. Hard. Seriously. Then I shall be too young for the fashion !

Hastings. No lady begins now to put on jewels till she's past forty. For instance, miss there, in a polite circle, would be considered as a child, as a mere maker of samplers.

Mrs. Hard. And yet Mrs. Niece thinks herself as much a woman, and is as fond of jewels as the oldest of us all.

Hastings. Your niece, is she ? And that young gentleman, a brother of yours, I should presume ?

Mrs. Hard. My son, sir. They are contracted to each other. Observe their little sports. They fall in and out ten times a day, as if they were man and wife already. (*To them.*) Well, Tony, child, what soft things are you saying to your cousin Constance, this evening ?

Tony. I have been saying no soft things ; but that it's very hard to be followed about so. Ecod !

I've not a place in the house now that's left to my-self but the stable.

Mrs. Hard. Never mind him, Con, my dear. He's in another story behind your back.

Miss Neville. There's something generous in my consin's manner. He falls out before faces to be forgiven in private.

Tony. That's a damned confounded——crack.

Mrs. Hard. Ah! he's a sly one. Don't you think they're like each other about the mouth, Mr. Hastings? The Blenkinsop mouth to a T. They're of a size, too. Back to back, my pretties, that Mr. Hastings may see you.[1] Come, Tony.

Tony. You had as good not make me, I tell you.

[*Measuring.*

Miss Neville. O lud! he has almost cracked my head.

Mrs. Hard. O, the monster! For shame, Tony. You a man, and behave so!

Tony. If I'm a man, let me have my fortin. Ecod! I'll not be made a fool of no longer.

Mrs. Hard. Is this, ungrateful boy, all that I'm to get for the pains I have taken in your education? I that have rocked you in your cradle, and fed that pretty mouth with a spoon! Did not I work that waistcoat to make you genteel? Did not I pre-scribe for you every day, and weep while the receipt was operating?

Tony. Ecod! you had reason to weep, for you have been dosing me ever since I was born. I have gone through every receipt in the complete housewife ten times over; and you have thoughts

[1 Cf. *The Vicar of Wakefield*, 1766, i, 158-9.]

of coursing me through *Quincy*[1] next spring. But, ecod! I tell you, I'll not be made a fool of no longer.

Mrs. Hard. Wasn't it all for your good, viper? Wasn't it all for your good?

Tony. I wish you'd let me and my good alone, then. Snubbing this way when I'm in spirits. If I'm to have any good, let it come of itself; not to keep dinging it, dinging it into one so.

Mrs. Hard. That's false; I never see you when you're in spirits. No, Tony, you then go to the alehouse or kennel. I'm never to be delighted with your agreeable, wild notes, unfeeling monster!

Tony. Ecod! Mamma, your own notes are the wildest of the two.

Mrs. Hard. Was ever the like? But I see he he wants to break my heart, I see he does.

Hastings. Dear Madam, permit me to lecture the young gentleman a little. I'm certain I can persuade him to his duty.

Mrs. Hard. Well! I must retire. Come, Constance, my love. You see, Mr Hastings, the wretchedness of my situation. Was ever poor woman so plagued with a dear, sweet, pretty, provoking, undutiful boy.

[*Exeunt Mrs.* HARDCASTLE *and Miss* NEVILLE.

HASTINGS. TONY.

Tony (singing). *There was a young man riding by, and fain would have his will.* *Rang do diddo*

[1 John Quincy, M.D. (d. 1723) author of a highly popular *Complete English Dispensatory,* a fourteenth edition of which was published in 1772.]

dee. Don't mind her. Let her cry. It's the comfort of her heart. I have seen her and sister cry over a book for an hour together, and they said, they liked the book the better the more it made them cry.

Hastings. Then you're no friend to the ladies, I find, my pretty young gentleman?

Tony. That's as I find 'um.

Hastings. Not to her of your mother's choosing, I dare answer! And yet she appears to me a pretty, well-tempered girl.

Tony. That's because you don't know her as well as I. Ecod! I know every inch about her; and there's not a more bitter cantankerous toad in all Christendom!

Hastings. (*aside*). Pretty encouragement, this, for a lover!

Tony. I have seen her since the height of that. She has as many tricks as a hare in a thicket, or a colt the first day's breaking.

Hastings. To me she appears sensible and silent!

Tony. Ay, before company. But when she's with her playmates she's as loud as a hog in a gate.

Hastings. But there is a meek modesty about her that charms me.

Tony. Yes, but curb her never so little, she kicks up, and you're flung in a ditch.

Hastings. Well, but you must allow her a little beauty.—Yes, you must allow her some beauty.

Tony. Bandbox! She's all a made up thing, mun. Ah! could you but see Bet Bouncer of these parts, you might then talk of beauty. Ecod,

she has two eyes as black as sloes, and cheeks as
broad and red as a pulpit cushion. She'd make
two of she.

Hastings. Well, what say you to a friend that
would take this bitter bargain off your hands?

Tony. Anon.

Hastings. Would you thank him that would
take Miss Neville, and leave you to happiness and
your dear Betsy?

Tony. Ay; but where is there such a friend, for
who would take *her?*

Hastings. I am he. If you but assist me, I'll
engage to whip her off to France, and you shall
never hear more of her.

Tony. Assist you! Ecod, I will, to the last
drop of my blood. I'll clap a pair of horses to
your chaise that shall trundle you off in a twinkling,
and may be get you a part of her fortin besides, in
jewels, that you little dream of.

Hastings. My dear 'Squire, this looks like a lad
of spirit.

Tony. Come along then, and you shall see
more of my spirit before you have done with me.

[*Singing.*

We are the boys
That fears no noise
Where the thundering cannons roar.

[*Exeunt.*

END OF THE SECOND ACT.

ACT III.

Enter HARDCASTLE *solus.*

Hardcastle.

WHAT could my old friend Sir Charles mean by recommending his son as the modestest young man in town? To me he appears the most impudent piece of brass that ever spoke with a tongue. He has taken possession of the easy chair by the fireside already. He took off his boots in the parlour, and desired me to see them taken care of. I'm desirous to know how his impudence affects my daughter.—She will certainly be shocked at it.

Enter Miss HARDCASTLE *plainly dressed.*

Hard. Well, my Kate, I see you have changed your dress as I bid you; and yet, I believe, there was no great occasion.

Miss Hard. I find such a pleasure, sir, in obeying your commands, that I take care to observe them without ever debating their propriety.

Hard. And yet, Kate, I sometimes give you some cause, particularly when I recommended my *modest* gentleman to you as a lover to-day.

Miss Hard. You taught me to expect something extraordinary, and I find the original exceeds the description!

Hard. I was never so surprised in my life ! He has quite confounded all my faculties !

Miss Hard. I never saw anything like it : And a man of the world, too !

Hard. Ay, he learned it all abroad,—what a fool was I, to think a young man could learn modesty by travelling. He might as soon learn wit at a masquerade.

Miss Hard. It seems all natural to him.

Hard. A good deal assisted by bad company and a French dancing-master.

Miss Hard. Sure, you mistake, papa ! a French dancing-master could never have taught him that timid look,—that awkward address,—that bashful manner——

Hard. Whose look ? whose manner ? child !

Miss Hard. Mr. Marlow's : his *mauvaise honte*, his timidity struck me at the first sight.

Hard. Then your first sight deceived you ; for I think him one of the most brazen first sights that ever astonished my senses !

Miss Hard. Sure, sir, you rally ! I never saw anyone so modest.

Hard. And can you be serious ! I never saw such a bouncing swaggering puppy since I was born. Bully Dawson [1] was but a fool to him.

Miss Hard. Surprising ! He met me with a respectful bow, a stammering voice, and a look fixed on the ground.

Hard. He met me with a loud voice, a lordly

[1 A Whitefriars bully and gutter-blood. He is immortalized in *Spectator*, No. 2, as having been kicked in a coffee-house by Sir Roger de Coverley.]

air, and a familiarity that made my blood freeze again.

Miss Hard. He treated me with diffidence and respect; censured the manners of the age; admired the prudence of girls that never laughed; tired me with apologies for being tiresome; then left the room with a bow, and, madam, I would not for the world detain you.

Hard. He spoke to me as if he knew me all his life before. Asked twenty questions, and never waited for an answer. Interrupted my best remarks with some silly pun, and when I was in my best story of the Duke of Marlborough and Prince Eugene, he asked if I had not a good hand at making punch. Yes, Kate, he asked your father if he was a maker of punch !

Miss Hard. One of us must certainly be mistaken.

Hard. If he be what he has shown himself, I'm determined he shall never have my consent.

Miss Hard. And if he be the sullen thing I take him, he shall never have mine.

Hard. In one thing then we are agreed—to reject him.

Miss Hard. Yes. But upon conditions. For if you should find him less impudent, and I more presuming; if you find him more respectful, and I more importunate——I don't know——the fellow is well enough for a man—Certainly we don't meet many such at a horse race in the country.

Hard. If we should find him so——But that's impossible. The first appearance has done my business. I'm seldom deceived in that.

Miss Hard. And yet there may be many good qualities under that first appearance.

Hard. Ay, when a girl finds a fellow's outside to her taste, she then sets about guessing the rest of his furniture. With her, a smooth face stands for good sense, and a genteel figure for every virtue.

Miss Hard. I hope, sir, a conversation begun with a compliment to my good sense won't end with a sneer at my understanding?

Hard. Pardon me, Kate. But if young Mr. Brazen can find the art of reconciling contradictions, he may please us both, perhaps.

Miss Hard. And as one of us must be mistaken, what if we go to make further discoveries?

Hard. Agreed. But depend on't I'm in the right.

Miss Hard. And depend on't I'm not much in the wrong.   [*Exeunt.*

Enter TONY *running in with a casket.*

Tony. Ecod! I have got them. Here they are. My Cousin Con's necklaces, bobs and all. My mother shan't cheat the poor souls out of their fortin neither. O! my genus, is that you?

Enter HASTINGS.

Hastings. My dear friend, how have you managed with your mother? I hope you have amused her with pretending love for your cousin, and that you are willing to be reconciled at last? Our horses will be refreshed in a short time, and we shall soon be ready to set off.

Tony. And here's something to bear your charges by the way. (*Giving the casket.*) Your sweetheart's jewels. Keep them, and hang those, I say, that would rob you of one of them !

Hastings. But how have you procured them from your mother ?

Tony. Ask me no questions, and I'll tell you no fibs. I procured them by the rule of thumb. If I had not a key to every drawer in mother's bureau, how could I go to the alehouse so often as I do? An honest man may rob himself of his own at any time.

Hastings. Thousands do it every day. But to be plain with you ; Miss Neville is endeavouring to procure them from her aunt this very instant. If she succeeds, it will be the most delicate way at least of obtaining them.

Tony. Well, keep them, till you know how it will be. But I know how it will be well enough, she'd as soon part with the only sound tooth in her head !

Hastings. But I dread the effects of her resentment, when she finds she has lost them.

Tony. Never you mind her resentment, leave *me* to manage that. I don't value her resentment the bounce of a cracker. Zounds ! here they are ! Morrice, Prance ! [*Exit* HASTINGS.

TONY, *Mrs.* HARDCASTLE, *Miss* NEVILLE.

Mrs. Hard. Indeed, Constance, you amaze me. Such a girl as you want jewels? It will be time enough for jewels, my dear, twenty years hence, when your beauty begins to want repairs.

Miss Neville. But what will repair beauty at forty, will certainly improve it at twenty, madam.

Mrs. Hard. Yours, my dear, can admit of none. That natural blush is beyond a thousand ornaments. Besides, child, jewels are quite out at present. Don't you see half the ladies of our acquaintance, my lady Kill-daylight, and Mrs. Crump, and the rest of them, carry their jewels to town, and bring nothing but paste and marcasites[1] back?

Miss Neville. But who knows, madam, but somebody that shall be nameless would like me best with all my little finery about me?

Mrs. Hard. Consult your glass, my dear, and then see, if with such a pair of eyes, you want any better sparklers. What do you think, Tony, my dear, does your cousin Con. want any jewels, in your eyes, to set off her beauty?

Tony. That's as thereafter may be.

Miss Neville. My dear aunt, if you knew how it would oblige me.

Mrs. Hard. A parcel of old-fashioned rose and table-cut[2] things. They would make you look like the court of king Solomon at a puppet-show. Besides, I believe I can't readily come at them. They may be missing, for aught I know to the contrary.

Tony (apart to Mrs. HARD.). Then why don't you tell her so at once, as she's so longing for them. Tell her they're lost. It's the only way

---

[1 A mineral often mistaken for gold and silver ore]

[2 Table-cut stones have flat upper surfaces. They are only cut in angles at the sides.]

to quiet her. Say they're lost, and call me to bear witness.

Mrs. Hard. (*apart to* TONY.) You know, my dear, I'm only keeping them for you. So if I say they're gone, you'll bear me witness, will you? He! he! he!

Tony. Never fear me. Ecod! I'll say I saw them taken out with my own eyes.

Miss Neville. I desire them but for a day, madam. Just to be permitted to show them as relics, and then they may be locked up again.

Mrs. Hard. To be plain with you, my dear Constance, if I could find them, you should have them. They're missing, I assure you. Lost, for aught I know; but we must have patience wherever they are.

Miss Neville. I'll not believe it; this is but a shallow pretence to deny me. I know they're too valuable to be so slightly kept, and as you are to answer for the loss.

Mrs. Hard. Don't be alarmed, Constance. If they be lost, I must restore an equivalent. But my son knows they are missing, and not to be found.

Tony. That I can bear witness to. They are missing, and not to be found, I'll take my oath on't!

Mrs. Hard. You must learn resignation, my dear; for though we lose our fortune, yet we should not lose our patience. See me, how calm I am!

Miss Neville. Ay, people are generally calm at the misfortunes of others.

Mrs. Hard. Now, I wonder a girl of your good sense should waste a thought upon such trumpery. We shall soon find them ; and, in the meantime, you shall make use of my garnets till your jewels be found.

Miss Neville. I detest garnets !

Mrs. Hard. The most becoming things in the world to set off a clear complexion. You have often seen how well they look upon me. You *shall* have them. [*Exit.*

Miss Neville. I dislike them of all things. You shan't stir.—Was ever anything so provoking to mislay my own jewels, and force me to wear her trumpery.

Tony. Don't be a fool. If she gives you the garnets, take what you can get. The jewels are your own already. I have stolen them out of her bureau, and she does not know it. Fly to your spark, he'll tell you more of the matter. Leave me to manage *her.*

Miss Neville. My dear cousin !

Tony. Vanish. She's here, and has missed them already. Zounds ! how she fidgets and spits about like a Catharine wheel.

Enter Mrs. HARDCASTLE.

Mrs. Hard. Confusion ! thieves ! robbers ! We are cheated, plundered, broke open, undone !

Tony. What's the matter, what's the matter, mamma ? I hope nothing has happened to any of the good family !

Mrs. Hard. We are robbed. My bureau has been broke open, the jewels taken out, and I'm undone !

Tony. Oh! is that all? Ha! ha! ha! By the laws, I never saw it better acted in my life. Ecod, I thought you was ruined in earnest, ha, ha, ha!

Mrs. Hard. Why, boy, I *am* ruined in earnest. My bureau has been broke open, and all taken away.

Tony. Stick to that; ha, ha, ha! stick to that. I'll bear witness, you know, call me to bear witness.

Mrs. Hard. I tell you, Tony, by all that's precious, the jewels are gone, and I shall be ruined for ever.

Tony. Sure I know they're gone, and I am to say so.

Mrs. Hard. My dearest Tony, but hear me. They're gone, I say.

Tony. By the laws, mamma, you make me for to laugh, ha! ha! I know who took them well enough, ha! ha! ha!

Mrs. Hard. Was there ever such a blockhead, that can't tell the difference between jest and earnest. I tell you I'm not in jest, booby!

Tony. That's right, that's right: You must be in a bitter passion, and then nobody will suspect either of us. I'll bear witness that they are gone.

Mrs. Hard. Was there ever such a cross-grained brute, that won't hear me! Can you bear witness that you're no better than a fool? Was ever poor woman so beset with fools on one hand, and thieves on the other?

Tony. I can bear witness to that.

Mrs. Hard. Bear witness again, you blockhead, you, and I'll turn you out of the room directly.

My poor niece, what will become of *her*? Do you laugh, you unfeeling brute, as if you enjoyed my distress?

Tony. I can bear witness to that.

Mrs. Hard. Do you insult me, monster? I'll teach you to vex your mother, I will!

Tony. I can bear witness to that.

      (He runs off, she follows him.

Enter Miss HARDCASTLE and Maid.

Miss Hard. What an unaccountable creature is that brother of mine, to send them to the house as an inn, ha! ha! I don't wonder at his impudence.

Maid. But what is more, madam, the young gentleman as you passed by in your present dress, asked me if you were the barmaid? He mistook you for the barmaid, madam!

Miss Hard. Did he? Then as I live I'm resolved to keep up the delusion. Tell me, Pimple, how do you like my present dress? Don't you think I look something like Cherry in the Beaux' Stratagem?[1]

Maid. It's the dress, madam, that every lady wears in the country, but when she visits or receives company.

Miss Hard. And are you sure he does not remember my face or person?

Maid. Certain of it!

[1 By George Farquhar. "Cherry" is the daughter of Boniface, the landlord of the inn at Lichfield. The part was originally played by Steele's friend Mrs. Bicknell.]

Miss Hard. I vow, I thought so; for though we spoke for some time together, yet his fears were such, that he never once looked up during the interview. Indeed, if he had, my bonnet would have kept him from seeing me.

Maid. But what do you hope from keeping him in his mistake?

Miss Hard. In the first place, I shall be *seen*, and that is no small advantage to a girl who brings her face to market. Then I shall perhaps make an acquaintance, and that's no small victory gained over one who never addresses any but the wildest of her sex. But my chief aim is to take my gentleman off his guard, and like an invisible champion of romance examine the giant's force before I offer to combat.

Maid. But you are sure you can act your part, and disguise your voice, so that he may mistake that, as he has already mistaken your person?

Miss Hard. Never fear me. I think I have got the true bar cant.—Did your honour call?——Attend the Lion there.——Pipes and tobacco for the Angel.—The Lamb has been outrageous this half hour!

Maid. It will do, madam. But he's here.

[*Exit* Maid.

Enter MARLOW.

Marlow. What a bawling in every part of the house; I have scarce a moment's repose. If I go to the best room, there I find my host and his story. If I fly to the gallery, there we have my hostess with her curtsey down to the ground. I have at last got a moment to myself, and now for recollection. [*Walks and muses.*

Miss Hard. Did you call, sir? did your honour call?

Marlow (*musing*). As for Miss Hardcastle, she's too grave and sentimental for me.

Miss Hard. Did your honour call?

[*She still places herself before him, he turning away.*

Marlow. No, child! (*Musing.*) Besides from the glimpse I had of her, I think she squints.

Miss Hard. I'm sure, sir, I heard the bell ring.

Marlow. No, no! (*Musing.*) I have pleased my father, however, by coming down, and I'll to-morrow please myself by returning.

[*Taking out his tablets, and perusing.*

Miss Hard. Perhaps the other gentleman called, sir?

Marlow. I tell you, no.

Miss Hard. I should be glad to know, sir. We have such a parcel of servants.

Marlow. No, no, I tell you. (*Looks full in her face.*) Yes, child, I think I did call. I wanted ——I wanted——I vow, child, you are vastly handsome!

Miss Hard. O la, sir, you'll make one ashamed.

Marlow. Never saw a more sprightly malicious eye. Yes, yes, my dear, I did call. Have you got any of your— a— what d'ye call it in the house?

Miss Hard. No, sir, we have been out of that these ten days.

Marlow. One may call in this house, I find, to very little purpose. Suppose I should call for a taste, just by way of trial, of the nectar of your lips; perhaps I might be disappointed in that, too!

Miss Hard. Nectar! nectar! that's a liquor there's no call for in these parts. French, I suppose. We keep no French wines here, sir.

Marlow. Of true English growth, I assure you.

Miss Hard. Then it's odd I should not know it. We brew all sorts of wines in this house, and I have lived here these eighteen years.

Marlow. Eighteen years! Why one would think, child, you kept the bar before you were born. How old are you?

Miss Hard. O! sir, I must not tell my age. They say women and music should never be dated.

Marlow. To guess at this distance, you can't be much above forty. (*Approaching.*) Yet nearer I don't think so much. (*Approaching.*) By coming close to some women they look younger still; but when we come very close indeed (*Attempting to kiss her.*)

Miss Hard. Pray, sir, keep your distance. One would think you wanted to know one's age as they do horses, by mark of mouth.

Marlow. I protest, child, you use me extremely ill. If you keep me at this distance, how is it possible you and I can be ever acquainted?

Miss Hard. And who wants to be acquainted with you? I want no such acquaintance, not I. I'm sure you did not treat Miss Hardcastle that was here awhile ago in this obstropalous manner. I'll warrant me, before her you looked dashed, and kept bowing to the ground, and talked, for all the world, as if you was before a justice of peace.

Marlow (*aside*). Egad! she has hit it, sure enough. (*To her.*) In awe of her, child? Ha! ha! ha! A mere awkward, squinting thing, no, no! I find you don't know me. I laughed, and rallied her a little; but I was unwilling to be too severe. No, I could not be too severe, curse me!

Miss Hard. O! then, sir, you are a favourite, I find, among the ladies?

Marlow. Yes, my dear, a great favourite. And yet, hang me, I don't see what they find in me to follow. At the Ladies' Club in town [1] I'm called their agreeable Rattle. Rattle, child, is not my real name, but one I'm known by. My name is Solomons. Mr. Solomons, my dear, at your service. (*Offering to salute her.*)

Miss Hard. Hold, sir; you were introducing me to your club, not to yourself. And you're so great a favourite there you say?

Marlow. Yes, my dear. There's Mrs. Mantrap, Lady Betty Blackleg, the Countess of Sligo, Mrs. Longhorns, old Miss Biddy Buckskin [2] and your humble servant, keep up the spirit of the place.

Miss Hard. Then it's a very merry place, I suppose.

[1 See the *Gentleman's Magazine* for 1770, pp. 414-5, which gives the rules of the so-called *Female Coterie* in Albemarle Street here intended, together with a list of the members. Horace Walpole, his friend Conway, the Walde-graves, Mr. and Mrs. Damer, C. J. Fox, Selwyn and many persons of quality belonged to it.]

[2 This is said to have been meant for Miss Rachael Lloyd, an elderly member of the *Female Coterie*.]

Marlow. Yes, as merry as cards, suppers, wine, and old women can make us.

Miss Hard. And their agreeable Rattle, ha! ha! ha!

Marlow (aside). Egad! I don't quite like this chit. She looks knowing, methinks. You laugh, child!

Miss Hard. I can't but laugh to think what time they all have for minding their work or their family.

Marlow (aside). All's well, she don't laugh at me. (*To her.*) Do *you* ever work, child?

Miss Hard. Ay, sure. There's not a screen or a quilt in the whole house but what can bear witness to that.

Marlow. Odso! Then you must show me your embroidery. I embroider and draw patterns myself a little. If you want a judge of your work you must apply to me. [*Seizing her hand.*

Miss Hard. Ay, but the colours don't look well by candle light. You shall see all in the morning. [*Struggling.*

Marlow. And why not now, my angel? Such beauty fires beyond the power of resistance.—— P'shaw! the father here! My old luck: I never nicked seven that I did not throw ames-ace[1] three times following. [*Exit* MARLOW.

Enter HARDCASTLE, *who stands in surprise.*

Hard. So, madam! So I find *this* is your

[1 Ames-ace = ambs-ace, *i.e.* a cast of double ace. "And *Ames-Ace* loses what kind *Sixes* won"—says a poem attributed to Prior.]

modest lover. This is your humble admirer that kept his eyes fixed on the ground, and only adored at humble distance. Kate, Kate, art thou not ashamed to deceive your father so?

Miss Hard. Never trust me, dear papa, but he's still the modest man I first took him for, you'll be convinced of it as well as I.

Hard. By the hand of my body, I believe his impudence is infectious! Didn't I see him seize your hand? Didn't I see him haul you about like a milkmaid? and now you talk of his respect and his modesty, forsooth!

Miss Hard. But if I shortly convince you of his modesty, that he has only the faults that will pass off with time, and the virtues that will improve with age, I hope you'll forgive him.

Hard. The girl would actually make one run mad! I tell you I'll not be convinced. I am convinced. He has scarcely been three hours in the house, and he has already encroached on all my prerogatives. You may like his impudence, and call it modesty. But my son-in-law, madam, must have very different qualifications.

Miss Hard. Sir, I ask but this night to convince you.

Hard. You shall not have half the time, for I have thoughts of turning him out this very hour.

Miss Hard. Give me that hour then, and I hope to satisfy you.

Hard. Well, an hour let it be then. But I'll have no trifling with your father. All fair and open, do you mind me?

Miss Hard. I hope, sir, you have ever found

that I considered your commands as my pride ; for your kindness is such, that my duty as yet has been inclination.   [*Exeunt.*

END OF THE THIRD ACT.

ACT IV.

Enter HASTINGS *and Miss* NEVILLE.

Hastings.

YOU surprise me! Sir Charles Marlow expected here this night? Where have you had your information?

Miss Neville. You may depend upon it. I just saw his letter to Mr. Hardcastle, in which he tells him he intends setting out a few hours after his son.

Hastings. Then, my Constance, all must be completed before he arrives. He knows me; and should he find me here, would discover my name, and perhaps my designs, to the rest of the family.

Miss Neville. The jewels, I hope, are safe.

Hastings. Yes, yes. I have sent them to Marlow, who keeps the keys of our baggage. In the meantime, I'll go to prepare matters for our elopement. I have had the Squire's promise of a fresh pair of horses; and, if I should not see him again, will write him further directions.   [*Exit.*

Miss Neville. Well! success attend you. In the meantime, I'll go amuse my aunt with the old pretence of a violent passion for my cousin. [*Exit.*

Enter MARLOW, *followed by a* Servant.

Marlow. I wonder what Hastings could mean by sending me so valuable a thing as a casket to keep for him, when he knows the only place I have is the seat of a post-coach at an Inn-door. I have you deposited the casket with the landlady, as I ordered you? Have you put it into her own hands?

Servant. Yes, your honour.

Marlow. She said she'd keep it safe, did she?

Servant. Yes, she said she'd keep it safe enough; she asked me how I came by it? and she said she had a great mind to make me give an account of myself.   [*Exit* Servant.

Marlow. Ha! ha! ha! They're safe, however. What an unaccountable set of beings have we got amongst! This little barmaid though runs in my head most strangely, and drives out the absurdities of all the rest of the family. She's mine, she must be mine, or I'm greatly mistaken!

Enter HASTINGS.

Hastings. Bless me! I quite forgot to tell her that I intended to prepare at the bottom of the garden. Marlow here, and in spirits too!

Marlow. Give me joy, George! Crown me, shadow me with laurels! Well, George, after all, we modest fellows don't want for success among the women.

Hastings. Some women, you mean. But what success has your honour's modesty been crowned with now, that it grows so insolent upon us?

Marlow. Didn't you see the tempting, brisk, lovely little thing that runs about the house with a bunch of keys to its girdle?

Hastings. Well! and what then?

Marlow. She's mine, you rogue, you. Such fire, such motion, such eyes, such lips——but egad! she would not let me kiss them though.

Hastings. But are you sure, so very sure of her?

Marlow. Why, man, she talked of showing me her work above-stairs, and I am to improve the pattern.

Hastings. But how can *you*, Charles, go about to rob a woman of her honour?

Marlow. Pshaw! pshaw! we all know the honour of the barmaid of an inn. I don't intend to *rob* her, take my word for it, there's nothing in this house, I shan't honestly *pay* for!

Hastings. I believe the girl has virtue.

Marlow. And if she has, I should be the last man in the world that would attempt to corrupt it.

Hastings. You have taken care, I hope, of the casket I sent you lock up? It's in safety?

Marlow. Yes, yes. It's safe enough. I have taken care of it. But how could you think the seat of a post-coach at an Inn-door a place of safety? Ah! numbskull! I have taken better precautions for you than you did for yourself.——I have——

Hastings. What!

Marlow. I have sent it to the landlady to keep for you.

Hastings. To the landlady!

Marlow. The landlady.

Hastings. You did!

Marlow. I did. She's to be answerable for its forth-coming, you know.

Hastings. Yes, she'll bring it forth with a witness.

Marlow. Wasn't I right? I believe you'll allow that I acted prudently upon this occasion?

Hastings (*aside*). He must not see my uneasiness.

Marlow. You seem a little disconcerted, though, methinks. Sure nothing has happened?

Hastings. No, nothing. Never was in better spirits in all my life. And so you left it with the landlady, who, no doubt, very readily undertook the charge?

Marlow. Rather too readily. For she not only kept the casket, but, through her great precaution, was going to keep the messenger too. Ha! ha! ha!

Hastings. He! he! he! They're safe, however.

Marlow. As a guinea in a miser's purse.

Hastings (*aside*). So now all hopes of fortune are at an end, and we must set off without it. (*To him.*) Well, Charles, I'll leave you to your meditations on the pretty barmaid, and, he! he! he! may you be as successful for yourself as you have been for me.   [*Exit.*

Marlow. Thank ye, George! I ask no more. Ha! ha! ha!

Enter HARDCASTLE.

Hard I no longer know my own house. It's turned all topsy-turvy. His servants have got drunk already. I'll bear it no longer, and yet, from my respect for his father, I'll be calm. (*To him.*) Mr. Marlow, your servant. I'm your very humble servant.   [*Bowing low.*

Marlow. Sir, your humble servant. (*Aside.*) What's to be the wonder now?

Hard. I believe, sir, you must be sensible, sir, that no man alive ought to be more welcome than your father's son, sir. I hope you think so?

Marlow. I do, from my soul, sir. I don't want much entreaty. I generally make my father's son welcome wherever he goes.

Hard. I believe you do, from my soul, sir. But though I say nothing to your own conduct, that of your servants is insufferable. Their manner of drinking is setting a very bad example in this house, I assure you.

Marlow. I protest, my very good sir, that's no fault of mine. If they don't drink as they ought *they* are to blame. I ordered them not to spare the cellar, I did, I assure you. (*To the side scene.*) Here, let one of my servants come up. (*To him.*) My positive directions were, that as I did not drink myself, they should make up for my deficiencies below.

Hard. Then they had your orders for what they do! I'm satisfied!

Marlow. They had, I assure you. You shall hear from one of themselves.

Enter Servant, *drunk.*

Marlow. You, Jeremy! Come forward, sirrah! What were my orders? Were you not told to drink freely, and call for what you thought fit, for the good of the house?

Hard. (*aside.*) I begin to lose my patience.

Jeremy. Please your honour, liberty and Fleet Street for ever! Though I'm but a servant, I'm as good as another man. I'll drink for no man

before supper, sir, dammy ! Good liquor will sit
upon a good supper, but a good supper will not sit
upon——hiccup——upon my conscience, sir.

Marlow. You see, my old friend, the fellow is
as drunk as he can possibly be. I don't know
what you'd have more, unless you'd have the poor
devil soused in a beer-barrel.

Hard. Zounds ! He'll drive me distracted if I
contain myself any longer. Mr. Marlow. Sir ; I
have submitted to your insolence for more than
four hours, and I see no likelihood of its coming to
an end. I'm now resolved to be master here, sir,
and I desire that you and your drunken pack may
leave my house directly.

Marlow. Leave your house !—Sure, you jest, my
good friend ! What, when I'm doing what I can
to please you !

Hard. I tell you, sir, you don't please me ; so
I desire you'll leave my house.

Marlow. Sure, you cannot be serious ! At this
time of night, and such a night ! You only mean
to banter me !

Hard. I tell you, sir, I'm serious ; and, now
that my passions are roused, I say this house is
mine, sir ; this house is mine, and I command you
to leave it directly.

Marlow. Ha ! ha ! ha ! A puddle in a storm.
I shan't stir a step, I assure you. (*In a serious tone.*)
This your house, fellow ! It's my house. This is
my house. Mine, while I choose to stay. What
right have you to bid me leave this house, sir?
I never met with such impudence, curse me, never
in my whole life before !

Hard. Nor I, confound me if ever I did! To come to my house, to call for what he likes, to turn me out of my own chair, to insult the family, to order his servants to get drunk, and then to tell me *This house is mine, sir.* By all that's impudent, it makes me laugh. Ha! ha! ha! Pray, sir, (*Bantering.*) as you take the house, what think you of taking the rest of the furniture? There's a pair of silver candlesticks, and there's a fire-screen, and here's a pair of brazen-nosed bellows, perhaps you may take a fancy to them?

Marlow. Bring me your bill, sir, bring me your bill, and let's make no more words about it.

Hard. There are a set of prints, too. What think you of the Rake's Progress[1] for your own apartment?

Marlow. Bring me your bill, I say; and I'll leave you and your infernal house directly.

Hard. Then there's a mahogany table, that you may see your own face in.

Marlow. My bill, I say.

Hard. I had forgot the great chair, for your own particular slumbers, after a hearty meal.

Marlow. Zounds! bring me my bill, I say, and let's hear no more on't.

Hard. Young man, young man, from your father's letter to me, I was taught to expect a well-bred modest man, as a visitor here, but now I find him no better than a coxcomb and a bully; but he will be down here presently, and shall hear more of it. [*Exit.*

Marlow. How's this! Sure, I have not mistaken

[1 By Hogarth.]

the house? Everything looks like an inn. The
servants cry " coming." The attendance is awkward; the barmaid, too, to attend us. But she's
here, and will further inform me. Whither so fast,
child? A word with you.

Enter Miss HARDCASTLE.

Miss Hard. Let it be short, then. I'm in a
hurry.—(*Aside.*) I believe he begins to find out his
mistake, but it's too soon quite to undeceive him.

Marlow. Pray, child, answer me one question.
What are you, and what may your business in this
house be?

Miss Hard. A relation of the family, sir.

Marlow. What? A poor relation?

Miss Hard. Yes, sir. A poor relation appointed
to keep the keys, and to see that the guests want
nothing in my power to give them.

Marlow. That is, you act as the barmaid of this
inn.

Miss Hard. Inn! O law!—What brought that
in your head? One of the best families in the
county keep an inn! Ha, ha, ha, old Mr. Hardcastle's house an inn!

Marlow. Mr. Hardcastle's house! Is this house
Mr. Hardcastle's house, child?

Miss Hard. Ay, sure. Whose else should it be.

Marlow. So then all's out, and I have been
damnably imposed on. O, confound my stupid
head, I shall be laughed at over the whole town.
I shall be stuck up in caricature in all the print-
shops. The Dullissimo Macaroni.[1] To mistake

[1 At this date the print-shops, and especially Matthew

this house of all others for an inn, and my father's old friend for an inn-keeper ! What a swaggering puppy must he take me for. What a silly puppy do I find myself. There again, may I be hanged, my dear, but I mistook you for the barmaid !

Miss Hard. Dear me ! dear me ! I'm sure there's nothing in my *behaviour* to put me upon a level with one of that stamp.

Marlow. Nothing, my dear, nothing. But I was in for a list of blunders, and could not help making you a subscriber. My stupidity saw everything the wrong way. I mistook your assiduity for assurance, and your simplicity for allurement. But it's over—this house I no more show *my* face in !

Miss Hard. I hope, sir, I have done nothing to disoblige you. I'm sure I should be sorry to affront any gentleman who has been so polite, and said so many civil things to me. I'm sure I should be sorry (*Pretending to cry.*) if he left the family upon my account. I'm sure I should be sorry people said anything amiss, since I have no fortune but my character.

Marlow (*aside*). By heaven, she weeps. This is the first mark of tenderness I ever had from a modest woman, and it touches me. (*To her.*) Excuse me, my lovely girl, you are the only part

Darly's in the Strand, were filled with engravings, generally satirizing well-known individuals and having titles of this kind, *e.g.*, *The Lilly Macaroni* (Lord Ancrum), *The South-wark Macaroni* (Mr. Thrale), *The Martial Macaroni* (Goldsmith's friend, Ensign Horneck) and so forth. See note to p. 128, vol. i, on the Macaronies.]

of the family I leave with reluctance. But to be plain with you, the difference of our birth, fortune and education, make an honourable connexion impossible ; and I can never harbour a thought of seducing simplicity that trusted in my honour, or bringing ruin upon one whose only fault was being too lovely.

Miss Hard. (*aside.*) Generous man ! I now begin to admire him. (*To him.*) But I'm sure my family is as good as Miss Hardcastle's, and though I'm poor, that's no great misfortune to a contented mind, and, until this moment, I never thought that it was bad to want fortune.

Marlow. And why now, my pretty simplicity ?

Miss Hard. Because it puts me at a distance from one, that if I had a thousand pound I would give it all to.

Marlow (*aside*). This simplicity bewitches me, so that if I stay I'm undone. I must make one bold effort, and leave her. (*To her.*) Your partiality in my favour, my dear, touches me most sensibly, and were I to live for myself alone, I could easily fix my choice. But I owe too much to the opinion of the world, too much to the authority of a father, so that—I can scarcely speak it— it affects me ! Farewell ! [*Exit.*

Miss Hard. I never knew half his merit till now. He shall not go, if I have power or art to detain him. I'll still preserve the character in which I stooped to conquer, but will undeceive my papa, who, perhaps, may laugh him out of his resolution. [*Exit.*

Enter TONY, *Miss* NEVILLE.

Tony. Ay, you may steal for yourselves the next time. I have done my duty. She has got the jewels again, that's a sure thing ; but she believes it was all a mistake of the servants.

Miss Neville. But, my dear cousin, sure, you won't forsake us in this distress. If she in the least suspects that I am going off, I shall certainly be locked up, or sent to my aunt Pedigree's, which is ten times worse.

Tony. To be sure, aunts of all kinds are damned bad things. But what can I do ? I have got you a pair of horses that will fly like Whistlejacket, and I'm sure you can't say but I have courted you nicely before her face. Here she comes, we must court a bit or two more, for fear she should suspect us.   [*They retire, and seem to fondle.*

Enter Mrs. HARDCASTLE.

Mrs. Hard. Well, I was greatly fluttered, to be sure. But my son tells me it was all a mistake of the servants. I shan't be easy, however, till they are fairly married, and then let her keep her own fortune. But what do I see ! Fondling together, as I'm alive ! I never saw Tony so sprightly before. Ah ! have I caught you, my pretty doves ! What, billing, exchanging stolen glances, and broken murmurs ! Ah !

Tony. As for murmurs, mother, we grumble a little now and then, to be sure. But there's no love lost between us.

Mrs. Hard. A mere sprinkling, Tony, upon the flame, only to make it burn brighter.

Miss Neville. Cousin Tony promises to give us more of his company at home. Indeed, he shan't leave us any more. It won't leave us, cousin Tony, will it?

Tony. O! it's a pretty creature. No, I'd sooner leave my horse in a pound, than leave you when you smile upon one so. Your laugh makes you so becoming.

Miss Neville. Agreeable cousin! Who can help admiring that natural humour, that pleasant, broad, red, thoughtless, (*Patting his cheek.*) ah! it's a bold face.

Mrs. Hard. Pretty innocence!

Tony. I'm sure I always loved cousin Con's hazle eyes, and her pretty long fingers, that she twists this way and that, over the haspicholls,[1] like a parcel of bobbins.

Mrs. Hard. Ah, he would charm the bird from the tree. I was never so happy before. My boy takes after his father, poor Mr. Lumpkin, exactly. The jewels, my dear Con, shall be your's incontinently. You shall have them. Isn't he a sweet boy, my dear? You shall be married to-morrow, and we'll put off the rest of his education, like Dr. Drowsy's sermons, to a fitter opportunity.

Enter DIGGORY.

Diggory. Where's the 'Squire? I have got a letter for your worship.

[1 Goldsmith does not seem to have invented this delightful perversion, for Gray uses it in a letter to his friend

Tony. Give it to my mamma. She reads all my letters first.

Diggory. I had orders to deliver it into your own hands.

Tony. Who does it come from?

Diggory. Your worship mun ask that of the letter itself.

Tony. I could wish to know, though. (*Turning the letter, and gazing on it.*)

Miss Neville (*aside*). Undone, undone! A letter to him from Hastings. I know the hand. If my aunt sees it we are ruined for ever. I'll keep her employed a little if I can. (*To Mrs.* HARDCASTLE.) But I have not told you, madam, of my cousin's smart answer just now to Mr. Marlow. We so laughed—you must know, madam—this way a little, for he must not hear us. (*They confer.*)

Tony (*Still gazing*). A damned cramp piece of penmanship, as ever I saw in my life. I can read your print-hand very well. But here there are such handles, and shanks, and dashes, that one can scarce tell the head from the tail. *To Anthony Lumpkin, Esquire.* It's very odd, I can read the outside of my letters, where my own name is, well enough. But when I come to open it, it's all—buzz. That's hard, very hard; for the inside of the letter is always the cream of the correspondence.

Mrs. Hard. Ha! ha! ha! Very well, very well. And so my son was too hard for the philosopher!

Miss Neville. Yes, madam; but you must hear

Chute of 1746. He has " not seen the face of a *Haspical*, since he came home." Probably it was a popular vulgarism.]

the rest, madam. A little more this way, or he may hear us. You'll hear how he puzzled him again.

Mrs. Hard. He seems strangely puzzled now himself, methinks.

Tony (Still gazing). A damned up and down hand, as if it was disguised in liquor. (*Reading.*) *Dear Sir.* Ay, that's that. Then there's an *M*, and *a T*, and an *S*, but whether the next be an *izzard* or an *R*, confound me, I cannot tell !

Mrs. Hard. What's that, my dear? Can I give you any assistance?

Miss Neville. Pray, aunt, let me read it. Nobody reads a cramp hand better than I. (*Twitching the letter from her.*) Do you know who it is from?

Tony. Can't tell, except from Dick Ginger the feeder.[1]

Miss Neville. Ay, so it is. (*Pretending to read.*) Dear 'Squire, Hoping that you're in health, as I am at this present. The gentlemen of the Shakebag club has cut the gentlemen of Goose-green quite out of feather. The odds—um—odd battle —um—long fighting—um, here, here, it's all about cocks, and fighting; it's of no consequence, here, put it up, put it up. [*Thrusting the crumpled letter upon him.*

Tony. But I tell you, miss, it's of all the consequence in the world ! I would not lose the rest of it for a guinea ! Here, mother, do you make it out? Of no consequence ! [*Giving Mrs.* HARDCASTLE *the letter.*

[1 That is—the cock-feeder. Compare the *Vicar of Wakefield*, 1766, i, 57.]

Mrs. Hard. How's this! (*Reads.*) Dear 'Squire, I'm now waiting for Miss Neville, with a post-chaise and pair, at the bottom of the garden, but I find my horses yet unable to perform the journey. I expect you'll assist us with a pair of fresh horses, as you promised. Dispatch is necessary, as the *hag* (ay, the hag) your mother, will otherwise suspect us. Yours, Hastings. Grant me patience. I shall run distracted! My rage chokes me.

Miss Neville. I hope, madam, you'll suspend your resentment for a few moments, and not impute to me any impertinence, or sinister design that belongs to another.

Mrs. Hard. (*Curtseying very low.*) Fine spoken, madam, you are most miraculously polite and engaging, and quite the very pink of courtesy and circumspection, madam. (*Changing her tone.*) And you, you great ill-fashioned oaf, with scarce sense enough to keep your mouth shut. Were you too joined against me? But I'll defeat all your plots in a moment. As for you, madam, since you have got a pair of fresh horses ready, it would be cruel to disappoint them. So, if you please, instead of running away with your spark, prepare, this very moment, to run off with *me*. Your old aunt Pedigree will keep you secure, I'll warrant me. You too, sir, may mount your horse, and guard us upon the way. Here, Thomas, Roger, Diggory, I'll show you that I wish you better than you do yourselves. [*Exit.*

Miss Neville. So now I'm completely ruined.

Tony. Ay, that's a sure thing.

Miss Neville. What better could be expected

from being connected with such a stupid fool, and after all the nods and signs I made him.

Tony. By the laws, miss, it was your own cleverness, and not my stupidity, that did your business. You were so nice and so busy with your Shake-bags and Goose-greens, that I thought you could never be making believe.

Enter HASTINGS.

Hastings. So, sir, I find by my servant, that you have shown my letter, and betrayed us. Was this well done, young gentleman?

Tony. Here's another. Ask miss there who betrayed you. Ecod, it was her doing, not mine.

Enter MARLOW.

Marlow. So I have been finely used here among you. Rendered contemptible, driven into ill manners, despised, insulted, laughed at.

Tony. Here's another. We shall have old Bedlam broke loose presently.

Miss Neville. And there, sir, is the gentleman to whom we all owe every obligation.

Marlow. What can I say to him, a mere boy, an idiot, whose ignorance and age are a protection.

Hastings. A poor contemptible booby, that would but disgrace correction.

Miss Neville. Yet with cunning and malice enough to make himself merry with all our embarrassments.

Hastings. An insensible cub.

Marlow. Replete with tricks and mischief.

Tony. Baw! damme, but I'll fight you both one after the other, —— with baskets.

Marlow. As for him, he's below resentment. But your conduct, Mr. Hastings, requires an explanation. You knew of my mistakes, yet would not undeceive me.

Hastings. Tortured as I am with my own disappointments, is this a time for explanations? It is not friendly, Mr. Marlow.

Marlow. But, sir——

Miss Neville. Mr. Marlow, we never kept on your mistake, till it was too late to undeceive you. Be pacified.

Enter Servant.

Servant. My mistress desires you'll get ready immediately, madam. The horses are putting to. Your hat and things are in the next room. We are to go thirty miles before morning.

[*Exit* Servant.

Miss Neville. Well, well; I'll come presently.

Marlow (*To* HASTINGS). Was it well done, sir, to assist in rendering me ridiculous? To hang me out for the scorn of all my acquaintance? Depend upon it, sir, I shall expect an explanation.

Hastings. Was it well done, sir, if you're upon that subject, to deliver what I entrusted to yourself, to the care of another, sir?

Miss Neville. Mr. Hastings. Mr. Marlow. Why will you increase my distress by this groundless dispute? I implore, I entreat you——

Enter Servant.

Servant. Your cloak, madam. My mistress is impatient.

Miss Neville. I come. Pray be pacified. If I leave you thus, I shall die with apprehension!

Enter Servant.

Servant. Your fan, muff, and gloves, madam. The horses are waiting.

Miss Neville. O, Mr. Marlow! if you knew what a scene of constraint and ill-nature lies before me, I'm sure it would convert your resentment into pity.

Marlow. I'm so distracted with a variety of passions, that I don't know what I do. Forgive me, madam. George, forgive me. You know my hasty temper, and should not exasperate it.

Hastings. The torture of my situation is my only excuse.

Miss Neville. Well, my dear Hastings, if you have that esteem for me that I think, that I am sure you have, your constancy for three years will but increase the happiness of our future connection. If—

Mrs. Hard. (*Within.*) Miss Neville. Constance, why, Constance, I say.

Miss Neville. I'm coming. Well, constancy. Remember, constancy is the word.   [*Exit.*

Hastings. My heart! How can I support this! To be so near happiness, and such happiness!

Marlow (*To* Tony). You see now, young

gentleman, the effects of your folly. What might
be amusement to you, is here disappointment, and
even distress.

Tony (*From a reverie*). Ecod, I have hit it. It's
here. Your hands. Yours and yours, my poor Sulky.
My boots there, ho ! Meet me two hours hence at
the bottom of the garden ; and if you don't find
Tony Lumpkin a more good-natur'd fellow than
you thought for, I'll give you leave to take my
best horse, and Bet Bouncer into the bargain !
Come along. My boots, ho !   [*Exeunt.*

END OF THE FOURTH ACT.

ACT V.

SCENE.—*Continues.*

Enter HASTINGS *and* Servant.

Hastings.

YOU saw the old lady and Miss Neville drive off, you say?

Servant. Yes, your honour. They went off in a post coach, and the young 'Squire went on horseback. They're thirty miles off by this time.

Hastings. Then all my hopes are over.

Servant. Yes, sir. Old Sir Charles is arrived. He and the old gentleman of the house have been laughing at Mr. Marlow's mistake this half hour. They are coming this way.

Hastings. Then I must not be seen. So now to my fruitless appointment at the bottom of the garden. This is about the time. [*Exit.*

Enter Sir CHARLES *and* HARDCASTLE.

Hard. Ha! ha! ha! The peremptory tone in which he sent forth his sublime commands.

Sir Charles. And the reserve with which I suppose he treated all your advances.

Hard. And yet he might have seen something in me above a common innkeeper, too.

Sir Charles. Yes, Dick, but he mistook you for an uncommon innkeeper, ha! ha! ha!

Hard. Well, I'm in too good spirits to think of anything but joy. Yes, my dear friend, this union of our families will make our personal friendships hereditary : and though my daughter's fortune is but small——

Sir Charles. Why, Dick, will you talk of fortune to *me?* My son is possessed of more than a competence already, and can want nothing but a good and virtuous girl to share his happiness and increase it. If they like each other, as you say they do——

Hard. *If*, man! I tell you they *do* like each other. My daughter as good as told me so.

Sir Charles. But girls are apt to flatter themselves, you know.

Hard. I saw him grasp her hand in the warmest manner myself; and here he comes to put you out of your *if's*, I warrant him.

Enter MARLOW.

Marlow. I come, sir, once more, to ask pardon for my strange conduct. I can scarce reflect on my insolence without confusion.

Hard. Tut, boy, a trifle. You take it too gravely. An hour or two's laughing with my daughter will set all to rights again. She'll never like you the worse for it.

Marlow. Sir, I shall be always proud of her approbation.

Hard. Approbation is but a cold word, Mr. Marlow; if I am not deceived, you have something more than approbation thereabouts. You take me.

Marlow. Really, sir, I have not that happiness.

Hard. Come, boy, I'm an old fellow, and know what's what, as well as you that are younger. I know what has past between you ; but mum.

Marlow. Sure, sir, nothing has past between us but the most profound respect on my side, and the most distant reserve on her's. You don't think, sir, that my impudence has been past upon all the rest of the family.

Hard. Impudence ! No, I don't say that—Not quite impudence—Though girls like to be played with, and rumpled a little too, sometimes. But she has told no tales, I assure you.

Marlow. I never gave her the slightest cause.

Hard. Well, well, I like modesty in its place well enough. But this is over-acting, young gentleman. You *may* be open. Your father and I will like you the better for it.

Marlow. May I die, sir, if I ever——

Hard. I tell you, she don't dislike you ; and as I'm sure you like her——

Marlow. Dear sir—I protest, sir——

Hard. I see no reason why you should not be joined as fast as the parson can tie you.

Marlow. But hear me, sir——

Hard. Your father approves the match, I admire it, every moment's delay will be doing mischief, so——

Marlow. But why won't you hear me ? By all that's just and true, I never gave Miss Hardcastle the slightest mark of my attachment, or even the most distant hint to suspect me of affection. We had but one interview, and that was formal, modest, and uninteresting.

Hard. (*aside.*) This fellow's formal modest impudence is beyond bearing.

Sir Charles. And you never grasped her hand, or made any protestations !

Marlow. As heaven is my witness, I came down in obedience to your commands. I saw the lady without emotion, and parted without reluctance. I hope you'll exact no further proofs of my duty, nor prevent me from leaving a house in which I suffer so many mortifications. [*Exit.*

Sir Charles. I'm astonished at the air of sincerity with which he parted.

Hard. And I'm astonished at the deliberate intrepidity of his assurance.

Sir Charles. I dare pledge my life and honour upon his truth.

Hard. Here comes my daughter, and I would stake my happiness upon her veracity.

Enter Miss HARDCASTLE.

Hard. Kate, come hither, child. Answer us sincerely, and without reserve ; has Mr. Marlow made you any professions of love and affection?

Miss Hard. The question is very abrupt, sir ! But since you require unreserved sincerity, I think he has.

Hard. (*To Sir* CHARLES.) You see.

Sir Charles. And pray, madam, have you and my son had more than one interview ?

Miss Hard. Yes, sir, several.

Hard. (*To Sir* CHARLES.) You see.

Sir Charles. But did he profess any attachment?

Miss Hard. A lasting one.

Sir Charles. Did he talk of love?

Miss Hard. Much, sir.

Sir Charles. Amazing! And all this formally?

Miss Hard. Formally.

Hard. Now, my friend, I hope you are satisfied.

Sir Charles. And how did he behave, madam?

Miss Hard. As most professed admirers do. Said some civil things of my face, talked much of his want of merit, and the greatness of mine; mentioned his heart, gave a short tragedy speech, and ended with pretended rapture.

Sir Charles. Now I'm perfectly convinced, indeed. I know his conversation among women to be modest and submissive. This forward, canting, ranting manner by no means describes him, and I am confident he never sat for the picture.

Miss Hard. Then what, sir, if I should convince you to your face of my sincerity? If you and my papa, in about half-an-hour, will place yourselves behind that screen, you shall hear him declare his passion to me in person.

Sir Charles. Agreed. And if I find him what you describe, all my happiness in him must have an end. [*Exit.*

Miss Hard. And if you don't find him what I describe—I fear my happiness must never have a beginning. [*Exeunt.*

SCENE.—*Changes to the back of the Garden.*

Enter HASTINGS.

Hastings. What an idiot am I, to wait here for
a fellow, who probably takes a delight in mortifying me. He never intended to be punctual, and
I'll wait no longer. What do I see? It is he,
and perhaps with news of my Constance.

Enter TONY, *booted and spattered.*

Hastings. My honest 'Squire! I now find you
a man of your word. This looks like friendship.

Tony. Ay, I'm your friend, and the best friend
you have in the world, if you knew but all. This
riding by night, by-the-bye, is cursedly tiresome.
It has shook me worse than the basket of a stage-
coach.[1]

Hastings. But how? Where did you leave your
fellow-travellers? Are they in safety? Are they
housed?

Tony. Five and twenty miles in two hours and
a half is no such bad driving. The poor beasts
have smoked for it: Rabbit me, but I'd rather
ride forty miles after a fox, than ten with such
varmint.

Hastings. Well, but where have you left the
ladies? I die with impatience.

Tony. Left them? Why, where should I leave
them, but where I found them?

Hastings. This is a riddle.

[1 Cf. C. P. Moritz, *Travels in England in* 1782.]

Tony. Riddle me this, then. What's that goes round the house, and round the house, and never touches the house?

Hastings. I'm still astray.

Tony. Why, that's it, mon. I have led them astray. By jingo, there's not a pond or slough within five miles of the place but they can tell the taste of.

Hastings. Ha, ha, ha, I understand ; you took them in a round, while they supposed themselves going forward. And so you have at last brought them home again.

Tony. You shall hear. I first took them down Feather-bed-lane, where we stuck fast in the mud. I then rattled them crack over the stones of Up-and-down Hill—I then introduced them to the gibbet on Heavy-tree Heath, and from that, with a circumbendibus, I fairly lodged them in the horsepond at the bottom of the garden.

Hastings. But no accident, I hope.

Tony. No, no. Only mother is confoundedly frightened. She thinks herself forty miles off.[1] She's sick of the journey, and the cattle can scarce crawl. So, if your own horses be ready, you may whip off with cousin, and I'll be bound that no soul here can budge a foot to follow you.

Hastings. My dear friend, how can I be grateful ?

Tony. Ay, now it's dear friend, noble 'Squire. Just now, it was all idiot, cub, and run me through the guts. Damn *your* way of fighting,

[1 A trick of this kind was afterwards played by Sheridan on Madame de Genlis (*Memoirs*, 1825, iv. 113-8).]

I say. After we take a knock in this part of the country, we kiss and be friends. But if you had run me through the guts, then I should be dead, and you might go kiss the hangman.

Hastings. The rebuke is just. But I must hasten to relieve Miss Neville; if you keep the old lady employed, I promise to take care of the young one.   [*Exit* HASTINGS.

Tony. Never fear me. Here she comes. Vanish. She's got from the pond, and draggled up to the waist like a mermaid.

Enter Mrs. HARDCASTLE.

Mrs. Hard. Oh, Tony, I'm killed. Shook. Battered to death. I shall never survive it. That last jolt that laid us against the quickset hedge has done my business.

Tony. Alack, mamma, it was all your own fault. You would be for running away by night, without knowing one inch of the way.

Mrs. Hard. I wish we were at home again. I never met so many accidents in so short a journey. Drenched in the mud, overturned in a ditch, stuck fast in a slough, jolted to a jelly, and at last to lose our way! Whereabouts do you think we are, Tony?

Tony. By my guess we should be upon Crack-skull Common, about forty miles from home.

Mrs. Hard. O lud! O lud! the most notorious spot in all the country. We only want a robbery to make a complete night on't.

Tony. Don't be afraid, mamma, don't be afraid. Two of the five that kept here are hanged, and the other three may not find us. Don't be afraid. Is that a man that's gallopiug behind us? No; its only a tree. Don't be afraid.

Mrs. Hard. The fright will certainly kill me.

Tony. Do you see any thing like a black hat moving behind the thicket?

Mrs. Hard. O death!

Tony. No, it's only a cow. Don't be afraid, mamma, don't be afraid.

Mrs. Hard. As I'm alive, Tony, I see a man coming towards us. Ah! I'm sure on't. If he perceives us, we are undone.

Tony (aside). Father-in-law, by all that's unlucky, come to take one of his night walks. (*To her.*) Ah, it's a highwayman, with pistols as long as my arm. A damned ill-looking fellow.

Mrs. Hard. Good heaven defend us! He approaches.

Tony. Do you hide yourself in that thicket, and leave me to manage him. If there be any danger I'll cough and cry hem. When I cough be sure to keep close. [*Mrs. HARDCASTLE hides behind a tree in the back scene.*

Enter HARDCASTLE.

Hard. I'm mistaken, or I heard voices of people in want of help. Oh, Tony, is that you? I did not expect you so soon back. Are your mother and her charge in safety?

Tony. Very safe, sir, at my aunt Pedigree's. Hem.

Mrs. Hard. (From behind.) Ah! I find there's danger.

Hard. Forty miles in three hours; sure, that's too much, my youngster.

Tony. Stout horses and willing minds make short journeys, as they say. Hem.

Mrs. Hard. (*From behind.*) Sure he'll do the dear boy no harm.

Hard. But I heard a voice here; I should be glad to know from whence it came?

Tony. It was I, sir, talking to myself, sir. I was saying that forty miles in four hours was very good going. Hem. As to be sure it was. Hem. I have got a sort of cold by being out in the air. We'll go in if you please. Hem.

Hard. But if you talked to yourself, you did not answer yourself. I am certain I heard two voices, and am resolved (*Raising his voice.*) to find the other out.

Mrs. Hard. (*From behind.*) Oh! he's coming to find me out. Oh!

Tony. What need you go, sir, if I tell you? Hem. I'll lay down my life for the truth—hem— I'll tell you all, sir. [*Detaining him.*

Hard. I tell you I will not be detained. I insist on seeing. It's in vain to expect I'll believe you.

Mrs. Hard. (*Running forward from behind.*) O lud, he'll murder my poor boy, my darling. Here, good gentleman, whet your rage upon me. Take my money, my life, but spare that young gentleman, spare my child, if you have any mercy.

Hard. My wife! as I'm a Christian. From whence can she come, or what does she mean?

Mrs. Hard. (*Kneeling.*) Take compassion on us, good Mr. Highwayman. Take our money, our watches, all we have, but spare our lives. We will never bring you to justice, indeed we won't, good Mr. Highwayman.

Hard. I believe the woman's out of her senses. What, Dorothy, don't you know *me?*

Mrs. Hard. Mr. Hardcastle, as I'm alive! My fears blinded me. But who, my dear, could have expected to meet you here, in this frightful place, so far from home. What has brought you to follow us?

Hard. Sure, Dorothy, you have not lost your wits! So far from home, when you are within forty yards of your own door! (*To him.*) This is one of your old tricks, you graceless rogue, you! (*To her.*) Don't you know the gate, and the mulberry-tree; and don't you remember the horsepond, my dear?

Mrs. Hard. Yes, I shall remember the horsepond as long as I live; I have caught my death in it. (*To* Tony.) And is it to you, you graceless varlet, I owe all this? I'll teach you to abuse your mother, I will.

Tony. Ecod, mother, all the parish says you have spoiled me, and so you may take the fruits on't.

Mrs. Hard. I'll spoil you, I will.

[*Follows him off the stage. Exit.*

Hard. There's morality, however, in his reply.

[*Exit.*

Enter HASTINGS *and Miss* NEVILLE.

Hastings. My dear Constance, why will you deliberate thus? If we delay a moment, all is lost for ever. Pluck up a little resolution, and we shall soon be out of the reach of her malignity.

Miss Neville. I find it impossible.   My spirits are so sunk with the agitations I have suffered, that I am unable to face any new danger. Two or three years' patience will at last crown us with happiness.

Hastings. Such a tedious delay is worse than inconstancy. Let us fly, my charmer. Let us date our happiness from this very moment. Perish fortune. Love and content will increase what we possess beyond a monarch's revenue.   Let me prevail.

Miss Neville. No, Mr. Hastings, no.   Prudence once more comes to my relief, and I will obey its dictates.   In the moment of passion, fortune may be despised, but it ever produces a lasting repentance.   I'm resolved to apply to Mr. Hardcastle's compassion and justice for redress.

Hastings. But though he had the will, he has not the power to relieve you.

Miss Neville. But he has influence, and upon that I am resolved to rely.

Hastings. I have no hopes. But since you persist, I must reluctantly obey you.   [*Exeunt.*

SCENE.— *Changes.*

Enter Sir CHARLES *and Miss* HARDCASTLE.

Sir Charles. What a situation am I in ! If what you say appears, I shall then find a guilty son.   If what he says be true, I shall then lose one that, of all others, I most wished for a daughter.

Miss Hard. I am proud of your approbation ; and, to show I merit it, if you place yourselves as I directed, you shall hear his explicit declaration. But he comes.

Sir Charles. I'll to your father, and keep him to the appointment.　　　　　[*Exit Sir* CHARLES.

Enter MARLOW.

Marlow. Though prepared for setting out, I come once more to take leave, nor did I, till this moment, know the pain I feel in the separation.

Miss Hard. (*In her own natural manner.*) I believe these sufferings cannot be very great, sir, which you can so easily remove. A day or two longer, perhaps, might lessen your uneasiness, by showing the little value of what you think proper to regret.

Marlow (*aside*). This girl every moment improves upon me. (*To her.*) It must not be, madam. I have already trifled too long with my heart. My very pride begins to submit to my passion. The disparity of education and fortune, the anger of a parent, and the contempt of my equals, begin to lose their weight; and nothing can restore me to myself but this painful effort of resolution.

Miss Hard. Then go, sir. I'll urge nothing more to detain you. Though my family be as good as her's you came down to visit, and my education, I hope, not inferior, what are these advantages without equal affluence? I must remain contented with the slight approbation of imputed merit; I must have only the mockery of your addresses, while all your serious aims are fixed on fortune.

C C

Enter HARDCASTLE *and Sir* CHARLES *from behind.*

Sir Charles. Here, behind this screen.

Hard. Ay, ay, make no noise. I'll engage my Kate covers him with confusion at last.

Marlow. By heavens, madam, fortune was ever my smallest consideration. Your beauty at first caught my eye ; for who could see that without emotion ? But every moment that I converse with you, steals in some new grace, heightens the picture, and gives it stronger expression. What at first seemed rustic plainness, now appears refined simplicity. What seemed forward assurance, now strikes me as the result of courageous innocence, and conscious virtue.

Sir Charles. What can it mean ? He amazes me !

Hard. I told you how it would be. Hush !

Marlow. I am now determined to stay, madam, and I have too good an opinion of my father's discernment, when he sees you, to doubt his approbation.

Miss Hard. No, Mr. Marlow, I will not, cannot detain you. Do you think I could suffer a connexion, in which there is the smallest room for repentance ? Do you think I would take the mean advantage of a transient passion, to load you with confusion ? Do you think I could ever relish that happiness, which was acquired by lessening your's ?

Marlow. By all that's good, I can have no happiness but what's in your power to grant me. Nor shall I ever feel repentance, but in not having

seen your merits before. I will stay, even contrary
to your wishes; and though you should persist to
shun me, I will make my respectful assiduities
atone for the levity of my past conduct.

Miss Hard. Sir, I must entreat you'll desist.
As our acquaintance began, so let it end, in indifference. I might have given an hour or two to
levity; but, seriously, Mr. Marlow, do you think
I could ever submit to a connexion, where *I* must
appear mercenary, and *you* imprudent? Do you
think I could ever catch at the confident addresses
of a secure admirer?

Marlow (*Kneeling*). Does this look like security? Does this look like confidence? No,
madam, every moment that shows me your merit,
only serves to increase my diffidence and confusion.
Here let me continue——

Sir Charles. I can hold it no longer. Charles,
Charles, how hast thou deceived me! Is this your
indifference, your uninteresting conversation!

Hard. Your cold contempt! your formal interview! What have you to say now?

Marlow. That I'm all amazement! What can
it mean?

Hard. It means that you can say and unsay
things at pleasure. That you can address a lady
in private, and deny it in public; that you have
one story for us, and another for my daughter!

Marlow. Daughter!—this lady your daughter!

Hard. Yes, sir, my only daughter. My Kate,
whose else should she be?

Marlow. Oh, the devil!

Miss Hard. Yes, sir, that very identical tall

squinting lady you were pleased to take me for.
(*Curtseying.*) She that you addressed as the mild,
modest, sentimental man of gravity, and the bold,
forward, agreeable rattle of the ladies' club: ha,
ha, ha.

Marlow. Zounds, there's no bearing this; it's
worse than death!

Miss Hard. In which of your characters, sir,
will you give us leave to address you? As the
faltering gentleman, with looks on the ground, that
speaks just to be heard, and hates hypocrisy: or
the loud confident creature, that keeps it up with
Mrs. Mantrap, and old Miss Biddy Buckskin, till
three in the morning; ha, ha, ha!

Marlow. O, curse on my noisy head. I never
attempted to be impudent yet, that I was not
taken down. I must be gone.

Hard. By the hand of my body, but you shall
not. I see it was all a mistake, and I am rejoiced
to find it. You shall not, sir, I tell you. I know
she'll forgive you. Won't you forgive him, Kate?
We'll all forgive you. Take courage, man.

[*They retire, she tormenting him to the back scene.*

Enter Mrs. HARDCASTLE, TONY.

Mrs. Hard. So, so, they're gone off. Let them
go, I care not.

Hard. Who gone?

Mrs. Hard. My dutiful niece and her gentleman,
Mr. Hastings, from town. He who came down
with our modest visitor, here.

Sir Charles. Who, my honest George Hastings?

As worthy a fellow as lives, and the girl could not have made a more prudent choice.

Hard. Then, by the hand of my body, I'm proud of the connexion.

Mrs. Hard. Well, if he has taken away the lady, he has not taken her fortune, that remains in this family to console us for her loss.

Hard. Sure, Dorothy, you would not be so mercenary?

Mrs. Hard. Ay, that's my affair, not yours. But you know, if your son when of age, refuses to marry his cousin, her whole fortune is then at her own disposal.

Hard. Ay, but he's not of age, and she has not thought proper to wait for his refusal.

Enter HASTINGS *and Miss* NEVILLE.

Mrs. Hard. (*aside.*) What! returned so soon? I begin not to like it.

Hastings (*To* HARDCASTLE). For my late attempt to fly off with your niece, let my present confusion be my punishment. We are now come back, to appeal from your justice to your humanity. By her father's consent, I first paid her my addresses, and our passions were first founded in duty.

Miss Neville. Since his death, I have been obliged to stoop to dissimulation to avoid oppression. In an hour of levity, I was ready even to give up my fortune to secure my choice. But I'm now recovered from the delusion, and hope from your tenderness what is denied me from a nearer connexion.

Mrs. Hard. Pshaw, pshaw! this is all but the whining end of a modern novel.

Hard. Be it what it will, I'm glad they're come back to reclaim their due. Come hither, Tony, boy. Do you refuse this lady's hand whom I now offer you?

Tony. What signifies my refusing? You know I can't refuse her till I'm of age, father.

Hard. While I thought concealing your age, boy, was likely to conduce to your improvement, I concurred with your mother's desire to keep it secret. But since I find she turns it to a wrong use, I must now declare, you have been of age these three months.

Tony. Of age! Am I of age, father?

Hard. Above three months.

Tony. Then you'll see the first use I'll make of my liberty. (*Taking Miss* NEVILLE's *hand.*) Witness all men by these presents, that I, Anthony Lumpkin, Esquire, of BLANK place, refuse you, Constantia Neville, spinster, of no place at all, for my true and lawful wife. So Constance Neville may marry whom she pleases, and Tony Lumpkin is his own man again!

Sir Charles. O brave 'Squire!

Hastings. My worthy friend!

Mrs. Hard. My undutiful offspring!

Marlow. Joy, my dear George, I give you joy, sincerely. And could I prevail upon my little tyrant here to be less arbitrary, I should be the happiest man alive, if you would return me the favour.

Hastings (*To Miss* HARDCASTLE). Come,

madam, you are now driven to the very last scene of all your contrivances. I know you like him, I'm sure he loves you, and you must and shall have him.

Hard. (*Joining their hands.*) And I say so, too. And Mr. Marlow, if she makes as good a wife as she has a daughter, I don't believe you'll ever repent your bargain. So now to supper, to-morrow we shall gather all the poor of the parish about us, and the Mistakes of the Night shall be crowned with a merry morning; so boy, take her; and as you have been mistaken in the mistress, my wish is, that you may never be mistaken in the wife.

EPILOGUE.

BY DR. GOLDSMITH.[1]

ELL, having stooped to conquer with
    success,
    And gained a husband without aid
    from dress,
Still as a Barmaid, I could wish it too,
As I have conquered him to conquer you:
And let me say, for all your resolution,
That pretty Barmaids have done execution.
Our life is all a play, composed to please,
" We have our exits and our entrances." [2]
The first act shows the simple country maid,
Harmless and young, of everything afraid ;
Blushes when hired, and with unmeaning action,
I hopes as how to give you satisfaction.
Her second act displays a livelier scene,—
Th' unblushing Barmaid of a country inn.
Who whisks about the house, at market caters,
Talks loud, coquets [3] the guests, and scolds the
    waiters.
Next the scene shifts to town, and there she soars,

[1 This Epilogue was spoken by Mrs. Bulkley as " Miss
Hardcastle."]

[2 *As you like it*, Act ii., Sc. 7.   What follows is of course
a variation on the speech of Jaques.]

[3 Coquet—to entertain with compliments (Johnson).]

The chop-house toast of ogling connoisseurs.
On 'Squires and Cits she there displays her arts,
And on the gridiron broils her lovers' hearts—
And as she smiles, her triumphs to complete,
Even Common Councilmen forget to eat.
The fourth act shows her wedded to the 'Squire,
And madam now begins to hold it higher ;
Pretends to taste, at Operas cries *caro*,
And quits her *Nancy Dawson*,[1] for *Che Faro*.[2]
Doats upon dancing, and in all her pride,
Swims round the room, the *Heinel*[3] of Cheapside :
Ogles and leers with artificial skill,
Till having lost in age the power to kill,
She sits all night at cards, and ogles at spadille.[4]
Such, through our lives, the eventful history—
The fifth and last act still remains for me.
The Barmaid now for your protection prays,
Turns female Barrister, and pleads for Bayes.[5]

[1 See note, vol. i, p. 132.]
[2 *Che farò senza Euridice* in Glück's *Orfeo*, 1764.]
[3 See note, vol. i, p. 128.]
[4 The ace of spades,—first trump in Ombre.]
[5 A character in Buckingham's *Rehearsal*, 1672, intended
for Dryden.   Here it is used by extension for "poet" or
"dramatist."]

EPILOGUE.[1]

To be spoken in the character of TONY LUMPKIN.

BY J. CRADOCK ESQ.[2]

WELL—now all's ended—and my comrades gone,
    Pray what becomes of *mother's nonly*
    son ?
A hopeful blade !—in town I'll fix my station,
And try to make a bluster in the nation.
As for my cousin Neville, I renounce her,
Off—in a crack—I'll carry big Bet Bouncer.
   Why should not I in the great world appear?
I soon shall have a thousand pounds a year ;
No matter what a man may here inherit,
In London—'gad, they've some regard for spirit.
I see the horses prancing up the streets,
And big Bet Bouncer bobs to all she meets ;
Then hoikes to jiggs and pastimes ev'ry night—
Not to the plays—they say it a'n't polite,
To Sadler's-Wells [3] perhaps, or Operas go,
And once by chance, to the roratorio.
Thus here and there, for ever up and down,

---

[1] This came too late to be spoken (Goldsmith's note).
[2 See note, vol. i., p. 105.]
[3 A popular pleasure garden by the New River Head,
the scene of Hogarth's *Evening.*]

We'll set the fashions too, to half the town ;
And then at auctions—money ne'er regard,
Buy pictures like the great, ten pounds a yard :
Zounds, we shall make these London gentry say,
We know what's damned genteel, as well as they.

SCENE FROM THE GRUMBLER,

A FARCE.

[*The Grumbler*, never printed, was adapted by Goldsmith from *Le Grondeur* of Brueys and Palaprat, or rather from Sir C. Sedley's version of that play, produced in 1702. It was written for John Quick, (d. 1831) the actor of "Tony Lumpkin," and produced at his benefit, in May, 1773. Prior printed the accompanying scene in the *Miscellaneous Works*, 1837, from the Licenser's copy. It exhibits the final expedient adopted by the heroine, who is in love with Sourby's son, to free herself from the unwelcome proposals of the father.]

DRAMATIS PERSONÆ.

Sourby (*The Grumbler*)	Mr. Quick.
Octavio (*his Son*)	Mr. Davis.
Wentworth (*Brother-in-Law to Sourby*)	Mr. Owenson.
Dancing Master (*called Signior Capriole in the Bills*)	Mr. King.
Scamper (*Servant*)	Mr. Saunders.
Clarissa (*in love with Octavio*)	Miss Helme.
Jenny (*her Maid*)	Miss Pearce.

SCENE FROM THE GRUMBLER.

Enter SCAMPER (SOURBY'S *servant*) *to* SOURBY, *and his intended wife's maid* JENNY.

Scamper.

IR, a gentleman would speak with you.

Jenny. Good! Here comes Scamper; —(*Aside.*) he'll manage you, I'll warrant me.

Sourby. Who is it?

Scamper. He says his name is Monsieur Ri—Ri—stay, sir, I'll go and ask him again.

Sourby (*Pulling him by the ears*). Take that, sirrah, by the way.

Scamper. Ahi! Ahi!   [*Exit.*

Jenny. Sir, you have torn off his hair, so that he must now have a wig: you have pulled his ears off; but there are none of them to be had for money!

Sourby. I'll teach him!—'Tis certainly Mr. Rigaut, my notary; I know who it is, let him come in. Could he find no time but this to bring me money? Plague take the blockhead!

D D

Enter DANCING MASTER *and his Fiddler.*

Sourby. This is not my man. Who are you, with your compliments?

Dancing Master (Bowing often). I am called Rigaudon, sir, at your service.

Sourby (To JENNY). Have not I seen that face somewhere before?

Jenny. There are a thousand people like one another.

Sourby. Well, Mr. Rigaudon, what is your business?

Dancing Master. To give you this letter from Madame Clarissa.

Sourby. Give it to me—I would fain know who taught Clarissa to fold a letter thus. What contains it?

Jenny (Aside ; while he unfolds the letter). A lover, I believe, never complained of that before.

Sourby (Reads). "Everybody says I am to marry the most brutal of men. I would disabuse them ; and for that reason you and I must begin the ball to-night." She is mad!

Dancing Master. Go on, pray, sir.

Sourby (Reads). "You told me you cannot dance ; but I have sent you the first man in the world." [SOURBY *looks at him from head to foot.*

Dancing Master. Oh Lord, sir!

Sourby (Reads). "Who will teach you in less than an hour enough to serve your purpose." I learn to dance!

Dancing Master. Finish, if you please.

Sourby (Reads). "And if you love me, you will

learn the Allemande."[1]   The Allemande! I, the
Allemande! Mr. the first man in the world, do
you know you are in some danger here?

Dancing Master. Come, sir, in a quarter of an
hour, you shall dance to a miracle.

Sourby. Mr. Rigaudon, do you know I will
send you out of the window if I call my servants?

Dancing Master (*Bidding his man play*). Come,
brisk, this little prelude will put you in humour;
you must be held by the hand; or have you some
steps of your own?

Sourby. Unless you put up that d——d fiddle,
I'll beat it about your ears!

Dancing Master. Zounds, sir! if you are thereabouts, you shall dance presently—I say presently.

Sourby. Shall I dance, villain?

Dancing Master. Yes. By the heavens above
shall you dance.   I have orders from Clarissa to
make you dance.   She has paid me, and dance
you shall; first let him go out.

[*He draws his sword, and puts it under his arm.*

Sourby. Ah! I'm dead.   What a madman has
this woman sent me!

Jenny. I see I must interpose.   Stay you there,
sir; let me speak to him; sir, pray do us the
favour to go and tell the lady that it's disagreeable
to my master.

Dancing Master. I will have him dance.

Sourby. The rascal! the rascal!

Jenny. Consider, if you please, my master is a
grave man.

Dancing Master. I'll have him dance.

[1 A German dance movement in triple time.]

Jenny. You may stand in need of him.

Sourby (Taking her aside). Yes, tell him that
when he will, without costing him a farthing, I'll
bleed and purge him his bellyfull.

Dancing Master. I have nothing to do with
that ; I'll have him dance, or have his blood.

Sourby. The rascal ! (*muttering*).

Jenny. Sir, I can't work upon him ; the madman will not hear reason ; some harm will happen
—we are alone.

Sourby. 'Tis very true.

Jenny. Look on him ; he has an ill look.

Sourby. He has so (*trembling*).

Dancing Master. Make haste, I say, make
haste.

Sourby. Help ! neighbours ! murder !

Jenny. Aye, you may cry for help ; do you
know that all your neighbours would be glad to
see you robbed and your throat cut ? Believe me
sir, two Allemande steps may save your life.

Sourby. But if it should come to be known, I
should be taken for a fool.

Jenny. Love excuses all follies ; and I have
heard say that when Hercules was in love, he
spun for Queen Omphale.

Sourby. Yes, Hercules spun, but Hercules did
not dance the Allemande.

Jenny. Well, you must tell him so ; the gentleman will teach you another.

Dancing Master. Will you have a minuet, sir?

Sourby. A minuet ; no.

Dancing Master. The loure.[1]

[1 *Loure,* a grave dance *à deux temps.*]

Sourby. The loure ; no.

Dancing Master. The passay !

Sourby. The passay ; no.

Dancing Master. What then? The trocanny, the tricotez,[1] the rigadon? Come, choose, choose.

Sourby. No, no, no, I like none of these.

Dancing Master. You would have a grave, serious dance, perhaps?

Sourby. Yes, a serious one, if there be any— but a very serious dance.

Dancing Master. Well, the courante, the hornpipe, the brocane, the saraband?

Sourby. No, no, no !

Dancing Master. What the devil then will you have? But make haste, or—death?

Sourby. Come on, then, since it must be so ; I'll learn a few steps of the—the—

Dancing Master. What, of the—the—

Sourby. I know not what.

Dancing Master. You mock me, sir ; you shall dance the Allemande, since Clarissa will have it so, or—

> [*He leads him about, the fiddle playing the Allemande.*

Sourby. I shall be laughed at by the whole town if it should be known. I am determined, for this frolic, to deprive Clarissa of that invaluable blessing, the possession of my person.

Dancing Master. Come, come, sir, move, move.
(Teaching him.)

Sourby. Cockatrice !

[1 *Tricotets*, an old lively dance.]

Dancing Master. One, two, three ! (*Teaching.*)

Sourby. A d——d, infernal——

Enter WENTWORTH.

Sourby. Oh ! brother, you are in good time to free me from this cursed bondage.

Wentworth. How ! for shame, brother, at your age to be thus foolish.

Sourby. As I hope for mercy—

Wentworth. For shame, for shame—practising at sixty what should have been finished at six !

Dancing Master. He's not the only grown gentleman I have had in hand.

Wentworth. Brother, brother, you'll be the mockery of the whole city.

Sourby. Eternal babbler ! hear me ; this cursed confounded villain will make me dance perforce.

Wentworth. Perforce !

Sourby. Yes ; by order, he says, of Clarissa ; but since I now find she is unworthy, I give her up—renounce her for ever.